# Thirty-One
## *and a*
# Half Regrets

A ROSE GARDNER MYSTERY

# Other books by Denise Grover Swank:

*Rose Gardner Mysteries*
(Humorous Southern mysteries)
TWENTY-EIGHT AND A HALF WISHES
TWENTY-NINE AND A HALF REASONS
THIRTY AND A HALF EXCUSES
FALLING TO PIECES (novella)
THIRTY-ONE AND A HALF REGRETS
THIRTY-TWO AND A HALF COMPLICATIONS (June, 2014)

*Chosen Series*
(Urban fantasy)
CHOSEN
HUNTED
SACRIFICE
REDEMPTION

*On the Otherside Series*
(Young adult science fiction/romance)
HERE
THERE

*Curse Keepers*
(Adult urban fantasy)
THE CURSE KEEPERS
THIS PLACE IS DEATH (Curse Keeper #1.5, February, 2014)
THE CURSE BREAKERS (May 20, 2014)

*New Adult Contemporary Romance*
AFTER MATH
REDESIGNED

# Thirty-One
## *and a*
# Half Regrets

A ROSE GARDNER MYSTERY

# Denise Grover Swank

This book is a work of fiction. References to real people, events, establishments, organizations, or locations are intended only to provide a sense of authenticity, and are used fictitiously. All other characters, and all incidents and dialogue, are drawn from the author's imagination and are not to be construed as real.

Cover art and design: Eisley Jacobs
Cover photography: Iona Nicole Photography
Developmental Editor: Angela Polidoro
ISBN- 978-1494738143

*To everyone who loved and lost but loved again*

# Chapter One

I had no idea how my life had gotten so complicated.

Sitting in an overstuffed chair in Jonah Pruitt's living room, I stared out the window as a steady rain beaded on the glass and rolled down the pane. The weather reflected my mood. Dark and gloomy.

"How often do you think of Joe?"

I swiveled my head to look at Jonah, my friend and now therapist. He offered me a warm smile. When I found out a few weeks ago that he'd been a practicing psychologist in Texas, I asked him to consider listening to my problems. We had been meeting twice a week ever since. I had offered to pay him, but he'd responded by saying that because I'd saved his life, *he* would forever be the one in *my* debt.

Shifting my gaze to my lap, I picked at a loose thread in the hem of my shirt. "Not as often as I did a couple of weeks ago. Working helps, but the weather has been horrible this past week. I've had more free time, which means I've been seeing a lot of Violet."

"How are things going with your sister?"

Now wasn't that the million dollar question. When Joe walked out of my life a month ago, Violet had been more than eager to step in and coddle me. But I'd found it difficult to step back into our childhood roles—Violet as the protector and me as the helpless victim. I was tired of playing the victim, which meant Violet didn't know how to relate to me anymore. But more importantly, the night before Joe broke up with me, Violet had confessed that she'd let half the town think I'd stolen her inheritance from our mother's estate and used it to open our gardening nursery, forcing Violet to work for me without pay. In truth, I'd financed the nursery and allowed her to be co-owner with little investment of her own. Worst yet, she'd let people think badly of me to help hide her own indiscretion—an affair with Henryetta's mayor, Brody MacIntosh.

I'd forgiven her, but I couldn't forget.

"Things are still rough. We don't see each other much except for what little interaction we have at the nursery. Until the rainy weather hit, I was away a lot working on landscaping jobs with Bruce Wayne."

"Does she seem contrite?"

I shook my head, looking at the window again. "She says she is, but she still sneaks calls to Brody."

Jonah sat up straighter. "What do her phone calls with Brody have to do with it?"

Closing my eyes, I heaved a sigh. Jonah knew about Violet's affair with Brody and how her soon-to-be ex-husband Mike had threatened to take their children away if he found evidence of it. But he didn't know everything.

"Is there something you're not telling me?"

"No." While I knew I could trust Jonah with my secrets, I still couldn't bring myself to tell him the real reason for my breakup with Joe. It was too horrible to think about, let alone talk about: Joe's father had blackmailed him into running for a state senate seat by producing false evidence that not only had Mike bribed county officials to grant him favors in his construction business, but that I had hired Daniel Crocker to kill my mother, and that Violet had been conducting an affair with Brody. Only Joe didn't know the evidence his father had on Violet was real. And while I knew that Mike and I were innocent and could clear our names, my sister would pay for her crimes with her children. She'd told me that she and Brody wouldn't see each other until things died down, but she talked to him in hushed tones on the phone multiple times a day.

Some days, I resented her. I resented how she'd pretended to be so perfect all these years when really she was as flawed as the rest of us. Her mistake had been colossal, and yet she only seemed to regret getting caught.

But I kept my mouth shut, because while I knew that Jonah would never tell a soul, he'd *know*. He'd look at her differently and treat her differently, and Violet would figure it out. I couldn't deal with the fallout of that.

But most of all, I kept quiet to protect myself. Resentment ran like a river through my soul, deep and ugly. Jonah was a man of God, and what would he think of *me* if he knew that?

"I just think she should feel more guilt over having an affair is all."

"You're not responsible for other people's feelings of guilt or lack thereof, Rose. Even Violet's. You can only be responsible for yourself."

"I know. I'm just not sure who I am anymore. The person I was before Joe is so different from the person I am now."

"Rose, you aren't Eliza Doolittle and Joe wasn't your Henry Higgins." His toothpaste-commercial smile reminded me why he was such a success in televangelical circles. "Sure, he played a part in your transformation, but you have to take ownership too." He paused. "Your past doesn't have to control your future. *You* are in charge of your future. Not your mother. Not Joe. You."

9

I sucked in my lower lip and snuggled deeper into the chair. Intellectually, I knew he was right, but my mother's voice was a constant hum in my head.

"I know your mother had a profound effect on your self-confidence, but it's time to leave her in the past. It's not going to happen overnight. Honestly, you might struggle with it your entire life. But the more you confront the negativity head-on, the less it can control you. When you hear that voice inside saying you can't do something, immediately confront it and tell it that you can."

I laughed. "I'm supposed to talk to myself? What kind of therapist are you, Jonah?"

He smiled. "Yes, talk to yourself all the time. Even out loud if you have to. We believe what we hear repeated over and over to us. Your mother told you that you were evil and worthless. You just need to retrain yourself to believe something different."

I nodded. When he said it, it made sense.

Jonah shifted in his wingback chair and reached for his mug of tea. "Have our talks helped?" He took a sip. "Do you feel like you're moving forward?"

"Yeah. I think I'm seeing things more clearly now. And I am moving forward. It's been five weeks since Joe broke up with me and although I still miss him, I've accepted that he's gone. I want to be happy again, and I think maybe that can really happen."

"That's good."

"But something's still not right."

"Well, it has only been a month, so you're still grieving. Still, I suspect the problem might be something non-Joe related. Something you seem to avoid every time I bring it up."

I lifted my gaze. "What are you talking about?"

"Your birth mother."

Closing my eyes, I pushed myself deeper into the cushions. "I didn't even know she existed until about six months ago. Why should talking about her make a difference?"

"Her inheritance enabled you to start your business with Violet. Her existence and her death shaped your life in ways that had a profound effect on you. In a way, I'm facing a similar situation with my own mother. I can't ignore how her actions have impacted my life, and neither can you when it comes to your birth mother. Of course it makes a difference."

I pressed my mouth closed.

"Have you ever been to your farm?"

"*Her* farm."

"No, Rose. *Your* farm. You own it. Aren't you curious?"

I lifted my shoulder into a half-shrug as I turned back to the window. "Maybe a little." But the truth was, I'd given a *lot* of thought to my birth mother over the last few weeks. Jonah asked about her almost every time we met and had done so even before our talks became official. The bottom line was that I was angry with Dora Middleton, the woman who'd given birth to me. I knew it was an irrational feeling, but there it was. If she hadn't died in a car accident when I was less than two months old, my life would have been different.

I didn't want to tell Jonah any of that. What kind of person would he think I was if I told him I was angry with a woman who'd died through no fault of her own, and might, in fact, have been murdered?

"I'm thinking of selling it. I put all my available money into the nursery and I can't withdraw anything from my trust for several more years. We're doing so well, we're considering expanding, and I could use the cash for that."

"Don't make a hasty decision. The farm might be your only tangible tie to your birth mother. At least consider seeing it before you decide."

I stared out the window at the dreary day. The thought of visiting the farm terrified me, I just wasn't sure why.

"Rose?"

I lifted my mouth into a tight smile. "I'm just tired. Bruce Wayne has been nursing a cold, and I've been doin' both our jobs the last two work days."

"It could be our sessions too. You're digging through a lot of emotions in a very short period of time and it's exhausting. Perhaps we should cut back."

My eyes flew up and I leaned forward, gripping the arms of the chair. "No. I don't want to cut back."

"Okay, we'll keep meeting twice a week *for now*." He set his mug on the coffee table and rubbed his left arm. "And now I need to get to my *own* therapy session."

"At least you're not wearing the sling any more. That's a good sign, isn't it?" Jonah had been going to physical therapy since his mother had shot him a month ago.

"Yes, but mine is progressing much more slowly than yours, I'm sorry to say."

I stood and picked up his mug, sparing a glance at his kitchen chair—the very one his mother had tied me to the night she almost killed me. I shuddered then moved to the sink. "Are you still having nightmares?" I asked, rinsing out the cup.

"Not as often. They're getting better." He stood and chuckled. "And I thought I was the one asking questions."

"Our session is done, which means we're back to being friends." I turned around and picked up my sweater. "And I'm allowed to worry about you."

"I'm healing, inside and out, so no need to worry."

"It looked like there were more people in attendance at church yesterday."

That mega-watt smile spread across his face again. "My TV viewership is higher than ever. Everyone loves a good scandal." He winked at me, but I knew him well enough to see behind his shiny façade. There was pain in his eyes.

I grabbed my purse and threw an arm around his neck, pulling him into a hug. "It's gonna be okay. For both of us."

"Be kind to yourself, Rose," Jonah said.

"Take your own advice, Jonah," I teased.

"Fair enough."

I drove back to the nursery, dreading a confrontation with Violet. We had been too busy over the weekend to do much talking, but I couldn't expect my luck to hold out. We'd had a lot of last minute pumpkin shoppers along with some return customers whose kids loved the hay bale maze we'd set up on the empty lot next door. But tomorrow was Halloween and business was bound to slow down. Despite Violet's character flaws, she had a good head for business and had already started preparing for a Holiday Open House with live trees, ornaments, and decorations.

She was sweeping the floor when I walked in. She paused mid-stroke and watched me brush past her. "Rose, we need to talk."

I froze. My increasing animosity must have caught her attention, but I wasn't sure I was ready to have this conversation. I spun around to face her, taking in a deep breath. "Okay."

"Tomorrow's Halloween, so I'll need to leave early to get the kids dressed in their costumes."

"Oh." The band around my chest loosened. "Okay."

"We can either close early or you can man the shop. Do you have any landscaping jobs tomorrow?"

I shook my head. "We're in the middle of one right now, but the job site's bound to be muddy with all the rain we've had the last couple of days. Besides, Bruce Wayne might not even be back to work tomorrow. He's still nursin' that cold."

She put her hand on her hip. "Are you sure he's sick? Maybe he's just off getting high with his friends."

"Bruce Wayne hasn't gotten high since he started working for me."

"That you know of."

"You don't know him like I do, Violet." The resentment reared its head in me, ugly and large, and there was more attitude in my voice than intended. I was tired of her always criticizing my friend and thinking the worst of him. "He loves his job and would never do anything to jeopardize that."

She started sweeping again. "Okay ... if you say so." She paused for a second. "Do you still want to go trick-or-treating with us? Mike's still coming," she grumbled. "I thought about talking him out of it, but he enjoys traipsing around the neighborhood more than I do."

She had asked me over a week ago, but since then things had gotten more and more intense between us. But I loved trick-or-treating with the kids. Maybe because Momma had never let me and Violet do it. "Yeah, I'd love to see the kids in their costumes."

"So why don't we just close early and you can come over and help? I'll make a pot of chili."

I smiled. "I'd like that." I'd been going to Violet's for Halloween since Ashley was a few months old and my sister dressed her as an Anne Geddes flower.

Her back straightened and she offered me a stiff smile. "Then we're good."

We were far from good, but we'd do for now.

# Chapter Two

I woke up the next day to my phone ringing on my nightstand. A dusky gray light filtered around my curtains, so I knew it was morning, just another overcast and dreary one.

My little dog, Muffy, whimpered when I leaned over to grab the phone. The display read 6:58 a.m., but no name appeared, just a phone number. "Hello?" I answered, still groggy.

"Rose, this is David."

David Moore? "What's wrong?" I shot upright, fear rushing through my veins. David was Bruce Wayne's lifelong best friend and roommate. And also a notorious pot smoker who didn't believe in getting out of bed before noon. So why was he calling me before seven in the morning?

"Nothin's wrong. I'm just callin' to tell you that Bruce Wayne can't make it in again today."

"Why are you calling and not Bruce Wayne?"

"Uh." He paused. "He's been up all night coughing and he finally got to sleep."

"What are you doing up so early?"

"Who could sleep with all that coughing?"

Something didn't feel right. "Has he gone to the doctor yet? He really needs to see one, David. I know he doesn't have insurance, so tell him the nursery will pay for it."

"Okay ... I will."

"He's still not going to go, is he?"

He didn't answer.

"Is he running a fever?"

"Well, yeah."

"He could have bronchitis or pneumonia. He probably needs antibiotics."

"Okay!" David sounded annoyed. "I'll tell him."

"David, you really need—"

"I said I'd tell him! I gotta go." He hung up before I could say anything else.

I threw on a fluffy robe and a pair of flip-flops and took Muffy outside. My next door neighbor, Heidi Joy, waddled out her front door while I watched Muffy relieve herself on her favorite bush.

"Oh, hi, Rose." She said, tucking her hair behind her ear self-consciously then cinching the belt of her robe over her protruding belly.

"How are you feeling?"

"Oh, you know. Tired. Same as always." She came around the side of her house toward her trash cans. "Andy's been picking up a lot more hours to help cover expenses, which is great, but it means he hasn't been around as much to help me." She spread her feet apart and leaned over to pick up a metal trash can.

I hurried over to her. "Heidi Joy, let help you with that." I gently pushed her to the side and picked up the heavy can. "What were you thinking, trying to pick this up? You're going to hurt yourself."

Tears filled her eyes. "Andy already left and forgot to carry the cans out. I can't let all these dirty diapers sit outside another week."

I put the can down and pulled her into an awkward hug. "Then let me help you. We're friends, right? Friends help each other. You've helped me plenty of times with Muffy."

"I guess."

I smiled. "Then *ask* me, okay?"

"Okay."

But I knew she wouldn't. She was too stubborn. I just needed to remember to offer my help more.

I carted her cans out to the curb and Miss Mildred, my eighty-two-year-old neighbor across the street, came out her front door wearing a housedress and curlers in her hair.

"Good morning, Miss Mildred."

"There ain't nothing good about a morning when women are strutting around in skimpy clothes only hours after the sun has risen."

I sighed. My robe hit mid-thigh. "Would you rather I wait until lunch time to prance around in my skimpy clothes?"

A scowl puckered her face. "Don't you get fresh with me, young lady. Your mother's probably rolling over in her grave right now."

I shook my head. I had no doubts about that, but I was sure some much bigger grievances were causing all that rolling around.

As I suspected, the job site was too muddy for more work, which was just as well. Our next task was to build a three-foot-tall retaining wall. And while I could have done it on my own, it would save time if Bruce Wayne was around to help me cart the stones.

I spent the rest of the morning at two other houses, creating landscaping plans and promising estimates within the next couple of days. The last house belonged to Mary Louise Milligan, one of Violet's friends from high school. "I saw what you did at the Murphy's. I loved the fountain, but I really have my heart set on a water garden. A little pond in the back with some of those big-eyed fish. You know the ones. What are they called?" She tilted her head to the side, a perplexed look on her face.

"Koi?"

"Yeah, them."

We'd never made a water garden before, but I was thinking about putting one in my own backyard and had been studying the logistics of building one. It didn't seem difficult. "Sure, we can definitely do that."

Her face lit up with happiness and she started listing what else she wanted, ticking off each item with a finger. "I want those flowers that float on the water and a waterfall. And also some rocks stacked around to make it look artsy like Betsy's pond." Her hands made a somewhat pornographic shape. "Only nicer." Her eyes widened as she nodded to stress this point.

I watched her as she continued to mime phallic shapes that were nicer than Betsy's. "Okay," I finally said, jotting down notes.

My head felt cloudy and my vision got fuzzy. I cringed at the familiar sensation, preparing for the awkwardness that would hit within a few seconds.

"You're going to have a baby."

Her eyes flew open, her face turning pale. "How did you know that?"

I forced a smile. "How could I not, Mary Louise? You've got a glow that's hard to miss." But that wasn't the reason. Ever since I was a little girl, I'd known things about people. Things I shouldn't have known. The information came from visions. I couldn't control my ability, and the visions were always for the people next to me. They were usually mundane, about an unexpected visit from an in-law or the color so-and-so was going to paint her bedroom. But they were almost always awkward, especially since only a few people knew about them.

She twisted her hands in front of her, biting her lip. "But my husband Brian doesn't know yet."

"He's going to be thrilled, Mary Louise."

"How can you be so sure?"

I'd seen his bright smile when she told him in my vision. "I just am."

When I finished my drawings—although I couldn't bring myself to draw the anatomical rock structure—I checked the time and realized I only had ten minutes to get back downtown and meet my best friend, Neely Kate, for lunch at Merilee's Café.

I parked my truck a block from the county courthouse where she worked and was putting change in the parking meter when I heard someone say my name from behind me.

"Rose."

I spun around, my heart in my throat. "Mason."

He stopped in front of me, wearing a dress coat over his grey suit. The wind blew his dark blond hair around his face. His cheeks were tinged with pink, making his hazel irises even greener than usual. I hadn't seen him in almost two weeks, and I was surprised by how nervous I felt.

"How are you?"

"Good. And you?" I brushed my hair back, suddenly very aware of how bad I had to look. I didn't have on any makeup and my hair was in a messy ponytail. The knees of my jeans were muddy from the first job site and my tan sweater had a coffee stain.

Why on earth was I worried about how I looked around Mason? I'd never thought about it before. But I knew why.

The last time we saw each other, we'd admitted that our feelings were more than just friendly. I'd told Mason I wasn't ready for a relationship yet, that I was working with Jonah to figure out who I was now. Mason had said he'd wait.

His eyes softened. "I miss you, Rose."

"I miss you too." But I still wasn't ready, and I could see in his eyes that he knew that. "I'm meeting Neely Kate for lunch at Merilee's. Would you care to join us?"

He looked over his shoulder at the café. "I'd love to, but I'm meeting my friend Jeff for a working lunch. Can I get a rain check?"

"Do you really have another lunch date or are you avoiding me?"

"Rose." Several people walked by and Mason grabbed my arm and pulled me closer to the entrance of an antique shop. "I'm not avoiding you. I'm giving you space. Do you really think I don't want to be with you?"

I stared at the button on his coat before looking up into his eyes. "No. But I'm worried you'll get tired of waiting for me."

He released a soft laugh. "It's been thirteen days since I last saw you. I've been waiting for you since the day you ran into me at the courthouse in July. Thirteen days is nothing."

My heart stuttered. He'd been counting days. "Not that day. You couldn't stand me that day." I'd showed up late for jury duty and literally ran into Mason, making him drop his papers all over the hallway. He'd been furious.

"Okay, maybe not that day, but you definitely piqued my interest. It was soon after that."

"But I was with Joe."

"I know. And I'd never put you in a difficult situation, which is why I kept my feelings to myself."

"If you've really waited that long, aren't you frustrated?"

"No." His eyes burned with an intensity I'd never seen before. "I know what I want, and I'm a patient man."

My face flushed at his bluntness. "I'm sorry."

"There's nothing to be sorry about."

"But I hate not seeing you. Can't we just be friends until I'm ready?"

His face lit up. "Of course. I just wanted to give you some time. And now that my feelings are out in the open, I'm sure I'll do a terrible job of keeping them to myself."

"I'm making great progress with Jonah."

"I'm glad to hear that."

"I'm considering selling my birth mother's farm, but Jonah thinks I should go visit it first." Before I could stop myself, I blurted out, "Would you be interested in going out there with me?"

His mouth dropped open in surprise.

"Oh, you don't have to. It's just that Violet and I aren't on the best terms right now and I don't want to go alone, although I'm sure that Neely Kate—"

"Rose, yes." His voice softened. "I want to come."

"You do?"

"Of course. I'm honored that I'm the one you asked. Do you want to go this weekend?"

I nodded. "If you can swing it."

"How about Sunday? I know you work at the nursery on Saturday."

"Yeah, that sounds good." But my stomach was in knots thinking about it.

"Great, we'll work out the details later in the week."

"Okay." I paused. "But can we see each other before Sunday?" Now that we'd established he wasn't avoiding me, I was eager to spend more time with him. Mason was one of the few people who made me feel at home with myself.

He laughed. "I have court tomorrow, but the case should be wrapped up by the end of the day. How about lunch on Thursday? At Merilee's. You can have Neely Kate join us if you'd like."

My chest warmed. "Lunch on Thursday. Sounds good."

Mason pulled me into a hug, lingering for a moment before dropping his arms. "It was good seeing you, Rose." He smiled then walked down the sidewalk to his car.

Neely Kate was already at a table when I walked into the restaurant. Her long blonde hair was curled and very full, and she was wearing a burnt orange cardigan sweater with rhinestones around the collar and a jack-o-lantern pin. Underneath was a beige button-down collared blouse. I did a double-take. I had never seen her in any shade of beige before. Neely Kate believed in living large and that included bright colors and bling. I sat down and shrugged off my sweater, feeling happier than I had in weeks.

"Does the smile on your face have anything to do with the fact I saw you talking to the Fenton County Assistant DA just now?"

I blushed. "Maybe."

"And…?"

"And what?"

"Are you going to go out with him or what?"

"I'm still not ready, Neely Kate. I'm working through things with Jonah."

"Rose." Disappointment was heavy in her voice. "Are you sure you're not just holding back because you're scared?"

She had a point. I'd let fear hold me back from living my life until Momma's death. Then as I waited to be murdered or arrested for her murder, I worked my way through a list of twenty-eight things I still wanted to experience. That list changed my life. But I knew it wasn't fear holding me back this time. I hadn't sorted me out yet. "No. I promise. I just want to take it slow and Mason understands that. If it makes you feel any better, we're having lunch on Thursday and he's going with me to visit my birth mother's farm on Sunday."

Her smile fell. "You're kidding."

"I thought you'd be happy."

"I am, but I'm stuck on the fact that you said you're going to your birth mother's farm."

"Jonah thinks I need to confront my past. And her farm is part of it."

"It's not a very romantic date. The last time I forced you to talk about the farm, you said it's run down and no one's lived there for years."

"It's still run down, but it's not a date, Neely Kate, not really."

"*That's* obvious."

"Mason seemed happy to go with me."

"The man would tie your shoelaces if you let him just so he could be with you."

"Neely Kate." The way she said it made me reconsider asking him. I didn't want to take advantage of his kindness. He'd done enough for me.

"I'm kidding. Kind of. I'm sure he's happy to go with you. And it could be romantic, just bring lunch and—"

"It's not supposed to be romantic, Neely Kate. It's supposed to be about me connecting with my past."

"And doing it with the man of your future…" Her face lit up. "I changed my mind. It *is* romantic."

"You're hopeless."

A dreamy look filled her eyes. "Yes, a hopeless romantic."

We ordered lunch, but Neely Kate only took a few bites of her sandwich before pushing it away.

"I'm not feeling very well. It must be all that Halloween chocolate Tiffany brought into our department. I'm a sucker for those mini Snickers bars, but even those have been turning my stomach."

"That's not like you."

She inhaled and sat back in her seat. "I know. I'd call it a stomach bug, but it's lasted for days. I'm so exhausted every night that I've been falling asleep before ten."

"Bruce Wayne hasn't been feeling well, either. He says it's just a bad cold, but he's missed three days of work, which means he's been sick even longer because today is Tuesday and he doesn't work on the weekends. I'm really worried about him. And what's even weirder is David was up before seven this morning. He called me to tell me that Bruce Wayne wouldn't be in."

"That pothead was up before the sun rose?"

"Well…it was *after* the sun rose, but obviously much earlier than he usually gets up. According to David, Bruce Wayne was up coughing all night, but he refuses to go to the doctor because he doesn't have insurance."

"Oh, dear. I can see why you're worried."

"Maybe I should check on him myself. I can bring him some chicken soup so I don't look so obvious. He hates attention."

"That's a great idea."

"And if he's really sick, maybe I'll kidnap him and take him to the doctor myself, like it or not."

"Well, if anyone can pull it off it's you. You have an influence over that man that no else seems to have. It's a good thing you use it for good instead of evil."

I laughed, but I could see how easy it would be for someone Bruce Wayne trusted to control him. I was just glad he was trying so hard to stick to the straight and narrow path.

After ordering Bruce Wayne's soup to go, along with a slice of apple pie, I said goodbye to Neely Kate and headed over to his house.

Bruce Wayne and David lived in a rental house in an older part of town. The first time I saw their house, the paint was peeling off the siding and the yard was overgrown. But when I stopped by again after Bruce Wayne started working for me, the bushes had been trimmed and all the weeds pulled out. Bruce Wayne had begun taking pride in his work, his life. I felt lucky to be a part of his transformation.

I wondered if Joe had felt the same about me?

The thought shot a stab of pain through my chest, but I took a deep breath and walked toward the front door. Joe was in my past. It was time to let him go.

I knocked and waited for someone to answer. After about ten seconds, I knocked again and called out, "Bruce Wayne, it's Rose. I brought you some chicken noodle soup and a piece of apple pie. It's from Merilee's. Your favorite."

When he didn't answer, I tried the door knob, surprised to find it unlocked. Pushing the door open, I looked around the tiny living room. "Bruce Wayne?"

I stepped inside, leaving the door cracked behind me. The living room was messy; the secondhand furniture had seen better days. I looked around the corner and saw dishes piled high in the kitchen sink.

"Bruce Wayne?"

Heading down the hall, I peered into the bathroom. The trash can caught my eye and I realized that there weren't any used tissues in it. Unless David had suddenly developed a type-A personality when it came to taking out the bathroom trash, it seemed strange.

Continuing down the hall, I peered into both empty bedrooms. One was generically messy, but it was the other that grabbed my attention. Several of the dresser drawers hung open. I walked in and found a photo of Bruce Wayne and his parents on the nightstand that looked like it dated back to his high school days. A silver necklace with a medallion lay on the dresser. I picked it up and recognized St. Jude. I'd seen him wear it a few times. But what concerned me the most was that two drawers were empty and there were multiple empty hangers in his closet.

Bruce Wayne wasn't sick.

Bruce Wayne was gone.

# Chapter Three

I ran to my car and pulled out my cell phone. "He's gone, Neely Kate! Bruce Wayne's gone!"

"Oh, my God! He's dead?"

"What?" I shook my head. "No! He's *gone*. As in he packed up his clothes and left."

"What? *Why?*"

"I don't know." My voice broke. "But if his parole officer finds out, they'll put him back in jail. And he might not get out this time."

She sighed. "So I guess telling Mason is out."

"Definitely." I fought to keep from crying. "I don't understand. Why would he take off? He was doing so well."

"I don't know, Rose. What're you goin' to do?"

"David wasn't at their house, so he must be at work. I'm going to swing by the Piggly Wiggly. Ten cents to the dollar he covered for Bruce Wayne this morning." Which meant David had lied to me. My hand gripped the steering wheel. "I'm going to make him tell me what he knows."

"Good luck. And keep me updated."

"Okay."

While Bruce Wayne had been making progress at becoming a productive member of society, David had been making strides of his own. He'd been working at the Piggly

Wiggly since Bruce Wayne's trial for murder three months ago, longer than most jobs he'd held.

Sure enough, I found him stocking a shelf with cereal. He stood bolt upright when he saw me, a box of Cap'n Crunch shaking in his hand. "Rose, what are you doing here?"

"I'm looking for you."

The color drained from his face. He put the box on the shelf.

"I stopped by your house a little while ago to bring Bruce Wayne some chicken soup and apple pie. Imagine my surprise when he wasn't home."

David picked up another box, his hand shaking so badly the cereal inside rattled. "Maybe he went to the doctor after all."

I put my hand on my hip. "Was he plannin' on spending a *really* long time in the waiting room? 'Cause it looks like he took most of his clothes with him."

He threw the box down and took off running.

"David! Wait!"

He headed for the back exit and I followed him out the door, cornering him on the loading dock.

He turned to face me, wide-eyed. "I didn't want to do it."

"Do what?" I took a breath and held up my hands in surrender. "It's okay, David. Just tell me where he is. I want to help him."

He shook his head. "The best way you can help him is to let this go."

None of this made any sense. My voice broke. "I don't understand. Why did he leave?"

"I don't know for sure. He was gone when I got home from work last night. I called you this morning to cover for him. In case he came back. If his parole officer finds out…"

"I know," I said, the words full of worry.

David squared his shoulders. "Are you goin' to turn him in?"

I shook my head. "No. I don't want him to get into trouble. I want to help, but I can't do that if I don't know where he went and why. He wasn't sick, was he?"

"No."

"So where was he instead of working?"

"All I know is that for the last few days he's been leavin' early in the morning and only coming home to sleep. And then last night, he didn't come home at all. The other day I asked him where he was goin', 'cause I knew he was calling in sick to work, but he insisted that I didn't want to know. I could tell he was scared."

"Scared of what?"

Pressing his lips together, he shook his head. "I don't know."

"If you hear from him, promise to call me immediately. Okay?"

He hesitated.

"*Please*, David. I'm worried sick."

"Okay." He nodded. I could tell from the look in his eyes that he was worried too, which only made me feel worse.

"Thanks." I headed out to my car and called Neely Kate. When she didn't answer, I left a message telling her what I'd found out. I was deep in thought when I pulled up to the nursery, unsure what to do about Bruce Wayne. I grabbed my drawings from the truck and headed for the back to work up some estimates.

Violet was standing behind the register, but she came around the end of the counter when she saw me. "Rose, I need to tell you something."

I stopped and blinked. "Okay."

"I got a phone call yesterday, from the Arkansas Small Business Administration. They've presented us with a wonderful opportunity."

"Oh, that sounds great." I swiped some loose hairs from my face, my mind still stuck on Bruce Wayne. "What is it?"

"Well…" She twisted her hands in front of her, looking at the floor. "They want to feature our business. We'll be part of a press conference and they'll post a story about us on their website. And they've promised to give us that grant I applied for, the one that will let us expand into the lot next door like we've been talking about."

I dropped my defenses and gave her my full attention. The grant meant I wouldn't have to come up with the extra cash. "That sounds great, Vi. Why didn't you tell me yesterday?"

"Well, there's a catch."

My back stiffened. "What is it?"

"The presentation is part of a campaign stop."

"Joe's?" A band constricted around my chest and I fought to take a breath. It couldn't be.

She cringed and her words rushed out. "When I agreed, I told them you wouldn't be here. That's why I didn't mention it yesterday. I didn't want to hurt you. But they called back today and said we both had to be present. And if we're not, we won't get the grant."

"I don't understand. We're not even in his district."

"They said the small business administration is part of his platform; that it's a great opportunity for both sides."

Feeling lightheaded, I leaned against the counter. "When is it?"

"Tomorrow at one. They need to have it done as soon as possible since the election's a week from today."

Joe was coming to the nursery. I was going to see Joe.

"The press will be here. Joe will hand us the grant check. They'll interview us, and that will be that."

I didn't know if I could stand with him in front of cameras and pretend nothing was wrong.

"Rose." She sounded worried. "Say something."

"I need to sit down."

She dragged a stool from around the counter and I perched on it, resisting the urge to put my head between my knees to keep from passing out. *I will not faint*. Thankfully, all the recent shocks in the last few months had helped me outgrow that reaction. But apparently some shocks were still strong enough to bring it back.

"How much is the grant?"

"Large enough to build a greenhouse. We'd be two years ahead of our business plan and you wouldn't have to get a loan or sell your farm."

I closed my eyes.

"I'd tell them no, Rose, but it's a grant. We don't have pay it back."

"Okay," I whispered.

She released a soft groan. "I'm gonna tell them no. It's not fair to you. Not after what that man did to you."

I looked up into her clueless face. She had no earthly idea what he'd done to protect her and her children.

I stood up. "No. We'll do it."

"Are you sure?"

I headed to the back room. "I have to work on some estimates."

She followed me to the doorway. "I'll tell them no, Rose."

I spun around. "No, you will not. I'm not gonna hide and pretend like I've done something to be ashamed of. Now I have to get to work on these estimates if we're hosting a press conference tomorrow."

The bell on the front door dinged and guilt covered Violet's face.

I sighed, weary of the conversation. "I'm fine, Vi. *Go.*"

I spent the next two hours trying to concentrate on my work, a difficult task given all the worries weighing on my mind. I tried to call Bruce Wayne three times. The first call rang with no answer, but the other two times it went straight to voice mail. I left messages all three times, begging Bruce Wayne to call me and let me know he was okay.

I struggled to come up with an explanation for why he had fled. After all, he hadn't run after witnessing a murder while robbing the hardware store. He'd gone to David for help. Of course, that hadn't turned out well, and as much as I loved Bruce Wayne, I'd be the first to admit he wasn't the sharpest tool in the shed. He'd been a pothead for years, notorious for making the same mistakes over and over again. It stood to reason that he'd repeat his earlier behavior by seeking help from David. So if he hadn't gone to David with his problem this time, where was he?

I was lost in thought when Violet came back and told me that it was five and she was closing the shop.

"Are you still comin' over?"

"Yeah. I just want to get Muffy." I felt guilty enough about leaving her home alone all day, and although our neighborhood didn't get a lot of trick-or-treaters, I didn't know how well she'd do if people were knocking on our door all night.

"Okay, get Muffy and come on over. The kids miss you." She sounded wistful and I wondered if she was implying that she missed me too.

But I couldn't bring myself to say it back.

I smiled as I pulled into my driveway, pleased by what I saw. I'd neglected my own yard most of the year, but I'd gone all out for Halloween and Thanksgiving. My front porch was decorated with hay bales and corn stalks, pumpkins and squash.

I went inside and took a short shower then changed into a clean pair of jeans and a long-sleeved T-shirt. Last year I'd dressed up as Red Riding Hood—I'd had to sneak out of the house past Momma—but I didn't feel like putting on a costume tonight. Bruce Wayne's disappearance had stolen what little joy I'd found since losing Joe.

Although I had decided not to dress up, I still wanted Muffy to have a costume. It was her first Halloween with me and I knew Ashley and Mikey would love it. My usually good-natured dog had other ideas. When I started to pull the bumblebee costume over her head, she tried to escape, but I managed to get it on after some wrestling. I put her on the ground, and she shook her body like she always did after a bath, tipping her head up to look at me, as if to say, "Are you *kidding* me?"

Since I didn't have any children and none were in the foreseeable future, Muffy would have to bear the brunt of my overzealous desire to participate in all the holidays. And while she might not like this costume, I was sure she wouldn't protest the Christmas presents I planned to get her.

My eyebrows lowered as I took in the yellow-and-black-striped stuffed costume that covered most of her trunk and the short gauzy wings that stuck out from its sides. The plumpness made her spindly legs look even skinnier, but her dark fur blended perfectly with the color scheme. My mouth twisted to the side as I debated whether it was worth my trouble and Muffy's obvious reluctance to try to get the cap with the antennae fastened on her head. Ultimately, I stuffed the little hat in the bag I'd packed to take along. No sense pressing my luck.

"Okay, girl. Let's go."

As I let Muffy outside and turned to lock up, Heidi Joy's four older boys came piling out of their front door, shoving and shouting, each of them clutching an orange plastic pumpkin. Muffy usually ran right to them, but this time she bolted into the front yard, throwing herself to the ground and rolling onto her back.

"Muffy! Stop that right now! You'll mess up your costume!"

The boys ran over and stood in a semi-circle around her, their mouths hanging open. Andy, Jr. grabbed his belly and burst out into laugher. "What in the world happened to your dog? Did she jump into a hill of fire ants?"

The other boys giggled.

"No."

"What's she wearing?"

"She's wearin' a Halloween costume, just like you. What's it look like?"

His eyes narrowed. "She looks like a hot dog with mustard stripes."

"She's a bumblebee, *not* a hot dog." I knew I sounded defensive and I was. I didn't like it when people made fun of her.

"Where's her stinger?" four-year-old Keith asked.

"She doesn't have one."

He shook his head and mumbled, "If she don't have a stinger, she'd be dead. She don't look like a dead bumblebee."

Muffy continued to roll around and let out a loud fart, the smell permeating the air.

A chorus of giggles and "Ewww..." erupted from the boys.

"But it smells like she's *dyin'*!" Andy, Jr. waved in front of his face and burst out laughing again.

I gave the boys a frown before scooping Muffy into my arms. "Y'all are gonna hurt Muffy's feelings." I looked down at Andy, Jr. "What are *you* supposed to be?"

"I'm a pirate." The six-year-old tugged on the patch covering his eye. His three little brothers crowded around him, dressed as Spider-Man, a dinosaur, and a cowboy. Heidi Joy came out her front door with the baby, who was dressed as a puppy, on her hip. She was wearing a long-sleeved black T-shirt with a baby-sized skeleton overlaying an adult-sized skeleton.

Andy, Jr. held up his plastic sword and spoke in a growl, "Give me your buried treasure or I'll make you walk the plank."

I considered telling him he wasn't getting anything after making fun of Muffy, but decided I could be more mature than a six-year-old. "I left you some treasure on my front porch, but it's not buried. It's hiding behind my pumpkins."

The boys ran onto the porch while I shifted Muffy's costume back into place and put her in the truck with my tote bag, hoping she wouldn't hurt herself by trying to get the costume off in there. The boys' squeals of delight made me smile.

"We each have our own bag!" four-year-old Keith shouted.

"You spoil them, Rose." Heidi Joy shook her head with a smile as she transferred the baby to her other hip.

"They're not bags full of candy, I promise. I put coloring books and a puzzle in each of them. I figured they'll get enough sugar tonight."

"Like I said, you spoil them."

"I'm headed to Violet's. Can you keep an eye on my house? After all the craziness in the neighborhood over the last few months, I'm worried about what the older kids might do, especially Thomas and his friends." Thomas was a high school senior who seemed determined not to graduate and had gotten mixed up with Daniel Crocker's friends. He'd made no secret that he didn't like me and had insinuated that Crocker's men were upset with me for helping putting their boss behind bars.

I suddenly wondered if Bruce Wayne's disappearance was somehow tied to Daniel Crocker. When the police threatened to arrest him for the murders committed by Jonah's mother, he'd sought refuge at Weston's Garage, the former headquarters of Daniel Crocker's drug and stolen car parts ring. Bruce Wayne had worked for Crocker a year ago, before he was arrested for the hardware store manager's murder, and Crocker's men were loyal to their own. But if Bruce Wayne had sought help at Weston's Garage, what had scared him in the first place?

Horror spread across Heidi Joy's face, and I realized that all the drama in our neighborhood had nearly toppled her over the edge. "Oh, don't worry." I tried to look comforting. "I don't *expect* anything to happen. It's a just-in-case type thing."

She nodded, worry furrowing her brow. "Sure. Of course."

My head tingled with the tell-tale sign of an oncoming vision. I saw a moving van outside Heidi Joy's house, her husband Andy and his friend carting furniture into it. Autumn leaves littered the yard.

"You're moving." I said.

Her eyes widened and her tongue seemed tied. Finally she said, "How did you know?"

I glanced at the baby skeleton on her belly. "Call it a hunch?"

"I love having you for a neighbor, Rose. You know that. But now that it's getting colder, it's harder than ever to entertain these boys in that tiny house. I told Andy when we moved in that it was too small. A two-bedroom house with five boys? And another on the way..." Her voice broke.

I didn't want to confess that I'd had those same thoughts when she'd moved in months ago. Instead, I pulled her into a hug. "I'm sorry."

"Listen to me, belly-aching. We're lucky to have somewhere to live after Andy lost his job and we lost our house. But he's been working all this overtime to try and save enough money to move us into a bigger house before the baby's born." A lopsided grin lifted her mouth, her eyes shiny with tears. "Especially since it's a girl."

Heidi Joy was going to move. I wasn't sure why that surprised me. It was probably the most logical decision they'd made in the few months I'd known them. I'd miss our chats, but I had to push my selfishness aside. "A girl! How wonderful! I know how badly you wanted a little girl." I forced myself to sound happy. "Have you found a new place yet?"

"No. But we're looking at a few options in a couple of days. The baby's due in three weeks."

"Well, that's wonderful news. And if I can help at all, just let me know."

"Thanks, Rose. I'll miss you."

"Well, it's not like you're leaving Henryetta, is it? We'll still see each other."

"Yeah." But she sounded sad. We both knew it wouldn't be the same.

The boys ran off the porch. "Mommy! Let's go trick-or-treating!"

I grabbed her arm and squeezed. "It will all work out, Heidi Joy. I promise."

She nodded then herded her boys into a group, forcing the bigger ones to hold hands with the little ones. I climbed in my truck and watched them walk down the street, a lump in my throat.

Change was the way of the world. Only it never seemed to work in my favor.

I shook my head, irritated with my wallowing. I had more blessings I could count. I needed to stop feeling sorry for myself.

Ashley was waiting at her front door dressed as a pink princess.

"Muffy!" she shouted as we walked up, Muffy still trying to shake off her costume. "You're so cute!"

At least somebody appreciated her costume.

Muffy jumped into her arms and licked her face, making the little girl giggle.

"Hello there, princess. Have you seen my favorite niece, Ashley?"

Giggles erupted. "It's *me*, Aunt Rose!"

"Oh, my goodness! It *is* you!"

"And I'm your only niece."

"When'd you get so smart?"

She put her hand on her hip and cocked her head. "I'm in kindergarten now."

"Well, no wonder then."

Violet was in the kitchen trying to get Mikey stuffed into a dragon costume. She twisted her head to look at me. "I thought you'd be here by now."

"I was dressing Muffy."

She just gave me a look.

39

I put a hand on my hip. "Well, she can't go trick-or-treating without a costume."

Her mouth pursed. "Hmm."

"Daddy's here!" Ashley shouted, running from the room.

Violet made an ugly face. "Yippee."

A few moments later, Violet's estranged husband walked into the room with Ashley on his hip, Muffy trotting behind them. He set his daughter down on the floor, laughing. "I stumbled upon this beautiful princess and her valiant mosquito."

"Muffy's not a mosquito, Daddy," she giggled. "She's a bee."

He bowed low, sweeping his hand wide. "Excuse my mistake, my royal insect. No insult intended."

Ashley covered her mouth, still giggling.

"I heard there was a fire-breathing dragon in the bowels of the kitchen, and as the princess's knight in shining armor, it's my duty to save her from the beast."

"I don't know about fire breathing," Violet muttered. "But he's passing enough gas that we could light his farts on fire. I have no idea what on earth your mother feeds him for lunch, but I wish she'd stop."

"Violet!" I hissed.

Mike shot her a glare and snatched up Mikey. "I'm not afraid to wrestle a dragon," he laughed as he carried the toddler into the living room, Ashley trailing behind. Muffy gave me a long look then ran after them.

Traitor.

"I don't know what's gotten into you, Violet Mae Gardner Beauregard, but you stop it right now!" I whisper-shouted.

Her eyes flew open in shock.

"I don't care how angry you are at Mike. You be nice to him in front of your children, and you sure as tarnation should not speak badly of his mother. That woman loves them more than life itself. Not to mention that she watches your children without pay." Unleashed, my bitterness spread through my body, saturating every word. "You have no idea how lucky you have it."

Violet's mouth fell open. "What in the world has gotten *into* you?"

"I think you should count your blessings because a lot of people have sacrificed to let you keep them."

Her eyes narrowed. "What's that supposed to mean?"

I couldn't believe I'd let myself say so much. "Nothing." I walked into the other room to get away from her.

Violet acted hurt until it was time to go trick-or-treating, and then she announced that she'd decided to stay home and hand out candy. Mike and I left with the kids, Muffy trotting next to me on her leash. Ashley and Mike had coerced her into wear her antennae while I was in the kitchen with Violet, but the look of indignation on her face told me that it hadn't been consensual. We walked down the street, Ashley not as excited as she was before we left. It felt awkward and sad without Violet, as if one leg of a three-legged stool was missing. The three of us had always taken Ashley and Mikey out together.

Mike and I stood at the end of a driveway and watched the kids walk up to a neighbor's front door. I held Muffy's leash, trying to keep her from flopping onto her back again. One of her wings was already dented and had a small hole in it.

"I was sorry to hear about you and Joe breaking up," Mike said, keeping his gaze on the kids. "I hope Violet didn't have anything to do with it."

I sighed and mumbled, "Not how you think."

He spun to face me. "What?"

"No. She didn't."

He relaxed and stuffed his hands in the front pockets of his jeans. "I miss seeing you, Rose. You've been like a little sister to me. I should have called to check on you, but I wasn't sure...with Violet." He cleared his throat. "How are you handling everything?"

"I'm better." I wrapped my arms around my chest, my heart aching. I'd lost so much in my life recently and I just kept losing more. "I miss you too, Mike. I hope you're doing well."

"I've been better," he sighed as the kids ran back to us. "I've been a helluva lot better."

Ashley held up her pink pumpkin. "I got M&Ms, Daddy!"

"That's awesome, my little princess!"

Melancholy hung over me the rest of the evening, seasoned with my dread of facing Joe the next day. Mike and I took the kids back to the house and went inside, stopping in the entryway. Violet was sitting on the sofa with a bottle of wine and two glasses, one partially full.

"I'm going to go ahead and head home, Vi. I'll see you tomorrow."

"Oh!" she exclaimed, jumping off the sofa and walking over to me, disappointment in her eyes. "I thought maybe you could stay and have a glass of wine with me and we could talk. We haven't really had a chance to for weeks."

I glanced at Mike, who awkwardly stood to the side.

"I'm really tired and I want to get plenty of rest for tomorrow. What time do I need to be there?"

"The presentation is at one, but we should both be there by twelve. I think it'll take the whole afternoon."

No way could I handle that. "Once my part is done, I'm out of there."

"Okay." She nodded.

"Aunt Rose?" Ashley tugged on the hem of my sweater. "Can Muffy sleep over with me?"

"I don't know…" I hadn't had any run-ins with Thomas in over a month, but I was still worried that he and his friends might try to prank my house. If Muffy was there, at least she'd be some kind of alarm system. "I kind of want Muffy to spend the night with me tonight. How about tomorrow night? If it's okay with your mommy."

"Can she, Mommy?" Ashley spun to face her mother. "I miss Muffy."

"Okay, maybe Aunt Rose can bring Muffy to the shop tomorrow. She should be there for the press conference anyway. She *is* the nursery mascot."

Her statement surprised me. She usually didn't like Muffy hanging around the store.

I flashed Ashley a smile. "Muffy will be *very* excited. She loves having sleep-overs with you."

Mike picked up little Mikey and put an arm around Ashley's shoulders. "How about I get you two ready for bed?"

Violet looked surprised. "You don't have to do that, Mike."

He stopped and stared at her for several seconds. "I know, but I miss this. Our family." His voice was raspy, so he cleared his throat. "I'd appreciate it if you'd let me get them ready for bed."

For once Violet seemed at a loss for words. "Sure, Mike," she finally said. "Thank you."

Violet watched them disappear down the hall, and there was a certain heaviness in her eyes when she turned back to me. "Are you sure you can't stay?"

My heart ached. I longed for the days when Violet and I had been close, but lately I'd begun to wonder how close we'd really been. My faith in Violet had wavered in everything, including her role in our shared past. If she'd managed to hide an affair from me for months, what else had she hidden? I couldn't stay tonight because it was too hard to hide my bitterness and anger. I knew I needed to confront her, but now wasn't the time. "I'm tired. I've been working more with Bruce Wayne gone."

"When is he coming back?"

"I'm not sure." I sure wished I knew. I needed to start figuring out where he was, and what I could do to find him.

I headed home, suddenly feeling more lonely than usual. I missed Joe, but I realized it wasn't an all-consuming feeling, like it had been for the past several weeks. The kind that sometimes stole my breath and threatened to suck me into an abyss of despair. No, the grief had turned to a nagging ache, and when I really stopped to examine it, I realized it wasn't even necessarily Joe that I missed. It was having someone in my life to share the little things no one else cared about.

Did that mean I was ready to move on?

I pulled into my driveway and walked up to my dark front porch, looking for any signs of mischief from Thomas and his friends, but everything was in its place.

When had I become so paranoid?

Muffy was still wearing her costume, and I considered taking it off before letting her loose to go to the bathroom in the front yard, but she didn't seem to mind it anymore, perhaps because she'd broke it in. One of her antennae had fallen off completely and the broken wing was hanging lopsided. Somehow it seemed to suit her even more now.

My eyes drifted to Thomas's house. He was in his driveway, sitting on the back of his car with two of his friends. When Bruce Wayne had disappeared last time, it was after an encounter with Thomas at Jonah's church. I was beginning to suspect that Bruce Wayne's disappearance definitely had some tie to Crocker's gang. I just didn't know what. The question was, would Thomas tell me anything?

There was only one way to find out.

I could only imagine the harassment Muffy would endure if I took her with me in her costume, so I stripped it off before clipping her leash onto her collar. She immediately began to jump around in excitement. If only my enthusiasm matched hers. Instead, dread filled my belly like a boulder, dragging me down my steps. I forced myself to straighten my back and lift my chin as I walked. I was about to confront a handful of teenage boys. What was I so worked up about?

A giant grin spread across Thomas's face as I approached his car. His two friends flanked him, each with a beer can in hand.

"Well, look who's come-a-callin'." Thomas laughed. "Here to party with us, Rose?"

I swallowed the lecture on the tip of my tongue. It would be wasted breath and wouldn't encourage him to help me. "Have you seen Bruce Wayne Decker lately?"

Thomas's smile turned wicked. "Nope, he's usually hiding up your skirt when I see him."

My face burned with anger and embarrassment. "Are you sure you haven't seen him? Maybe out at Weston's Garage?"

He hopped off the back of the car and strutted toward me. He was a tall and lanky seventeen-year-old who hadn't quite grown into himself. But he could still cause me physical harm. The question was whether he'd cross that line.

"Maybe you'd like to come pay a visit and see for yourself. I know a few friends who'd love to have a chat with you."

The hairs on my arms stood on end. "Have you seen him or not?"

He cocked an eyebrow with a smirk. "You didn't say the magic word. Please." The street light caught the medallion at the base of his throat.

I drew in a breath, trying to rein in my impatience. "Thomas, would you please tell me if you've seen Bruce Wayne?"

He leaned his face into mine, his beer breath nearly making me gag. "That wasn't so hard, now was it?" he whispered, then grinned wider and stepped back. I got a better look at the medallion, which was a St. Jude's charm. Funny, Thomas didn't strike me as the religious type and his mother was Pentecostal. "I haven't seen him since last week."

"And when and where was that?"

"Last Friday. At Weston's Garage. Now you owe me something."

I took a step back. "What could I possibly have that you want?"

"I'll let you know when I want it." Then he started laughing again, his peanut gallery joining in, and turned his back to me.

Muffy lowered her head and released a growl. I tugged on her leash. "Come on, Muffy."

Their laughter filled the darkness as I walked back to my house. I was surprised Miss Mildred hadn't called the police on them yet for disturbing the peace. When I got inside, I locked all the doors and windows, more irritated than scared.

Thomas was a lot of talk, but I knew one day he'd cross a line that couldn't be uncrossed.

Muffy seemed agitated, but I finally got her calm enough to settle down for bed. I had trouble sleeping, worried as I was about Bruce Wayne and where to look for him. No, I *knew* where to look. I just didn't want to go there. While I knew Thomas was a bunch of talk, I had no delusions that Crocker's associates at Weston's Garage wouldn't back their threats with action. I was tempted to tell Mason what was going on, but I didn't want to put him in a difficult situation. If I told him Bruce Wayne was missing, he'd be forced to report it. And if I asked him not to, I'd be putting his job at risk. I couldn't do that.

I woke up the next morning to the sound of Muffy whimpering. After I checked her over to make sure she wasn't hurt, I took her outside through the kitchen door. But she instantly bolted around the corner to the front of the house. I raced after her, but stopped in my tracks when I caught sight of my front yard.

Smashed pumpkins littered the yard and covered the porch. The hay bales had been ripped apart and strewn across the grass and the street.

With a heavy sigh of disappointment, I walked up the front steps to see if Thomas and his friends had done any permanent damage to the house. Dried-up gobs of the pumpkins and squash splattered the porch, but I didn't see anything that couldn't be fixed. My gaze landed on the table between my rocking chairs. Smack in the middle was a half-finished bottle of tequila.

So Thomas and his friends had staged a party on my porch.

Something shiny on the table next to the bottle caught my attention. I leaned over and picked it up, immediately recognizing it as a St. Jude's medallion necklace. When I flipped it over, I saw an engraved snake on the other side. Here was my proof that Thomas was involved, but the necklace sparked another memory too. A month ago, someone had tried to break into the house next door to Thomas and the police had found a St. Jude's necklace in the yard. And then there was the necklace I'd found in Bruce Wayne's apartment. Was it some symbol of being loyal to Crocker? I let it drop from my fingers onto the table.

I considered calling the police and filing a report so I could press charges, but I doubted that Henryetta's finest would take me seriously. When I gave my statement to Detective Taylor the day after Jonah's mother had tried to kill me, he insinuated that I was responsible for the predicaments I'd gotten sucked into over the last few months. I could only imagine how he would react if I made the call.

"Let me get this straight, Ms. Gardner. You confronted a known hoodlum and his friends, and then you were surprised when they trashed your porch? And you say you don't bring these things on yourself?"

The police were out. Once again, I was on my own.

# Chapter Four

I got dressed and spent the next half hour cleaning my yard. I was putting my rake in the shed when my cell phone rang. I dug it out of my pocket, surprised to see it was Mason.

What was he doing calling me at eight in the morning?

"Rose, have you left for work yet?"

My forehead furrowed in confusion. "No. But I'm about to leave soon."

"Would you meet me somewhere for coffee?"

My stomach fluttered in anticipation, but my head told it to be still. Mason was using his business voice. This wasn't about us. "Sure. Merilee's?"

"Not this time. How about the new coffee shop south of town, The Coffee House. Do you know where it is?"

"Yeah," I said, still confused. "But I have to run by a job, so I'll be in my work clothes."

"That's okay. I just need to talk to you and the sooner the better. Can you meet me in about thirty minutes?"

"I was about to leave, so I can meet you in fifteen."

"See you there."

After I put Muffy in the bathroom, I drove across town, anxiety prickling the hair on the back of my neck. Why did he sound so business-like? Had he changed his mind and decided to tell me he was moving on?

I pulled into the parking lot, recognizing Mason's car several spots away. A patch of new houses and businesses had sprung up south of town over the last few years, and Violet's neighborhood was part of the transformation. The Coffee House had opened after our nursery and had replaced us as the most buzzed about new business. For a town a full hour from the nearest Starbucks, an establishment that specialized in espresso drinks was a big deal.

Mason stood outside the front door, wearing a dark suit and looking more handsome than ever. It made me blush to realize that I noticed. "Thanks for meeting me, Rose."

"You know I wouldn't refuse you anything."

He had opened the door for me, and I was walking through it when he stared down into my eyes. The longing in his gaze stole my breath away. "Be careful or I'll take you up on that sooner than I intended."

A shiver ran down my back and I let my imagination wander to what that might entail, which surprised me even more. This morning was full of shocks.

We walked up to the counter and placed our orders, then stood at the end of the counter waiting for our drinks.

"So...are you going to tell me why you asked me here?"

"Can't I just ask you to coffee?"

"Well, yesterday we decided we would spend more time together as friends. And I definitely would have still come if it was just a friendly invitation. But your Mason Deveraux III, assistant DA voice convinced me this was something other than a coffee date."

"No wonder you solve so many mysteries," Mason teased as he took our cups from the barista. But I noticed his smile didn't reach his eyes, and his shoulders were tense. "You pay attention to the details."

We found a table next to the window that overlooked the parking lot. Once we were settled, I couldn't shake my nerves. Why would Mason ask to see me over here about something DA-related?

My stomach fell to my feet. What if it was about Bruce Wayne?

"So what's up, Mason?" I tried to keep my voice from quivering.

He took a breath, his forehead wrinkling with concern. "I wanted you to hear this from me first."

The seriousness of his expression left me lightheaded. "What?" I whispered.

"There was a prison break last night."

My eyes flew open. "Miss Rhonda escaped?" Mason had promised me weeks ago that if Jonah's mother ever got out of jail, he'd make sure to tell me as soon as he knew. Only after I said the words did I realize I'd used her fake name. "Does Jonah know?" I could only imagine how upset he'd be.

He shook his head, looking even more worried. "No, not Wanda Pruitt."

"Then who? Why are you telling me in person—?" I sank back into my chair as the truth hit me like an anvil.

Daniel Crocker.

"The sheriff's office is following several leads and the state police are also part of the manhunt." He reached across the table and took my hand. "They'll catch him, Rose."

I nodded in shock, clinging to his fingers.

"He's probably miles away. He's had enough time to leave the state, so I'm sure you have nothing to worry about, but I wanted you to hear it from me. I'm sure you're safe, but as a precaution, the police are going to increase their patrols of your neighborhood."

"Like that's done me any good in the past." I pulled my hand from Mason's and forced myself to take a sip of my coffee, which was so hot it burned my tongue. "How sure are you that he's left the state?"

"My friend Jeff at the sheriff's office is very sure. Their most solid lead points to Shreveport."

"Not the sheriff's department. *You*. Do *you* think he left the state?"

Mason grabbed his cup and spun it in his hand. "I don't have a good handle on the guy. I read all of his files after you told me that his former associates threatened you last month. The smart thing for him to do would be to leave the state."

"You still haven't given me an answer."

"All of the law enforcement offices are certain he's left, but they're neglecting to take into consideration that he's a psychopath. And from my experience, psychopaths never behave as they should."

"So you think he could still be around the area."

His eyes searched mine. "I don't know. Maybe. So I need you to report anything unusual. A phone call. Anything strange that makes you uneasy."

"The decorations on my front porch were destroyed last night. But I'm fairly certain that my neighbor Thomas and his friends did it."

"Why him?"

"Because I talked to him last night and he was antagonistic."

Mason sat up straighter. "Why were you talking to him?"

Oh, crappy doodles. I couldn't tell him about Bruce Wayne. "I took Muffy on a walk and his friends were sitting on his car drinking beer."

"Rose, if you feel unsafe in your neighborhood, you need to call the police."

"Yeah," I snorted. "Officer Ernie will come running to protect me."

"He'll do his job."

I didn't want to discuss the loyalty or lack thereof of the Henryetta Police Department.

"Did you at least call the police to file a report?"

"No. We both know what little good that would have done."

Mason sighed and leaned forward. "If you really feel that unsafe with the Henryetta police, perhaps you should consider moving out of the city limits. To the sheriff's jurisdiction. Maybe you'd feel more protected."

"And leave my house?" But the truth was that it was really Violet's house. We'd both grown up in it, but Momma had left it to Vi in her will. I paid Violet rent to live there. Maybe moving really was a good idea. "I'd never considered it."

"There are some condos close to here, just outside the city limit but in Fenton County. Your commute wouldn't be much longer. Maybe ten minutes."

But I wasn't sure if I could live in some cookie-cutter condo like Violet's house. I liked older houses with character. Not that it mattered. Momma's house was Violet's and all my available cash was tied up in the business. I couldn't afford to buy a new house even if I wanted to. Unless I decided to sell the farm. One more reason to strongly consider it.

"You're probably right about the vandalism being the work of some teens. It doesn't seem likely that Crocker would break out of jail then swing by your house to smash pumpkins on your front porch when half the law enforcement officers in Arkansas are hot on his tail. But humor me and file a report, okay? Especially since we know Thomas has ties to them."

"Okay."

"Until Crocker's caught, you should lay low."

I grimaced. "That might be difficult. The Gardner Sisters Nursery is part of a press conference today and I *have* to be there."

"What press conference?"

"The small business administration is giving us a grant. It's big enough for us to expand our business onto the empty lot next to the nursery."

"Rose, that's wonderful."

"Yeah, well…it comes with strings. They contacted her on Monday and said they were giving us the check as part of a campaign stop."

Realization drained the blood from his face. "Joe?"

I nodded with a sigh. "Yeah."

"Did you agree?"

"I did, but only because it could make a huge difference to our long-term goals. I can suffer through this for the good of the business."

"Why's he coming to Henryetta? This isn't even his district."

"His father has ties to the Arkansas SBA. Joe is including it as part of his platform. They're highlighting successful small businesses."

"So Violet takes care of the press conference and you get the check."

I shook my head. "No. They said we both have to be there."

Mason cursed under his breath, then reached across the table and took my hand again. "Sometimes the money is tempting, but the cost associated with it is too much. I urge you to give this more consideration."

My blood turned cold. "You think I shouldn't do it."

"No, Rose. Only you can decide what you should or shouldn't do. I'm just asking you not to be blinded by all the zeros on a check."

I nodded. He was right.

"On the other hand, it could be empowering for you to see Joe again and let him know you're doing okay without him, that you're moving on. But don't feel like you have to do that, either. You don't have to prove anything to him...or me. If you decide to do it, do it to prove it to yourself."

"How'd you get so smart?'

He winked. "Let's just say I've made plenty of mistakes of my own."

I took a sip of my coffee and studied Mason's face. Something was different—in a good way—only I couldn't figure out what it was.

Mason's eyebrows lifted in derision. "You do know that this has Joe's father's stink all over it?"

"I know. I just can't figure out why he'd want us together."

Mason leaned his elbow on the table. "Why does J.R. Simmons do *anything*? To get Joe out of trouble or keep him in line. The question is how could this situation take care of either one of those things?"

I closed my eyes. Mason was right. Joe was being punished somehow and I was just a pawn for his father to use in his game of manipulation.

"What time's the press conference?"

My stomach knotted. "One."

"And when is Joe getting there?"

"I don't know. Violet said to be there around noon."

"I'd like to come." He hesitated. "If that's okay with you."

"Oh, Mason. I'd love for you to be there." I was amazed at how true my statement was. I worried how I'd react when I saw Joe, and I couldn't count on Violet to be supportive. Mason had proven in the past that I could always count on him. "But I thought you had court."

"I'll get a postponement. With Crocker loose, I'll just worry about you all day anyway. If you don't mind having a shadow today, I'd like to be there to support you."

The thought of spending the day with Mason made me happier than I'd expected. "You don't *have* to, Mason."

"I know, but I want to. There's a difference."

"Okay then." As grateful as I was to have Mason by my side, I couldn't neglect the fact that Bruce Wayne probably had no one. I needed to figure out where he was and all the evidence was pointing to the one place in town where I definitely wasn't welcome. "I have an appointment with Jonah later this morning. At the church." I hated lying to him, but it couldn't be helped. Bruce Wayne disappearing within twenty-four hours of Daniel Crocker's escape from prison was too big of a coincidence to ignore. And while I still wasn't ready to tell Mason, I felt safe telling Jonah, especially since he ran a program for troubled youths who were mentored by rehabilitated criminals. Jonah had access to resources I didn't.

"How about you talk to Jonah, and I'll meet you at the nursery around noon. But tell Bruce Wayne what's going on and make sure he's with you at any job sites today. You really shouldn't be alone."

Mason was right. The fact that Daniel Crocker was running around loose freaked me out more than I cared to admit. "That might be a problem. Bruce Wayne has called in sick every day since last week."

He paused. "Is he okay?"

"I don't know. David told me that he thinks it might be bronchitis." Technically, it wasn't a lie.

"So you're working alone? That's not a good idea."

"I know. But there's nothing too pressing that can't wait. We were supposed to start building a retaining wall today, but I'd barely have time to get started before I'd have to leave to get ready for the press conference."

"Good." He glanced at his watch and grimaced. "I'd love nothing more than to spend the morning with you, but if I'm taking the afternoon off, I need to get some work done."

I nodded, hating the fact he was taking off work because of me.

"Rose, don't feel guilty." He laughed when my eyes widened. "What? You think I don't know how much you hate inconveniencing people? Just remember this: It's not an inconvenience for me. I'm grateful for an excuse to spend the afternoon with you. Even if the situation is less than ideal."

He walked me to my truck and stood in front of me, pushing my back against the driver's side door. Being this close to him made my heart beat faster.

"Be careful, Rose," he murmured, tucking a piece of my hair behind my ear. "I couldn't bear it if something happened to you."

"I don't intend to let anything happen to me."

A grin lifted his mouth. "You're like a cat with nine lives, but don't press your luck. You have great instincts. Listen to them. If you feel like you're in a dangerous situation, call 911. Even if you don't think the police will help, they'll do their job. I promise."

"I will."

He reached around and opened my door. "I'll see you at the nursery around noon."

As Mason took off for the courthouse, I checked my cell phone for any missed calls and tried calling Bruce Wayne again, getting his voice mail. "Bruce Wayne, I know Daniel Crocker escaped from prison. If you're in some kind of trouble, *please* just call me so I can help." I hung up, feeling like my pathetic efforts were a waste of time. Maybe it was time to tell Mason. After all, Bruce Wayne could be in real danger. But Mason had just told me to listen to my instincts, and they were telling me not to let the police know just yet.

At the moment, my best hope for an ally was in the pastor's office of the New Living Hope Revival Church.

# Chapter Five

Every time I walked into the main office of Jonah's church, I always stopped and blinked when I saw the secretary who looked nothing like Miss Rhonda, aka Wanda Pruitt. His new secretary was much younger than the older women who loved to flock to him. Jonah definitely had a way with the grandmothers of our town, but the scandalous rumors had no truth to them. The older women were lonely and Jonah spent time with them, actually listening, which came as no surprise to me. He'd listened to me for weeks before we officially called it therapy.

"Hi, Jessica. Is Jonah in his office?"

The young woman looked up at me with a fake smile. Her bleached blonde hair was big and curly and her shirt was tighter than necessary and slightly inappropriate for a church office. She'd arranged little knick-knacks around the office, and a candle burned on her desk, filling the room with the scent of snickerdoodle cookies. "I'll let him know you're here." But she didn't look happy about it.

She pressed her intercom button and Jonah's office door opened within seconds.

A toothy, too-white smile spread across his face as he leaned against the door jamb. "What's the wonderful smell?"

Turning in her seat, Jessica beamed. "That's my candle, Jonah. But I brought you some cookies. Would you like some?"

He rubbed his stomach. "I'm gonna gain ten pounds if you keep bringing in those delicious baked goods." He turned his attention to me. "Rose, what's the pleasure of this visit? I thought we were seeing each other at my house tomorrow afternoon."

The young blonde woman shot me an ugly glare. She obviously liked Jonah and thought I was trying to steal him from her, especially since we spent so much time together.

Were all secretaries destined to hate me?

"Something important came up and I didn't want to wait until tomorrow to talk. Do you have time now?"

He held his door wider in invitation. "Of course. Come on in." He leaned out the door after I brushed past him. "Jessica, hold my calls, please."

I sat in one of the wingback chairs in front of his desk. Rather than sitting behind the desk, he sat next to me, crossing his legs, looking very much like the televangelist I'd first met. He'd updated his hairstyle from its former eighties pompadour, but though it was shorter and more stylish, he hadn't been able to resist adding highlights. "What's going on?"

I gripped the chair arm. "Bruce Wayne is missing."

He paused. "What do you mean, missing?"

"You know how he's been calling in sick? Well, it turns out he's not. David says he was leaving in the mornings and coming back late at night, but when David asked where he was going and what he was doing, Bruce Wayne told him it would be better if he didn't know."

He sank back in his chair, his shoulders slumping. "Oh dear."

"Then yesterday morning, David called me before seven a.m. to tell me that Bruce Wayne wouldn't be in, that he was still sick, but it made me suspicious. I doubt David Moore even knew seven a.m. existed before yesterday morning. So after I ate lunch with Neely Kate at Merilee's, I stopped by their house and brought him some chicken noodle soup. Only Bruce Wayne wasn't home and half his clothes were missing. When I asked David, he told me Bruce Wayne never came home the night before."

Jonah squeezed his eyes shut. "This isn't good."

"It gets worse."

His eyes flew open and his back stiffened.

"Mason told me this morning that Daniel Crocker escaped from the county jail last night."

Jonah jumped out of his chair and started pacing. "What? How?"

"I don't know. He didn't give me details. But I got to thinking that Bruce Wayne worked for Crocker before he got arrested for murder. And he still has a connection to Crocker's guys. It seems too coincidental for Bruce Wayne to disappear twenty-four hours before Crocker's prison break."

"Agreed. This is bad." He stopped pacing. "What does Mason think?"

"I haven't told him."

"Why not? He can help you."

I twisted my hands in my lap, questioning whether I'd made the right decision. "Jonah, if I tell Mason, he'll be obligated to report it. And what if Bruce Wayne took off for something stupid? He's on parole! They'll toss him in prison. I just need a day or two to see if I can figure out where he went and why he's gone. I'd go out to Weston's Garage—"

Jonah released a heavy sigh. "You and I both know that's a terrible idea. Especially in light of Crocker's prison break."

"Well…if it makes you feel any better, the sheriff's office and the state police think Crocker has left for Louisiana."

"That doesn't mean it's safe for you to go out there."

"I know…" My voice trailed off as I looked up at him.

He rolled his eyes and groaned. "Rose."

I sat on the edge of my seat. "Jonah, Bruce Wayne is in trouble. I know it and those guys out there like you."

He shook his head with a grimace. "I'm not sure I'd call it *like*. They come to my group for the community service hours. They only do it to stay on the right side of the law and their parole officers. Honestly, some days I question how effective it is. I've probably only turned around one boy since starting the group a few months ago."

I stood and put a hand on his arm. "Maybe it's only happening one boy at a time, but at least you made a difference to that one boy. I suspect you're making more of an impact than you realize. And those guys from Weston's Garage don't have to come here. They could do something else."

He released a wry laugh. "You were the one who suggested—quite rightly, I might add—that those guys from Weston's Garage were probably using my group to recruit boys like your neighbor Thomas."

I turned and leaned my butt against the desk. "I'm desperate, Jonah. I really care about Bruce Wayne and I know in my gut that something's wrong. I can't just sit around and do nothing. I'm open to suggestions."

He was silent for several seconds. "One of Crocker's former guys really seems to be trying to turn his life around—Scooter Malcolm."

My eyebrows lifted. "The brother of Skeeter Malcolm, the bookie at the pool hall? Their momma must have trouble coming up with names."

"Yep, that's him. And we both know that no one wants to get on Skeeter's bad side."

I knew that from personal experience with Skeeter when I was looking for evidence to clear Bruce Wayne's name. I shivered. I hated to think what might have happened if Mason hadn't shown up. "I didn't know the Malcolms had ties to Crocker."

"Rose, everyone in this town had ties to Crocker one way or the other."

"Oh." But it wasn't surprising I didn't know. Before Momma's murder, I had lived a completely sheltered life. I went to work at the DMV each morning, went home and took care of Momma, then got up the next day to do it all over again. With Violet's backing, I'd convinced myself that I was the town outcast, but I'd recently begun to question how much of that was caused by my own isolation, which had perpetuated the idea that I really *was* strange and different.

"Scooter's been trying to turn his life around, just like Bruce Wayne, but he has a harder road ahead of him because his brother keeps trying to pull him back in." He shifted his weight. "In any case, I'll find Scooter and ask him if he's heard anything. But don't get your hopes up. If Bruce Wayne's disappearance really does have something to do with Daniel Crocker, I'm not sure Scooter will help us."

"Okay," I said, trying to keep the disappointment out of my voice. Jonah was trying to help, which was more than I should have been asking. "We'll just hope that he knows something."

"But if I don't find anything, you need to tell Mason."

I sucked in my lower lip.

"Rose."

I stood and moved to the window, looking down at the church grounds. I had hired Bruce Wayne and David out of desperation when Jonah commissioned us to landscape the entire church grounds in less than five days. But it turned out that Bruce Wayne loved it. He'd been working for me for a little over a month and I couldn't imagine the Gardner Sisters Nursery without him.

"*Rose.*"

"I've been leaving Bruce Wayne messages on his cell phone. Maybe he'll call me back and tell me that this has all been a big misunderstanding."

Jonah's mouth pursed as his eyebrows rose.

"When do you think you can talk to Scooter?"

"I'll track him down as soon as we're done here."

"Okay," I groaned. "If Scooter can't help us, and if I haven't heard anything by the end of the press conference, I'll tell Mason."

"What press conference?"

I spun around and offered him an awkward smile. "The Gardner Sisters Nursery is being awarded a huge grant this afternoon from the Arkansas Small Business Administration." I told him everything I'd told Mason earlier.

He frowned while he listened, then asked, "Are you sure you want to do this?"

"How can I turn it down?"

"You do realize that his father is counting on that very reaction. He offered you something that you think you can't live without. Just more of his manipulation."

"You don't think I know that?" I asked, my irritation increasing. "But how can I turn this down? Violet's counting on it."

"Forget Violet. What do *you* want?"

"If we don't do this, Violet will—"

Jonah moved closer to me and bent his knees so we were eye to eye. "I don't give a Fig Newton about Violet right now. I'm asking about *you*. What does *Rose* want to do? Do you want to see Joe?"

I walked back toward the desk and sank into the chair. "Would it make me a terrible person if I did?"

"It would make you perfectly normal."

"I know he's with Hilary now."

"And we both know that's staged."

"But still."

"What do you hope to get out of seeing him? Ask yourself that before you go."

"I think I just want to know that he's okay. That he's making the best of it."

"Do you want him to tell you it's all a terrible mistake? That he wants to come back to you?"

"No. I don't know." I ran a hand over my hair, smoothing back several loose strands. "I used to think I wanted that, but Mason..." I took a deep breath. "I think what I really need is closure. I need to say goodbye while I'm not sobbing my eyes out. Does that make sense?"

"Perfect sense. And it's a very good reason to go through with it. I just wanted to make sure you're doing it for you."

"I guess I am."

"When is it scheduled? I'll try to come. I was a big part of the first press conference at the grand opening of your business. I should make a habit of attending all of them."

I grinned, trying to settle my nerves. Not too long ago, I'd been alone in the world, but now I had supportive friends who were there for me when I needed them. Facing Joe at the press conference would be hard, but I felt stronger knowing Mason, Jonah, and Neely Kate would be there to support me. "You're the one who got our landscaping business rolling, but I think you've run out of land for us to work with."

"There's still my backyard." He winked.

I laughed. "When we were working on the front yard, Bruce Wayne checked out the back and actually came up with a few ideas. He's a natural." My voice broke.

Jonah placed his hand on my shoulder. "He'll turn up, Rose. We'll find him."

I sure hoped Jonah was right.

# Chapter Six

A crowd was already gathering in the nursery parking lot when I pulled up a few minutes after noon. My phone dinged and I checked to see I had another message from Mason. He'd been checking in with me all morning to make sure I was safe. His latest text told me he was running late, but he'd be at the nursery by one.

Violet burst out of the door as I walked to the entrance, Muffy trotting along behind me. "Where have you been?" she said through gritted teeth. "You're late."

I glanced at my phone. "By three minutes."

"I needed you here, Rose. People are already showing up." Her gaze took me in from head to toe. "Have you spent all morning getting dressed? Because I know you weren't building Mrs. Miller's retaining wall. Which means you weren't *working*."

After leaving Jonah's, I'd run by our latest job to check on the site and tell the homeowner it might be a few days before we wrapped things up. When I got home, I spent five full minutes staring at the clothes in my closet. Did I want to wear jeans and a sweatshirt and try to make Joe think this was no big deal? Did I want to put on a dress and curl my hair? But would he think I was trying to win him back? I ultimately decided to dress for me. I was going to be on camera and I wanted to look good whether Joe was there or not. I chose a suede skirt and cream-colored sweater with dark brown boots. I'd even curled my hair and fixed it into a style Neely Kate had tried out the weekend before.

I knew Violet lashed out when she was stressed, but I was stressed too. "Violet, I'm already going above and beyond by doing this today. Don't push me."

Her mouth fell open in shock, but she quickly closed it and gave me a disapproving look. "I don't know what's gotten into you lately, Rose Anne Gardner, but I'm not sure I like you very much right now."

"Well, that makes two of us, because I haven't liked you for a good month."

Tears welled in her eyes. She started say something but then turned around and walked into the back room, leaving me to feel like the worst sister in the world. What I said may have been true, but that wasn't the way to tell her. At least not according to the role-playing games Jonah and I had practiced when preparing for this confrontation.

I glanced around the shop and wondered why she had freaked out about me being late. I couldn't see a single thing that needed to be done. But then again, I had no idea what we were supposed to do in the first place.

She came back out after a few minutes, her smile screwed on and her eyes shining bright, pretending like nothing had happened. "The campaign people won't be here until close to one, but the SBA people should be here at any moment."

My stomach flip-flopped. "Do you know who's coming with the campaign people?"

She turned to give me a smug smile. "Nope."

It was my turn to gasp.

She glanced out the window, her eyes lighting up as the front door opened. "Mayor MacIntosh. It's so wonderful that you could make time in your busy schedule to come today."

Brody sauntered through the door and shook her extended hand, holding on longer than necessary. "I wouldn't dream of missing it, Violet. What's good for the Gardner Sisters Nursery is excellent for all of Henryetta."

I glanced around, wondering who they were putting on their little show for. There were a few customers in the store, but I was the only one watching, and I wasn't falling for it. I cleared my throat. "Muffy, let's go in back."

"That's right," Violet called after me. "You run off and hide like you always do, leaving me to do all the work."

I stopped in the doorway and spun around while Muffy ran for the dog bed I kept in the back room. Smart dog.

Brody stood next to her, looking like someone had just pointed a shotgun in his face.

I put my hand on my hip. "Is that what you think I do?"

Brody took two careful steps backward as though he was worried he was about to step on a landmine.

She put both hands on her hips and cocked her head. "Isn't it?" she asked in her syrupy sweet voice.

I took several steps toward her. "I do plenty of work around here. I work six days a week, and I'm out doing manual labor while you stand around behind a cash register all day."

She gasped. "I do more than that!"

The customers had stopped perusing the store, turning their full attention to Violet.

Brody had his hand on the door. "I'll just wait outside."

Violet spun her head around to him so quickly it was a wonder it didn't fly off her head. "No you won't! You wait right there."

My sister's raised voice had attracted the attention of several busybodies outside and they stood in rapt attention outside the windows, as if they were watching an episode of the *Real Housewives of Fenton County*.

"You're right," I conceded. "You do more than run a cash register. You let everyone think that I'm some evil tyrant who's made you into an indentured servant."

Her face reddened. "You know full good and well that I've been trying to set the record straight since I confessed that to you."

I took several steps closer. "Really, Vi? How hard are you trying? Because Mrs. Hershel's eyes nearly fell out of her head while she was glaring at me at the bank last week."

"How can you be sure that it was over my little misunderstanding? It could be because of the company you keep. Think about it! Jonah Pruitt's mother killed five women and tried to kill you, but you spend more time with him than me. Then take Bruce Wayne. He's a criminal, for heaven's sake. I'm sure we'd get even more landscaping jobs if someone more respectable worked with you. Joe was right. No wonder he broke up with you."

I shook my head in disbelief, tears springing to my eyes. "You have no idea, Violet." I clenched my fists at my sides. "No idea at all why we broke up."

"Mason will see it too. He'll see that you're not like everyone else. I've tried to protect you, but you got a bee in your bonnet and decided to prove me wrong. And everything's falling apart around you now, just like I knew it would."

"Violet!" Brody said, his voice full of shock.

"Even Bruce Wayne is proving to be a disappointment. You actually believe he's sick and not off getting high somewhere? You really are naïve. This is why you need to let me make all the business decisions, Rose. I'm the one with common sense."

"You're just like Momma," I whispered.

"*What?*"

"Oh, my word." I sagged against the counter. "How did I never see this before? You're exactly like her."

Her back became ram-rod stiff. "I'm *nothin'* like her."

"You think your way is the right way, and when I don't do things your way, you berate me until I think I was wrong." I shook my head. "I'm done. I'm done with letting you or anyone else tell me what to do."

"*Tell you what to do*? Good heavens." She scowled in disgust. "You haven't done a *thing* I've told you to do since Joe Simmons showed up in your life! I knew he'd hurt you! When I found out about his family, I told you that you'd never be good enough for them. And who was right, Rose? It kills you to admit it, doesn't it?"

"Is that what this is about?" I shouted. "Joe destroys my heart and you're waiting for me to tell you that *you're right*?"

The crowd outside the windows had grown larger and several onlookers dared to come inside and gather around the front door.

"Congratulations, Violet. You were right." I took a step toward her, lifting my eyebrows. "I'm too white trash for the high-and-mighty Simmons family of El Dorado, Arkansas. But if I'm white trash because of my roots, stop and think about what that makes you."

Her smile fell.

I leaned into her ear and whispered, "And the reason Joe and I broke up was to save you, Violet. His father has photos of you and Brody coming out of a motel room and was using them to blackmail Joe into running for office." I took a step back, my heart dark with anger and bitterness. "But I don't expect a thank you. You'll just twist it around somehow so you won't have to accept responsibility. Because that's what you do." I turned around and headed into the back room. "And for the record," I said as I walked. "I'm not hiding in the back room. I'm trying to stay away from *you*."

I left her standing in the middle of the shop, pale-faced and in obvious shock, but for once I didn't care. And if that didn't make me wicked, I wasn't sure what would.

Neely Kate was sitting at my potting table, her eyes as big as quarters. "Did that just happen?" she whispered.

I had invited her the night before, but with all the commotion, I hadn't seen her sneak in. My legs started to quiver as I nodded.

She hopped off the stool and grabbed my arm. "Let's go out and get some fresh air."

I let her pull me out the back door and Muffy followed us. I leaned against the brick wall, reminded of the night of Momma's visitation when Joe and I had ducked out to escape the stares of the people who were certain that I'd bashed in my mother's head and then hid the rolling pin in the folds of my skirt.

"Thanks for coming early, Neely Kate. You didn't have to."

"And miss that confrontation? That was the best thing I've seen in…well, *ever*."

Muffy lay on the concrete next to my feet, looking up at me in confusion.

"It was horrible." I squeezed my eyes, hoping all the mean, vile things I'd just said would somehow disappear. "I've never talked to anyone that way."

She grabbed my arm. "Well, then that was a long time coming, wasn't it? Besides, what about all the ugly things she said to you? She was much more hateful than you would ever even consider being. How can you work with her every day?"

"I'm not with her every day. I'm usually out at the job sites."

"Well, there you have it. You can just stay away from the shop," she teased, but my heart ached.

Spewing my anger had made me feel good temporarily, but now I felt hollow and sick to my stomach. "What am I going to do?" I turned to Neely Kate, her bright blue eyes gazing at me while her long blonde curls blew in the wind behind her. "I should apologize."

Her eyes flew open. "No, you will not! Are you *really* sorry you told her how you felt?"

"Well, no. But I *am* sorry I was so hateful. I regret that part."

"I suspect that's the only language Violet Beauregard understands."

I sighed. "It still doesn't make it right."

"I suppose." She was silent for several seconds. "I heard about Daniel Crocker getting out."

"Yeah, I'm surprised so many people are out front waiting for this press conference with a hardened criminal on the loose."

She stepped away from the wall. "You don't know, do you?"

"Know what?"

She turned to look at me, studying my face. "A good portion of Henryetta supports Daniel Crocker. He provided a lot of jobs that disappeared after he was arrested. Some people are happy he escaped. They think he's innocent and that it was all a setup. You may have seen his evil side, but he was an excellent schmoozer and an even better liar. Heck, people loved him so much that I suspect he would have been the next mayor if he'd decided to run."

"You're kidding." But I wasn't too surprised when I stopped to think about it. Thomas had pretty much told me the same thing, only he'd added that a lot of people blamed his arrest on me.

"I wish I was." She sighed and pressed her back to the wall again. "Aren't you worried?"

"It makes me nervous knowing he's on the loose, but Mason says the state police think he's in Louisiana." I paused. "Mason is taking this afternoon off from work to come to the press conference and spend the rest of the day with me."

"Aww…"

I shook my head, but I couldn't stop my grin.

"Will you just date the guy already?"

"I can't, Neely Kate. Not yet."

"I'm an old married woman now. I need to live vicariously though you."

I laughed and bumped into her arm. "Yeah, you're about to hit your four-month anniversary. That's like *forever*."

"When time does Joe show up?"

"I don't know." My chest tightened and my heart sped up. "I think right before one."

"How are you doing? Really?"

I took a deep breath. "Honestly, I'm scared to see Joe. I don't know what he's going to say or do. He might ignore me for all I know."

"The way you look? There's no way that man could ignore you. I'm glad you're showing him what he walked away from."

"That's not why I wore this."

"I know. You don't have a manipulative bone in your body. I think Violet got all the bitchy genes."

"Neely Kate!" I chastised, but I couldn't hold back my laughter.

"So what are you supposed to do at this thing anyway?"

"I have no idea how this works. I think I'll hide back here until someone comes looking for me."

"Good idea. Better steer clear of Violet right now, though. She'll be on a war path." Neely Kate moaned and leaned her head against the building, closing her eyes. "Something is *not* agreeing with me."

"Still not feeling well?" I asked, worried about her. Neely Kate rarely complained of physical ailments.

"It's probably those dog-gone hot wings. My grandmother made me take her to Big Bill's Barbeque for buffalo hot wings last night and then to the VFW for bingo night." She shot me a pretend glare. "Since it was Halloween and you were with your niece and nephew, I couldn't use you as an excuse to get out of it."

"Surely it's not that bad."

"Fine. Next week you go with her and help her set out all her good luck charms just so. Then every time she gets any kind of bingo, she tells everyone she's a psychic and she knew she was gonna win. By the end of the night, she has several new clients for her psychic readings."

"Do you think she's really psychic?"

"I used to kinda believe. Until I met you." She laughed. "In any case, those damn hot wings are my curse. Not only do they send my guts into a panic whenever they're within ten feet of my mouth, but they seem to do the same to my grandma. Yet she still won't give 'em up. Not even after the time she took them to the Maryville Southern Baptist Church Valentine's Sweetheart Potluck and tried to pass 'em off as her own." She shook her head with a laugh. "Oh, my word! The uproar! The church board had to call an emergency meeting to see about getting her kicked off the ladies auxiliary."

We giggled over her grandmother's antics for another twenty minutes before the back door opened and Mason poked his head around the corner.

"So this is where you two are hiding? Is it just me, or does Violet seem even more tense than usual?"

"It's not just you." Neely Kate laughed. "You missed the fireworks."

Mason's gaze shifted to the back room to see what he might have missed.

I walked toward him. "I'll tell you about it later. Is Jonah out front?"

"I didn't see him, but I wasn't looking for him, either. I was more worried about finding you."

"I take it that means they haven't captured Daniel Crocker yet?"

"No, but they're still pretty confident that they've tracked him to Shreveport."

"That's what you said this morning."

"I'm sorry." He grimaced apologetically. "I wish I had better news. Just get through this press conference, and then how about I take you to Magnolia for the rest of the day? We can see a movie and eat dinner. It'll take your mind off of everything."

I smiled up at him, my stomach fluttering. "I'd like that."

Neely Kate moved behind Mason and waggled her eyebrows at me with a lascivious smirk. I shot her a glare.

Keeping his eyes on mine, Mason grinned. "You're not helping, Neely Kate."

She laughed and disappeared through the open back door.

Mason let it close behind her, hesitating. "Are you sure you want to do this?"

I nodded. Part of me didn't want to, but I needed to for so many more reasons.

Too bad that didn't make me any less nervous.

He stared into my eyes, his smile fading. "I hope you find what you're looking for, Rose."

"Me too."

# Chapter Seven

When we went back inside, Muffy found her bed in the corner of the back room and hunkered down. I wondered if my little dog could see the future too, but it didn't take a psychic reading to know things were about to get even tenser. I found Violet in a huddle of several people I didn't recognize, all wearing suits and business attire. Her head swiveled as I emerged from the back room, and she shot me a glare. All the customers had vanished.

A woman with graying hair straightened and took several steps toward me. "You must be Rose," she said with a smile.

"Yes, ma'am." I extended my hand, glad that Mason was standing behind me. My nerves were about to overtake me.

She shook with a firm grasp. "I'm Thelma Peterman and I'm with the Arkansas Small Business Association. When J.R. Simmons brought your business to our attention, we were excited to process your grant."

My stomach tightened and I felt Mason place a hand on the small of my back for support. I wasn't sure why I was shocked. I had already guessed that Joe's father was behind this set-up, but suspecting something and having it confirmed were two different things.

"We don't usually spotlight businesses as new as yours, but Mr. Simmons insisted we feature you as part of Joe

Simmons's political campaign, which, of course, will provide great exposure for both of you."

"We're just so honored to be considered," Violet gushed, clutching her hands in front of her.

Thelma cleared her throat, speaking loud enough to get everyone's attention. "Here's what's going to happen: Joe's running behind schedule, so we'll film some footage of you and Violet puttering around the shop and ask some informal questions while we wait. Then we'll stand outside when he shows up, and Joe will give a speech about Arkansas' entrepreneurial spirit. He'll hand you an envelope, saying that he's giving you the check, but in reality it will be empty. Instead, we'll deposit the money directly into your account. Then Joe will take questions from the press and be on his way. If we need more footage of you two, we'll stick around after he leaves. This should take no more than two hours max."

"Okay," I said, looking out the window at the growing crowd. "Why are there so many people showing up for this? I didn't know Joe was so popular in Henryetta."

"It's probably because there are going to be news crews from Little Rock here filming the press conference," Violet said with a snip in her voice. "They want to be on TV. If you'd been in here ten minutes ago, you would know that."

"Excuse me, Ms. Peterman." Mason stepped around me. "You say that the money will deposited into the Gardner Sisters Nursery's bank account. I'd like to know exactly when that transaction will be processed."

Thelma's bushy eyebrows shot up, and her mouth pursed into the shape of a heart. "And you are...?"

Mason extended his hand, assuming his official countenance. The one that had intimidated me when we first met on Bruce Wayne Decker's trial. "Mason Deveraux III. Fenton County Assistant District Attorney."

Her eyes widened in alarm. "I assure you that there is nothing to worry about, Mr. Deveraux. We're a state-run department and all the paperwork has been processed. The money will be deposited by the end of the week."

"I was told that there were conditions placed on awarding the grant. One of them was that Rose has to be present for the press conference, is that correct?"

"Well...yes..."

"May I ask who placed those conditions?"

The blood drained from Violet's face. "Mason, I'm sure you're getting all worked up over nothing."

Thelma had recovered enough to become indignant. "It was a decision of the board, Mr. Deveraux. The business does include the name *sisters*. We needed both sisters."

Mason shifted his weight, lifting his eyebrows but maintaining his death stare. "How curious that you would think it necessary to make that stipulation. I would presume that both sisters would be thrilled with such an honor and that neither would consider missing the opportunity to show off their business."

"Well..."

"I want assurance—in writing—that if Ms. Gardner participates in this presentation, the money will be deposited into the business's account."

Thelma's face reddened. "Mr. Deveraux—"

"Mason!" Violet protested. "That really isn't necessary."

Mason stared her down. "Violet, I'm positive you can appreciate that I'm looking out for your best interest."

Her eyes glittered with suppressed anger. "You mean Rose's." She turned to me. "Rose, tell Mason that you don't need his intervention."

I looked up into Mason's determined face then turned back to Violet. "No. He's right. If I'm gonna do this, I want to know that they won't change their minds."

Thelma turned and talked to the people behind her in hushed tones before addressing Mason. "This is highly unusual, Mr. Deveraux."

"Nevertheless, we'll need that agreement in writing."

Her back stiffened. "I'm not authorized to create such a document."

"Then find someone who is."

Violet marched over and grabbed Mason's arm, her fingers digging so deep she was bound to leave bruises. "Mason, can we talk for a moment?"

His gaze shifted to Thelma. "It looks like we have a few moments while we're waiting."

Violet dragged him into the back room and I followed them, numb with shock.

Violet jabbed him in the chest with her finger. "You have *no right* butting your nose into our business, Mason. *Our business.*"

Mason's face softened. "And as Rose's friend, I can't in good conscience stand in the background without offering her legal counsel when I feel she needs it." He shifted his weight. "Violet, you know good and well that this was instigated by J.R. Simmons. You don't think that man will double-cross you both with a smile on his face? I want you to have this money as much as *you* want it, but I'd hate to see these people put you two through the Joe Simmons Puppet Show without anything to show for it. Trust me, Violet. I am looking out for your best interest here too, not just Rose's. J.R. Simmons has used every trick in the book to get what he wants. I want to make sure both of you get what you were promised."

His speech seemed to calm her down. She put her hands on her hips and looked at the floor, nodding. "Yeah, maybe you're right."

"Thank you." He put his hands on her arms and squatted to meet her gaze. "I promise you, I would never do anything to hurt your business. I care about Rose and I see how happy it makes her. I want it to succeed, but as her friend—and yours—I can't stand back and watch you be taken advantage of."

She chewed on the inside of her lip for a moment. "Okay."

He dropped his hold, becoming more official again. "And when that document shows up—and I'm certain it will—I want to look it over to make sure it's legally binding."

"How can you be so sure they'll do it?" I asked.

Mason's face hardened. "Because J.R. Simmons is desperate to put you and Joe together. Desperate enough to offer you several hundred thousand dollars to make it happen."

"Oh."

Violet was indignant again. "No, we're getting that money because *I* applied for this grant."

"And how long ago did you apply? A month?"

She scowled. "Three weeks."

"And when was the last time you heard of the government working that quickly?"

Her scowl deepened.

Mason's face softened as he searched Violet's eyes. "Trust me."

She took a deep breath then released it. "Okay."

Several minutes later, one of Thelma's associates appeared in the doorway of the back room. "Do you have a fax machine?"

Violet's eyes widened. "Yeah." And she rattled off the number.

The document arrived several minutes later and Thelma tapped her foot impatiently while Mason read it over. When he was done, he turned to Violet and me. "This says that you will both be present for the press conference and that the money will be deposited into your account by noon tomorrow. There are no other stipulations or requirements. It also asks you to agree to let them use whatever footage they get for promotion or any other way they see fit. While I admit the wording of the last part concerns me a bit, I think you'll be fine."

Violet already had a pen in her hand. "Where do we sign?"

When I signed it, I wasn't surprised to see J.R. Simmons's own signature next to ours. "How did they send it so quickly?" I whispered to Mason after I handed Thelma the document.

"Because I suspect he already had it prepared."

"We need to hustle, people," Thelma shouted, clapping her hands together. "We're officially behind schedule."

The small business group had brought two cameramen and while waiting for the document, they set up the lighting for the interview. They put a microphone on Violet and filmed her walking around the shop straightening the pots and gift items we sold. After a few takes of that, they had her stand by the register and asked her questions about opening the nursery. Another cameraman asked me to go outside so he could get some shots of me with the plants we had lining the sidewalk.

I was thankful the camera crew didn't seem interested in talking to me, only filming me watering the flowers and talking to a pretend customer. Mason stood off to the side, watching in silence. While they followed me around for the next fifteen minutes, three news vans drove up and parked on the street. The crews emerged and they began setting up for the press conference. Someone had set up a rope barrier between the sidewalk and the parking lot. The crowd on the other side of the rope had swelled even more.

The cameraman turned to see where my attention had gone. "Ms. Gardner, we need you to pretend the people on the street aren't there."

Easier said than done. I knew Joe would arrive at any moment, and I felt like I was going to be sick. I took a deep breath. I had agreed to do this. It would all be over soon.

When they finished filming, Joe still hadn't arrived even though it was well past one. I'd noticed Jonah in the crowd earlier and since the camera crew was done with me, I waved him over. He pushed his way through the gathered mass of people and I couldn't help but think how different this was from the first time I met him at the grand opening of the nursery. That time, he'd arrived with an entourage and his own camera crew. I had to say I liked this new Reverend Jonah much better.

Someone called out, "Reverend Jonah!"

Jonah's television smile switched on and he turned to wave. He may have changed, but his on-screen persona had endured the transformation. I had to admit he was a great showman.

When he reached me, I grabbed his arm and pulled him around the side of the building. "Did you have a chance to talk to Scooter?"

He leaned his head closer to mine and lowered his voice. "I did, but I didn't get much information."

I glanced at Mason, who stood at the edge of the parking lot, looking official. He seemed to be scanning the crowd for something. His gaze landed on mine and his mouth tipped into a sexy smile. My stomach fluttered and my skin heated despite the chilly wind. Flustered, I returned my attention to Jonah, trying to concentrate on the task at hand. "What did he say?"

"Scooter has been out at Weston's Garage quite a bit over the last week. He says there was lots of activity and he knew something big was about to go down but claims not to know what. He saw Bruce Wayne there on Friday and over the weekend."

My heart sunk. "It sounds like they were helping Daniel Crocker break out of jail, but I just can't believe Bruce Wayne would be a part of that."

"We don't know for sure that he *was*. Maybe that's why he disappeared. Because he refused to cooperate." His voice lowered. "I really think it's time for you to tell Mason."

Movement in the parking lot drew my attention. As a dark sedan pulled into a parking spot, Thelma came outside with Violet and her cameraman in tow. I drew in a breath of anticipation as the rear car doors opened. When Joe got out, he was already waving to the crowd, wearing a smile I'd never once seen on his face the entire time we'd known each other. He shook several hands before he walked toward us. He was handsome in his dark gray suit with a red tie and several women in the crowd shouted his name and whistled. Joe ignored them as his gaze landed on me and Jonah, his face hardening.

My chest tightened and I tried to take a breath. Of all the reactions I'd expected from him the first time we saw each other again, this disdain was stunning.

Thelma intercepted him on the sidewalk and it took him several seconds to give her his attention.

I blinked to ease the tears burning my eyes. What had I done to earn that look from him?

I barely had time to recover when the next person to emerge from the car sent the blood rushing from my head—Hilary. She wore a cream colored dress with a green vine print as though she were playing along with the whole gardening theme. Her long auburn hair was pulled back from her face and hung in waves. If I didn't know the real her, I would have believed she was the sweet, dutiful fiancée of an up-and-coming political star. She was pretty enough to be a Hollywood celebrity.

My gaze strayed to Mason, who was watching me with a worried expression. I had no doubt he'd seen Joe's reaction. I flashed him a tight smile even as I fought to take a breath.

Hilary waved to the crowd, her smile lighting up her face as she made her way to Joe. She looped her arm through his, pulling him like she was staking her territory. Her left hand rested on his forearm and the massive diamond on her finger caught the sunlight, sparkling like one of Ashley's glitter-encrusted art projects. I couldn't help comparing her engagement ring to the one Joe had given me. The one that now sat in a box in my underwear drawer. The rings were so vastly different it was like they had been given by two different men. But then again, I wasn't surprised.

This man who was working the crowd wasn't the one I'd known. He smiled and shook hands, talking to strangers as though they were his close friends. I had no idea why he was wasting time on people who weren't even his constituents, but maybe he was thinking long term. After all, I'd seen a vision in which Hilary was his wife and he was winning a U.S. Senate seat.

I searched the crowd that had now swelled to over a hundred people. There were more people here today than had shown up for our grand opening. A group of middle-aged women held up signs with pictures of Joe and Hilary with crowns drawn on their heads with black marker and the word "Jolary for President!" handwritten at the top. It took me three whole seconds to figure out *Jolary* was their version of *Brangelina*.

Several younger women near the front were wearing T-shirts with Joe's photo emblazoned across their chests with the phrase, "I want to be your *First Lady* on the street and the *First Slut* in your bed." I wondered if they had truly thought that slogan through. My mouth dropped open when I realized Samantha Jo Wheaten was one of the women. She'd waited on us several times at the Suds and Spuds diner without ever giving Joe a second glance. But now that he had TV cameras on him, they all wanted him.

Joe watched as Jonah rejoined the crowd after offering me a smile and a thumbs up. Then Joe turned back to me, his cold eyes searching my face for a moment before he faced the crowd.

The blood drained from my head. Who *was* this man?

I considered bolting, the stupid grant be damned. I'd deal with Violet later. But as I went to leave, Thelma grabbed my arm and ushered me in front of the nursery doors. I caught a glimpse of Mason, who was hanging close to the building but staying away from the cameras. He offered me an encouraging smile.

I smiled back, not because I was happy with the situation, but because I could always count on him to be there when I needed him. The surety of this surprised me. Truth was, he'd been my rock for a while now. From getting me out of jail to saving me from Jimmy DeWade to helping me choose my truck, he had always been waiting in the wings to lend a helping hand. Now he was standing on the periphery again, and I realized I didn't want him there anymore. I wanted him beside me. As soon as this nightmare press conference was over, I was going to address that.

But at the moment, I had to stand in front of the crowd in a straight line with the other official participants of this press conference, smack in front of the nursery. Violet and I hung to the right, while Joe and Hilary were on the left, Thelma between us. Joe stood less than four feet from me, close enough for me to see the tremor in his hand as he reached into his jacket and removed a folded piece of paper.

Several women shouted Joe's name again and I noticed a sign that read *Joe, will you marry ME?* Hilary grabbed Joe's hand and laced her fingers with his, smiling coyly at the crowd. "Sorry, girls. He's all mine." And without warning, she grabbed his face and gave him a kiss on the lips. Joe resisted for a moment before relaxing into her embrace. When he broke loose, he flashed a hundred-watt smile in response to the catcalls.

Violet stiffened next to me, and I was surprised when her hand slipped into mine. All my anger at her faded as we reverted to our familiar roles. The supporter and the victim. But I was tired of playing the victim, I reminded myself. I wanted to be the strong one for once. I squeezed her hand to show her how much I appreciated her effort, then released it.

Joe laughed. "We're here today to recognize the Gardner Sisters Nursery, not give y'all a show." He winked at Hilary, then looked down at his paper and gave a five-minute speech about Arkansas being built on the backs of hardworking entrepreneurs and how the Gardner sisters were carrying that legacy into the twenty-first century. To hear him speak of us, no one would ever guess he'd been there from the beginning, even reconstructing part of the greenhouse that stood twenty feet behind us.

When he finished, Thelma handed him a cream-colored, legal-sized envelope. He turned to us and presented the envelope to Violet. "It is with great pride and respect that the Arkansas Small Business Administration presents the Gardner Sisters Nursery with a two-hundred-thousand dollar grant to expand their business."

The crowd cheered and cameras flashed as Violet took the envelope and shook Joe's hand. He moved on to me next, his hand engulfing mine and holding on for several seconds as he stared into my face with a longing that stole my breath.

Hilary pulled on his arm until he released me, then he turned back to the crowd. "We'll now take any questions y'all might have."

Hands shot up in the air and Joe pointed to a blonde newswoman. "I'm sure you're both used to the comparison of you two to Jackie and John F. Kennedy. What we want to know is when is your wedding and will it have a Camelot theme?"

Joe grinned, then shook his head. "We don't—"

Hilary looped her arm through his and smiled up into his face. "It's okay, Joe, we might as well tell everyone our big secret."

His body tensed.

She stared down the cameras, her face beaming. "Joe and I are planning a December wedding and it *will* have a royal theme."

The crowd began shouting questions.

"What are your colors?"

"Will the wedding be at the Simmons Estate?"

*December.* While my vision had shown him married to a very pregnant Hilary, learning that they'd set a date made me want to throw up.

Joe seemed to regain his senses. "Okay, we'll take the next question. A *non*-wedding question."

But the blonde reporter shouted, "How do you feel about your upcoming nuptials, Joe?"

His mouth opened then closed; he looked like a fish out of water struggling to breathe.

"Do you get any say about the colors or the ceremony?"

A grim smile lifted his mouth. "Hilary seems to be in charge of all of the details. I guess I'll just show up when and where I'm told like any dutiful husband-to-be." He released a chuckle, but it sounded forced. "Next question." He pointed to a man in the back.

"Joe, you're a last-minute entry into what might be your first political office. What makes you qualified?"

"Well…" Joe drawled. "That's an excellent question. After graduating from the University of Arkansas law school and rankin' third in my class, I've spent the last five years working for the Arkansas state police as an undercover officer. I've seen firsthand the effects of crime, and as an Arkansas State Senator, I will help ensure that criminal laws are upheld. I see it as a natural extension of my experience."

"Do you think your father's reputation and money make you more qualified?"

Joe's grin froze. It was such a subtle reaction that no one else would notice. But I did. I knew this man…or thought I did. The Joe Simmons standing in front of this crowd was different from any of the variations of Joe that I'd met, from Joe McAllister, his pseudonym while he was undercover, to the Joe Simmons who had walked out my door five weeks ago. This Joe Simmons was a schmoozer who said what people wanted to hear. But the set of his mouth told me that he didn't like what he was doing and I couldn't help but feel partially responsible for that.

"No," Joe answered. "I'd like to think I'm my own man and I'm making my own way in this world. I'd like to stand on my own merit. Next question."

An older man with a notepad turned his attention to me, self-consciously sweeping long strands of thinning hair over a large bald spot on top of his head. When he lowered his hand, the gusty wind instantly blew them to the side. "Anthony Blund from the *Henryetta Gazette*. My question is for Rose Gardner."

"Uh…" Joe's eyes widened slightly and he turned to me. "I'm not sure the Gardner sisters are here to answer questions."

"We were assured that they would."

That damned contract.

I felt a comforting hand on the small of my back, and I looked over my shoulder into Mason's expressionless face. "Take the question," he said, leaning down to my ear, "but don't answer if it's a setup."

I nodded at the reporter. "All right."

"What do you have to say about the allegations that you have defrauded your sister of her inheritance?"

My chest constricted and I turned to Violet. Her face paled and she shook her head, turning toward the reporter. "That's not true. Rose has done no such thing."

"There are witnesses who testify that you, Violet, made such a claim. Are you backing down from your accusations?"

"I…" Violet fumbled.

Mason stepped between us. "As the Gardner Sisters Nursery's legal counsel, I advise my clients to not respond to rumors and gossip."

"Excuse me, Mr. Deveraux," the Henryetta reporter called out. "If you're the assistant DA, why are you their legal counsel? Wouldn't that be a conflict of interest?"

"I can assure you, Mr. Blund, there has been no wrongdoing, so there can be no conflict of interest."

"What about the fact that she hires a known felon? Doesn't that present an issue?"

I cringed, but Mason kept his resolve. "Mr. Decker has served his time and reports regularly to his parole officer. Ms. Gardner has offered him employment when most people in this town would not. Ms. Gardner believes that everyone deserves a second chance and I commend her efforts."

"Rose, is it true that you and Jonah Pruitt are dating? Was that why his mother tried to kill you? Because she didn't approve?"

My mouth dropped open.

Mason cleared his throat. "Rose's personal relationships are not up for public discussion." He turned his head toward Joe and flashed a good-ole-boy grin. "I thought we were here to quiz Joe, not my clients."

Joe tried to take control. "Mr. Deveraux is right." He spread his hands open. "I've got six more days until the election. What else do you have for me?"

"Joe," a TV reporter shouted. "You've based a good portion of your fight against crime on your bust of alleged murderer and drug dealer Daniel Crocker. Do you think his escape will hurt your campaign?"

Joe's face froze. "What?"

"Surely you're aware of his escape."

His eyes widened and he gave a slight shake of his head. "Uh…"

"Daniel Crocker escaped from the Fenton County Jail last night, starting the biggest manhunt in the state of Arkansas in the last twenty years. I'm surprised that someone with a campaign against crime wouldn't be aware of that."

Joe shot a glare at Hilary and then turned back toward the crowd. "I've been traveling all morning and have been away from the news. My people neglected to inform me."

"Rose," a woman shouted. "Aren't you worried about Daniel Crocker being on the loose after you helped get him arrested?"

I glanced up at Mason and he nodded. I turned back to the crowd. "I've been told that the state police have that matter under control."

"Joe," someone called out. "Is this a sign of how well you'll be kept apprised if you're elected?"

"No," Joe's eyes narrowed. "I can assure you that I will be addressing my staff's huge error in judgment." He looked at his watch. "Now if you'll excuse me, we're out of time. Thanks for coming today!" He waved to the crowd and disappeared into the nursery.

I stepped back while reporters shouted my name. Mason moved in front of me and grabbed my arm, leading me through the door.

I stood just inside it, shock hitting me like a freight train. "What just happened?" I whispered.

He leaned into my ear, keeping his gaze on Joe and Hilary as they disappeared into the back room. "I don't know, but I think we know who was behind part of it."

I didn't want to believe it. "Doesn't that seem a little paranoid?"

"We're talking about a man who probably forked out several hundred thousand of his own money to set this up. When you look at it that way, it doesn't seem so paranoid." He pulled me into the corner as a camera crew followed Violet making her way through the shop. "But what does surprise me is that Joe of all people didn't know about Crocker's escape. He's already four points behind in the polls. That lack of information is bound to hurt him even more."

A man in a suit emerged from the back room and searched the shop until his eyes landed on me. He walked over, studying me before he grinned. "Rose? I'm Teddy Bowman, Joe's campaign manager. Joe's in the back and would like to meet with you."

"Uh...I..."

"It's not part of the conditions, Rose," Mason whispered into my ear. "You don't have to see him."

The thought of seeing Joe filled my heart with equal amounts of joy and dread. Did I want to talk to him? I wasn't so sure after the way he'd treated me. I glanced up at Mason. "I need to do this. If I don't, I think I'll always regret it."

His eyes searched mine and I struggled to lay name to the emotion I saw there. I knew he didn't want me to go, but Mason would never make demands of me. It made me appreciate him all the more. I threw my arms around his neck. "Will you wait for me? Then we'll go to Magnolia and spend the rest of the afternoon together. A date."

A smile quivered on his lips. "You know that I'll wait as long as you need me to."

I kissed his cheek and released him, smoothing my skirt. I followed Teddy through the shop, past the camera crew that was now filming Violet talking to a customer. As we neared the back room, I could hear Joe shouting.

I pushed the door to the back room open and stood in the threshold for a moment before shutting the door behind me. Joe was yelling and pointing his finger at two college-aged kids, whose faces were red from Joe's verbal berating.

Muffy was still sitting in her dog bed, hunkered down, but when she saw me she hopped up and ran over, jumping and begging for me to pick her up. She'd been subjected to more confrontation in one afternoon than she'd probably seen in her entire life. I had no idea what was about to happen, but I didn't want her to be traumatized any more than she already had been. I bent down and whispered in her ear, "Go find Violet, Muffy."

She whimpered when I stood up, and when I opened the door a crack, she slunk into the front room.

Joe continued his tirade. "What the hell were you thinking by keeping something like this away from me? I looked like an idiot out there! I've never worked with such incompetent idiots in all my life!" he shouted, running his hands through his hair as his gaze spun around the room. His eyes finally landed on me, and he stopped as though a switch in his head had been flipped. Dropping his hand to his side, his face hardened. "Everybody out. *Now.*"

Their mouths dropped open as they turned their attention to me.

"You heard him." Hilary slid off my stool at the potting table and wrapped her hand around Joe's arm. "Joe needs a few moments alone to regroup."

Joe shook off her hand. "That includes you, Hilary."

She turned up her chin, her eyes darting hate toward me. "I'm not going anywhere."

"So help me God, if you don't—"

An angry glare made her look five years older. "If you think I'm leaving you alone with her—"

Joe pointed to the doorway, shouting, "Get the hell out of here now, or I'll go out there and tell the press our engagement is off."

"Don't do anything stupid, Joe," she hissed. "You know your father will be quizzing all your people tonight. He'll know you saw her."

The veins on his temple throbbed. "Get. *Out!*"

Hilary walked past me, bumping into my arm. I took a step backward, gasping at her rudeness.

"Lock the door," Joe barked. "I don't want to be interrupted."

I spun around to see who he was talking to. When I realized I was the only person in the back room with him, my anger surged. "You may think it's acceptable to talk to your staff that way, but I don't work for you, Joe Simmons."

He stomped past me and turned the lock, then pulled me into his arms, lowering his mouth to mine. His breath reeked of alcohol.

I turned my head to the side, his lips brushing my cheek. "Let go of me, Joe."

"Are you saving yourself for Jonah Pruitt now?"

I shoved his chest to break his hold. "What in tarnation are you talking about?"

Anger filled his eyes. "I know about you and Jonah, and I have to say I'm surprised that you moved on so quickly. Especially with *him*."

"*Me* move on?" I hissed in a low voice. I refused to provide this god-forsaken town with more gossip. "*You're* the one who announced your engagement to your old girlfriend within two days of breaking up with me!"

"You know I don't care about her!"

"And yet you're still engaged to her."

"Rose," he ran his hand through his hair and sank onto my potting stool, where Hilary had been sitting just moments ago. "How could you sleep with Jonah Pruitt?"

Had he lost his mind? "You have no right to accuse me of that."

He looked up, his eyes red and glassy. "I saw the pictures."

"What pictures?"

"Of Jonah holding you and you two sitting close together, holding hands. Photos taken less than two weeks after we broke up. I *know*, Rose."

"You have photos of me? *You're watching me?*"

"My father." His voice was tight.

Of course he was. I shook my head. "You think that you meant so little to me—that *we* did—that I could just move on with someone else in two weeks? How could you see us hugging and jump to the conclusion that we were sleeping together?" And then I knew why he would make that leap. "You've slept with Hilary. Your engagement isn't pretend."

Guilt flooded his face.

"Who *are* you?" Tears stung my eyes. "My Joe would never sleep with her." But even as I said the words, I knew they weren't true. How many times had he run back to her? Running back to Hilary was what he did. "Why am I back here, Joe? Why did you want to see me?"

He slid off the stool and moved toward me, taking my hand in his. "I miss you so much it hurts, Rose. I don't know if I can live without you."

A lump formed in my throat, and it took everything I had not to let my tears loose.

He slowly slid his hand around my lower back and pulled me to his chest. "You're the first thing I think of when I wake up in the morning and the last thing on my mind when I close my eyes."

"I can tell from the way you and Hilary were kissing outside."

"I don't want to be with her, Rose. You have to know that."

"And yet you are. I understand why you're engaged to her. I get it. But it's not a total sham and we both know it. You're sleeping with her. You've been sleeping with her for weeks."

"I…It's just…"

"Thank you for not insulting me by denying it." I closed my eyes, smelling his alcohol-laden breath. It wasn't even two o'clock yet. I slowly pushed on his chest, but his hand covered mine.

"Rose, I love you. You are my reason for living. Without you, I have *nothing*. I am *nothing*." His voice broke and tears filled his eyes.

My conscience fought a battle with my guilt. How much of his misery should I lay claim to? "I'm sorry, but we both have to accept that we're done."

"I can't."

"Joe, even if your father changed his mind, I couldn't go back to you now. Not after this. All I can see is you with Hilary."

Anger contorted his face. "And you don't think it kills me to think of you with Jonah Pruitt of all people? How could you, Rose? *Jonah Pruitt*," he spat. "And what the hell is going on between you and Mason?"

I shoved his arm off my waist. "I don't owe you an answer. Not after I found out about you and Hilary, but I'm going to tell you anyway: I'm not sleeping with Jonah Pruitt. He's my friend and he's my therapist. There's nothing between us."

He jolted and seemed dazed. "And Mason?"

I shook my head, anger seeping into my words. "That is none of your business."

"So you're with him."

"I'm with no one. *No one.* I could hardly breathe when you left me, Joe. I struggled to get up every morning and survive. How could I possibly consider being with someone else before now?"

He looked like I'd shot him.

"But I'd like to thank you. I wasn't sure why I felt the need to see you today, but now I know. I needed closure and you've definitely given me that. Now I can move on without feeling guilty."

His eyes pleaded with me. "Rose, I love you."

"Do you? I thought so, but now I'm not so sure. I think you love the escape from your family that I seemed to offer. But you're not strong enough to stay away from them and I'm obviously not reason enough."

He grabbed me again and buried his face in my hair. "No, Rose. No. I love you more than I've loved anyone in my whole life. But I'm not as strong as you. Without you everything seems hopeless and pointless."

I closed my eyes and tried to keep from crying. Could I blame him for what he'd done? We were over and he was lonely. *But Hilary?* I took a step back. "No. I could forgive you for anyone else, but not her. Not after my vision, and not after what happened to Savannah. How could you, Joe? Hilary's partially responsible for her death."

His hands clenched at his sides. "Go ahead and finish it. Who else is responsible?"

"You," I choked out. "You. And I could forgive you for that too, even though you destroyed Mason in the process—" I shook my head. "But I can't forgive this."

"So that's it? We're just over?"

"We were *already* over. You told me that we were over when you walked out my door. Has anything changed? Has your father taken back his threat?"

He closed his eyes and turned away. "No."

"There's nothing to discuss. We're done."

He turned back to me, his eyes pleading. "How can you say that? I gave up everything including you to save you!"

I fought to catch my breath. "I know. And I'll always be grateful for that. But why are you set on destroying your entire life? I can't accept responsibility for that. You have to." I looked up at the ceiling, trying not to cry. "I have to go."

"Don't leave me, Rose. I'm begging you."

"I can't do this, Joe. I can't. I can't be with you after you've been with her. Can't you see? I would never be able to trust you. I'd always be waiting for you to go back to her." I turned around and walked toward the door.

"What about Daniel Crocker?"

I stopped but didn't face him. "What about him?"

"He's going to be out for revenge. I want to protect you."

I slowly spun around. "The state police think he's in Shreveport."

"But they don't know that for sure, do they?"

"No."

"You're unprotected." He took several breaths and I could see he was trying to work out a plan.

"No. I'm not."

His jaw clenched.

"I have Mason. Just like I did a month ago when he stopped Jonah's mother from shooting me. And last July when he scared away Jimmy DeWade after he attacked me in my house. Mason's there for me now, just like he's always been."

Before Joe could answer, I unlocked the door and opened it, a dozen pairs of prying eyes focused on me.

Hilary stood two feet on the other side of the curtain and if looks could kill, I'd have a dozen knives in my back. I offered her a grim smile. "He's all yours. I wish you a very happy life together, but somehow I find that unlikely."

Her mouth dropped open, then she recovered and disappeared into the back.

Violet held Muffy, smiling sweetly and talking to a cameraman, but her smile faded as her gaze turned to me. I could see she was dying to ask what happened, but there was only one person I wanted to see right now. He was standing in the back corner where I'd left him. I moved through the crowd and slipped my hand into his.

"Let's go."

# Chapter Eight

W hat about Muffy?" Mason asked as he led me to his car.

"I told my niece Muffy could have a sleepover with her tonight. I was supposed to leave her with Violet anyway."

He nodded as he opened the passenger door and shut the door behind me before getting in and starting the car. He stayed silent until he'd pulled out of the parking lot and onto the street. "Are you okay?"

"Surprisingly better than expected." I couldn't believe it was true. I felt badly for Joe, but I had realized something in that back room. He had spent his life making messes and then scrambling to clean them up. While he'd told me that very thing, seeing firsthand proof of it was eye-opening and freeing.

"Do you still want to go to Magnolia?"

I grabbed his hand and twined his fingers with mine. Part of me wanted to go home and cry, but most of me was done mourning the life I'd never have with Joe. I'd squandered twenty-four years before Joe, and there was no reason to squander another day now that I had a chance at a life with the man next to me. "You have no idea how much I want to go to Magnolia with you."

He shot me a surprised look before returning his attention to the street. "Is there any particular movie you want to see?"

I stared at him, amazed that I was here with him now. Part of me screamed that this was too much, too soon, but the rest of me was tired of waiting.

Mason swung another glance at me, waiting for my answer.

"I don't even know what's playing."

He rattled off several movies and I picked a romantic comedy. He kept shooting me curious glances, probably expecting me to fall to pieces after my encounter with Joe. But instead I felt more empowered. Joe was supposed to be the strong one, but he was the one who'd fallen apart. Maybe I was stronger than I thought I was.

I turned in my seat to face him. "How did you get the afternoon off?"

"I already told you."

"Mason, you're the assistant DA and you canceled court to take me to Magnolia for the afternoon. Given the fact I'm not one of Judge McClary's favorite people, I doubt he'd give you permission for that. What's really going on?"

His free hand tightened on the steering wheel. "I didn't want to worry you, especially since you had enough to worry about with seeing Joe."

"I'm not some fragile flower, so don't treat me like one."

He nodded. "You're right. I'm sorry. I didn't mean to insult you."

"You are the very last person I would ever accuse of insulting me. Just tell me the truth."

He took a breath. "The police and the FBI think they have Crocker cornered in a four-block area in Shreveport."

"But?"

He shot a grim smile at me. "But I have a bad feeling in the pit of my stomach. I think he's still around. I have no evidence to back it up, just a gut feeling."

"So why are we going to Magnolia?"

"Because if Crocker's still around Henryetta, I doubt he'd look for you in Magnolia."

"So that's why Judge McClary agreed."

"Reluctantly, but yes."

I didn't want to think about the possibility of Daniel Crocker lurking in Henryetta.

"Don't worry, Rose. They'll find him."

I nodded. They had a better chance because the state police were involved.

"Did I tell you that my mother is coming to visit in a couple of weeks?" Mason asked.

"No." I'd met his mother after Sunday service at Jonah's church over a month ago and I'd loved her from the moment she uttered her first sweet word.

"She asked if she could collect on that rain check for Sunday lunch."

I smiled, happiness filling my heart. "I'd love that."

We spent the rest of the forty-five-minute drive talking about Mason's childhood and antics he and Savannah had gotten into as kids.

"My dad was an attorney. He practiced estate law, but he encouraged Savannah and me to practice the art of persuasive arguing. I think he secretly wished he'd become a defense attorney." He laughed. "My father would secretly give us a topic at breakfast, and we'd spend the day coming up with our arguments. Then we'd argue our points at dinner. We drove my mother insane. No one was surprised that we both went to law school."

"I can tell that you love what you do."

His eyebrows rose in surprise. "Really, how can you?"

"Because your eyes light up when you talk about it. Do you ever worry that you're prosecuting an innocent person?"

"Honestly, I never thought about it very much until Bruce Wayne's trial. A lot of things changed for me after that case."

The smile he flashed me said his attitude wasn't the only thing that had changed.

We went to see the movie, but I couldn't stop thinking about how I was safe and cozy in a movie theater in Magnolia while Bruce Wayne was God only knew where. He could be in serious trouble. Jonah was right. It was time to tell Mason.

After the movie, we went to dinner at a local restaurant. To calm my nerves, I kept telling myself that our meal was just like our lunches at Merilee's, but it wasn't. At least not for me. The air was charged with anticipation, although I wasn't sure of what. Mason had made little physical contact with me other than holding my hand. It was just as well since I was distracted enough just sitting next to him. I couldn't imagine being able to concentrate if he had made any other kind of move, and I really needed to concentrate on something important. I took a deep breath after we ordered. "Mason, I have something to tell you."

The smile fell from his face. "Okay."

"It's about Bruce Wayne."

His shoulders relaxed. "Okay."

"Wait. What did you think I was going to say?"

"Never mind. Tell me about Bruce Wayne."

"He's missing."

His eyes narrowed. "What do you mean, *missing*?"

"You know that he's been calling in sick, but after I ate lunch with Neely Kate yesterday I took Bruce Wayne some chicken noodle soup and he wasn't there. Not only that, but half his clothes were gone."

Mason looked worried. "Where did he go?"

"That's just it. I don't know. David said that for the past several days, Bruce Wayne would call in sick to work and then leave early in the morning and come back late. The last time he saw Bruce Wayne was on Monday night. Then Scooter Malcolm told Jonah that he saw Bruce Wayne at Weston's Garage on Friday and over the weekend."

"Do you think he had anything to do with Crocker's prison break? We know he had some outside help."

"No. I just can't see him agreeing to do that. He's protective of me and he knows that Crocker is upset with me. But what if he refused to help and they hurt him?"

"Why didn't you tell me sooner?"

"I didn't want to get him into trouble. I was worried that he might have run away, and I figured you'd have to turn him into his parole officer if I told you."

"It sounds like he's in trouble. I'll notify the sheriff's office and we'll file a missing person report."

"What if he's hiding from Crocker's guys?"

"We'll take that into account. Rose, I know how hard Bruce Wayne has been working to straighten out his life and his parole officer is bound to have noticed too. Plus, I can put a good word in for him."

"You'd do that?"

"Of course. Bruce Wayne has made remarkable progress since he's begun working for you. Everyone can see that."

"Thanks."

"Next time, tell me, okay? We really are on the same side."

That was going to take some getting used to.

An hour later, we arrived at the Fenton County sheriff's office to file a missing person report on Bruce Wayne. Mason asked the receptionist if his friend Jeff was around and a few minutes later, a deputy wearing a warm smile walked out from the back. Mason took a step toward him. "Rose, I'd like to introduce you to my friend, Jeff Dimler. He's the Chief Deputy Sheriff and we've worked together quite a bit."

I shook his hand, thrown off by his friendliness. "Hi."

"So you're the infamous Rose Gardner."

I cringed. "You know about me?"

He laughed. "You have a better case record than the Henryetta Police Department. There's a running bet here at the sheriff's department that you'll solve more crimes this year than they will."

I scowled. "Yeah, they're not too fond of me over there."

"So we've heard. Not to worry, we'll take you seriously here."

I couldn't hide my surprise.

"It's hard to argue with a three for three record, Ms. Gardner." He winked. "If you ever consider a career in law enforcement, keep the sheriff's department in mind."

I laughed. "Thanks."

"Say, Mason." Chief Deputy Dimler leaned his shoulder against the wall. "The guys were impressed with your three-point shot in the last seconds of the basketball game. They're talking about making you a permanent member of the team even after Gonzales comes back after his dislocated shoulder. Interested?"

Mason laughed. "The deputies are willing to have a lawyer on their team?"

"As long as you help us beat those guys at Martin Heating and Cooling, you could be a three-eyed Martian as far as their concerned. What do you say?"

He grinned. "Count me in."

"Great!" He looped his thumbs over his belt. "Exciting day in Henryetta today apart from the Crocker escape, huh? I heard that Joe Simmons even made a campaign stop in Henryetta." The deputy turned to me. "At your nursery, right?"

"Yeah," I said.

"He applied for a sheriff's deputy position and we offered it to him, but he turned it down to run for the state senate. Turning out like his daddy, huh?"

I shifted my weight, uncomfortable to be reminded of my past with Joe.

"You have no idea," Mason muttered, casting a glance at me. "But we're here to talk about Bruce Wayne."

Chief Deputy Dimler gave Mason a puckered smile. "Fair enough." He motioned to his office and we sat in front of his desk.

"Bruce Wayne worked for Daniel Crocker before Bruce Wayne's arrest last year, so we know he has ties to Crocker's boys," Mason began. "But he's been working for Rose this past month and has shown a real aptitude for landscaping. He's gone above and beyond as an employee. He seems to love his job, and I'm certain he wouldn't throw all that hard work away on a whim. I'm worried his old ties have gotten him into trouble." Mason and I filled Chief Deputy Dimler in on what we knew.

The deputy looked up from his notes. "We've noticed a lot more activity at Weston's Garage these last few weeks. We'll see what we can do. It could be they were putting some pressure on Decker to come back to the fold, so to speak, and he's lying low to avoid getting mixed back up in it. Hopefully we can get Decker's roommate to cooperate."

I wasn't sure they'd ever manage that.

Chief Deputy Dimler's cell phone rang and he glanced at the caller ID. "Excuse me, I need to take this."

Mason stood. "I think we're done here. Thanks for the assistance, Jeff."

We got up and walked out of the room as the deputy took the call.

Mason put an arm around my back and leaned close to my ear. "Bruce Wayne's not in any trouble and they'll start looking for him soon. Feel better?"

I was more than relieved. "Yes. Much. And the fact that Chief Deputy Dimler doesn't hate me is reassuring."

"Rose, I was serious about moving out of the city limits. The sheriff's deputies would be much more responsive when you need help. I know *I'd* feel better if I knew law enforcement was going to respond to your calls more quickly."

I scowled. "Why do you keep suggesting there will be a next time?" His eyebrows rose as he smirked. "I've been considering the idea since you mentioned it to me. But financially, it's just not an option right now. Not unless I sell the farm and who knows how long it will take for that to happen."

"We can talk about it later. And if you're serious about moving, we can figure out a way to make it happen." He pushed the front door open. "Now let's head home."

I grinned up at him. "What was Jeff talking about you making a three-point shot?"

He shrugged. "Fenton County has a men's rec basketball league. A lot of the businesses have teams, the sheriff's department included. Deputy Gonzales dislocated his shoulder several weeks ago and when Jeff and I met for lunch a couple of days later, he asked me to help out. I've filled in three games."

"Sounds like you impressed them. I didn't know you played basketball."

He shook his head. "I haven't in years. But it's been fun and I've started hanging out with some of the guys after the games."

Mason opened the car door for me to get in when Chief Deputy Dimler stood in the doorway and called out to us. "Hey, Mason. I think you're gonna to want to hear this. The FBI just phoned and said they have Crocker cornered in a warehouse in Shreveport."

Mason released a long breath. "That's great news."

"They're in the middle of a stand-off, but they should have him apprehended within several hours."

"Thanks for the information. I'd appreciate it if you'd let me know when he's back in custody."

"Sure thing."

We got in the car and I called David, warning him that a sheriff's deputy would be dropping by to ask questions about Bruce Wayne. I knew he'd freak out if law enforcement officers just showed up on his doorstep.

When I hung up, Mason seemed unusually quiet and tense for several minutes. "Do you want to talk about anything that happened earlier this afternoon?"

Part of me wanted to forget the afternoon altogether, but I knew Jonah would call that unhealthy. Plus I didn't want to keep secrets from Mason. "Joe thought I was sleeping with Jonah."

The expression left his face. "Excuse me?"

"His father had someone take photos of me with Jonah a couple of weeks after Joe broke up with me. He said they showed us hugging and sitting close to each other."

"How did he jump to that conclusion?"

"Because the Joe and Hilary engagement isn't so fake. Joe's sleeping with Hilary."

He cringed. "Rose. I'm sorry."

"There's nothing for you to be sorry about. I just don't understand. He says he can't stand her, but he keeps going back to her time and time again."

"Some habits are hard to break. Even when they're bad for us."

We drove in silence for several minutes until Mason pulled into my driveway and turned off the engine.

I stared out the windshield at my front porch. "He told me he can't live without me," I blurted out.

"And how do you feel about that?"

I turned to Mason, searching his eyes. I hated that he looked worried. "I told him that I can't forgive him for running to Hilary so soon after we broke up. Even if we got back together, I wouldn't be able to trust him not to go back to her."

His expression was still guarded. "Is that how you really feel or what you thought you should say?"

If anyone other than Mason had asked me that question, I'd be angry. But there was no malice in his voice, and he of all people deserved an answer. "I have to be able to trust the man in my life, Mason. I've been hurt by too many people. If I give my heart to someone, I want him to be truthful with me. The fact is, Joe hid so many things from me. He wasn't truthful with me over the majority of our relationship."

He didn't answer.

"He said he wanted to protect me from Daniel Crocker, but I told him that I didn't need him. I told him I had you. Just like I've had you for months. I just didn't realize it."

"Rose." His hand slid up my arm.

"I'm glad I saw that side of him today. It freed me to move on and not feel guilty for wanting to be happy with someone else."

His gaze fell to my mouth. "Someone else?"

"You, Mason," I whispered. "I want it to be with *you*."

His mouth lowered and my breath stuck in my chest as his lips lightly brushed against mine, like he was worried he'd scare me away.

I rested my hands on his shoulders and parted my mouth as his tongue explored mine. A fire erupted in my chest and I wrapped my arms around his neck, pulling him closer. My reaction removed his hesitancy and he wrapped one arm around my back, moving the other behind my head.

Desire flowed through my veins and I turned awkwardly in the passenger seat to press myself against more of him.

His head lifted, leaving us both panting. "I suspect your neighbor is watching us."

I grabbed his hand. "Come inside."

He got out of the car and came around to open my door, pulling me into his arms and kissing me until I was lightheaded.

Why had I been resisting him for weeks?

Leaning back with a grin, he took my hand and dragged me up to the front porch. "Keys," he mumbled before he kissed me again. When he lifted his head, he said it again. "Your keys."

I stared up at him.

"Your keys? So I can unlock your door."

"Oh." But I still studied his face in a daze. Mason had literally kissed me senseless.

"If you keep staring at me like that, I'm liable to skip going inside, which wouldn't be so great for my career given that your neighbor makes bi-weekly calls to my office to report indecent activity at your house."

I laughed as I dug through my purse and found my keys. Mason took them from me and quickly unlocked the doorknob and the deadbolt. But instead of opening the door, he pushed my back up against it and kissed me again. One hand cupped my cheek while the other slid under my sweater and skimmed the bare skin of my waist, setting my hairs on end. I grabbed the back of his neck, clinging to him as my knees weakened. My heart pounded in my chest and my skin flushed.

Mason lifted his head, his eyelids heavy with lust.

"Are you coming in?"

He watched me for several seconds. "No."

I blinked, certain I'd heard him wrong. "No?"

"I've waited for months, but you haven't. I don't want to push you into something you're not ready for."

"You're not pushing me into anything. I want you."

"I don't want you to regret this, Rose. We have time. We can wait."

"What if I don't want to wait?"

His hand caressed my cheek. "If *I* can wait, so can *you*. I just want you to be sure. You only decided today to move on."

I buried my face into his chest and groaned. I could see the sense in his words, even though I didn't want to admit it. "I hate that you're right."

His arms wrapped around my back. "You have no idea how hard this is for me. I'm going to have to go home and take a cold shower."

I looked up into his eyes and pressed my lips against his before I could stop myself.

He groaned and deepened the kiss as I clung to him. "Rose, you're not making this any easier."

"Sorry," I mumbled against his lips.

"Liar." He laughed and took a step back. "Go inside and lock the door. They have Crocker cornered, so you should be safe, but I'll have the police do several drive-bys tonight."

"Okay."

"Will you meet me for lunch at Merilee's tomorrow?"

"I should tell you no for being so mean."

He kissed me again, murmuring against my lips, "I'm doing my best to convince you."

"If you kiss me like this tomorrow, then definitely yes."

His face lit up with a grin. "I have court in the morning, but it's Judge McClary and you know how he likes his noon lunch recesses."

"So noon? I'll be working at a job site by myself tomorrow, so I might not be too pretty."

"You're always beautiful, Rose."

I blushed.

"Are you building the retaining wall? By yourself? Can you get someone to help you temporarily until Bruce Wayne shows up?"

"I could ask David, but he hated working for me before. He only did it because I promised he'd earn *recreational* money."

"Try him again. And maybe he'll tell you more about Bruce Wayne while you're working."

"Okay." I had to admit it was a good idea, although I suspected he'd be resistant, particularly since this would be even harder manual labor than what I'd hired him for the first time.

"Now go inside. I'll call you in the morning and let you know that Crocker was officially apprehended."

I opened the door and stood in the doorway for a moment. "Goodnight, Mason."

He leaned over and gave me one last kiss, proving that meeting him for lunch was the best idea since the invention of the microwave.

"Goodnight, Rose." He gently pushed me inside and closed the door behind me.

After flipping the lock I turned on a lamp and peered through the curtains as his car backed out of the driveway.

I leaned my back against the door and sighed as a strange feeling washed through me. I tried to put my finger on what it was. It was weird not having to let Muffy outside, but that wasn't it. My body was filled with surging hormones and an unsatisfied craving, but that wasn't it, either. I felt unsettled, as if my life were on a teeter-totter and I didn't know where I was going to land. Was this what it was like dating someone else? Dealing with the uncertainty of the future?

With a tired sigh, I pushed away from the door. It was only nine o'clock, and I was nowhere near ready for bed. I put on my pajamas and called Neely Kate, filling her in on my day with Mason. When I told her about Mason kissing me, she squealed so loudly in my ear that I had to hold the phone away. "You're going to make me deaf, Neely Kate."

"Hearing is overrated. So he's a good kisser?"

"Well, I don't have much to compare it to, but when he finished, I was pretty fuddled."

"Oh!" She squealed again. "I knew you two would have great chemistry. You're a rising Scorpio and he's a Cancer. You're a perfect love match."

"How do you know Mason's birthday?"

She gasped. "I can't believe you of all people are asking me that!"

"No kidding." I laughed. Neely Kate was known far and wide for her extensive knowledge regarding everything and everyone around her. But incredibly, she wasn't prone to gossip. "I can't believe he's making us wait."

"I think it's romantic. He really cares about you, Rose."

"I've known that for weeks. I don't need him to wait to prove it."

"Well, you rushed into sleeping with Joe and look how that turned out."

I sighed. "That was different. I was sure I was about to be murdered and I didn't want to die a virgin."

"Still, I like it. It makes him more chivalrous. If I wasn't married to Ronnie, I'd go after him myself."

"I'm eating lunch with him tomorrow. I'll be sure to tell him he has options."

She snorted. "It would be a waste of breath. The guy only has eyes for you, Rose. Be sure to kiss him in public, though. He's turned down so many eligible Fenton County women that rumors have been going around that the poor guy is gay."

I laughed. "I'll see what I can do."

"Call me tomorrow after your lunch. Unless you're too *busy*."

"You're terrible. Goodnight."

I turned on the TV and started a new episode from season two of *Grey's Anatomy*. After I found out about Joe's engagement to Hilary a few weeks ago, Neely Kate had brought over the first few seasons. Now I was hooked. But tonight I couldn't concentrate, remembering the way Mason had kissed me and how much I wanted more. I'd worried that dating Mason would feel like I was cheating on Joe. But I hadn't given Joe any thought whatsoever just now. I tried to pay attention to who was sleeping with whom at Seattle Grace, which seemed to change from episode to episode, but my mind kept drifting to Mason and our moment on my porch. Finally, I gave up in the middle of the second episode and turned off the TV.

After making sure all the doors were locked, I climbed into bed, missing Muffy so much it took me longer than usual to get to sleep. My dreams made me restless and when I woke up in the morning, I felt uneasy, like something was wrong.

Cracking my eyes open, I glanced around the room. Everything looked fine until I noticed specks of red all over my ivory comforter.

Red rose petals were strewn all over my bed.

Shrieking, I sat up and scrambled backward, bumping into the headboard.

Rose petals were scattered in a path that led from my bed out the open doorway into the hall.

My heart hammering in my chest, I got out of bed and rounded the corner into the hallway, terrified of what I'd find. The petals continued down the hall and led to my sofa, which was now covered in red splatters, eerily similar to Momma's sofa after her head had been bashed in by Daniel Crocker with her rolling pin. I fought hysteria and swallowed to keep from throwing up as I inched closer, terrified the red stains were blood. A wooden rolling pin covered in red on one end lay on the middle cushion next to a geode with purple crystals, both pinning a piece of paper in place. I carefully pulled the sheet out, my hand shaking so hard I could barely read the handwritten note.

*My dearest Rose,*

*You and I have business that I'm <u>very much</u> looking forward to finishing.*

*Eternally yours, Dan*

# Chapter Nine

I stumbled into the bedroom and grabbed my phone off the nightstand, trying to get my fingers to cooperate to dial Mason's number. But I was having trouble breathing and my vision was blackening around the edges. *I will not pass out.* After two more deep breaths, my vision returned to normal, but a new thought hit me.

What if Daniel Crocker was still in the house?

My clumsy hand dropped the phone and I fumbled to pick it up as I ran down the hall and out the kitchen door. Standing in the driveway in my spaghetti strap nightgown and barefeet, I struggled to see the numbers on my phone through my tears.

*Get it together, Rose.*

I blinked and the screen cleared enough for me to find Mason's speed dial.

"Rose?" He sounded alarmed. "What's wrong?"

*Do not freak him out.* I was freaked out enough for both of us. "How did you know something's wrong?"

"Because you're calling me at six-thirty in the morning and you're crying."

"Someone's been in my house."

"Get out of there. *Now!*"

"I did. I am." I shook my head. "I'm standing in my driveway."

"Go to Heidi Joy's. Or even better, Mildred's."

That cleared my head. "I'm not going to *Mildred's* house."

"Did you call 9-1-1?"

"No, I called you. And he's not here anymore." I was starting to feel more in control. "He got his point across."

"*Who*? What happened?" He sounded breathless. "Never mind. Tell me when I get there. Just go to Heidi Joy's. *Now*."

"Do you want me to call 9-1-1?"

"No. We're already on our way."

"We? You're with the police? At this time of morning? Why?"

"I'm with the sheriff and he's already got someone on the way. Are you at Heidi Joy's yet?"

"No, I'm on the phone with you."

"*Go over there!*"

"He's already gone, Mason. I'm safe." For now.

"Rose, just humor me. *Please*."

"Okay. I'm going," I said, climbing her front porch.

"Stay put. I'll be right there," Mason said before hanging up.

But I couldn't bring myself to wake Heidi Joy up. She had looked so exhausted the last few times I'd seen her that I didn't want to steal her precious sleep and scare her half to death by telling her that someone had broken into my house. Again.

I sat on a chair on her front porch and wrapped my arms across my chest. Now that my shock had worn off, I was getting cold. I considered going back inside my house to get a robe, but I couldn't bring myself to do it. I hadn't lied to Mason when I said that I was sure Daniel Crocker was gone. But the horror of what happened was hitting me.

Psychopath Daniel Crocker had been in my house—while I'd slept—and I hadn't known it. He could have easily killed me; he'd chosen to taunt me instead.

But how? The last I heard, Daniel Crocker was cornered in a warehouse in Shreveport.

Two police cars turned the corner and pulled up in front of my house, lights flashing and sirens blaring. This had happened so often over the last six months that I was surprised my neighbors hadn't signed a petition to get me kicked out of the neighborhood. I couldn't say I would blame them.

A car from the sheriff's office pulled up next, and Mason's car was right behind it. His door flew open and Mason bounded across the yard, shrugging off his jacket. "Rose, I told you to go into Heidi Joy's house." He pulled me out of the chair and put his coat around my bare shoulders.

"No. You told me to go *to* Heidi Joy's. I just couldn't wake her and scare the living daylights out of her. Although I'm sure the sirens did it for me."

He glanced down at my feet. "You don't even have any shoes on."

"I saw...*it* and just grabbed my phone and ran out the door."

"What is *it*?"

"Go see for yourself."

Heidi Joy's front door opened and Andy, Sr. came out wearing flannel pajama bottoms and a stained T-shirt, running his hand through his bed-head hair. "What's going on?"

Mason put his arm around my shoulders. "Can Rose wait inside for a bit? Someone's broken into her house."

"*Again?*"

I cringed.

"Rose, there's something I have to tell you first," Mason said. Taking a deep breath, he turned me to face him, keeping a strong arm around my back. "Daniel Crocker wasn't in the warehouse in Shreveport."

"I know."

His face paled. "How do you know?"

"He left me a note."

He pushed me inside the front door and turned to Andy, his face hardening. "Do *not* let her out of your sight." Then he hurried across the yard, intercepting the policemen who were about to go through my open kitchen door.

I stared out the front window, wondering why these things kept happening to me. I had lived a simple, boring life until Daniel Crocker showed up at the DMV that Friday in May, just five months ago.

Mason came back about ten minutes later, carrying a pair of shoes and clothing wadded up in a ball. He handed them to me, looking embarrassed. "I figured you'd want some clothes. Why don't you get dressed and I'll take you for breakfast. We can talk about what we found."

"Okay." I grabbed the clothes and started down the hall. As I unwrapped the wad, I quickly found the source of Mason's embarrassment. He'd gotten me a pair of jeans and a long-sleeved T-shirt, but he'd also picked out a pair of panties and a bra. It had to be pretty apparent that I was braless in my nightgown. I closed my eyes, taking a moment to wallow in my humiliation.

When I finished changing, I put on my shoes and Mason slipped his hand into mine and led me outside to his car.

"Don't you have to stick around?"

"No, Sheriff Foster and Jeff are in there and I trust them to do a thorough investigation." He opened the passenger door and climbed behind the steering wheel. "Are you okay, Rose?"

"Yeah," I said, watching several sheriff's deputies walk into my house. This was a new twist to the law enforcement invasion of my house. I'd never entertained the sheriff before. "I'm fine."

We were silent as Mason drove through town, heading away from most of the restaurants that were open this early. He kept his gaze focused on the road, but I could tell he was upset.

I turned toward him. "I thought we were getting breakfast."

"We are. At my house. I don't think you should be in public right now."

"You mean out in the open."

He didn't say anything and my stomach revolted. I looked in the side mirror and realized the car behind us had been following us through several turns. Inhaling sharply, I turned to Mason in a panic. "Somebody's following us."

He reached over and grabbed my hand. "It's okay. It's a sheriff's deputy in an unmarked car. He's protecting us."

Nodding, I pressed my knuckles to my lips. How was this happening? Panic bubbled up in my chest and I took deep breaths to calm down.

Mason squeezed my hand. "It's okay, Rose. It's going to be okay."

I closed my eyes, telling myself I had nothing to worry about. Half the law enforcement officers in southern Arkansas were looking for Crocker. But it was the reassurance of the man next to me that made me believe everything could be okay.

He turned into a section of condos in the newer part of town, one that bordered Violet's cookie-cutter neighborhood. The condos were all upscale, with stone and brick and stucco exteriors. But as we drove past the well-manicured lawns, I couldn't help noticing how boring the landscaping looked.

When he pulled into a driveway, I looked through the windshield at the two-story four-plex that loomed ahead. "So this is where you live?"

"This is it." As he led me through the front door I noticed the car that had been following us was parked at the curb across the street. Mason locked the door.

"Do you think he'd come here looking for me?"

Mason stopped and hesitated as he searched my eyes. "Yes. Crocker is bat-shit crazy and obsessed with making you pay for what he thinks you've done to him. I have no doubt he'd come here or anywhere looking for you."

"Oh." That wasn't the answer I expected.

"Stay away from the windows." He disappeared upstairs and came back out carrying a handgun.

"Is that really necessary, Mason?"

"Yes." He set it on the kitchen counter.

He was being so matter-of-fact, so different from how he'd been last night, that I suddenly worried he'd decided I was too much trouble. "Mason, are you mad at me?"

His head swung around, his eyes wide as he placed a box of pancake mix on the counter. "Why on earth would I be angry with you?" He came around the counter and pulled me into his arms. "No, I'm freaked out. He was in your house with you and he could have..." His voice trailed off. "I should have stayed with you. I should never have left but I was worried that I wouldn't be able to resist you if I stayed and Jeff was so sure—"

"Mason, stop."

He squeezed me tighter. "Jeff said they had Crocker cornered in Shreveport, but it just didn't make sense to me that he would have run that far."

"Why?

"Because he's obsessed with you." He released me. "Do you like pancakes?"

I blinked, stunned by his bombshell followed by a complete change in topic. "Yeah."

He grabbed a bottle of syrup out of the cabinet.

"I'm beginning to think everyone eats better than I do."

He glanced over his shoulder as he spooned pancake mix into a measuring cup. "What do you usually eat?"

"Canned soup."

He grimaced. "Then just about everyone *does* eat better than you."

"Thanks." I laughed, but it was forced. I was eager to find out what Mason knew. "I know that I shouldn't have touched the note he left, but I wasn't thinking straight." I shrugged. "I saw the sofa and I just—"

Mason turned around to face me. "It's okay. You didn't do anything wrong."

"Do we have to eat now? I keep thinking about him being in my house and it makes me feel like I'm going to throw up."

He was around the counter in seconds, pulling me off the stool and into his arms.

I rested my cheek on his chest and wrapped my arms around his back. "You found the note?"

"Yes."

"Was that blood on the sofa?"

"No, it was catsup."

"Thank God. I was worried someone or some animal had gotten hurt."

"No one got hurt. That I know of."

I leaned my head back to look up at him. "How do you know he's obsessed with me?"

"I did some digging after what that boy from your neighborhood said about Crocker's guys threatening you."

"Oh."

"The sheriff's department has been investigating, but they didn't do much legwork because they seemed like idle threats. Crocker's known associates had been lying low and Crocker was behind bars. Until the guards at the county jail realized he wasn't in his cell around three a.m. two days ago."

I shuddered.

"I get the rose petals and the rolling pin." His voice softened. "But why the geode?"

I stiffened, remembering the day of Crocker's arrest. "I guess it wasn't in the report." I forced a smile. "And I know you've read the report. Sometimes I think you know more about me from reports than I do."

He grimaced.

"I'm teasing—or trying to. If you were investigating Crocker's threats, of course you would have looked at the report."

"There was nothing about a geode in there."

"When I went to the warehouse to save Joe, I got Crocker to take me upstairs to keep him distracted so he wouldn't shoot Joe. I may have...questioned his masculinity."

"That wasn't in the report, Rose. All it says is that he took you up to the office, then the bust unfolded and Joe came upstairs to save you."

I shook my head. "That's not how it happened."

He guided me to one of the chairs at the kitchen table and then disappeared for a moment, returning with a legal pad and pen. "Start from the beginning. The first time you saw Daniel Crocker was at the DMV, correct?"

"Yeah, when I saw the vision of me dead on Momma's sofa with my head bashed in. I passed out before I could blurt out that he was going to murder me. He left his paperwork and disappeared."

He nodded. "Okay, I have that part down."

"The next time I saw him was at the bar in Jasper's. My blind date had left while I was in the bathroom, so I decided to head to the bar and scratch an item off my wish list—drink wine."

Mason looked up from writing. "Wait. Some guy left you at Jasper's?"

"To be fair, he didn't want to go out with me at all. Violet coerced him into it. And he was terrified that I had killed Momma."

Mason shook his head and lowered his gaze to the paper. "What an idiot. What happened next?"

"Sloan was the bartender."

He looked up again, his eyes wide. "Sloan Chapman?"

"Yeah, just one more coincidence that dug me even deeper into the whole mess. I'd never had wine before, so I had no idea what to order. He was really sweet and helped me figure it out. Then Daniel Crocker came in. He'd seen me in the restaurant with my date, but he didn't recognize me because I had a different hairstyle and was wearing makeup. I looked different. Still, he said he knew he'd seen me somewhere, and it was driving him crazy that he couldn't place me." I paused, taking a breath. "Sloan saw Crocker hitting on me and came over to intervene. He told Crocker that I was his sister and to back off. Crocker did, but he wasn't happy about it."

Mason looked up. "Do you realize the risk Sloan took defending you?"

I nodded, tears in my eyes. "He was shot a few days later, after Crocker came back to the DMV and figured out who I was. He had been looking for me every day while I was off for Momma's funeral. He figured out that Sloan wasn't my brother, and then he asked me if he was an undercover cop. I was horrified and told him no. But I didn't know anything then. I had no idea that Sloan was working with the state police. I got him killed." My voice broke. "I've lived with the guilt of that ever since."

"Rose. It wasn't your fault. You had no way of knowing."

I shook my head. "The next time I saw Crocker was at Sloan's visitation. That was the night that I had another vision of myself dead. It was also when I finally figured out why he was interested in me: He thought I was the DMV informant with a flash drive of information. He told me to meet him the next night at The Trading Post at 10:00 p.m. and bring him the flash drive. But I was clueless about what was supposed to be on it."

Mason kept his eyes on the legal pad. "The report says you went and gave him a flash drive with false information, and then Joe showed up and helped you escape out the back window. That's pretty skimpy." He looked up again. "What else happened that night?"

"Why do you think something else happened?"

His face hardened. "Crocker has a...reputation."

I hesitated. "When Joe realized I really wasn't part of the whole mess, he drove me to my car, which was still at the funeral home, and gave me the fake flash drive. The reason I agreed to meet with Crocker was that I was trying to save Violet—Crocker had put a photo of her under my door to remind me what was at stake." I swallowed and looked toward Mason's shiny stainless steel refrigerator. "He'd expressed an interest in how I was dressed at the funeral home the night before, so I wore a low-cut shirt and tried to dress sexy, hoping to distract him from the fact that I didn't have what he wanted.

When Joe gave me the flash drive, he told me I had the right idea but warned me not to let Crocker get me into bed. He was known to be...rough."

Mason continued writing, his knuckles turning white from his strong grip on the pen.

"When I showed up, Crocker seemed eager to show me how interested he was in me. After his men did a quick check of the flash drive and it passed, Crocker insisted on celebrating with tequila shots."

I heard Mason's pen scribbling.

"After the first three shots and some sloppy kissing, I excused myself to the bathroom to throw up. Joe was in there waiting for me. He told me to go back out and said that he'd help me escape the next time. So I did three more shots with Crocker, with some kissing in between, and then I went to the bathroom to throw up again. And I escaped with Joe."

Mason scribbled down several more lines and then looked up, expressionless. "And when did you see Crocker again?"

"The next day. After we left The Trading Post, Joe took me to his house and hid me in his attic. Crocker's men showed up, but Joe swore he hadn't helped me, that he'd been home alone all night. They said they'd kill him if he was lying. When Joe went off the morning of the big bust, I had a vision of him getting shot, but he insisted he'd be fine and that I needed to stay in his house until it was done.

"Instead, I chased Muffy behind Joe's house. While I was out there, Crocker's men showed up and busted Joe's door down and found my shoes in his house. The ones I'd been wearing the night before. I knew my vision was going to come true, so Muffy and I stole Miss Mildred's car and drove out there with a gun that Joe had planted in my shed. We broke in the back of Crocker's warehouse. Muffy and I hid in a storage room until Crocker came storming out of his office, demanding that Joe tell him where I was. So I rushed out and told Crocker that Joe had nothing to do with it. I said I'd left on my own because I was looking for a real man."

Mason stopped writing and looked up at me wide-eyed.

"What?" I shrugged. "I had to come up with something."

He still didn't say anything.

"Crocker was going to shoot me, but I told him he should prove he was a real man before killing me, so he dragged me up the stairs to the office."

Mason kept watching me, expressionless.

"When a commotion broke out downstairs, I bit his lip and he stumbled backward, then I pulled out my gun and shot him in the leg. But Joe heard the gunshot and ran upstairs with Muffy. She attacked Crocker and he started hitting her. I had to make him stop, so I picked up a geode off his desk and threw it at his head, knocking him out. Joe tied him up with a light cord, and then the state police took him away."

Mason was silent for several seconds. "Do you know what his unfinished business is?"

I swallowed the bile rising in my throat. "I have a good idea."

# Chapter Ten

They're going to catch him," he said, his eyes focused on the gun on the counter. "The sheriff's office and the state police are canvassing the county right now. Maybe he'll realize that stalking you isn't worth getting caught, but that's what a sane person would do. Crocker is a psycho. You can't go home."

"What am I supposed to do? I don't want to stay with Violet."

He shook his head. "No. You'd only put her in danger, anyway. The sheriff's office wants to put you into witness protection."

"But what about my landscaping job? How long will I be gone?"

"As long as it takes. I suspect they'll try to flush him out, but Crocker is smart, so he might realize that you're not really at your house."

"Where will I stay if I can't go home and I can't go to Violet's?"

"You can stay with me until they find a safe place for you. We're outside Henryetta city limits, which is why the undercover sheriff's deputy who followed us is watching my condo."

"So why can't I just stay with you until it's over?"

"Because I have to go to work, and even though the deputy can stay with you while I'm gone, it would be too obvious. Crocker and his men would find you in no time. We need to keep you hidden."

"But how long will it take to catch him?"

"Hopefully they'll be able to flush him out in a day or two. But I don't want to take any chances. It needs to be somewhere outside of Henryetta city limits but still in Fenton County."

Suddenly the answer came to me, so obvious that I felt blind for not seeing it before. "My birth mother's farm."

His mouth parted. "Where is it?"

"About thirty minutes out of town. My Uncle Earl has kept it up. When I asked him about it a week ago, he told me he's been paying the electric and gas bills with my trust. He said the water comes from a well."

"Who else knows about it?"

"Uh…" I wrinkled my brow as I counted. "Violet, of course. And her husband, Mike. Joe. Jonah. Neely Kate and my aunt and uncle. But only my aunt and uncle know where it is. Like I told you yesterday, I haven't been out there yet."

"And who knows about the existence of your birth mother?"

"The same people. No one else. Well, except for you, of course."

"This could be good. It's a secret and it's remote. Give me the address and I'll have the deputies check it out."

"So I'll just hide out at the farm?"

"If the sheriff thinks it's a good idea, then, yeah. With sheriff's deputies there to guard you."

Even though I'd been the one to suggest the farm, I was having second thoughts. What if I was stuck there for days or even weeks? "I suppose I was going on Sunday anyway," I said.

"*We* were going on Sunday."

I smiled at him. "We." We'd only made those plans two days ago, but it seemed like weeks. A new worry hit me. "Unless you changed your mind."

He looked incredulous. "Why would I have changed my mind?"

I looked down at the table. "I don't know…last night you couldn't keep your hands off me and now you're acting like Mr. Assistant DA. Maybe you decided I'm too much drama. Joe considered breaking up with me last July after the whole Bruce Wayne and Jimmy DeWade mess. Maybe you've decided to escape while you still can."

"Is that what you think?" he asked in disbelief. "You think this has become too intense and I've changed my mind?"

I looked up into his face. "I wouldn't blame you."

He shook his head. "Come here." He reached over and grabbed my wrist, pulling me around the side of the table and into his lap, wrapping an arm around the small of my back. He looked up at me with a soft smile. "Are you forgetting how we met? You were like this tornado that swept into the courthouse with the sole intent of throwing my entire life off its axis. I knew you were a pack of trouble the moment I laid eyes on you. And when you stood in front of me, completely lopsided because of your broken heel, and verbally berated my lack of manners, threatening to hunt down my mother and tattle on me, I knew I could search to the ends of the earth and never find another woman like you."

I cringed. "I was horrid."

"I deserved every word you unleashed."

"Mason, I'm like a magnet for trouble. Joe hated it."

"Joe's an imbecile. And lucky for me that he is." He kissed me softly and I sighed into his lips. Even in this situation, with Daniel Crocker after me, I felt safe with Mason. Cherished.

I turned to face him better, grabbing the sides of his head and holding him in place in case he changed his mind.

But my actions ignited something in him and he slid his hands under my T-shirt and up my back, setting my skin on fire.

Mason groaned and grabbed my shoulders, pulling me back. "I didn't touch you because I knew I wouldn't be able to stop once I started. As much as I want you, it's more important for me to make sure you're safe. And if I'm the one in charge of protecting you, I'll do a shitty job of it, because when I'm kissing you a damn nuclear bomb could go off and I wouldn't even notice."

"Oh." I could see his point. "So does that mean you're not going to kiss me?"

His eyes watched my mouth. "I don't see how I can be this close to you without kissing you, but we can't get too carried away. At least not until we get you somewhere safe, somewhere with a real protection detail."

"Then why are we still here?"

He laughed and when he kissed me again, I could see what he meant about a nuclear bomb going off. There was a knock at the door, but the sound didn't register until Mason set me on the ground and reached for his gun.

"Why are you getting your gun? Do you really think Daniel Crocker would knock on the door?"

"I wouldn't put anything past that mental case." He checked the chamber. "Now go hide in the bathroom. It doesn't have any windows."

The blood fled my head. "You're serious."

He looked down at me, determination squaring his jaw. "I'm dead serious. Now go."

"No! What if it's him and he shoots you?" Panic made my voice tighten.

His face softened. "Rose, no one's going to shoot me. It's probably Jeff. He told me he was going to come by after he checked out the crime scene, but I don't want to take any chances, okay?" The pounding grew louder. "Now, go." He pointed to a partially open door under the staircase.

I did as he asked, mostly because I didn't know what else to do. I went inside and he pulled the door to the powder room shut on his way to the windowless front door. I sat on the toilet lid, my ears straining to hear what was happening while I studied his décor. It was all sleek and shiny with chrome and dark wood with straight lines. His living room and kitchen were the same—stainless steel and granite counters, contemporary looking sofa and chairs with glass tables. I couldn't imagine a house more different from mine.

"Come on in, Jeff." Mason's voice filtered through the bathroom door. Then the door opened and his face appeared in the crack. "It's safe."

I stood and he pushed the door open, taking my hand and pulling me into the hall. "Rose, you remember Chief Deputy Dimler?"

"Have you heard anything about Bruce Wayne?"

He ran a hand over his head. "I confess that we haven't. Once we got word that Crocker wasn't in the warehouse in Shreveport, we had to regroup and focus all our attention on that. It's why I'm here."

Mason gestured to his living room and we sat on the sofa while the deputy took the chair across from us, leaning forward.

Mason put his arm around my back and the gesture drew Chief Deputy Dimler's attention. "I'm sure you can appreciate that I have a personal interest in Rose's safety," Mason said, tightening his grip.

A frown flickered on his face before it metamorphosed into a grin. "I can see that. I didn't realize you were dating. You never mentioned it."

"We just started dating recently," Mason said, then cast a glance at me as though asking permission after the fact.

I gave him a soft smile.

He turned back to his friend. "What do you know?"

"We don't have confirmation on the prints yet, so we don't know for sure that Crocker was the one in Rose's house, but someone obviously was. For all we know, it could have been one of his boys."

"How'd they get in?"

"The back window. The Henryetta Police swore they were parked in front of your house, Rose, after we notified them at three this morning, but they wouldn't have seen anyone who came in that way."

"So what's your plan?" Mason asked.

"Whether this was Crocker or one of his guys, the fact that someone was in her house while she was asleep is a huge concern."

"Do you think it was Daniel Crocker?" I asked.

The deputy hesitated.

"It was him," Mason said, his voice low. "He swore to get revenge for what he thought Rose did to him. In his mind, she not only got him arrested, she damaged his pride. He's gonna want the satisfaction of scaring her. I don't think he'll stop until he makes her suffer."

Cold chills ran up my back.

Chief Deputy Dimler rested his forearm on his knee. "With all due respect, Mason, you just admitted you have a personal interest in her safety. That could make you jump to conclusions. You're no longer impartial."

"No, Jeff. It makes me more invested, so I might look at things you would miss. Who told you Crocker was still around town?"

He groaned. "You did."

"Crocker's dead set on making Rose pay. He won't leave her alone until he's satisfied. I'm even more certain after hearing everything that happened to Rose when Crocker thought she was his informant. Most of it wasn't in the reports."

The deputy scowled. "Who took the damned reports?"

"Hilary," I said, remembering how nice she'd pretended to be. "She's with the state police, but she was Joe's ex-girlfriend at the time."

"Wait. Joe Simmons?"

"Yes," Mason said. "He and Rose became romantically involved. I suspect Officer Wilder may have let that influence her report." Mason grabbed his notes off the table and shared the rest of my story with the deputy.

Jeff released a frustrated breath. "That information would have been helpful two days ago. There's no question that Crocker is behind this, whether he was physically in Rose's house or not. She needs to be protected until further notice. She's not safe here so I'm going to take her to our safe house."

"And where's that?" Mason asked.

A grin lifted one corner of the deputy's mouth. "It wouldn't exactly be our secret safe house if I went around telling everyone where it was."

"I'm not everyone."

"Nevertheless..." He stood. "Rose, you're going to come with me now."

I blinked, startled. "What about Mason?" I looked at him for reassurance.

There was a strange expression on his face, like a mixture of regret and indecision.

"Mason's not the one in danger," Jeff said in a firm voice. "You are. And with all the craziness goin' on, he's needed at the courthouse."

Mason's arm tightened around my waist. "Maybe I should take the rest of the day off to be with her."

"We'll keep her safe, Mason. You'll be of much more use at the courthouse. You and I both know the sooner we catch this bastard the better."

A war of emotions played out across his face.

I leaned toward him and put a hand on his chest. "I'll be fine. You go to work and I'll hang out somewhere secret for the day." I grinned and tried to keep my chin from quivering. "A day off! Imagine that. Maybe I'll read a book. I heard Jana Deleon has a new mystery out."

He didn't look convinced.

"Mason, you're already in hot water with McClary and the DA as it is," Jeff warned. "Not to mention that incident with the Baumgartner trial."

Mason's eyes widened. "You know that wasn't my fault."

"And we both know the DA blamed you anyway. Think this through."

Mason swore under his breath and began to pace.

I knew Jeff Dimler and Mason were friends, but the way Mason listened to the chief deputy told me that they were more acquainted than I'd realized.

The deputy turned to me. "We need to go *now*, Rose. I would have taken you sooner, but the safe house wasn't ready."

"Okay." My voice was shaky as I stood. "But can I call my sister and check on her?"

He shook his head. "We really don't have time and once we leave, you can't have contact with anyone."

"Bull shit," Mason growled as he pulled my cell phone out of his pants pocket and handed it to me. I'd forgotten he still had it. "She can take a couple of minutes to call her sister."

Jeff sighed. "Fine, two minutes. But don't tell her anything except that you're safe."

I swallowed the lump in my throat. "Okay."

The two men stepped into the kitchen to talk while I dialed Violet's number. Mason's temper seemed like it was getting the better of him. Violet answered on the first ring, catching me off guard.

"Hello?" she asked hesitantly. After yesterday, she probably wasn't sure what to expect.

"Vi, it's me. I don't have much time, so listen."

"What do you mean you don't have much time?" Her tone was one part concerned and two parts irritated.

Mason's voice rose in the kitchen. "You know that I don't give a damn about that!" I heard him say.

"Well, you should!" Jeff answered, hands on his hips.

I shook my head. I needed to focus on my conversation with Violet, not eavesdrop on Mason and Jeff's. "Daniel Crocker broke into my house last night and left me a threatening note."

"*Oh, my word!*"

"The sheriff's deputies are taking me somewhere so he can't find me."

"Are you okay?" Her voice broke. "Did he hurt you?"

"No, I'm fine. I promise. The sheriff is going to make sure I'm safe, so there's nothing to worry about." I tried to make it sound believable. I succeeded enough that *I* almost believed it. "But I wanted to be the one to tell you. I don't know if they'll call you once I'm settled."

"Where are you going?"

"I don't know. They won't tell me." I tried to keep my voice from breaking. "But I'll call you as soon as I can."

"Okay." I could tell she was crying. "Rose, I'm so sorry about yesterday."

"I love you, Vi. No matter what. No argument will ever change that."

"I love you too."

Jeff moved toward me, or more accurately, away from Mason, who looked close to erupting.

"I have to go, Vi. Be safe."

"You too."

I hung up the phone and stuck it in my pocket.

"I'm sorry, Rose." Jeff grimaced apologetically. "You'll have to leave your phone behind."

I reluctantly handed my phone to Mason, and he pulled me into a tight embrace.

I desperately wanted him to come with me. I was terrified and Mason was the only one who could give me any kind of reassurance. But I also didn't want to be selfish. What if he lost his job over me? I had caught enough of their conversation to figure out that Chief Deputy Dimler thought it was a possibility. I couldn't do that to Mason.

I leaned back and cupped his cheek, looking into his eyes. "It's okay. I'll be fine."

"I have a really bad feeling about this, Rose."

My mouth lifted in a half-smile. "I do too. But Jeff is right. There's no need for you to sit around doin' nothing with me. Besides," I glanced over at the deputy "that's what the sheriff's deputies are trained to do. Protect people." It didn't seem like a good time to remind him that I'd been kidnapped from the sheriff's office a month ago right under their noses.

"I'll come see you as soon as I can."

"Mason," Jeff groaned. "You know we'll need to limit outside contact."

His face reddened with anger. Before he could open his mouth, I grabbed his shoulders and stood on tiptoes so I could look him in the eye. "Just do your part and help me come home," I whispered. "To you."

Mason pulled me into the kitchen and kissed me with a ferocity that surprised me. I clung to him, scared to death to go into hiding without him, but I didn't have a choice. Instead, I absorbed as much strength from him as I could.

"Be careful," he murmured, searching my eyes. "Do what they say and don't put yourself in unnecessary danger."

"You too," I said, tears burning my eyes.

Alarm spread across his face when he saw a tear fall down my cheek.

"I'm fine." I pulled away from him and walked toward the chief deputy. "I'm ready." If I didn't leave now, I'd change my mind and beg Mason to come with me. And I knew I'd always regret that.

"Rose," Mason called out from behind me, but I ignored him as I followed Jeff to the door.

The deputy's phone rang and he scowled when he looked at the caller ID. "Wait here," Jeff said. He ducked outside, closing the door behind him.

I sniffed, hoping I could hold it together long enough to get out of the house.

Mason pressed his chest to mine, pushing me backward until my back was against the wall. His mouth devoured mine, working me into a frenzy of desire and need. "I'll see you tonight," he whispered in my ear. "I'll find a way to get to you."

"I don't want you to get into any trouble, Mason."

"Don't worry about me. Just worry about you."

"Will you call Neely Kate and let her know? She'll be so worried. And Jonah?"

His face softened. "Of course."

"And check on Muffy." My voice broke. "I'm sure she'll be fine with Violet, but I forgot to ask about her, and—"

He grabbed my hand and lifted it to his mouth, kissing my knuckles. "I know how much she means to you. I'll make sure she's okay."

"Thank you."

The door opened again and Jeff poked his head through the crack. "Okay, we're ready."

Mason opened my hand and placed another kiss in my palm. "I'll see you soon."

I leaned into him and murmured against his lips, "I'm counting on it." Forcing myself to step away, I followed Jeff out the door.

"Rose, why don't you ride in the back and I'll have you duck down as we drive through downtown Henryetta, okay?"

I nodded and slid into the back of his unmarked car.

Jeff climbed behind the wheel and started the engine while I watched Mason stand there in his doorway. Our eyes locked and we stared at each other, both of our faces expressionless, while Jeff backed out of the driveway. As he drove down the street, I turned to watch Mason grow smaller and smaller. And when he disappeared completely, I swallowed a sob.

I had never felt so alone in my life.

# Chapter Eleven

I took several deep breaths to keep from breaking down and embarrassing myself in the back of Chief Deputy Dimler's car.

"Rough morning, huh?" he asked.

My gaze strayed up to the rearview mirror and found him looking back at me. "Yeah."

"Mason seems very attached to you. How long have you been dating?"

He'd already asked Mason that inside, so why was he asking me? Who knew how far the safe house was, maybe it was far enough that he wanted to pass the time with conversation. "Our relationship is...complicated." Just like the rest of my life.

He laughed. "People say that, but either someone's worth fighting for or they're not. Nothing so complicated about that."

It was a presumptuous thing to say, but he had a good point. "Are you married, Chief Deputy Dimler?"

He looked over his shoulder with a grin. "If you're a good friend of Mason's, we're past the formal stage. Call me Jeff." He turned back to look in the rearview mirror.

I looked behind us, too, and noticed that the unmarked police car that had been parked in front of Mason's house was trailing us.

"And yep, married with three kids. Expensive little buggers." He paused. "Funny that Mason has never mentioned you to me before—other than professionally, of course."

"Well…" I wasn't sure how much I wanted to say.

"Mason's a great guy. He got a raw deal in Little Rock. Who can blame him for beating the shit out of the bastard who killed his sister?"

While I agreed, the edge in his voice made me uncomfortable. Not to mention Mason didn't go spreading that information around. "He seems to be making the best of the situation."

"True, but that's Mason for you. He believes in white knights and chivalry and justice for all."

"And you don't, Jeff?"

He shook his head with a chuckle. "Let's just say I'm a bit more jaded than Mason. I'm a good ten years older, so I've been around long enough to lose some of that idealism."

I wasn't sure how to answer that, either.

"Like I said, he's a great guy, but he tends to throw himself whole-heartedly into his projects. And he gets too emotionally involved."

I bristled. I was sharp enough to know he was insinuating something but I was too tired to play games. "What are you getting at, Chief Deputy Dimler?"

He chuckled again. "Back to formal, huh? There's no need to act defensive, Rose. We're both on the same team here. We both want what's best for Mason."

"And let me guess, you don't think I'm what's best for him?"

He didn't answer.

"You don't know anything about me or us."

"You're right." He stopped at a four-way intersection and turned back to look me in the eye. "I don't know anything about you...besides the fact that you're a thorn in the Henryetta Police Department's side. And like I said, I've been a friend of Mason's for months, and he's never mentioned you other than in professional conversations. It just seems coincidental that you're in trouble and he's suddenly taken a shining to you. I can't help but wonder if his white knight complex has kicked into gear."

I didn't owe him an explanation and I considered telling him off, but two things stopped me. One, he was in charge of guarding my life, so it wouldn't be wise to antagonize him. And two, he really did seem to have Mason's best interests in mind. Could I fault him for trying to be a good friend? "I can assure you that we've been friends for months and we've had...feelings for each other for some time."

"What happened with Joe Simmons?" He studied me in the mirror.

"We broke up over a month ago."

"So Mason's your rebound?"

Now I was angry. "It's none of your business how we define our relationship!"

He pulled the car to the side of the road and looked over the seat, his eyes blazing with anger. "You're wrong. When my good friend is ready to threaten his career because of a woman he only recently started dating, it becomes my business. What kind of friend would I be if I let him throw everything away without thinkin' it through?"

I was right. He was right. We were both right. But I was too tired to argue. "I don't want to talk about it anymore."

"Rose." His voice softened. "It's not personal. I just want to make sure Mason doesn't get hurt."

I looked out the window, tears burning behind my eyes.

"He's gonna try to come stay with you. I'm urgin' you to make him reconsider. His professional image was already damaged enough by the incident with his sister. We'll do everything in our power to protect you, but I'm begging you, if you talk to Mason, ask him to stay away."

My tears broke free, spilling down my cheeks. I wasn't sure I was strong enough to do that, even if it really was the right thing to do.

"It's obvious you care about him," the deputy said, softly. "So just think about what I said." He turned around and started driving again.

My head tingled and I cringed, knowing a vision was right around the corner. I closed my eyes, and suddenly I was in the sheriff's office. Mason was standing in front of me, angrier than I'd ever seen him. "You have no right to keep her location from me, Jeff! This is my life, not yours!"

I squared my shoulders, resting my hand on my gun. "I did what I thought was right. Hopefully, you'll understand and thank me for it later."

The vision faded and the back of the deputy's head came into view. "You're gonna have an argument with Mason."

The deputy sighed loudly. "I suspect you're right about that one."

Did the vision mean I should I tell Mason to stay away or not? I wasn't sure I'd even get the chance to talk to him.

We drove the rest of the way in silence except for a short phone call he took, during which he did a lot of grunting and didn't sound very happy, but he pulled a U-turn and headed the opposite direction.

"Is there a problem?" I asked.

"Nothing that won't be straightened out soon enough," he responded with a frown.

His answer wasn't exactly reassuring. I had no idea where we were going other than south of Henryetta until we stopped in the parking lot of a rundown motel in Pickle Junction, a small town known for its annual pickle festival and not much else. The motel looked like it had seen its hey-day back in the sixties and seventies, when the festival had been in its zenith. Now the establishment needed a new paint job and roof and, judging from the empty parking lot, a few customers. No wonder they picked this place. The deputy turned off the engine and turned to look at me. "I'm going to leave you here with an officer. Trust me."

As we got out of the car, the unmarked car pulled into the space next to the chief deputy's. One of the motel doors swung open and a man in a police uniform stepped out. Chief Deputy Dimler walked me to the doorway. "Rose, this is Officer Sprout with the Henryetta Police Department, and he's going to take care of you for now."

Officer Sprout looked like he was fresh out of high school. He had short, light-brown hair; brown eyes; and a face full of freckles. But he offered me a warm smile, which I desperately needed. "Nice to meet you, ma'am."

And then it hit me. "Wait!" I spun to face Jeff. "I thought the sheriff's department was going to protect me."

The deputy at least had the courtesy to grimace. "That phone call I took was telling me that the Henryetta police won the custody battle for you. Since the incident occurred in city limits, they claim it's theirs."

"But..." Why in the world would the Henryetta police *want* to look after me?

"If you need anything, tell Officer Sprout. He'll see to it."

I nodded, but I was less than confident about this whole mess. I suspected I'd be a lot safer hiding somewhere on my own.

Some unnamable emotion flickered over Jeff's face. "Rose, I suspect you probably think I'm a prick after our conversation about Mason and now this, but I assure you that it's not personal." He lowered his voice. "And while you might not feel very safe right now, I promise that you are. I'm doing everything in my power to get you transferred back to the sheriff's department. But for now, just sit tight."

Rather than answering, I walked over the threshold, leaving the two law enforcement officers murmuring to each other in the doorway. I took a minute to examine my temporary new home. Two double beds covered in nasty jewel-toned polyester bedspreads filled the room. The décor was completed by an old television chained to the dresser on the opposite wall, and a wooden chair with a vinyl seat in a corner by the window. Giant dancing pickles with faces, top hats, and stick arms and legs resembling the Planter's Mr. Peanut adorned artwork that hung over each bed. The door to the bathroom stood ajar, giving me a glimpse of a yellow laminate counter, only I was fairly certain it hadn't been yellow when it was new forty years ago. The floor was covered in a stained brown carpet I had no intention of standing on barefoot.

After Jeff left, I found myself alone with the barely legal boy who'd been charged with guarding my life.

Officer Sprout motioned to one of the beds and the TV. "I know it's not much, but it's remote, so there's little chance of him finding you here. Do you want to turn the TV on?"

I looked toward the back of the room. I wasn't sure how much longer I could keep from breaking down. "I need to go to the bathroom." The words sounded strangled.

His eyebrows lifted. "Oh. Okay."

I hurried into the one private place left to me, shutting and locking the door behind me. I turned on the sink faucet, sat on the yellow stained toilet, and started to cry. Once I let the dam break, I couldn't stop my tears. My shoulders shook as I tried to keep the officer from hearing me.

Daniel Crocker scared the bejiggers out of me. I had no delusions that we'd have a polite "let's get reacquainted" chat if he found me. I was sure he'd make me wish for death long before he granted it. And I had serious doubts that the officer outside my door could protect me. Crocker's men were hardened criminals. There wouldn't even be a contest if they showed up. My only hope was that the motel was really remote and secretive enough that Crocker was captured before he found me.

But it also occurred to me that as far as I knew, no one other than Jeff, the deputy in the unmarked car, and Officer Sprout knew where I was. If Crocker's men showed up and killed or kidnapped Officer Sprout, the sheriff's office wouldn't even know I was missing for hours.

I gasped for breath when the officer knocked on the door. "Ms. Gardner? Are you okay in there?"

I jumped up and turned off the water before opening the door.

When the officer caught sight of my tear-streaked, reddened face, his mouth fell open like it was on a hinge. I pushed past him and grabbed the phone on the nightstand.

"Ms. Gardner," he said, following me. "You can't call anyone."

I sank into one of the beds, the receiver cradled against my shoulder. "I need to call Mason." I wouldn't ask him to come, but I at least needed him to know where I was. And I needed to hear his voice telling me everything was going to be okay.

"You can't do that. I have orders that you aren't allowed to call anyone. Especially him."

"Please." I wasn't ashamed to beg. "I just need to talk to him for a minute."

His eyes filled with sympathy. "I'm sorry."

I was still holding the receiver in my hand. Would he really stop me? "Are you going to shoot me if I try it?" I started pressing in Mason's number. "Or are you going to wrestle the phone out of my hand?"

He stood between the beds, his thumbs hanging inside his belt. He looked remarkably relaxed considering he'd been ordered not to let me call anyone. As soon as I finished entering Mason's phone number, I realized why. The phone was dead. I put the receiver down and started to cry again.

Officer Sprout's face twisted with horror. "I'm sorry! I didn't make the rule. We always use this room because the phone is broken. I hear that witnesses tryin' to make a call isn't uncommon."

That got my attention. "This is the police department's room? Do you rent it by the *month?*"

His eyes bugged in surprise. "I don't rightly know. I was just told that they use this particular room because the phone's out."

"Who else has stayed in here?"

"You know, people who get themselves into trouble and then testify to cut themselves a deal. Drug dealers, prostitutes, the works."

I glanced at the nasty bed beneath me. "When was the last time the sheets were changed?"

Confusion crinkled his forehead. "I don't know…"

"So how many people have you protected?"

"Countless."

I doubted that. "No, you. How many have *you* protected?"

He gave me a sheepish look. "You mean like this? Here?"

"Yeah."

"You're the first."

I really didn't feel reassured. But if he was a newbie, I might get him to bend the rules for me. My tears seemed to horrify him, so hopefully I could use that to my advantage. "I'm really scared, Officer Sprout. My boyfriend Mason isn't just anyone. He's the assistant district attorney." The words felt odd rolling off my tongue, but my stomach fluttered just from thinking about him that way.

"I know." Officer Sprout didn't sound very happy.

"He's always there for me when something bad happens and he makes me feel safe. I know he can't come here, but if I could just hear his voice..." My voice trailed off. "I'm sure your girlfriend feels exactly the same way about you."

He cleared his throat. "I don't have a girlfriend."

"I find that hard to believe." And I did. He might be young, but he *was* cute even if he seemed a bit inept. I gave him a shy smile. "Here's the thing, Officer Sprout. When a girl's scared, she just wants her boyfriend to tell her everything's okay. I'm sure you can understand that."

He hesitated.

"I'll make it really short."

"I'll get in trouble."

I clasped my hands together. "No one will ever know."

He closed his eyes and inhaled, then released a long breath. "If I were to go to the bathroom, the witness could potentially leave the room and go to the office."

"What about your cell phone?"

He shook his head. "No way. That can be tracked."

"Leave the room? Is that safe?" I was shocked he would suggest it.

"No one knows we're here." He shrugged. "It's safe."

Given his cavalier attitude, I had all the more reason to call Mason. "Okay."

He walked over to the chair by the window.

I tilted my head to the side, squinting in confusion. "I thought you were going to go to the bathroom."

He looked at me with a blank expression. "I don't have to go yet."

My mouth dropped open. "Are you serious?"

"I usually have three cups of coffee in the morning, but with all of the excitement, I only had one."

I could argue with him and risk him changing his mind or wait. There was more than one way to handle this. I found a plastic cup on the dresser next to the ice bucket. I grabbed the bucket and headed for the door.

He jumped out of the chair and blocked my path. "Whoa! Where do you think you're goin'?"

"I'm goin' to get ice so you'll drink a big glass of water and go to the bathroom."

He shook his head. "I can't let you leave."

"But you..." I stopped. I didn't want to press my luck. Setting the ice bucket down, I grabbed the cup and filled it at the bathroom sink before handing it to him.

"Thanks." He took a small sip and set it down.

This was going to take a while.

I pulled back the greasy bedspread and thoroughly examined the sheets before lying down on the bed. I'd woken up early and it had been a stressful morning to say the least. I'd learned that my body's way of dealing with stress was to sleep. If I had to wait for the deputy to go to the bathroom, I might as well take a nap.

"Do you mind if I turn on the TV?" Officer Sprout asked.

"Go ahead."

I closed my eyes and let the talk show host's voice lull me to sleep. When I woke up later, the room was dark and the news was on. Groggy, I sat upright and looked around. The officer wasn't in his chair and the bathroom door was closed.

He'd gone to the bathroom without waking me.

I jumped off the bed and fumbled with the locks on the door, ignoring the rumbling in my stomach. I hadn't eaten since the night before and it was close to six o'clock. No wonder I was starving.

An older man at the reception desk was watching a television that looked even more ancient than the one in our room.

I leaned against the desk, my heart racing. I wouldn't put it past the deputy to find me and drag me back to the room even though he'd been the one to suggest this plan. "I need to use the phone."

The man didn't even look up. "Customers only."

"I am a customer!"

"Then use the one in your room." He sounded bored.

"I can't. It doesn't work."

Perking up, he swiveled his head toward me. "Yer in room six?"

I nodded.

"That's the Henryetta police's witness protection room. The phone's not *supposed* to work."

How many people knew about this room? So much for secrecy. "Please! I'm begging you!"

"I don't know…"

I ran around the desk and grabbed the phone.

"You can't do that!" he shouted.

Ignoring him, I dialed Mason's cell phone. Thankfully, he answered on the second ring.

"Mason Deveraux." It was his no-nonsense voice.

I picked up the phone and moved to the other side of the counter as the older man made a grab for it. "Mason, I need your help."

"*Rose*?" he sounded panicked. "Where are you?"

"I'm at the safe house, but it's anything but safe. I think *everyone* knows where this place is."

"Everyone but me," he grumbled bitterly. "Jeff refuses to tell me. Where are you?"

I looked out the window at the motel sign. "I'm at the Pine Motel in Pickle Junction. Did do you know the police department has a room they regularly use for all their witness protection cases?"

"You're shitting me."

"I wish I was."

He sounded breathless. "I'm comin' to get you. Do you feel safe right now?"

I looked at the owner, who had resumed watching the news, apparently no longer interested in getting the phone back. "For the moment."

"I wish you had your cell phone on you. *Goddamn it*. I knew I shouldn't have let you go alone."

"Just hurry, Mason. Please." I realized I was putting him in danger, both physically and professionally, but I couldn't stop myself from begging.

"I should be there in thirty minutes. Call me if something happens."

"That might be difficult given the fact that room six is the police department's room and they purposely have a broken phone."

"Then how are you calling me?"

"I'm in the motel office."

"You have got to be—" He broke off into a slew of obscenities then paused, trying to calm himself. "See if you can get into another room."

"The officer's going to come find me any minute now. He was in the bathroom when I left the room."

As if on cue, Officer Sprout appeared in the doorway. "Ms. Gardner," he growled.

"Mason, I've gotta go."

"Wait!" he shouted. "What's going on?"

"Officer Sprout found me."

"*Officer Sprout?* The guy who's been rejected from every police academy in Arkansas? The guy who the HPD hired anyway?"

That explained *so* much. "Yeah, that's him."

"I'll be there in *twenty* minutes."

I hung up the phone and turned to face the officer.

I was done. "I'm not goin' back in there with you."

Officer Sprout's eyes bugged out. "You can't just *leave*."

"Watch me." I started for the door, but that was when an image appeared on the television screen. Daniel Crocker.

I froze in my tracks.

"Crocker was believed to have been in an abandoned warehouse here in Shreveport, but after a lengthy standoff, police discovered the suspect was actually a homeless man with a gun. Arkansas State Police now believe Crocker is still in the southern Arkansas area. He is considered armed and deadly. Use extreme caution if you spot him."

"Ah…" the older desk clerk groaned, plopping his feet on the desk. "He ain't so bad. Everyone knows he was framed."

I gasped in shock, delaying long enough for the officer to grab my arm and drag me back into the room. I tried to pull out of his grasp, but he was deceptively strong. When we were almost inside, I had a vision. I was in the motel room, hiding behind the bed as gunshots zinged over my head.

"Come on out!" a man shouted. "We've got no beef with you. We only want Rose."

"Okay!" I shouted. "Stop shooting! You can have her!"

I looked next to me and my own shocked face appeared in the shadows.

My vision faded and I said, "You're going to turn me over to save yourself."

He scowled. "What are you talking about? I'm not doin' any such thing. I only want to get you back inside before I get in trouble."

He pushed me inside and locked the door. Two things hit me: one, Officer Sprout was going to turn me over without a second thought. And two, Crocker's men were going to find us; it was just a matter of when.

I couldn't wait for Mason to show up. I had to get away *now*.

I grabbed my lower abdomen. "I have to go to the bathroom."

Officer Sprout made a weird face, like he wasn't sure what to do with that piece of information.

"I just thought you might want to know that I'll be in there for a while."

He shrugged and sat down in his chair.

I stepped into the bathroom and immediately figured out how I'd bought so much time in the office. Officer Sprout must have paid a visit to Buffalo Bill's Hot Wings. Gagging, I batted my hand in front of my face and found the exhaust fan switch. I needed the noise anyway.

I spun around to inspect the feature that had inspired me to lock myself into the reeking room: the frosted glass window over the toilet.

Climbing on top of the toilet lid, I grabbed the bottom handle and lifted. Nothing happened. I reached on top of the casing to make sure the window was unlocked, then gave it another jerk. Nothing.

*No. No. No.* I had to get out of here. Now.

After I'd been working on the window for several minutes, I heard a pounding on the door. "Pizza delivery," a man shouted.

"I didn't order a pizza," Officer Sprout said.

Shit.

My heart beating wildly, I hopped off the toilet and pushed up, grunting and straining until the window finally popped up, throwing me off balance. I fell on my butt, which was the least of my worries if the shouting outside the bathroom door was any indication.

Scrambling on top of the toilet, I pushed my upper body through the window, dismayed to see a five-foot drop in front of me. I'd learned a lot about climbing out windows over the last several months, but I didn't have time to do it gracefully. The first gunshots echoed through the night as I dove head-first from the window, somersaulting to land on my butt in the grass. I climbed to my feet and looked around, considering my options. Behind the motel and to the left, there was a patch of woods; to the right was a storage unit surrounded by a tall chain link fence.

I headed for the woods.

I felt a little guilty for leaving Officer Sprout behind, but then I remembered my vision. I tried to keep quiet, but there was no disguising the crunch of leaves beneath my feet. Judging from the continuous sound of gunfire behind me, though, I was safe for now. Part of me was surprised no one was in the back looking for me, but they'd probably expected to catch us by surprise. Still, I wasn't sure how much time I'd bought. Crocker wanted me alive, so they would soon figure out I wasn't in the room and start searching the woods.

I ran about fifty feet, deep enough for the darkness to make it difficult to move around. Hopefully that same darkness would help conceal me. The gunshots stopped after about a minute and my heart lurched. How long until Crocker's men came looking for me? Just as I was about to turn and go deeper, sirens started to wail in the distance. I closed my eyes, for once relieved to hear them. Tires squealed as cars sped from the parking lot. Some of the sirens continued down the road in pursuit, but I could see red lights bouncing off the trees now.

I started to get up but hesitated, unsure who to trust. Did I really want to be under the protection of the Henryetta Police Department?

Several minutes later a shadowed man appeared around the side of the motel, a flashlight beam jiggling on the ground in front of him.

"Rose!" Mason's panicked voice called out.

I started to cry as I stood and ran toward him. "Mason," I called out, almost knocking him over as I rushed into his arms.

He wrapped me in a tight embrace. "Thank God. I thought they took you." I sobbed into his chest, but he tilted my head back to look at me. "Are you okay? Did you get hurt?"

"My butt's a little sore from falling out the window, but other than a few scratches from the trees, I'm okay." I wrapped my arms around his neck, clinging to him.

"You're safe now."

Was I? I wasn't so sure.

"Mason, what are you doing here?" Jeff asked as he walked around the corner.

Mason's head jerked up and his body stiffened. "Imagine my surprise when I found out that Rose was under the protection of the *Henryetta* Police Department and not the Fenton County Sheriff's Office as I'd been told."

Jeff shifted his gaze and kicked a stump on the ground. "Mason..."

"We're friends. Which means you should have told me."

"That fact that you're here right now is exactly why I didn't tell you. How did you even find out where she was?" He shook his head with a sigh. "You're the judicial leg in this system, Mason. You have your own job to do and you need to leave Rose's protection to the people who were trained to provide that type of help, the law enforcement officials!"

"Jeff, she was almost killed!"

"No. They wanted her alive."

"*And that's supposed to make me feel better?*" Mason shouted.

"Mason, you're too personally involved to be objective."

"You told me she'd be protected. She obviously wasn't."

"She was, Mason. Why do think my men got here so quickly? Those Henryetta bunglers may have official protection of her, but I knew they'd screw up. So while we were waiting to get her protection transferred to us, I had men stationed in the area, close enough to get here within a minute or two. The desk clerk alerted us as soon as he saw the first sign of trouble."

Mason huffed in a breath and I rubbed his arm. I knew I had to help defuse this situation. "Mason, I'm fine. Really."

"You're fine after you dove out a window," he said, but he seemed to be calming down. He looked up at his friend. "How did they find her?"

"How did *you* find her?"

I hoped Mason wouldn't rat me out to Jeff. But he must have felt me tense beside him because he said, "From what I hear, the Henryetta safe house isn't so safe. They use the same damn place every time. Once I knew they had her, it wasn't hard to figure it out."

"Exactly," Jeff said. "All Crocker's men had to do was find a previous occupant and they put two and two together. It's a miracle that none of the Henryetta Police Department's witnesses have been killed by now." He grimaced. "After this fiasco, we shouldn't have any trouble getting her officially transferred to our watch."

"So what happens now?" I asked Jeff. "You're telling me you'll put me under your protection, but what does that mean?"

"We'll find our own safe house, but for now you and Mason will come to the sheriff's office. Even Crocker wouldn't try to get you there."

I looked up at Mason, who nodded his agreement.

"Well, that's settled," Jeff said. "We'll take her to the sheriff's office and met you there."

Mason's arm tightened around my waist. "I'll take her."

"Mason." Jeff shook his head. "She'll ride to the office in a sheriff's patrol car. You can meet her there."

He started to protest, but I put my hand on his arm. "It's fine." I turned to the deputy. "Can we go soon? I don't want to stay here any longer than I have to."

"We can go now."

I grabbed Mason's hand and followed Jeff around the building to the parking lot full of Henryetta Police cars and Fenton County Sheriff cruisers.

Jeff stopped next to a marked sheriff's car and talked to the deputy standing next to it before turning to me. "Rose, you'll ride in this patrol car and we'll have another car follow." He paused. "Just in case."

I didn't want to think about what "just in case" entailed.

# Chapter Twelve

Mason got to the sheriff's station moments after I did and disappeared into Jeff's office with him. Someone ordered sandwiches, and I ate two of them while delivering my statement. Afterwards, I sat at an empty desk and waited for Mason. Someone gave me a Sudoku book, but I couldn't concentrate. I kept eyeing the phone. Jeff had told me he hadn't heard anything about Bruce Wayne, but I also knew the department was more concerned with finding Crocker. Jonah was still looking, though, and might have a lead.

Still, it was close to midnight and too late to call him. Jonah was an early-to-bed kind of guy and although he wouldn't mind me waking him up, I couldn't do it. I also considered calling Violet. I wanted to hear how Muffy was doing. I hadn't seen my little dog in a day and a half and missed her more than I would have thought possible.

Just when I'd started to think they'd be in there forever, Jeff's door flew open and Mason and Jeff hurried out of the office. Mason stopped at my desk and sat on the edge, his no-nonsense expression on his face. "I have to go out for a little while. Jeff had a couple of cots set up in the back. If you're tired, you can lie down and get some sleep."

"So I'm going to spend the night here?" I wasn't about to complain. I felt safer here than I did hiding at the motel.

"Yeah, it looks like it."

163

I could tell he was distracted. "Mason, is everything okay?"

He leaned over and kissed me lightly. "Yeah, get some rest, okay."

He was lying. Something was wrong, but I decided to let it go. I had to trust that he had a good reason for not telling me. If they'd found Crocker I'd be told soon enough. Unless…

My eyes flew open. "Is Violet okay?"

"What?" He blinked. "Yes. She's fine. But I'll have Jeff send someone to check on her to ease your mind, okay?"

"Okay. And could they check on Muffy?" My mouth twisted into a grimace. "I know she's just a dog…"

He took my hand. "Rose, she's not just a dog. She's important to you." He gave me another kiss and then stood. "I should have checked on her for you. I'm sorry. But Neely Kate and Jonah were okay when I talked to them this afternoon. I'll have the deputy make sure she's okay when they check on Violet. Now I have to go."

"Okay." I couldn't help but worry as I watched him and Jeff head for the exit. Something was really wrong.

He still hadn't returned a couple of hours later, but when I asked the other deputies about it, they only gave me vague answers. I tried waiting up for him, but I kept dozing off and writing nonsense numbers on the Sudoku puzzle I was trying to solve, so I finally gave up and went to the back storage room to rest on one of the cots.

When I awoke, Mason was sleeping in the cot next to mine. I watched him for several minutes, wanting to reach across the three feet between us and smooth the worry lines from his face. I hated to think that I was the one who put them there.

As though he sensed me watching him, his eyes opened and a lazy grin spread across his face. "All the times I've imagined sleeping with you, this was not what I pictured."

A shiver ran down my spine and my mind turned to dangerous thoughts. "You've imagined sleeping with me?"

He didn't answer, but his grin grew wider.

"Where'd you go last night?"

I'd asked the wrong thing. His expression turned serious as he angled his body toward me, still lying on his side. "My office."

"Why the big secret?"

"It was broken into."

"Why would someone break into your office?"

He hesitated. "They were looking for files. On you."

I sucked in my breath. "And did they get them?"

He rubbed his face. "Yes."

"I don't understand. Why would someone want my files?"

"Not *someone*. Crocker. Or more likely, his men."

I sat bolt upright, and he did too. "Why would he want my files?"

"I don't know. To find out what you've said about him? To get more information on you? Because he's obsessed with you? I'm not sure, but one thing is certain: files are gone."

I tried to absorb the information. "Why were you away for so long?"

"Because my office was trashed... And because Crocker left a note."

I gasped. "What did it say?"

"'Smart men don't take what is mine.'"

I felt like I was going to be sick. "He threatened you because he knows we're together..."

He stood and pulled me off my cot, taking me into his arms. "It's going to be okay."

"But they still don't know where he is."

His tightened his embrace. "No."

"He's going to hurt you, Mason. Because of me."

"No, Rose. Jeff's worried enough that he wants me to go into protection with you."

I buried my face in the nape of his neck. Was it wrong that I was relieved that he was going with me? Even if his life was in danger? I pulled back to look at him. "Where will they take us?"

A hesitant smile lifted his lips. "Your farm."

Not my farm. My *mother's* farm. Fear washed through me, not of Daniel Crocker but of the unknown from my past that awaited me there.

"I told Jeff about the farm and he had two deputies he trusts check it out yesterday afternoon. It's perfect because so few people know it exists. But we're only telling a few key people. We think there might be a leak in the department."

"*What?*"

"Jeff and I have suspected as much for a couple of months. Our lunch date the other day was just one of many meetings we've had to try and piece it together. Even though the Henryetta safe house wasn't so secret, the sheriff thinks Crocker's men might have gotten a tip from someone inside the Henryetta or Fenton County law enforcement departments."

"Then how can we trust them to protect us?"

"Because Jeff has handpicked a handful of men whom he's positive he can trust."

I struggled to breathe.

"By going to your farm, we've added an extra layer of protection. It's not one of their usual safe houses and no one knows anything about it. We'll hide there with the detail and wait for them to catch Crocker." He cupped my cheek and leaned down to kiss me. "I know you're scared, but trust me."

"Always." I grabbed his face and kissed him to show him not only how much I needed him, but how much I wanted him.

He wrapped his arms around my back and pulled me to him, kissing me until I was breathless.

He groaned and pulled back, staring at me with eyes full of longing. "As much as I want this to go further, a cot in the back room of the sheriff's department doesn't seem like the best place."

I rested my cheek on his chest. "Is it wrong that I want you on the farm with me?"

His hand stroked my arm. "No. It would be wrong if you didn't."

The door opened and Jeff appeared in the doorway. "Oh, good. You're awake. It's early, so half the county's still asleep. Now would be a good time for us to head to the safe house."

"Yes, we're eager to get settled," Mason said.

"Then let's get going."

After ordering his men to pull two unmarked cars behind the building, Jeff led us to the back door, stopping with his hand on the door handle. "I'll be in contact a couple of times a day. You'll have one guard during the day and two at night. Here's the list of guys who will be watching you." He handed Mason a folded sheet of paper. "Hopefully, we'll catch the bastard soon and you won't have to be out there for very long."

Mason shook Jeff's hand and pulled him into a guy hug, thumping him on the back. "Thanks. You have no idea how much I appreciate all your help."

"Don't mention it."

We followed Jeff into the parking lot. "You're going to take separate cars just to be on the safe side." He opened the back door of the first car and I slid onto the seat, then looked back to watch as Mason climbed into the other car.

Mason's car pulled away from the curb immediately, but Jeff still hadn't closed my door. He squatted down in the opening. "Rose, I'd like to apologize for yesterday. I think we got off on the wrong foot. When we were in Mason's office last night, he confessed that he's had feelings for you for months and that you two have been friends for even longer." He took a deep breath. "I was just being an overprotective friend and I jumped to the wrong conclusion. No hard feelings I hope?"

"No. Of course not."

"I'd appreciate it if you wouldn't mention yesterday's talk to Mason." His face reddened. "It'll make him angry and he has enough to deal with right now. Maybe we can all sit around and laugh about it someday."

"I don't see any reason to tell him. And I appreciate that you're such a good friend to him."

"Thanks. And don't worry. We'll catch this guy." He stood and shut my back door, thumping the roof with his hand.

# Chapter Thirteen

I watched out the back windows, the rising sun casting a warm glow over the pine trees lining the county road. Of all the times I'd thought about visiting my birth mother's farm, I had never once considered going there in the back of an unmarked sheriff's car.

I glanced at the front of the car and noticed the deputy was watching me in the rearview mirror.

He smiled. "It shouldn't take much longer."

"Thanks." I leaned my head against the window.

"I'm Deputy Miller and I'll be on watch today."

"Nice to meet you, Deputy Miller. I'm Rose." But he already knew that. I took another look at him. It was hard to get a full-fledged impression, since I could see little more than the back of his head, but his eyes looked kind in the mirror and he didn't seem to hate me. Both were steps in the right direction.

Neither of us spoke as he drove for several miles on the two-lane road before turning onto another county road and driving for several more miles past a few farms and sections of untouched woods. Finally he turned onto a one-lane gravel road, the entrance nearly hidden by overgrown tree branches.

"So far, so good," the deputy said, looking in his rearview mirror. He dropped his speed to keep from flinging gravel. "It'll work in our favor that the drive is so hard to find."

My stomach twisted into a knot as the tree branches thinned and a clearing spread out before us, a war of emotions stirring inside me. With all the commotion and stress, I hadn't really had time to absorb the fact that this would be my first visit to my birth mother's home.

A two-story, white clapboard, Victorian-style farmhouse sat at the end of the drive, the other sheriff's car parked in front of it. A large red barn with a wooden fence enclosure was situated several hundred feet behind the house on top of a small hill. Several acres of overgrown fields lay to the left of the farmhouse and several acres behind the house was a gently sloping hill covered in evergreen trees.

The deputy pulled up next to the other car. I climbed out and shut the door, staring at the front porch that wrapped around the right side of the house. Mason was already standing on the porch, surveying the land, but he came down the steps and wrapped an arm around my shoulders. "What do you think?"

I had wanted to hate it out of anger. Dora hadn't chosen to die, but my childhood had been ruined after her death. I recognized the ridiculousness of my reaction, but that didn't change the way I felt. Still, as I stared at the peeling paint of the Victorian-style house, my anger started to fade. "I'm reserving judgment."

"Fair enough." He spun around and took in the circular drive. "But this is an amazing safe house. We're completely secluded here with open space all around the house. And from the looks of it, there's only one way in and out. It couldn't be more perfect," he said and whistled.

Well, I was glad something was going our way.

When we walked onto the porch, I realized we had a problem. I turned to Mason, who was still looking all around, absorbing the details of the place. "I don't have the keys."

"I've got a couple of sets," Deputy Miller said, walking up behind us. "Once we determined it was a safe location, we had a locksmith come out to change the locks."

I got my first full look at him. He was young, but not as young as Officer Sprout, and he had an air of confidence and competence the other man had lacked. His dark hair was cropped short and his dark brown eyes still looked friendly.

Mason joined me on the porch. "Let's check out the inside and then investigate the barn."

The deputy swung the screen door aside and unlocked and opened the door. He moved aside so that I could be the first one to enter the house. I took a couple of steps into the foyer and stopped in my tracks, barely aware that Mason had followed me inside. The exterior of the house didn't do the interior justice. We were standing in an entryway across from a large wooden staircase that led to a landing with a wood banister. To our left was a dining room with white wood paneling halfway up the wall, furnished with a long ornate dining room table and chairs, a buffet stacked with china, and a glass cabinet stuffed full of crystal. To my right was a living room filled with old Victorian-style furniture. A small baby grand piano resided in the back corner. A brick fireplace was flanked on each side by four-foot-tall bookcases with windows above them. Much to my amazement, books still filled the cases. Jutting off the living room was a library with wood-paneled walls, a large desk, and more bookcases crammed with books.

I continued toward the back of the house, Mason trailing behind me. We passed through a swinging solid wooden door into a large kitchen. The walls were painted a pale yellow and white cabinets and appliances lined two of the walls. A large farmhouse-style table sat at the back of the room, beneath a pane of windows that looked out onto the backyard and barn. A door to the left led to a small powder room.

"When you said farmhouse, this isn't what I was expecting," Mason said.

"Yeah, I know." I'd expected rustic, and although the house wasn't ostentatious, it was far from a simple farmhouse.

We went upstairs next, and filed into the first bedroom on the right. A full-sized four-poster bed was pushed against one wall and a huge armoire filled another. The other two walls featured huge windows that looked out onto the land.

Mason parted the sheers, sending dust flying into the air. "Rose, I can see the county road at the end of the drive from here. This house really is the perfect place for us to hide out."

I could only stare, trying to sort out my confused emotions. As if he could read my mind, Mason gave me a hug and said, "I'm going to give you a few moments alone while I check the other rooms."

I nodded and he left me staring out at the acres and acres of land that belonged to me. While I'd used some of the money from my inheritance for the nursery, I'd ignored the farm until a shortage of liquid assets had made me consider selling it. But as much as I hated to admit it, I felt an immediate sense of belonging here.

"There are three more bedrooms and two bathrooms," Mason called out. "You can pick whichever room you'd like to use, but there's a bigger bedroom in the back that looks like it's the master with a canopy bed."

"Muffy would love it here," I said, looking down at the overgrown bushes in the yard. I was already starting to come up with a landscape design.

Mason pulled me into his arms, searching my face. "What about you? How do you feel about being here?"

"I'm not sure yet."

A car came down the gravel drive, sending dust flying into the air. I tensed, but Mason kissed my temple. "Don't worry. That's probably just one of the deputies with our things."

I looked up at him in surprise.

"After I finished at my office last night, a deputy took me to my condo and your house to get some clothes and personal items. I called the sheriff's department to ask you what you wanted but you were already asleep and I didn't want to wake you. So I guessed."

"Don't worry. I'm sure you did fine."

"We'll find out soon enough. Let's go on down. There's a surprise for you."

I couldn't imagine what it might be, but when we descended the stairs and I opened the front door, I saw a brown streak bolt from the car and head straight for an overgrown azalea bush.

"*Muffy?*"

I pushed the screen door open and ran outside, right past Deputy Miller. My little dog's head popped up and she bolted to me, jumping onto my lap when I squatted.

Mason followed me and stopped at the bottom of the steps. "I knew you were missing her, so I asked Jeff to have someone pick her up from Violet's house."

Muffy licked my face and I stood, holding her in my arms. "Thank you," I pushed past the lump in my throat.

His smile faltered. "Rose, you should know that the sheriff put Violet and her kids into protective custody." He saw the panic in my eyes and put a comforting hand on my shoulder. "They weren't threatened in any way, but he wants to be on the safe side."

I took a deep breath and nodded. "That's good, right?"

"Yes."

The new deputy opened the trunk of his unmarked car and lifted out a box. I noticed the car that had brought Mason was already gone.

Mason smiled down at me. "Why don't you let Muffy learn her way around, and I'll help the deputy take our things in?"

"Okay." I put Muffy down and followed her around the entire perimeter of the house while Mason and the new deputy carried in boxes and a couple of pieces of luggage. I recognized one of them as my own.

Deputy Miller was still standing on the front porch, dividing his time between watching us and the drive. "Your dog is cute. What's his name?"

"Muffy. And she's a she." I put a hand on my hip, wondering if he was making fun of her. "You really think she's cute?"

"Well, yeah." He looked confused by my question.

I was fairly certain he was the first person to ever have called her cute. I liked him already.

After Muffy had sniffed everything twice and run out of surfaces to pee on, I took her inside. Mason was in the kitchen with the man who had brought our things.

"Rose, this is Deputy Fitzgerald. He's one of the five men who will be rotating on and off duty."

"Good morning, Deputy." I reached my hand toward him and he shook it. "Thank you so much for bringing my dog along with our things."

"No trouble, ma'am." Muffy sniffed at the deputy's feet and he gave her an annoyed look before returning his gaze to me. "Well, I need to get going. This is the biggest manhunt in Fenton County history since the horse thief ring of 1884 and we need all available men."

Mason shook his hand. "Thank you, Deputy. With any luck at all, he'll be captured before you're scheduled to report for duty here at the farm."

Deputy Fitzgerald grimaced. "The way Crocker's hidden, I wouldn't be so sure about that."

I shivered and Mason wrapped an arm around my waist as we watched the deputy leave.

"Don't listen to him, Rose. Sheriff Foster himself assured me they were following up on several solid leads."

Maybe so, but I was inclined to believe Deputy Fitzgerald. "What's in the boxes?"

"Food."

My eyebrows rose.

"We have a working kitchen." We both took in the dusty mess. "Well, *almost* working, so I figured we could cook."

"Good idea."

The refrigerator wasn't working so we pulled it away from the wall and I squeezed behind it, searching for the electrical cord. After I plugged it in, I shimmied out of the space, dusty but grateful to hear the humming of the motor.

"I feel like I've stepped back into the mid-twentieth century," Mason mumbled, gesturing to the vintage cabinet and the laminate counters.

"That's because you have. No one's lived here in over twenty years."

"I can't believe all of this is yours and you just found out a few months ago."

"Uncle Earl told me I own the house and over a thousand acres."

"This place is amazing, Rose."

I couldn't bring myself to agree out loud, but I was getting there. The back part of the house faced southeast and sunlight poured through the windows, giving the room a cheery feeling despite the grime clinging to everything. "Uncle Earl has the house cleaned a couple of times a year, but it looks like it's due for another cleaning. I think I'll start with this room. We'll need to eat, after all."

He grabbed his laptop out of his bag. "I need to get some work done and then I'll help. But there's something I'd rather do first." He leaned down and kissed me until my knees were weak.

Deputy Miller walked in and cleared his throat. "Excuse me, Mr. Deveraux."

Mason looked up with a wicked grin, keeping his gaze on me. "Yes?"

"I think I'll walk around the property to make sure everything looks all right."

"Sounds great."

I pushed on Mason's chest and moved around the table to look in the boxes. "Did you bring a lunch, Deputy Miller? I'm going to make something after I clean up a bit. I'm not sure what's in here, but I'll come up with something when lunchtime rolls around."

"That's mighty kind of you, ma'am, but not necessary." His eyes darted to the boxes on the table.

"How about you do whatever you need to do and I'll save you something. And please call me Rose."

A grin spread across his face. "That would be great...Rose."

"Good. I'll be in here cleaning when you get back."

He disappeared through the door to the front of the house.

"Feeding the sheriff's deputies isn't part of your job," Mason said with a chuckle. "Or perhaps you think you can sway them to like you if you feed them. I suspect it will take more than canned soup to do that."

I swatted his arm. "I'm perfectly capable of cooking. I used to cook for Momma all the time, but after she died, I kind of rebelled against it because it had been expected of me for so long."

"If you plan to feed the deputies too, I suspect we'll need more food."

I grabbed the kitchen rags and turned on the water, waiting for the stream to get hot. It didn't. "We don't have hot water."

"It's probably been turned off. No sense heating water that's not getting used. I'll see if the hot water heater is in the basement." He left the kitchen and disappeared through the door under the staircase.

While I was surveying what needed to be done in the kitchen, I noticed a long bag on the table. I unzipped it, gasping when I saw the shotguns and handguns inside.

Mason came back up a few moments later, brushing dust off the shoulders of his light blue dress shirt. "Just as I suspected. The pilot light was out. I got it lit, so we should have hot water in about an hour. Also, there's a washer and dryer down there. They both seem to work, so we're set if we need to do laundry."

I looked up at him. "Why is there a bag of full of guns on the table? Where did they come from?"

"They're mine." His faced tensed. "Just in case."

Again with the *just in case*. *Just in case* made my stomach churn. "I thought Jeff asked you to leave our protection to his men."

"If it comes to a gun fight, there's no way in hell I'm willing to sit back defenseless. I'll do whatever it takes to make sure you're safe."

I narrowed my eyes. "Does Jeff know?"

"Rose—" He hesitated and his voice softened. "Sheriff Foster is the one who suggested it."

"Oh." That piece of knowledge made this all the more real. We were in so much danger we needed multiple lines of defense.

He cupped my cheek and tilted my face up. "It's just in case. Crocker won't find us here."

"Okay."

But he pulled a handgun out of the bag and put it on the table next to his laptop.

I spent the next two hours sneaking glances at his gun, trying to keep my mind off what would happen if Crocker *did* find us. I needed to stop borrowing trouble. It made me anxious and never came to any good. Instead, I focused on cleaning and unpacking the boxes the sheriff's department had sent, which, I was grateful to discover, contained all the staples I'd need to make several meals. Mason sat at the table with his laptop and legal pads, lost in his work. I leaned against the counter to study him. It wasn't the first time I'd watched him work, but I'd never seen him like this outside of the courtroom. The way his brow lowered when he was concentrating on something was incredibly sexy.

He glanced up from his computer, his gaze landing on me with a hungry look that made my knees weak.

Sitting back in his chair, he glanced around the room. "Rose, you don't have to clean it all at once. You're making me feel bad about not helping."

"You're working. And don't worry. I want to do this," I said, surprised by how true it was. Cleaning made the house seem more mine.

I found the ingredients to make three turkey sandwiches and put them on the paper plates from one of the boxes. I handed Mason his. "Would you prefer to work in the room that looks like an office? It's pretty private."

"I'd rather be in here with you."

I grinned, lifting my eyebrows. "Now what kind of work are you talking about?"

He groaned and shook his head. "It's going to be next to impossible to be alone in this house with you without taking you upstairs to one of those beds."

A shiver of excitement shot up my spine. "So why wait?"

"I still think you need some time. Especially in light of what's going on."

"What does that have to do with it?" I rested my butt on the table in front of him.

He reached for my waist, pulling me so close I was standing between his legs. "It has everything to do with it," he said, looking straight into my eyes. "You're under duress, Rose. Now is not the time to make a decision about sleeping with me."

"But I wanted to sleep with you two nights ago, and I wasn't under duress then."

"Then there's the fact that I'm supposed to be here guarding you. If I'm in bed with you, I'll be too preoccupied to keep you safe."

I sat on his lap, straddling him. "I thought you said this was the perfect place to hide."

He groaned, shifting beneath me. "You're not making this easy."

I grinned. "Good."

He reached a hand behind my head and pulled my mouth to his. When he finally stopped kissing me, I leaned back and stared into his eyes.

"If this is any indication of what's to come," he said, his voice husky, "I'm close to saying to hell with it and making love to you right here on the kitchen table."

A fire raged in my blood and I kissed him again, pressing my body to his.

Mason pushed me to my feet, still kissing me as he lifted my shirt over my head and tossed it to the floor, breaking contact with my lips for less than two seconds. I sat on the edge of the table and wrapped my legs around his waist as he unclasped my bra and pulled it down. His hand found one of my breasts and I gasped as I threaded my fingers through his hair, clinging to him. His mouth skimmed down my throat and over my chest as his arm wrapped around my back, pinning my pelvis against his. I closed my eyes and arched my back to give him better access.

"Um… Mr. Deveraux." Deputy Miller's voice cracked.

Mason's head shot up and he swiveled me around so the deputy couldn't see me, not that he was looking. He was standing with his back to us.

"Chief Deputy Dimler wanted you to call him. He said he hasn't been able to reach you on your phone."

Mason's hold tightened. "Thank you, Deputy."

"I…uh…I didn't mean to interrupt. Ms. Gardner told me to come back to the kitchen." The back of his neck was as red as a radish.

"It's okay," I said, breaking away from Mason's arms and scanning the floor for my bra. "If you'll wait just a minute, I'll bring a sandwich out to you."

"I'll be on the front porch," he said, bolting from the doorway.

"We've traumatized that poor boy," I murmured, picking my bra up off the dusty floor. I had to admit I was slightly traumatized myself.

"We can't do that again," Mason said, his face strained.

"In the kitchen?"

"At all. At least until they've caught Crocker."

My smile fell. "You're serious."

"Rose, neither one of us even heard him come in! He could have walked in and shot you, and I wouldn't have even realized it until you were already dead."

A shiver ran down my back. "Mason, don't you think you're overreacting?"

"*No*. I'm not." He grabbed his gun off the table.

This was the closest I'd seen him to being furious with me since Bruce Wayne's trial.

He stormed toward the back door.

"Are you really so angry with me that you have to leave?"

He already had his hand on the doorknob when he spun to face me, his eyes wide. "You think I'm angry with *you*? Why would I be angry with you?"

"I…" My face blazed with embarrassment. "I pretty much pushed myself on you just now."

"God." He leaned his head back and took a deep breath before meeting my gaze. "Why would I be angry with you for that? To have *you* come on to *me* after months of wanting you…" He shook his head. "I'm angry at myself, Rose. I can't lose you to that psycho now that I finally have the chance to be with you."

I stood still, unsure of what to say.

He opened the door, turning his attention to the yard. "I'm going to go call Jeff. Go ahead and take Deputy Miller his sandwich, but please don't leave the house."

Tears burned in my eyes, but I blinked them away, not even sure why I was upset. I hated that Mason had waited so long to be with me. I hated that he felt like my safety was his responsibility, but mostly I hated that I wanted to be naked with him right now. If kissing Mason was this passionate, what would it be like in bed with him? Guilt washed over me. Mason was outside berating himself and feeling miserable and here I was thinking about him naked and on top of me, staring into my eyes as he—

*Stop!* I squeezed my eyes shut.

Miss Mildred was right. I *was* wicked.

But my traitorous mind couldn't banish the image of him naked. I'd never seen him with his shirt off. What would he look like? What would his skin feel like against mine?

No one other than Joe and my doctor had ever seen my naked breasts. I wasn't flat-chested, but I wasn't particularly well-endowed either. What if Mason had been disappointed?

That thought cooled me off. I took the deputy his sandwich, then went back into the kitchen and channeled my sexual tension into cleaning the counters and the table so we'd have somewhere to eat for dinner.

I decided to go upstairs and figure out the bedroom situation. The beds appeared to have been made, which meant we had bed linens, but judging from the dusty state of the entire house, they would needed to be washed.

As I passed the front living room window, I spotted Mason sitting on a tree stump in the middle of the front yard, watching the gravel driveway as he talked on the phone.

With a sigh, I climbed the stairs. Muffy followed me, her tail wagging. I was pretty sure Mason would want his own room. And given his excitement over the view of the road from the front room, I suspected that was the one he'd choose.

I stripped the bed and carried the sheets and blankets down to the basement, starting the first load. The powdered laundry detergent was hard as a rock, but I broke off a small chunk and tossed it in, hoping some of it would dissolve.

Heading back upstairs, I searched the rooms to figure out where I wanted to sleep. I examined two bedrooms with full-size beds and antique dark wood furniture. I also found a bathroom that looked like it had been modernized in the 1970s.

Muffy was waiting for me in the fourth bedroom, curled up in the middle of the canopy bed Mason had mentioned earlier. A small attached bath was off to the left, with a toilet and a giant claw-foot bathtub that I suddenly ached to climb into. The back bedroom wall was covered with huge windows and I was about to turn and leave when something caught my eye through the gauzy curtains. There was a deck or maybe a porch outside the room.

I found the door and opened it, nearly falling to my knees when I realized what it was.

A baby's nursery.

# Chapter Fourteen

The room was painted a pale pink, and a white wooden baby bed was pushed against a solid wall. White gauzy curtains hung from above the many windows. Without finding any evidence to prove it, I knew that this had been my room. I'd slept in that bed against the wall. My birth mother had rocked me in that pink and white plaid rocking chair.

I gasped for breath and tried to hold back my sobs.

Proof of my mother's love filled the room, from the homemade diaper stack hanging from the wall to the painstakingly stitched comforter and bumper pads in the crib. A cross-stitched throw was neatly folded on top of a dresser. I opened it and saw the final proof: *Rose Anne Gardner, November 8* was stitched in scrolling cursive.

I sat in the rocking chair clutching the throw in my lap and cried. How different would my life had been if I'd lived with Dora, the woman who'd given me life and obviously love? How different would my father have been if he hadn't gone back to Momma? Would I have grown up in a house full of love and acceptance, or would Dora have locked me in the closet like Momma did when I began to have visions?

I closed my eyes and imagined growing up in this house, eating dinner in the dining room with a happy family. I let myself cry for the life I'd always wanted and would never have.

I sat up. That wasn't true. While I might not have had the family I'd wanted growing up, I could have a family of my own someday. I had thought it would happen with Joe, but while that dream was broken, I could still find happiness with someone else.

I closed my eyes and leaned back in the chair, jolting when I heard Mason's panicked voice shouting my name.

"I'm in here," I called out.

He appeared in the doorway seconds later, holding a shotgun. The fear in his eyes faded to relief when he saw me. "I couldn't find you anywhere. Didn't you hear me calling for you?"

"No, I didn't hear anything. Why are you carrying a shotgun?"

"I got worried when I couldn't find you. The deputy is searching over by the barn." He pulled out his cell phone and called Deputy Miller to tell him he'd found me. When he hung up, he took two steps into the room, pivoting as he studied the décor. "A nursery?"

I held up the blanket and forced a smile. "Mine."

From the look on his face, I could tell he understood what that meant to me. "Rose. I'm sorry."

"I'm okay now, but it came as a shock. For some reason I never suspected that I'd lived here. Uncle Earl called it Dora's family farm, but *of course* she would have lived here with me. Which means Daddy probably stayed here too for a while."

"Do you want me to leave you alone for a little while longer?"

"No. I've spent too much of my life alone." I stood and moved toward him.

He wrapped his arms around my back and rested his chin on top of my head. "I've spent the last fifteen minutes searching for you. I didn't realize this room was back here when I searched the upstairs, so after going through the house without finding you, I grabbed my gun to search the barn. I was going to do one more search of the house while the deputy did a second sweep of the barn before I called Jeff."

"I'm sorry. I didn't mean to scare you."

"You didn't do anything wrong. I suspect the kitchen was expanded at some point, and since this space is over the kitchen, they probably added this sunroom over top of the new part. That means this room is built against an exterior wall, so it's insulated enough to muffle sound, which is why you couldn't hear me. I about had a heart attack."

"I thought you said we'd be safe here."

"I can still be worried."

"What did Jeff want earlier? Or are you not supposed to tell me?"

"Sure, I can tell you. They thought they had a good lead that Crocker was holed up ten miles south of Henryetta, but he wasn't there, and they couldn't find any sign that he had been. I knew about the lead, so Jeff just wanted to keep me updated."

"He seems like a good friend to you."

"Yeah, I think we started our meetings at a time when he needed someone to talk to. One of his kids got sick a couple of years ago and he's focused a lot of energy on his care. But his son's doing better and I think he needs someone who hasn't been part of all the drama. He needs to get away from his troubles even if it's just over a beer watching a game. And I'm grateful to have a friend closer than Little Rock."

He moved over to the baby bed and picked up the comforter, sending dust everywhere. "While I was looking for the hot water heater I stumbled across a couple of boxes of old photos."

I sucked in a sharp breath then exhaled. "Oh."

"I know you originally wanted to come out here just to see the place, but there are obviously more connections to your past than you expected." He turned to look at me. "This is putting you through a lot emotionally, particularly on top of the whole Crocker mess." He set the blanket down and picked up my hand. "If exploring the pieces of your past that your mother left behind is too much, don't beat yourself up about it. Investigate at your own pace. You can always come back another time."

I smiled up at him. "Thanks."

"I've decided to set up my work in the office if that's still okay with you." He sounded anxious.

"Of course. Is everything okay?"

"I've been working on a project during my off hours. I figure I should take advantage of this free time to work on it now." He kissed me then smiled. "If you need me to help with anything, let me know." After he left, I rearranged the baby blanket on the crib and went back into the bedroom. Muffy was still lying on the bed, watching me.

"I take it you want this room?"

She wagged her tail so hard I thought it was going to fly off.

"Okay, this room it is." Moving to the dresser, I opened the top drawer, wondering if there'd be anything inside. I gasped when I found a stash of underwear and socks. Uncle Earl had maintained the property, but it was obvious he hadn't removed anything. Had he left it all for me to investigate?

I opened another drawer—this one filled with nightgowns—and noticed a leather-bound book. Pulling it out, I opened the cover, shocked to discover it was a journal. I flipped through the pages, stopping at a random passage written in a large, scrolling script.

*He's telling her tonight, even as I write this. He's so torn between me and our baby and his sweet Violet, but he says he can't stay with her another day. He's going to ask for a divorce.*

I snapped the book shut. I couldn't handle this right now.

If Muffy and I were going to sleep in here, I'd need to change the sheets. It took a few rounds of tug of war, but I finally convinced her to hop off the bed. After I carted the bedding to the basement and got the load started after putting Mason's in the dryer, I found my suitcase next to a sofa in the living room. I picked it up and stopped to take a peek into the office. Mason had multiple papers spread out across the desk and was flipping through a legal pad, an intense look on his face.

Whatever Mason was working on looked serious. For a moment, I wondered if it was related to Daniel Crocker, but I reminded myself that he was working on multiple cases that had nothing to do with my stalker.

I carried the bag up to my temporary bedroom and set it on the bed. Since I had no idea what Mason had packed, everything inside was a surprise. My purse and wool coat were on top. Under that was a toiletries bag I set to the side. I pulled out two pairs of jeans, a few long-sleeved T-shirts, and a couple of sweaters. To the side were several pairs of socks, underwear, a couple of bras, a nightgown, and two pairs of pajamas.

I sat on the unmade bed, holding up the grannie nightgown I had last worn months ago when Joe stayed over in my spare bedroom before we started dating. I had purposefully picked it that night because it was the most unflattering nightgown I owned. The panties and bras Mason had packed were my most utilitarian pieces of lingerie too. I had a half a drawer full of sexy stuff, yet Mason had chosen against packing it.

What did it mean?

I set it all on the bed, while I dug through my purse and pulled out my cell phone. It was still half charged.

I had about ten missed calls—Jonah, Violet, Neely Kate, and one that made me suck in my breath.

Bruce Wayne.

I listened to my voice mails, clicking through them until I got to the one I was hoping for.

"Miss Rose, you're in danger." Bruce Wayne's voice was shaky, like he was nervous and scared. "You have to hide and stay hidden until I tell you it's safe to come home. I wish I could tell you more, but I've already said too much. Be careful and I'll call you back when I can."

I held the phone in my hand, scrolling through the records to see when he'd called. Yesterday around five-thirty.

Less than a half an hour before Crocker's men showed up at the motel in Pickle Junction.

My phone began to ring, startling me. I jumped and dropped it on the hardwood floor. It bounced and slid under the bed.

I dove for it, praying it was Bruce Wayne. I found it halfway under the bed and grabbed it, only slightly disappointed to see it was Jonah.

"Jonah!" I said, hoping that I'd answered in time.

"Rose!" He sounded relieved. "I didn't think you'd answer. Mason told me you had to go into hiding."

"Honestly, I'm not sure if I was supposed to answer." I was on my stomach, but I rolled to my side, staying under the bed. I usually hated dark, cramped places, but for some reason I liked being under there.

"Should I hang up?" he asked, sounding concerned.

"Doesn't matter. I need to talk to you."

"Is everything okay?"

"Yes, no. I don't know." I rubbed my forehead. "Bruce Wayne called me."

"*He did? Is he okay?*"

"I don't know," I sighed. "I just found my phone, or more accurately, Mason packed my purse with my belongings, and I found the phone while I was unpacking. Bruce Wayne left me a voice message."

"What did he say?"

"Something very vague about me being in danger. But the odd thing is that it's time stamped less than thirty minutes before Crocker's men found where the police were hiding me."

"*Are you okay?*"

"Yeah, I climbed out the back window of the motel room. And then the sheriff's deputies showed up. But I'm somewhere safe now. Or as safe as I can be."

"So the police are watching out for you?"

"The sheriff's department now."

"Your house is blocked off with crime scene tape. I saw it after Mason called me. What happened?

"Daniel Crocker was in my house two nights ago. In my room while I was sleeping. That's why they decided I needed to go into hiding."

"Crocker was in your house? He could have killed you."

"I'm trying not to think about that too much."

"You can't ignore it, Rose."

"I know, but I'm dealing with enough right now."

"This morning I heard Mason's gone too. Is he with you?"

"Yeah."

"So they have you both under surveillance somewhere?"

"Yeah."

"There's something else going on. I hear it in your voice. What is it?"

"I can't tell you where I am, but I'm doing what you told me I needed to do the other day. I'm confronting my past."

"Oh," he said, his voice heavy with understanding.

"I used to live here, Jonah. As a baby. My mother's things are everywhere. Mine too."

"And how does that make you feel?"

"Confused. But it's obvious Dora loved me. It makes me feel good and bad all at the same time, which makes no sense."

"It's a complicated situation, Rose. Your emotions are bound to be all over the place."

"I found a journal in her drawer. I flipped through it and landed on an entry where Dora talks about how Daddy was going to ask Momma for a divorce. She even mentions Violet. It's so surreal."

"You've got a lot going on at the moment. Now might not be a good time to confront your past. It can wait until later."

"Mason found some old photos, but when he told me about them he said the same thing."

"Mason's an intelligent man. I'm not surprised he'd tell you that. He was the one who suggested you needed to confront your past in the first place. We both want the same thing for you. For you to be happy and at peace with your past."

"We…" I hesitated. "We decided we were ready to start a relationship."

"You mean *you* decided. Mason has been ready for a long time."

"Is it that obvious?"

"To anyone who knows you two, yes."

In light of the Crocker situation, I wasn't so sure that was a good thing.

"Have you found out anything else about Bruce Wayne? He didn't give me any information about where he is or what he's been doing."

"No, but I found out something else while I was poking around. Crocker's guys have been doing a lot of recruiting lately. In fact, they're growing so much, they've had to get a symbol and a secret code to show each other they're part of the fold."

"What's the symbol?"

"They all wear St. Jude's medallions. But not just any St. Jude's medallions. They're oval with a border that says 'Saint Jude Pray for Us,' two stars on either side, and a snake on the back."

That made sense. "The police found a St. Jude's necklace in poor Miss Dorothy's backyard last month. But I don't know what was on the back."

"Didn't Bruce Wayne tell you that Crocker's guys were involved in those break-ins?"

"Yeah. There was also a medallion on my front porch after it was vandalized. There was a snake on it." I released a heavy sigh, my throat tight as I decided to share another piece of information. "And I found one on Bruce Wayne's dresser when I discovered he was missing." I didn't want to think about the implications.

"Rose," Jonah pleaded. "You know he has ties to them, and we know he was at Weston's Garage several days before Crocker escaped. But you and I both know he didn't have a part in it."

"Unless he was forced to." I sniffed, looking up at the bed frame over my head. "How did he know that Crocker's guys were about to come find me?"

"I don't know." Jonah paused. "But I do know one thing: Bruce Wayne would never hurt you, and he wouldn't allow anyone else to either."

"I know." I blinked to keep from crying. "Do you know the secret code?"

"No, not yet, but I'm meeting a guy tomorrow who might be able to help."

"Be careful, Jonah. I'd hate it if you got hurt helping me."

"Hey, Bruce Wayne is my friend too. I want to find him as much as you do. Besides, people are more likely to share information with Reverend Jonah than they are with a police officer."

"Still…"

"One more thing that might be on your side: Crocker's men are getting irritated. They understood his need for revenge, but they think it's taking too much time and effort. There's some grumbling in the lower ranks that might actually bring about his downfall within."

"If only we could be so lucky."

"I'll let you know if I hear anything. Be careful, Rose."

"Bye, Jonah."

I laid under the bed for several minutes, telling myself that as long as I was under it, I could worry as much as I wanted over whatever I wanted, but as soon as I crawled out, I had to let it go.

I couldn't ignore the fact that Bruce Wayne had run to Crocker's guys a month ago. He could very well be there now. But Jonah was right. Bruce Wayne would never hurt me. After the last time, he'd promised to tell me if he was in trouble and I'd learned he didn't take promises lightly. I had to trust him.

I also realized that I'd more than likely told Jonah more about our location than was wise. I needed to let Mason know. I started sliding out from under the bed, when something shiny caught my eye. I reached for it, and my hand jerked back when I realized what it was. Tucked between the bed slats and the box spring was a gun.

Why was there a gun under Dora's bed?

# Chapter Fifteen

I found Mason in the office, still absorbed in his work. I stood in the doorway and leaned against the frame for nearly a minute before he looked up.

A tired smile spread across his face. "Hi."

"Hi. I found out a few things I think you should know about."

He set his pen down on his legal pad and leaned back in the seat.

I moved into the room and circled the desk, resting my bottom on the edge of the desk so that I was facing Mason. "I found my bag and unpacked it. You put my purse in there. Thank you."

"I thought you might need it."

"My cell phone was in there."

He watched me, unconcerned. "I put it in there so it wouldn't get lost."

"I had a missed call from Bruce Wayne."

That got his attention. He bolted upright. "Did he leave a message?"

"Yeah." I played it for him, watching his face, surprised by how little he reacted.

"This is all there is?"

I nodded. "But look at the time it came in. A little before Crocker's guys showed up at the motel."

His mouth pursed. "I noticed."

"Mason, there's something else."

He looked up at me, waiting.

"My phone rang immediately after I played the message and I answered without thinking. It was Jonah."

He looked startled at first, then relieved when I mentioned Jonah's name.

"I asked if he had any information about Bruce Wayne, and he didn't but he did find out something about Crocker's guys." I shifted my weight. "They've been recruiting a lot of new people and they needed something to help them recognize each other. They all wear St. Jude's medallions."

Mason blinked. "How did he find out?"

"He didn't say. It must be one of the sources he's been contacting about Bruce Wayne's whereabouts. But Thomas has a St. Jude's necklace. He was wearing it on Halloween night. And I found one on my front porch after it was trashed. The police found one in Miss Dorothy's backyard after the break-in." I paused. "And there was one on Bruce Wayne's dresser."

His squeezed his eyes shut and leaned back in his seat, rubbing his forehead. "Damn."

"Did you know about the St. Jude's medallions?"

He shook his head. "No. We knew there was something, but we didn't know what."

"Jonah also said there was a secret code or password, but he hasn't found out what it is yet."

He stared at the wall for several seconds before looking up at me. "We don't either."

"There's one more thing."

He chuckled. "You provide one more clue we've been searching months for, and I'll deputize you on the spot."

"What?"

He shook his head. "Never mind. What else?"

"I found a gun stuffed underneath Dora's bed."

His mouth gaped. "You're kidding."

"Nope."

He stood and moved around the desk. "Show me."

I led the way upstairs and Muffy trotted along behind us, probably confused about why we kept going up and down the stairs. When we reached Dora's room, I got to my knees and pointed under the bed. "There."

He dropped to the floor and scooted into the small opening between the floor and the bed frame. "Well, I'll be damned."

"I wonder if she bought it for protection."

"If she lived out here alone, she might have."

"No, I'm not talking about that. I'm wondering if someone was after her...if maybe she was murdered."

He slid out, still on his back, and looked up at me. "When you told me about your birth mother, you said she died under mysterious circumstances."

I lifted my eyebrows. "Good memory. She died in a car accident. Her car ran off the road and into a tree. According to my aunt, the brake lines looked like they'd been cut, but the Henryetta Police messed up the investigation."

He grimaced. "They do have a reputation." He moved back under the bed. "Can you hand me a towel or a piece of cloth?"

I grabbed one of the long-sleeve T-shirts he'd packed for me and handed it to him. When he re-emerged and stood, he was holding the gun wrapped in my shirt.

"Who do you think killed her?" he asked softly. "Something in your voice tells me you have an idea."

"Momma. I think Momma killed her. They had argument and then Dora crashed on her way home."

"When this Crocker mess is behind us, I'll help reopen the investigation, okay?"

I was surprised how much that meant to me. "Thank you."

"Come downstairs and I'll show you what I've been working on."

Muffy and I followed him to the office. He put the still-wrapped gun in the drawer of the office desk and motioned for me to come around and join him. He gestured to the spread-out papers. "Like I said, I've suspected for a while now that there's a leak somewhere in either the police or sheriff's office. What I didn't tell you is that it's tied to Crocker, and I'm certain it started long before his arrest. In fact, as far as Crocker and his men were concerned, his arrest should have never happened. They had a source who clued them in on any ongoing investigations and helped keep the heat off them. And in the cases that *did* make it to trial, witnesses suddenly changed their testimony or disappeared." Mason leaned against the desk. "Crocker could have used his informant to find you yesterday, but we can't be sure since the Henryetta safe house is so well known."

"Why would a deputy or police officer give them information?"

"Money. We estimated that before his arrest, Crocker was the third biggest industry in Fenton County. He actually had some legit businesses that hired a lot of county residents, many of whom have since lost their jobs."

"I've heard a lot of people think he's innocent."

"There are two sides to Daniel Crocker. His public persona as the guy who sponsored Little League teams and donated money to church raffles, and the very dark side of him that a lot of people chose to ignore or disbelieve."

No wonder so many people thought he was framed.

"Guys like Crocker don't get as far as they do without help, and I'm sure he's supplemented the income of more than one law enforcement official. But I think this goes deeper than some guy on patrol giving Crocker's guys a head's-up. I think a high-level official is involved, and I'm determined to find out who."

I remembered our conversation after I was arrested for obstruction of justice for investigating Bruce Wayne's case when I was a juror. I had asked Mason why he was an assistant district attorney. He told me that he wanted to make the world a better place and put the bad guys away. And, for some reason, the fact that he'd started this investigation before he ever knew Crocker had it out for me was even more admirable. He really did believe in fighting for justice.

"What Crocker *didn't* count on was that the state police would start their own investigation without him learning about it. The state police also suspected that Crocker had inside help, which is one of the many reasons they didn't clue the Henryetta Police Department in on the bust."

"But Weston's Garage is in Henryetta city limits. Why investigate the sheriff's office? Wouldn't it make more sense for the source to be in the local police department?"

"We thought so, but then a few interesting cases popped up before his arrest—some break-ins and an assault. They all occurred outside of city limits, which would implicate the sheriff's office. When I made that connection, I reached out to Jeff. I'd been investigating the cases on my own, but Jeff is as eager to find the source as I am, especially if he can pin it on the Henryetta police. There's no love lost between the two departments. We've been meeting regularly to discuss our individual findings."

"I had no idea."

"No one does. Or so we thought until last night."

"The break-in at your office."

He nodded. "We've kept this between the two of us, so no one should have even known this investigation existed. I kept most of the files in a safe at home, but I had a few at the office. They were missing after the break-in. Along with your files."

"I don't understand. Were they after the investigation files or mine?"

"Or both?" he asked. "Or was one a cover for the other? We don't know—at least not yet."

I sat down heavily on the desk chair.

"I've been going through these cases one by one, trying to find a connection and I just haven't yet. Both law enforcement agencies are involved at this point."

"Could there be a leak on both sides?"

"Or maybe somewhere else? Like I said, no one knew about this investigation other than Jeff and me. We didn't even tell the sheriff or the DA. It wasn't out of suspicion, more a *the less people who know the better* decision." He rubbed the back of his neck. "We planned to take our findings to both men."

"But could it be one of *them*?"

He sighed. "The sheriff is a good ole boy but he seems to be on the right side of justice. And I'm fairly certain *someone* is lining the DA's pockets. I just thought it came from higher up the food chain, from a guy like J.R. Simmons."

"If it's someone higher up, are we safe?"

He looked out the window and shook his head. "After yesterday, Jeff and I worried about that too. When I told Jeff about this farmhouse, he jumped on it. To be safe, he's told everyone else—including the sheriff—we're at another location. In fact, Jeff has set up decoys at the other location so we'll be notified in case it's compromised."

"So who's our immediate threat? Crocker or the informant?"

"Possibly both." He took a deep breath. "I've been going back through the files and notes trying to connect a high-level source to the cases. So far I have nothing."

I stood and pressed my hands to his chest. "If I can do anything to help, let me know."

"Thanks."

"I've got my own list of *very important* things to accomplish. Mine is focused on the house. I'm washing bedding," I teased. "I thought you'd want the front room with the view, and Muffy picked Dora's room for us."

His eyebrows lifted slightly. "Okay."

After giving him a quick kiss, I headed down to the basement to transfer the laundry. The washing machine was done, but the dryer was still running. I leaned against a folding table and took a moment to look around. Gray stone walls lined the space and I didn't see any windows other than one in a door at the top of a set of stairs that led to the back of the house. The hot water heater and furnace took up one end of the basement, but a row of wooden shelves stacked with boxes was on the other. Two were clearly labeled *photos*, which must have been what Mason had seen.

I wandered over to them, suddenly curious. I pulled one of the boxes down and carried it over to the folding table. I stared at the folded top for a long moment. Did I really want to explore the contents? Was I ready to see the photographic evidence of the life I'd almost had?

The dryer dinged, catching me by surprise. I had come down here to move the sheets to the dryer so I'd have a bed to sleep in, not to open a Pandora's box. I put the warm bedding on the folding table and moved the wet laundry to the dryer.

As I folded the sheets, my eyes kept returning to the box. Why *didn't* I want to look inside?

I'd convinced myself that I didn't want to know anything about Dora or the life I could have had. Knowing would be like rubbing salt in my wounds. But what if I found something inside the box that killed my fantasies about Dora and Daddy? Would that be worse?

After I folded the last piece of bedding, I rested my hand on top of the box, closing my eyes. If I had learned one thing over the past few months, it was to face my fears instead of letting them control me. Because when I really examined the source of my hesitation, it was fear. I was afraid of the past.

It was time to conquer that fear.

I piled the stack of folded sheets on top of the box, then hauled them up to the living room. After I stacked the sheets on the sofa, I set the box on the old wool rug and sat cross-legged beside it. Muffy curled up next to me, pressing her little body against my leg, giving me comfort.

Taking a deep breath, I carefully opened the box and peered inside. There was an assortment of old photo albums and loose photos—some ancient black and white square pictures and other newer rectangular ones. I pulled out the album on the top, flipping through the pages. I didn't recognize anyone in the pictures, but I did recognize the exterior of the house. In the pictures, it was freshly painted and in much better shape. They looked like they had been taken in the forties since the women wore flowing skirts, Victory rolls in their hair, and dark lips—probably red lipstick that didn't show up in the two-tone pictures. Since I didn't recognize the people or the names scrawled on the back—Betty, Floyd, Margaret, William—I paid more attention to the changing features of the house. At one point there had been a porch swing and I liked the idea of putting up another one.

I moved through two more photo albums, finding nothing of interest until I got to a small square album. The first pictures were of Daddy and Dora, looking so happy they could burst. In one, Daddy was holding a small Violet, a huge smile on his face. Next were photos of Dora in maternity clothes, progressively more pregnant in each passing photo. The next photos were of a newborn baby screaming in a hospital bassinet. Aunt Bessie was holding me in one with Uncle Earl next to her, his usual stoic expression on his face.

I tried to let the significance of the moment sink in.

Sensing someone's presence, I looked up. Mason stood in the doorway of the office, watching me. His gaze drifted to the photos in my lap then back up to my face. "How are you doing?"

"Better than expected."

"Can I look with you?"

"Don't you want to keep working?"

"I could use a break." A look of contrition crossed his face. "Unless you'd rather be alone." He took a step backward. "Which I understand. Just let me know if you need anything, okay?"

"Mason, wait."

He paused in the doorway.

"I want you to join me."

"Are you sure? I don't want to intrude."

I smiled and scooted some of the loose photos away, making a spot for him to sit. "Please."

"Thank you." He sank to the floor beside me, picking up the album. "Is this you?"

"Yeah."

"You were a beautiful baby."

"I was ugly. Look at my pointed head and red face."

He shook his head with a grin. "All babies are beautiful, Rose. Think about it. They *truly* are a miracle. Two cells from two different people join together to create this…" He held out his hand toward the photo. "This life. It's unbelievable when you think about it."

I grinned at him. "I never knew you were so philosophical, Mason."

"I'm usually not. I've just been doing a lot of reevaluating over the last few months."

"What's prompted that?"

He shrugged. "Savannah. The way my life took an unexpected turn."

I reached into the box and pulled out a stack of eight-by-ten black and white photos that looked like they'd been taken in a photography studio. Once I set them on the floor, I recognized the baby in the top photo as myself, but the first few didn't have the Sears portrait studio look. I began to turn them over, intrigued. They were all of me, and in a few of the photos, a woman was with me. My mother.

She faced the camera, smiling as she cuddled the baby—*me*—on her lap. The photos were all staged, with an artistic background of a gauzy white curtain hanging from a window.

Mason picked up one of the photos. "There's a darkroom in the basement."

My head jerked up. "What?"

"When I was lighting the pilot light in the furnace, I snooped around for potential entrances and exits. I found a room in the corner. It had been set up as a photography darkroom. There were negatives stacked on the table." He grimaced. "I'll admit that I looked at a few. Most were landscapes and flowers, but there were some of a woman and a baby—you and Dora."

"Dora was a photographer? I definitely didn't inherit any artistic tendencies."

"I wouldn't say that. Landscaping is an art and has an aesthetic. But I don't think Dora was the photographer." He paused. "I think it was your father."

Daddy? It seemed unlikely since I'd never seen him hold a camera, let alone take and develop portrait-style photos. But I couldn't dismiss it either. It was like Daddy had been an entirely different man with Dora.

I flipped through the rest of the stack of photos. There had to be close to thirty of them, and the last two portrayed a family of three. Me, Dora, and a much younger Daddy. He was kneeling next to the chair, one knee up, gazing at her with more love in his eyes than I'd ever seen on his face.

Dora had been the love of his life. He'd lost her and never recovered.

And Violet and I had paid the price.

# Chapter Sixteen

An unexpected fury ignited in my chest. How could my father give up on everything after losing her? How could he condemn me to the hell I'd experienced as a child?

Mason covered my hand with his.

Tears burned behind my eyes. "I'm so angry with him, Mason. He just gave up when she died. He let Momma destroy me."

"No, Rose. She didn't destroy you. You're a fighter. That's one of the things I admire most about you. No matter what happens, you pick yourself up and go on." He leaned over and caressed the side of my face. "It's okay to be angry with him. You *should* be."

"Maybe he deserves it, but why am I so angry with her?"

"Who?"

"Dora."

His eyes widened slightly.

"I know she couldn't help dying. But I'm just so *mad*. What kind of person does that make me?"

"It makes you human. I'm not a saint and neither are you. Your childhood sucked. Your mother was a terrible bitch and I wish to God that I could go back in time to file child abuse charges against her. But I'd like to think you're partially the person you are today because of her. Whether she meant to or not, she made you into the strong woman you are."

"But that doesn't excuse my anger at Dora." My voice broke as tears trailed down my cheeks. "She couldn't help dying, so how can I be angry with her?"

"Because her death sentenced you to that horrible life. I don't think you're angry with *her*, Rose. I think you're angry at her death."

I burst into tears and he pulled me close, his arms tightening around my back as I laid my cheek against his chest. He didn't say anything; he just held me as I cried. When I finally got a hold of myself, I wiped at the wet spot on his shirt and smiled, my chin quivering. "What did I tell you? You're good for offering perspective and shirts to cry on."

He looked into my eyes, wiping the tears from my face with both hands. "I'm so proud to know you, Rose. Most people would run from this because it hurts so much."

"And I have you to thank for that. I'd still be running if it weren't for you."

"No, I think you would have faced your past eventually."

"I don't know. If I were still with Joe, I might have hidden forever. He was so busy hiding from his own past that he never would have thought I needed to face my own."

"It doesn't matter. Because you're facing it now. And you're with me. I'm sorry for the pain you've been through, and I'll do everything in my power make up for it."

I kissed him softly. "You already have."

I jumped at the sound of a knock on the kitchen door and Muffy released a low growl. I started to move away, but Mason's arm tightened around my waist. "Come on in, Deputy Miller," he said.

Deputy Miller pushed the door open, averting his gaze when he saw how close I was to Mason.

The deputy turned his gaze to Muffy who ran over to his feet and danced around. "Sir, I got the truck in the barn to turn over and I left the keys in the ignition. It's really old, but someone's been taking care of it. I think it would be safe for you to take it out."

I glanced up at Mason in surprise.

"Thanks, Deputy."

He nodded and went back outside, clearly eager to escape any more PDA.

Mason turned toward me with a small smile. "I wanted to drive around the land, and I figured you'd probably welcome the chance to get out of the house." He stood. "Do you want to see the farm?"

"Yeah. I do," I said, surprised that I actually did. "But don't you need to get back to work?"

He shook his head. "I've gone over these files and cases so many times I've lost perspective. I'm hoping a little fresh air will help bring me some clarity." He reached down to help me up.

I ran upstairs to grab the jacket Mason had packed for me and met him in the kitchen. He was loading a shotgun when I walked in—a grim reminder that this wasn't just an afternoon drive.

"Does Muffy like car rides? Do you want to take her?" he asked, looking up.

"She loves them. And yeah." She'd been my shadow all day, and she was standing at my feet. "Muffy, do you want to go bye-bye?"

She jumped up on my legs and released an excited bark.

Mason laughed. "I'll take that as a yes."

"Muffy is definitely her own person."

He smirked. "Well, she's a lot like her owner." He slung the strap of the gun over his shoulder. "No wonder you two are so close."

We went out the back door and hiked out to the barn, following the path the tires had made in the tall weeds. The sun had begun to sink in the sky and the air had gotten colder since yesterday. I pulled my coat closer, thankful Mason had thought to grab it.

"There's snow in the forecast tomorrow."

I turned to him in surprise. "This early in November?"

He chuckled. "So much for global warming."

Muffy romped excitedly through the grass, stopping every couple of feet to sniff.

"Do you worry she'll run off?" Mason asked, pausing to watch her.

"Not really. Not unless she's scared. The only time she ran off was when Joe called the police with an anonymous tip that the gun that had killed Sloan was in my shed. The police showed up and a crowd gathered and Thomas's car backfired. Muffy freaked out and took off. I tried to run after her, but the police handcuffed me and left me in the driveway in front of everyone."

He slipped his arm around my shoulders and I leaned my head against him as I watched Muffy run to a new stretch of weeds.

"Joe was on his front porch watching the entire thing. He took off after her, but he couldn't find her. I was sure I'd never see her again. And then she came back the next day and saved my life. Now I listen to her. She has a sixth sense about things."

"I'm glad she's with us." He kissed my temple before releasing me.

When we reached the barn, he pulled open the big wooden doors. I walked into the darkness, letting my eyes adjust. An old pale blue pickup truck that I remembered from some of the old photographs filled the front of the building. I walked around the barn, discovering empty stalls and musty hay.

"They kept horses," I murmured, moving to the wall covered with reins and halters.

"Looks like it," Mason said, following me. "Do you ride?"

"I did when I was a girl. I spent a couple of summers with Uncle Earl and Aunt Bessie. They have a farm in Lafayette County."

We wandered around the barn for several minutes, Muffy sticking close to my side. Mason stood in the open doors for a few moments, staring out at the fields. "Let's go see the land," he finally said.

"Okay."

"Do you want to drive? It's a stick shift. I can teach you how."

Warm memories of Mason helping me buy my own truck washed through me. Then I remembered the last time I drove a stick shift was when a crazy drug addict held me hostage at gun point and we ended up crashing into the back of a truck. I didn't feel like pressing my luck. "I think I'll pass. Why don't you drive?"

He held open the passenger door and Muffy jumped in first, claiming her seat in the middle.

"This reminds me of my Nova," I said as Mason slid behind the steering wheel. I turned the knob on the radio, watching as a dot rolled back and forth over the line charting the stations. "I love my truck, but sometimes I miss that car."

He turned over the ignition and the engine sputtered to life. "They don't make 'em like they used to." He gave me an ornery grin.

After pulling out of the barn, he started to follow the one-lane dirt road abutting the fields north of the house.

"This road looks like it's been used within the last few weeks," he said. "It's not overgrown like the fields. But the question is who was out here and will they be back?"

"It could have been Uncle Earl. He checks on the property regularly."

"Maybe." But he didn't seem convinced. "Someone's worked these fields." He pulled to a stop and leaned over the steering wheel for a better look. "Do you know the layout of the land you own? Are these fields part of the farm?"

"Yeah, I think so. Uncle Earl said most of the land is to the north and east of the house and barn."

Mason cruised slowly past fields that had been cut and carved into the dirt with straight lines. "Then I'll bet he rents out the land. He's probably earning enough to pay the taxes on the property and the minimal utilities he keeps hooked up to the house. Smart."

"You're probably right. He's a smart businessman. He took the money Dora left me and invested it, more than doubling it. What does that mean for us if someone rented the fields?"

"It means that if someone we don't recognize pulls into the driveway, they might have a legitimate purpose to be on the property, but I suspect whoever works this land uses a back road. I figured there had to be one. That's part of the reason we're out here. Now I really want to find it. Crocker could reach us that way."

I shuddered.

"This is all precaution, Rose. From what you've told me, there's no paper trail connecting you to this place."

"I hope you're right."

We drove for almost a mile until we saw a road on the other side of a barbed wire fence. Mason drove up to the gate and parked. "Since we're so close to the road, I think you should stay inside," he said and hopped out the door, shutting it behind him.

Muffy put her paws on his door, watching him with her tongue hanging out of her mouth.

"Not this time, girl," I murmured, rubbing her head to settle her down. "We're going to stay inside."

He walked over the cattle guard in the road and examined the gate before climbing back over it. "The gate isn't locked. Right now anyone can open it and drive through." He exhaled and leaned his forearm on the steering wheel. "I'll see if I can find a padlock in the barn. It wouldn't stop Daniel Crocker, but it might slow him down."

"Is this a problem?"

"No. Whoever works the land isn't likely to make the connection between you and your uncle. We're probably fine."

"Probably?"

"It's the best I've got other than running off somewhere hundreds or thousands of miles away."

I felt sick to my stomach. "That's starting to sound like a better option."

"I think we're safer here, Rose. Jeff has seen to it that very few people know where we are. And at least we have armed protection here."

"One man, Mason."

"We'll have two at night," he said in a low voice. "With one inside watching the entrances. And we're armed too, don't forget."

"Mason."

"Rose, I'm so close to figuring out who the leak is, I can feel it. I have to keep connecting the dots. Once we have a strong case, we can make sure that the people who are after you will go away for a very long time. But I promise you, if I thought this place was unsafe, I'd be the first to move you. I would never knowingly put you at risk. Okay?"

Muffy hopped onto his lap and he reached down to absently to stroke her head.

"Okay." I only hoped he was right. "Why are you the one who thought of the back road? Shouldn't the sheriff's deputies have thought to check this out?"

"Yeah," he scowled.

That didn't exactly fill me with confidence.

"After I figure out how to secure the gate, I want to canvass the woods behind the barn. Do you want to come with me or head back to the house?"

I looked out the window, noticing the lowering sun. "Why don't I go back and start dinner? I don't feel like walking around in the cold right now."

"Okay, but stay inside until I get back."

Mason pulled the truck up in front of the house and I gave him a kiss goodbye, worry tightening my stomach. Something didn't feel right, but I wasn't sure what. "Be careful."

"I'll be back soon. Stay inside."

He pulled away as Muffy and I walked up the steps. Deputy Miller was sitting in a wicker chair on the porch, a gun across his lap. Muffy ran right up to him, sniffing his feet as though she were assessing him.

"Are you cold?" I asked. "It's freezing out here."

"I'm fine."

"Do you drink coffee?"

He nodded. "Yes, ma'am."

"I found some coffee grounds in the boxes of food. How about I make you some to warm you up?"

A smile spread across his face. "Thank you. I wouldn't say no."

"Great," I said, standing. "I'll be right back. Cream or sugar? But I don't have cream, only milk."

"Nah, black is fine."

Muffy and I went inside and after I put on a pot of coffee, I checked the food supply to see what I could fix for dinner, settling on pasta and a jar of spaghetti sauce. I also found a package of cookies and put a couple on a plate.

After I slipped out the front door, juggling a mug of coffee and the plate, Muffy on my heels, I gave the refreshments to the deputy and sunk into the chair next to his. Muffy settled on the floor between the chairs.

He took several sips of the coffee and shoveled one of the cookies into his mouth. He was obviously starving.

"I'm about to start dinner, nothing fancy, just spaghetti. But I'll bring some out to you when it's ready."

He hesitated. "I don't want to be any trouble, ma'am."

"I'm no ma'am. I can't be more than a year or two older than you. Call me Rose. How long have you worked for the sheriff?"

He shrugged, inhaling the other cookie. "A few years."

"Did you always want to be a policeman?"

"Nah, I got into some trouble when I was a kid. I decided to use the energy for something positive and got my associate's degree in criminal justice."

"Do you like working for the sheriff? Isn't it dangerous?"

"Not too much. No offense, Rose, but this is the most exciting thing that's happened in ages. Even the original Daniel Crocker bust was within Henryetta city limits, and the

214

state police took over. If it *had* been under the HPD's control, we still wouldn't have been involved. There's no love lost between our departments."

"That's not a surprise." I looked up into the darkening sky, worried that Mason wasn't back yet. "You said this is the most exciting thing that's happened in ages. I don't see how sitting outside could be very exciting. Aren't you bored?"

"A lot of police work is sitting around and waiting. And I specifically requested to be on this case."

"Really? Why?" I was genuinely baffled. I couldn't think of anything that sounded less appealing than sitting on someone's porch in the cold, looking for trouble.

He shrugged. "So you own this farm?" the deputy asked after a moment of silence.

"Yeah, I guess so. I didn't know until a few months ago. This is the first time I've been here."

"Wow. It's pretty awesome."

"It's really peaceful, isn't it?"

He took a sip of his coffee. "It doesn't scare you to be out here?"

"You mean other than worrying about Daniel Crocker?"

"Yeah."

"No more so than being in my own house in Henryetta. I've lost track of how many times it's been broken into. That tends to make you feel less safe. But when my little dog Muffy is with me, she's a pretty good guard dog."

Hearing her name, Muffy sat up and looked at me.

My head tingled, announcing a vision. The porch disappeared and I was in the woods in the daylight.

"It's okay, girl," I said, pushing my way through thick brush to find a wet and muddy Muffy huddled on the ground and shivering. I gently picked her up and cradled her to my chest. "Don't you worry. We'll find your mommy."

Suddenly, I was back on the porch staring into Deputy Miller's face. "You're gonna find my dog."

"What?"

Muffy jumped up and propped her front paws on his legs.

I stood, rattled by the vision. What did it mean? "I've got to go cook dinner." I headed for the door and held it open. "Coming, girl?"

Muffy stayed by Deputy Miller, who gave me an apologetic look.

"She can stay out here with me if she wants," the deputy said. "It would be good to have the company. I'll bring her inside if she gets restless."

I hesitated. After my vision, I was worried she'd run off, but I'd meant it when I told Mason she had a mind of her own. "Thanks." I turned my attention to her. "You be a good girl and don't run off."

I went inside and started boiling the water for dinner. The sun had set and Mason still wasn't back. I was getting really worried.

Finally, the back door swung open and Mason came through it, his cheeks pink, his hair windblown.

Relieved, I ran over to him and threw my arms around his neck, planting a kiss on his mouth. Caught unaware, his arms encircled my waist and his lips pressed against mine, his passion taking over.

Fire ignited inside me and I pressed my body against his. His arms pulled me closer, but it wasn't close enough. Still kissing him, my fingers found the zipper of his jacket and pushed it open.

One of his hands moved to my face, tilting my head back so his mouth had full access to mine. Then he stopped abruptly, his head lifting.

Panting, it took me a second to figure out why he had stopped. The pasta was boiling over.

Mason closed his eyes and took a step back, seemingly trying to recover as I moved to the stove and turned the heat down, stirring the pot. The spaghetti was done, so I found the colander and drained it.

"I'm sorry," I said as I put the pot back onto one of the cold burners.

He came up behind me and pressed his stomach to my back, slowly sliding his hand over my waist and down to my lower abdomen. He mouth lowered to my neck, his lips skimming up to my ear. "If you greet me like that every time I come home, I'll be sure to leave a lot."

Closing my eyes, I leaned back into him. "You were gone a long time and I was worried. I was about to try you on my phone."

"It wouldn't have done any good." His mouth concentrated on my ear lobe, lightly nibbling. "My cell service cut out a hundred feet past the tree line."

"Don't scare me like that again." I tried to sound gruff, but I was about to moan. While his mouth on my ear was driving me crazy, his hand glided up my abdomen and underneath my breast.

He stopped his exploration of my body, but he held me close before sighing and letting me go. "You're right. I was gone longer than intended. I'm sorry."

I turned around. "I'm not mad, Mason."

"I know, but I can still be sorry about worrying you."

"You really are determined not to sleep with me, aren't you?" I asked.

Resolve filled his eyes. "Not yet."

"What are we waiting for? Because I want this, no regrets."

"When I make love to you, I want to give you my full and undivided attention. I don't want to be worried that someone is going to sneak up on us and kill you."

"Or you. Crocker's after you too."

"True enough." He searched my face. "You have to know that resisting you is one of the hardest things I've ever done, but I have to put your safety above my own needs."

"I know." Reluctantly, I stepped out of his arms and grabbed plates from the cabinet. "Perfect timing. Dinner's ready, as simple as it is."

I scooped up three plates and, since we didn't have any dog food, a small one for Muffy. I put our two plates on the table and then picked up the third. "I'm going to take this out to Deputy Miller and check on Muffy. She wanted to stay out there with him."

He gave me a soft smile. "Okay."

Muffy was lying by the deputy's feet, but she jumped up when I opened the front door. "I brought you some spaghetti. And there's plenty more if you're still hungry."

Deputy Miller's grin stretched from ear to ear. "Thank you, Rose."

Muffy followed me inside and I went to the kitchen. Mason had gotten us glasses of water and was setting them on the table.

"I'll bet Deputy Miller was thrilled to see you," he said.

"I can't let that poor boy starve. You should have seen the way he devoured the cookies I took him earlier."

He gasped in fake shock. "You took him cookies and didn't give me any? I'm feeling slighted."

"Please," I scoffed, sitting down. "You yourself told me that Henryetta's single women were dropping so many baked goods off at your office that you could have had your own bake sale."

"I didn't ask for that."

"And who knows how many free pieces of pie or cake you've gotten at Merilee's. You get most your meals there, which is why all the waitresses have a crush on you."

His eyes widened. "No they don't."

I laughed, twirling spaghetti on my fork. "Hello, Mr. Henryetta's Most Eligible Bachelor. For someone who's so observant, in this instance you are so *not*."

"You know I don't encourage them, Rose."

"I know, which is why they all think you're gay now."

"*What?*"

"Don't worry. I'll help straighten that out for you. If you live up to my expectations."

His eyes lit up with a smirk. "Is that a *challenge*?"

"Take it as you will." I tilted my head and gave him a saucy grin.

Before I realized what he was doing, he had grabbed my wrist and pulled me out of my chair and into his lap. His mouth found the nape of my neck, trailing kisses up to my ear. "I accept your challenge. If you intend to make my wait difficult, I can make it just as difficult for you."

I laughed. "You play dirty."

"You have *no* idea."

Butterflies flapped in my stomach and I took a deep breath. "Then I call uncle because I don't have the will power you do. If you keep this up, I'll be begging you."

With a groan, he pushed me off his lap.

We needed a neutral subject and the farm seemed like a safe one. "I don't think I want to sell this place."

He looked surprised.

"I've been thinking about it since this morning."

"Well, you don't need the money for the nursery anymore. The SBA has already deposited the money for the grant into your business account."

Thinking about the grant reminded me of Joe. The memory of him begging me to take him back nearly brought me to tears.

Mason picked up on my mood, although not the reason for it. "It's a big decision, and I know this place is bittersweet with all its reminders of the life you didn't have, but I can't help but notice the way you've been lighting up as you investigate the house. I can see how much you love it."

"But it's so far from Henryetta."

"It feels remote, but it's only twenty minutes to your nursery." He stabbed several noodles with his fork. "Rose, I'm not telling you to move here," he said after a moment. "But you feel unsafe in Henryetta and you said you can't afford to move somewhere new. I just think it's something you should consider."

I'd add it to my ever growing list.

# Chapter Seventeen

After we finished eating, Mason helped clean up and then disappeared into the office to continue going through his files. As I headed upstairs to make both beds, my cell phone began to ring. I dug it out of my pocket, gasping when I saw the name on the screen.

Joe.

Turning the ringer off, I sank onto the top step and stared at the still-vibrating phone. Part of me wanted to answer to find out why he was calling. But most of me wanted him to leave me alone. If I was moving toward a future with Mason, I needed Joe to remain in the past.

The phone stopped ringing, but I stared at it for several more minutes, taking several deep breaths to calm down.

It was only eight o'clock when I finished making the beds, and I wasn't sure what to do with my time. I was too tired to dig up any more emotional hornet nests, but the TV didn't work. At the risk of interrupting Mason, I went into the office to find a book to read.

When I stood in the doorway, he glanced up at me and smiled. "Hey. Did you come to visit? Do I get to greet you like you greeted me when I came back tonight?"

He reached for me as I walked past him, and I swatted his hand away.

"You may be a self-proclaimed patient man, Mr. Deveraux, but I am not. So I've decided to keep my distance from you until this impasse has been resolved." I scanned the shelves, finding mostly medical journals and non-fiction books.

He leaned back in his seat and belly-laughed. "I hope to God you aren't a patient *man*."

I shot him a glare and fought to keep from giggling.

"I never took you for a cruel woman, Rose Gardner."

"It's not about cruelty. It's about self-preservation." I found a section with classical fiction but kept moving. I needed something lighter than a leather-bound copy of *Moby Dick* or *Anna Karenina*.

He turned back to his work but kept sneaking glances at me.

I found a section of romances dating from the seventies and eighties and picked one up to read the back blurb.

"I take it that you're looking for something to read."

I put my hand on my hip and turned to face him. "Aren't you supposed to be working?"

His eyes darkened. "You're far too distracting."

While I loved this game, Mason was working on something important and I didn't want to take his attention away from it. I headed for the door, still holding the old romance novel.

"You can read in the chair in the corner," he suggested, nodding toward it.

I turned back to him with a grin. "I'll read in the living room so you're not *distracted*."

I plopped into an overstuffed chair, but it wasn't very comfortable. In fact, none of the furniture in the living room looked all that cozy. I suddenly imagined my own furniture in here and how I would arrange it.

I jerked upright. Was I really considering this?

Maybe so, but I'd been through too much in the last forty-eight hours to make a big decision.

I read for fifteen minutes and was just starting to get sucked into the plot when my phone rang again. I pulled it out of my pocket expecting to see Joe's name.

But when I saw the number on the screen, my heart leapt into my throat.

The call was from Violet's home phone.

She had to know she wasn't supposed to call me, which meant it must be important. Then I remembered she wasn't even supposed to be at home. Hoping it wasn't a mistake, I answered. "Violet, are you okay?"

Silence greeted me on the other end.

I held my breath for a couple of seconds. "Violet?"

The voice that answered turned my blood to sludge. "Long time no see, Rose. I've missed you."

Daniel Crocker.

"How did you get into my sister's house?" I asked, trying to control my panic.

"Aren't you going to tell me that you missed me too?"

"No." Tears welled in my eyes, but I refused to let them fall. "Why are you at Violet's house?"

"Baby, I'm the one who's supposed to be asking the questions. Then I'll tell you about Violet."

"No, tell me about Violet first."

"Violet is somewhere safe and sound. For now."

I forced myself to take a deep breath.

My voice must have sounded panicky because Mason appeared in the doorway, worry in his eyes. He reached for my cell phone and turned on the speaker, holding it up between us.

"Why are you hiding from me, Rose? I just want to pick up where we left off before we were interrupted by the state police last June. Good call on dumping Joe McAllister, by the way."

I wanted to ask Daniel Crocker how he knew about me and Joe, but Joe was all over the news. "What do you want?"

"You." His raspy voice sent terror searing through my body. "I'll meet you tonight at ten at The Trading Post, just like old times. Be sure to bring the tequila bottle I left on your front porch."

"That was you?" I whispered.

"I'm hurt that you didn't get the reference. I'm beginning to think I care about us more than you do, Rose."

"I just never thought you'd break out of prison…or that you would come smash pumpkins on my front porch if you did. It seems like there would be other things you'd want to do. Like flee the state."

"And leave you? Not happening, baby. I'm not going anywhere until we've finished our business. Besides, I wanted to give you a gift. Did you like the rose petals?"

I couldn't find enough air to respond.

"It was so hard to watch you lying there so peacefully when I wanted nothing more than to climb into bed with you. But we both know it's all about the chase and the anticipation. You weren't ready. You needed to prepare yourself."

Mason's hand clenched so tightly around the phone I couldn't believe he didn't crush it.

"Tell your DA friend—who I'm sure is rudely listening to our private call—that he's not welcome to our party. In fact, I've got my own surprise for him for taking what's mine."

"Leave Mason out of this."

"I'll be more than happy to. If he lets us have our party of two. Come see me tonight, my sweet Rose. You know where to find me. Don't forget the tequila."

The phone went silent and Mason lowered it to the coffee table. "Why did you answer the phone?"

"He called from Violet's house, Mason. I knew she wouldn't call unless it was important. Does he have Violet? I thought she was safe." My voice rose in panic.

"She is. Jeff told me that she and the kids are with your aunt and uncle."

"But he's in her house."

"Because he wanted to talk to you and he knew you'd answer if he called from her number."

"What if he has her? He wants me to meet him tonight at The Trading Post."

"He didn't say it was a trade. He's bluffing. I'll have Jeff check on Violet, but I'm sure she's fine."

"You don't know that! You're just trying to keep me from getting more hysterical."

He grabbed my shoulders and looked into my face. "Take a deep breath. He's trying to spook you and it's working. We'll make sure your family's safe, okay?"

I nodded. It was all I could manage at the moment, but I couldn't stop myself from crying.

He dug out his phone and called his friend, filling him in on what he'd heard.

"One more thing, Jeff." Mason's voice was tight. "Crocker threatened me personally." He paused. "Could you ask the state police to check on my mother?"

I gasped, new tears coming to my eyes. I'd never forgive myself if something happened to his mother. Not after the way he'd lost his sister.

Mason frowned in response to something Jeff said. "Just get back to me as soon as possible. Rose is pretty worried about Violet." Mason hung up and took my hand in his.

"If Violet's missing, I'll have to go meet with him," I said after several seconds.

"Like hell you will." His voice was deceptively calm. "He knew I was listening and he's bound to know the sheriff's office is protecting you after the Henryetta Police Department's failures yesterday. There's no way he's going to announce where he's headed. He knows he'd be arrested on the spot."

What he was saying made sense, but I could never live with myself if something happened to Violet and I could have prevented it.

The chief deputy called back twenty minutes later and Mason began to pace as he told him that Violet and the kids were safe, but her house in Henryetta had been broken into and vandalized. Mason knelt in front of me. "Rose, I need to know if there's anything in Violet's house that could lead Crocker here. Did she have the address or any papers relating to the farm?"

I shook my head. "No. Nothing."

"You're sure?"

"Yeah."

"Jeff's going to send deputies to The Trading Post, but there's no way Crocker will show up. He doesn't expect you to be there either, but when he calls back, he'll try to use the fact that you weren't against you."

"*When* he calls back?"

"This isn't moving fast enough for him. And it's only going to get worse. He'll call again to try and flush you out."

My stomach twisted.

"Don't answer your phone. It will just encourage him."

I had no desire to talk to him again. "If he finds me and you're with me, he's going to hurt you, Mason."

He grabbed my hand and rubbed the back of it with his thumb. "He's not going to find you."

The sense of foreboding from earlier returned, this time twice as strong. "I think you should go somewhere else. It's too dangerous for you to be here with me."

His face softened. "Rose, where would I go?"

"I don't know."

"I'm not going anywhere. I'd be worried sick if I wasn't with you." He stood. "I found a bottle of wine in the pantry. I think we need some." He disappeared into the kitchen and came back with a bottle and two wine glasses. He poured some for each of us and handed me a glass before sitting next to me on the sofa.

I took several gulps, then spun the glass in my hand, staring at the scarlet liquid. "If he finds me—"

"He's not going to."

I jerked my head around to look into his eyes. He had to listen to me. "If he does, he's going to kill me. He'll torture me first, and then he'll kill me."

He turned to face me. "You can't think about it. That's why he called you. He wanted to make you worry. By dwelling on it, you're letting him win."

"No, Mason. I *have* to think about it. If he finds us, you can't let him get me."

"Shh…" He pulled my head against his chest. "Crocker was at Violet's house. There are bound to be witnesses. He's getting sloppy. They're going to catch him. We have to believe that."

"I think you're underestimating Daniel Crocker."

"If he knew where you were, he'd already be here. You're safe."

I closed my eyes and sank into him. "I don't know what I'd do if you weren't here with me. I'd go crazy."

"That would make two of us, so no more talk about sending me away."

My silence was my agreement, but it still felt selfish. Selfish or not, though, Mason was here to stay.

# Chapter Eighteen

Shortly before nine, Deputy Miller knocked on the front door and poked his head through a crack. "Mr. Deveraux?"

Mason and I were still on the sofa. He had an arm around my back and I was curled up against him. "Yeah," he answered.

"I'm about to leave. I know you don't want Ms. Gardner outside after dark so I thought I'd take Muffy out for her."

Mason glanced at me for permission.

I nodded and turned to the door. "Thank you, Deputy Miller."

"Do you want me to put a leash on her?"

My vision worried me, but I didn't have a leash. "No. I think she'll be okay." Muffy was on the sofa next to me, so I looked down at her and rubbed her behind the ears. "Go outside with Deputy Miller, but don't run off."

She hopped off the sofa and ran to the front door.

The deputy opened the door wider to let her out and gave me a smile. "I'll take good care of her, Rose."

"Thank you."

Mason's arm tightened around me. "The two deputies who are replacing Deputy Miller for the night should get here soon."

"And they're here all night?"

"Yes, until nine tomorrow with their replacement shows up."

I stood up. "I've taken up too much of your time. You need to get back to work."

He got up and took my hands. "You haven't stolen my time, Rose, so please don't feel like you have. I was exactly where I wanted to be. Hearing Crocker threaten you was hard for me to take. I couldn't have just gone back to work after that. I needed to be with you."

I gave him a kiss, wanting to show him how grateful I was to have him here.

He leaned back and cupped my cheek. "You look exhausted. Do you want to go to bed soon?"

The thought of going upstairs and sleeping alone freaked me out, but I wasn't going to tell Mason that. "Maybe in a bit. I want to wait for Muffy. I had a vision of her with Deputy Miller today. She was lost and he found her in the woods."

Mason's mouth twisted with worry. "Then we shouldn't let her out without a leash."

"The deputy who brought her didn't bring one."

"Tomorrow I'll find some rope in the barn you can use. We'll figure something out, okay?"

"Thank you for being so concerned."

"Of course I'm concerned. She's important to you and she's growing on me. I don't want her running off."

"Thanks." I picked up our empty wine glasses and the bottle and started for the kitchen. "I found some tea bags with the supplies, and I think I'm going to make some tea. Do you want some?"

He smiled softly and gave me a gentle kiss. "Yeah, sounds good."

I was pouring hot water into our mugs when Deputy Miller walked through the back kitchen door with Muffy.

I looked up and smiled. "Would you like a cup of tea?"

"No thanks, ma'am. I'm going home to get a good night's sleep before I come back in the morning. I wanted to let you know that Muffy did both kinds of business—" his voice lowered "—if you know what I mean."

I grinned. "Thanks, and I'm glad to hear you'll be back." And I was. Muffy trusted him so I did too.

"You have a good night, Rose." He started for the door and stopped. "Oh, I forgot to tell you. I noticed Muffy didn't have any dog food here, so I'll bring her some tomorrow."

"Thank you."

"No problem."

I finished making the tea and carried both cups into the living room. The front porch light was on and through the windows I could see Mason talking to two men on the porch. I set his mug down on his desk and headed upstairs.

I hadn't taken a shower for two days, so I took a quick one in the bathroom off the master bedroom. Muffy stayed close, as though she could sense I was nervous.

While Mason had grabbed my toothbrush, toothpaste, deodorant, shampoo and conditioner, he hadn't included any makeup, not that I expected him to know what to pack. It wasn't like I needed it for the morning anyway. I didn't usually wear any when I was working on job sites, but now that Mason and I were beginning something, I wanted to look my best.

I had to wonder if he hadn't packed makeup or sexy lingerie on purpose. I had a drawer full of sexy things I'd accumulated over the last several months. I still couldn't help thinking it was odd that Mason choose the underwear I'd worn pre-Joe that looked like something Miss Mildred would wear. Was it insurance so he wouldn't be tempted to sleep with me?

But I reminded myself that I was here because my life was in danger, not to impress my potential boyfriend.

Potential boyfriend. Was that what he was? I was amazed that kissing him felt so natural since Joe was the only other man I had ever kissed. Daniel Crocker didn't count.

But the thought of Crocker reminded me of his phone call. He had been in Violet's house and he'd specifically threatened Mason. What if he hurt someone I cared about because of me? As far as I could tell, the law enforcement agencies were no closer to finding him. Would it be selfish of me not to turn myself over to him? I took a deep breath. I wasn't sure I could do it.

I pulled back the covers on the bed, but I knew I wasn't tired enough to sleep. I decided to go down and get my discarded book. Besides, I wanted to tell Mason goodnight.

When I went downstairs, all the lights inside were turned off except for the one in the office. Mason was pacing behind the desk, his hands in white-knuckled fists by his sides.

Not wanting to disturb him, I hung back in the shadows. But when he glanced up and saw me, his look of irritation transformed into one of affection.

"Did you have a nice shower?" he asked. The look of surprise on my face made him flush. "I came up to check on you and heard the water."

I grinned. "I did. But I can't sleep so I thought I'd trying reading in bed. Are you going to keep working for a while?"

He inhaled sharply. "I don't know. I've looked at the evidence again and again, but I still can't find a commonality."

I put a hand on his arm. "You'll find it."

"I wish I was so sure."

"My grandma always used to say that sometimes you can't see the yarn fibers for the skeins."

Mason's brow lifted with an amused grin. "Excuse me?"

"It was Grandma's way of saying sometimes you can't see the forest for the trees."

He rubbed the back of his neck. "Yeah, well...I've examined the trees too."

"Maybe it's something so minuscule you'd never notice. It's like when I used to grow prize-winning roses."

He sat in his chair and looked up at me, his eyes shining. "You grew prize-winning roses?"

"That's not the point." I rested my hip against the desk. "Out of nowhere they developed a virus. I did everything I could to stop the infection from spreading, but most of my roses died. The next spring I planted new bushes and they came down with it too. It wasn't until I took a couple of steps back that I figured out the cause."

"And what *was* it?"

"It was a spade in my shed. I didn't even use it on the bushes, but it was in contact with the pruners I used. The virus had spread from the spade to the pruners. I had to disinfect everything and then I was finally able to grow healthy roses again."

Mason's mouth dropped open in shock, then he jumped up and pulled me into a hug. "Rose, you are a genius."

"What?"

"You may be on to something."

"You have an infected spade?" I teased.

"I'm positive I do. I just need to find it."

I grinned up at him. His excitement was contagious. "You will. Like I said, take a step back." I placed a hand on his chest and stood on my tiptoes, my mouth an inch from his. "I take it that you're going to stay up for a while?"

"Yes, I'm eager to look at all of this from a new perspective."

I kissed him softly then backed away. "Well, I'll leave you to it. Good night."

His eyes turned serious. "If you need me, come find me."

"Okay."

"Sleep well, Rose."

I headed upstairs and climbed into bed with my book, leaving the door cracked open and the lamp on the nightstand on. I propped up the pillows behind me and tried to read with Muffy curled up beside me, but my mind kept drifting to Daniel Crocker.

I jumped out of bed and went into the nursery, taking a seat in the rocking chair. I looked out the back window toward the barn and tried to get my mind to shift to something—*anything*—else. As I looked around the room, I tried to imagine what it would be like if I moved into this house.

The house was huge, so much so that I could fit Momma's house in the first floor. Would it be wasteful if I lived out here by myself? But then I thought about how much Muffy had loved running around the fields earlier. She could do that every day if we lived here. And I could get cats to live in the barn, maybe a horse.

But the house needed work and I was cash-poor. Did I really want to move out to an old house that was out in the middle of nowhere? I wasn't saying yes yet, but I wasn't saying no, either.

The rocking made me sleepy, so I got up after a while and switched on the bathroom light before climbing into bed, thinking about what color I'd paint this bedroom.

My sleep was restless, and I dreamed of Daniel Crocker finding me in the barn. I awoke with a start, bolting upright in bed. My breath came in heavy pants as I tried to settle down.

"Rose?"

Mason stood in the doorway, wearing pajama pants and a T-shirt. "Are you okay?"

"I had a bad dream."

He came into the room and sat on my bed, pulling me into his arms. "You're shaking."

"I'm okay."

"Do you want me to stay with you for a bit?"

"Would you mind?"

"No, of course not." He scooted back so he was sitting upright against the pillows. He tugged me back with him so I lay in the crook of his arm, my cheek on his chest. His hand lightly stroked my arm in a soothing motion.

"Did you find anything?" I asked, yawning.

"Not yet, but I'm seeing new correlations. Now if I can just tie them all together..." His arm squeezed around me. "Jeff's coming out tomorrow and I plan to fill him in. Maybe he'll see something."

"Good."

I closed my eyes as I felt a vision coming, but I relaxed into it. I was with Mason and I was safe.

I was lying in bed, in this room. Golden sunlight made the room glow. I turned to my side and saw *me*. I was curled on my side, the sheet exposing my naked chest. Mason's hand brushed some loose hairs that lay over my shoulder. I stirred and my eyelashes fluttered against my cheeks.

"Good morning," the me in my vision murmured lazily.

Mason rolled me onto my back and leaned down to kiss me. "Yes, it is," he said in a husky voice.

The vision faded and I was back in the dark, Mason's arm around me. "We're gonna wake up together."

He tensed slightly and looked down into my face. "Do you want me to stay?"

I knew I should tell him about my vision, but I couldn't bring myself to do it. And even if my vision didn't come true, I still wanted him with me. "Yes," I whispered. "I'm scared to be alone."

"I'm glad you said yes," he murmured. "I didn't want to leave." He reached for my face, trailing his fingertips down to my chin and then lifting my face so I could look into his warm eyes. He stared at me for several seconds, as though taking in the sight of me. Slowly, he lowered his face, his lips skimming across mine, his tongue darting into my mouth.

My mouth parted in surprise as desire rushed through my body like wildfire. I put a hand behind his head, holding his mouth against mine in case he changed his mind.

But he showed no intention of changing his mind, and as he continued to kiss me, he rolled me onto my back and pressed his chest against mine.

Need pulsed through my body and I could no longer wait to feel his naked body next to mine.

My fingers found the hem of his shirt and tugged it upward. He broke our kiss as I pulled the shirt over his head and tossed it aside. He loomed over me, his chest naked, and all I could think about was that I wanted to see more.

When I pushed him onto his back and straddled his waist, his eyes flew open in surprise. I ran my hands over his bare skin, marveling that I was finally touching him.

"This hardly seems fair," he said, his voice rough. "I'm naked from the waist up and you're not."

"That can easily be fixed." I lifted my long-sleeved knit pajama shirt over my head. "Better?"

"Much."

My hair hung over my right shoulder and Mason slowly reached up to brush it aside, then his hand lowered to my breast. His other hand lifted to my other breast and I leaned my head back and moaned as an ache shot to my core.

Mason sat up, shifting my legs so that they were wrapped around his waist. His right hand continued to fondle my breast while his other arm snaked around my back and held me in place so his mouth could devour mine, driving me crazy with want.

His hand slid up into my hair at the nape of my neck, pulling my body back as his mouth lowered to my breast.

"Oh God, Mason," I moaned, squirming on his lap. "*Please* don't change your mind."

He pushed me onto the bed and grabbed the waistband of my pajama pants, tugging them over my hips and down. I reached past him and pulled them over my feet. When I leaned back, I looped my thumbs in the waistband of his pajama pants, slowly sliding them down. He placed his hands over mine and helped me push them down to his hips, then he lay on his side and kicked them off as he leaned over me, his mouth finding my breast again as his hand slipped between my legs.

I gasped, arching my back. My hand threaded in his hair, holding on as he licked and kissed his way to my other breast. His hand continued to drive me closer to the edge.

His mouth found the spot on my neck that drove me crazy, his teeth nipping, his tongue licking.

I reached for him, but he stopped me, grabbing my hand and pinning it to the bed over my head, which turned me on even more.

"I don't know how much longer I can wait, Mason."

His tipped his face up. "Birth control?" he asked.

"Yes," I gasped, trying to catch my breath. He was asking me to think, which was almost more than I could handle at the moment. "The pill."

"I have a condom in the other room."

"*No*." I reached for his waist with my free hand and pulled him toward me.

He released my hand and climbed to his knees between my legs. The hungry look on his face made me groan with want and I lifted my hips toward him.

He lowered himself over me, pulling my leg around his waist as he slowly entered me.

I leaned my head back with a moan as he filled me.

Releasing my leg, he pinned both my hands over my head and I gasped at the shiver that ran through my body.

"God, Rose. You are *so* perfect." He plunged in slow strokes, as I wrapped my other leg around his waist.

He buried his face in the nape of my neck as his pace quickened, releasing one of my arms so he could cup my butt. When he tilted my pelvis, I squeezed my eyes shut, my world imploding as I called out his name.

Mason groaned and collapsed on top of me, then rolled to the side, pulling me with him as he kissed me senseless. "I could get used to spending every night this way," he smiled against my lips.

I sighed with contentment. "You'll get no complaints from me." I laughed when I realized our heads were at the foot of the bed. "We're upside down."

He sucked my lower lip between his teeth then released it. "I'm used to it. You turned my life upside down months ago."

Before I could answer, he kissed me, our passion climbing again. And I wondered how my life had become so wonderful in the midst of such chaos.

# Chapter Nineteen

I woke up to Mason's lips trailing down my stomach.

"Mason Deveraux," I sighed. "You are insatiable."

He lifted his head and looked up at me with a wicked grin. "I didn't hear any complaints last night or very early this morning."

"It's not a complaint. It's an observation." I giggled, then gasped as his mouth made my back arch. "Isn't there something you should be doing?"

"Yes, and I'm doing it."

Half an hour later, I was still nuzzled in his arms. My head was tucked under his chin and his fingers were stroking my side.

"I never want to leave this bed," I murmured.

"There's no place I'd rather be, but I need to find out what's going on downstairs."

I lifted up on my elbow. "You'd leave me all alone in this bed? Naked?"

"Now who's insatiable?" he asked, pushing my head back onto the pillow and thoroughly kissing me before lifting himself up with a wicked grin. "I thought sleeping with you would make me less obsessed with thinking about you naked, but I think it's actually worse now that I have the real image in my head. It's a good thing I'm not in court or I might be too distracted by the memories of my tongue on your—"

"Mason!" I giggled. "You would not. You'd be Mr. No-Nonsense, only happier than usual."

"Not just happier, more content," he whispered. "Hopeful."

"Me too."

"Rose, I know we should take things slow, but I've waited for this for months, and I'm struggling to put on the brakes after last night. If you need me to slow down, please tell me."

I shook my head. "No. I don't want to slow down. I want to feel all of this with you without worrying that something's too much, too soon. Let's not set any rules except to be honest with each other." A lump lodged in my throat. "And no secrets. I've had enough secrets to last a lifetime."

"No secrets." He kissed me softly.

My stomach growled and I laughed. "I think I've worked up an appetite."

"Let's get dressed and eat. I'm not sure when Jeff's coming."

He got up and found his pajamas on the floor.

I slid out of the bed and walked toward the bathroom, looking over my shoulder to see Mason watching my naked backside. "I'm going to take a shower. If you want to join me."

He took a deep breath then stepped into his pants. "You have no idea how much I want to—"

I turned around to face him, leaning against the doorframe.

His gaze traveled from my face to my toes. "—but I need to...um..."

I laughed. "Get ready for when Jeff comes?"

"Yeah, that." He crossed the room within seconds and pulled my body against his, his arms wrapping around my back.

He kissed me possessively, making me dizzy with desire and ready to climb back into bed. Obviously he felt the same way since he started to drag me in that direction.

Muffy scampered to the bedroom doorway and started barking.

Lifting his head, Mason asked, "Does she bark for no reason?"

"No," I forced out. "Not usually."

"Don't leave this room," he said. Then he rushed out of the room, still shirtless, shutting the door behind him.

I didn't know how he expected me to sit here and do nothing, but I also realized that I'd only get in his way if there was real danger. Still, I was sitting naked on my bed. If Daniel Crocker had found us, no need to make it so easy for him.

I was rummaging around the rumpled bed for my pajamas when the door opened.

"It's Jeff." Mason stepped into the room.

I released a breath. "Oh, good."

He bent down and retrieved his T-shirt and pulled it over his head. "If you still want to shower, feel free. We'll be in the office going over my files."

"Okay. I'll be down in a bit."

He started to leave then stepped into the room and tugged me to his chest, kissing me again. He lifted his head with a grin. "Let's pick up where we left off later."

I watched him walk out, wondering how he could set me ablaze in only a matter of seconds.

After I showered and dressed, I checked my cell phone on the nightstand then stuffed it into the pocket of my jeans. It was only ten percent charged and wouldn't make it through the day. I had thought about turning it off before I went to bed, but I hadn't wanted to miss a call from Jonah or Bruce Wayne.

When I went downstairs I wasn't surprised that the two men were in the office, but I hadn't expected that the French doors would be closed.

I grabbed my jacket off the hall tree and opened the front door to let Muffy out. Deputy Miller was in the same spot on the front porch, but this time another deputy was sitting beside him. Muffy ran out the door and stopped at the top of the steps, releasing a low growl as she looked at the deputies.

"Good morning, Deputy Miller." I glanced over at the new guy. "And Deputy...?"

"Good morning, Rose." Deputy Miller glanced at his partner. "Don't mind Deputy Gyer. He's not much of a morning person."

Muffy continued to growl.

I bent down and rubbed the back of her neck. "It's okay, girl, go potty."

She slunk down the stairs, turning back to give me a look that assured me she wasn't happy about it. I watched the deputy from the corner of my eye. He was young too, but probably a little older than Deputy Miller. He had short dark blond hair and his dark eyes were hard and unfriendly. He obviously took his job very seriously, which I supposed was a good thing in this situation. I just felt more comfortable around Deputy Miller.

"Are you going to be with us all day, Deputy Gyer, or are you just here with the chief deputy?" I asked, leaning against the support post.

Deputy Gyer looked up at me and smiled, but the expression didn't reach his eyes. "I'll be here all day, ma'am. You just let me know if you need something."

A chill ran down my back. "Thank you."

After Muffy finished her business, we went inside. I could see that Mason and Jeff were still in the office through the glass panes of the closed doors. Mason was sitting in the desk chair and Jeff had pulled up a seat beside him. The chief deputy looked up and smiled, motioning for me to join them.

I opened the door and stood in the entrance. "Good morning, Jeff." I still felt shaky from my experience with Deputy Gyer. "I don't want to interrupt your discussion."

"No, we were just wrapping up. Mason told me that he'd shared with you some of what we've been doing."

I glanced from Jeff to Mason, worried he'd be in trouble. "He didn't tell me much."

Jeff saw my concern. "Not to worry, Rose. No one's in trouble here. Mason said you helped him look at things in a new light. That spark helped him make some startling connections that neither of us had seen before"

"So you've figured out the leak?"

He grinned and clapped a hand on Mason's shoulder. "No, but Mason's *very* close."

Mason rubbed his forehead. "But not close enough." He looked up. "Still, I've determined the leak is from the sheriff's department."

Jeff nodded. "I'm leaving Deputy Gyer with Miller today."

Mason looked up, surprised.

I motioned toward the front door. "I just met Deputy Gyer when I let Muffy out."

Jeff grimaced. "Ah… Well, I hope he was polite and professional. Deputy Gyer is *not* happy to be out here. He thinks he'd be much more effective on the Crocker manhunt, but he's one of my most trusted men. While he's unaware of the internal leak, he'll react quickly if something happens. I'll feel better knowing he's out here with you two."

"Do you have any leads on Daniel Crocker?" I asked.

Frowning, Jeff patted Mason's shoulder. "That leads me the second reason I'm leaving Gyer here. There's something I need to tell you, Mason. I just wanted to get through this business first and wait for Rose."

Jeff's tone caught Mason's attention.

"Why don't we go sit in the living room?"

"Okay." Mason stood, giving me a worried look.

I waited in the doorway and took Mason's hand in mine, squeezing it before we sat down on the sofa.

Jeff sat on the coffee table in front of us, his fingertips pressed together. He suddenly looked exhausted. He closed his eyes and sighed, then looked at Mason. "There's no easy way to tell you this."

Mason tensed and I put my other hand over our clasped ones.

"Crocker burned down your condo."

I gasped.

Mason's jaw clenched but his face remained expressionless. "How do you know it was him?"

Jeff sat up straighter and ran a hand through his short graying hair, releasing a sigh. "He—or more likely one of his buddies—wrote you a note on your driveway in spray paint."

Mason's hand tightened around mine. "What did it say?"

Jeff pulled out his cell phone and drew up a picture before passing it to Mason.

Mason stared at it and started to hand it back, but I grabbed it from him. The image made me gasp.

*You've taken what's mine and now you'll pay* was scrawled in red spray paint on the concrete.

I dropped the phone onto the table next to Jeff and jumped to my feet, releasing Mason's hand.

"Don't you dare," Mason growled, turning toward me. "Don't try to accept responsibility for what he's done."

"He's going to hurt you." My voice broke as terror washed over me.

"Rose." Jeff stood and moved in front of me. "Crocker has no idea where you or Mason are hidden. We have a lead we're following. A neighbor saw two cars at the scene and got some partial license plate numbers. We're running those now. Crocker's been out of jail for a few days and is no closer to getting what he wants. He's getting desperate, which means he's going to get sloppy. But that's why I have Deputy Gyer here. While he may not have much personality, he's sharp and he'll protect you." He picked up one of my hands and squeezed. "It's my job to take care of you, and I promise you that I'll do everything in my power to do that. What's more, I have a personal investment in this case now." He released my hand and gestured to Mason. "Mason's not only my friend; he's exactly what Fenton County needs in the DA office. For the first time in a long time I feel like we can break free of the good ole boy mentality and corruption. But Mason needs to be a part of that." He steeled his back. "Don't worry. We'll catch him."

I nodded even though I wasn't so sure.

"How bad is it?" Mason asked.

"It's a total loss. The fire marshal says they doused everything in some type of accelerant."

Mason sat back on the sofa, his face paling. "What about my neighbors? Was anyone hurt?"

"No. Your neighbors got out in time. But they lost everything too."

Mason nodded and stood up, starting to pace.

Jeff grabbed Mason's shoulder and held on. "I'm sorry. I probably should have told you when I first got here, but I wanted to see what you had first, and I was worried the fire would distract you. And there was nothing to be done about it. What's done is done." His voice was tinged with sadness.

Mason shook his head, still looking dazed. "I understand."

"I'm sorry, Mason. But like I said, we'll catch the bastard." He dropped his arm. "I have to go. Walk me to the door?"

Nodding, Mason followed him.

They stood in front of the door and Jeff leaned his mouth close to Mason's ear, lowering his voice. I could still hear him. "I don't think he'll find you, but if he does, don't hole up. Try to outrun him. It might not be a bad idea to establish some kind of escape plan. You and two deputies won't be able to hold off Crocker and all his posse."

Mason's mouth pressed into a thin line and he nodded. He walked Jeff outside and I headed into the kitchen, my feet carrying me there without conscious thought. Muffy stayed close, more subdued than usual.

I had started a pot of coffee when I caught movement in the doorway. Startled, I jumped and dropped a mug on the floor, the pieces flying everywhere.

"I'm sorry," Deputy Miller said, hanging his head. He was holding a bag of dog food in his hands. "Since Mr. Deveraux was outside with the chief deputy I thought it would be safe to come in."

I shook my head, bending to pick up the bigger fragments. I blushed, realizing what he meant. "I'm just jumpy. Thank you so much for bringing Muffy some food. She loves people food, but it doesn't necessarily love her."

He set the bag on the table and squatted to help me clean up the floor.

"You don't have to do that, Deputy."

"I know, but the company is a lot friendlier in here than outside."

I gave him a smile and then stood up and threw the broken pieces in the trash.

"You shouldn't be walking around in here barefoot, Rose," he said, moving toward me as he spoke. Grabbing my waist, he lifted me onto the counter. His hands stayed on my hips and he stared into my eyes.

I grabbed his hands and pushed them away. "Thank you, Deputy Miller. I think you should go back outside now."

He opened his mouth to say something, still leaning close, but I said, "*Now*, Deputy."

Mason appeared in the doorway. "Rose, is there a problem here?"

I didn't want Deputy Miller to get into trouble because he had a crush on me, even if his behavior had been unprofessional. It just saddened me that I wouldn't be able to be friends with him now. "No. Deputy Miller brought Muffy some dog food, but he was just leaving."

The deputy's face reddened. "Rose dropped a cup and broke it. I was helpin' clean it up."

"Thank you," Mason said, his words gruff. "I'll help her now."

Deputy Miller brushed past Mason and stood in the doorway for a moment, giving me one last look before leaving.

"What really just happened, Rose?"

I shook my head and brushed the hair out of my face. "I'm not totally sure. He brought Muffy some dog food, but he startled me when he came in. So I dropped a cup and when I started to pick up the pieces, he insisted on helping. Then he said I shouldn't be walking in here barefoot and lifted me onto the counter." I paused, feeling sad. "I'm sure it was nothing."

"Then why do you look so upset?"

We'd agreed on honesty, so I had to tell him even if it was embarrassing. "I thought we were friends, but I don't want to encourage him if he has a crush on me." I paused, looking up into Mason's eyes.

He nodded and kissed me lightly. "But he was right about walking around barefoot. You stay here and let me find a broom."

Mason grabbed a broom from the mudroom and started to sweep up the shards.

"I'm sorry about your house," I said, wishing there were more adequate words.

He shook his head, keeping his gaze on the floor. "It's just a house."

"Mason, it's not just a house. It was your *home*."

He stopped and turned to me, leaning into the broom. "Yes, it was my home, but what happened with Savannah taught me that some things in life are far more important than material possessions." He swallowed and looked up at the ceiling, his eyes glassy. "She called me about a week before her death. She wanted to come stay with me for a few days, but she didn't tell me why. She'd taken her breakup with Joe hard and she'd resorted to some...unseemly behavior." He paused. "She'd begun to drink heavily. I suspected she might be dabbling with some recreational drugs. Enough of a problem that she was having issues at school." He swallowed, lowering his gaze to mine. "But when confronted about it, she refused to stop. So when she asked, I thought she was losing her apartment due to her bad choices and told her no. Not until she got her shit together."

My eyes sank shut for a moment under the weight of his pain. "Oh, Mason."

"I was trying to show her tough love, to get her to straighten out her life." His tone hardened. "But part of it was that I didn't want her in my apartment, screwing up my life. What kind of brother does that make me?"

I slipped off the counter and went to him, putting my hands on his chest. "It makes you human. Yesterday you told me neither one of us are perfect. We've both made plenty of mistakes we regret. But you loved Savannah and she knew it."

"It wasn't enough."

I wrapped my arms around his neck, burying my face in his chest. "It was the best you could do at the time."

"Maybe losing my condo was penance for not letting Savannah stay. That's what a voice in my head told me as soon as Jeff gave me the news."

Tilting my head back, I said, "No. Losing your condo was the result of a psychopath."

He handed me the broom and headed for the living room. "I need to get back to work."

"Mason."

He stopped in the doorway, waiting.

I didn't know what to say. Nothing would make him feel better. So I just did what came naturally. I went to him and kissed him for all I was worth, twining my fingers in his hair. "You are a *good* man, Mason Deveraux, and don't you dare let yourself believe differently."

His expression was pained, but I thought I saw hope in his eyes. "You make me feel like I can be one again." He broke free of my hold and went into the office.

An overwhelming sadness washed over me. Unsure how to handle it, I looked through the cooking supplies and found a biscuit mix. I was still starving, so I made biscuits, taking my frustration out on the dough. When they came out of the oven,

I put some in a basket and took them outside to the deputies, setting them on the table between them. Deputy Miller might have inappropriate feelings for me, but he still needed to eat. And maybe I could get the other deputy to warm up to me.

"I just made some biscuits if y'all want some. I can bring you coffee too."

"Thanks," Deputy Gyer said. He pointed to a couple of thermal mugs on the floor and offered me a forced smile. "Got it covered."

I headed back inside and took Mason a biscuit and a cup of coffee. He glanced up at me. "Have you seen my cell phone? I could have sworn I left it on the desk and now I can't find it anywhere."

I tugged my phone out of my pocket and pulled up his number. After I pressed enter, I looked up at him in surprise. "It went straight to voice mail."

He grimaced. "It must be dead. I forgot to charge it last night."

"I'll look around for it if you want."

He closed his eyes then opened them, looking exhausted. "You don't have do that, Rose. It's not why I asked."

"I know, but you're working and I'm looking for something to do." I shrugged. "Perfect match."

The corners of his mouth lifted and his face softened. "Perfect match."

I grabbed a biscuit and coffee from the kitchen, looking for his phone there before heading upstairs. I checked the front room first, feeling like I was snooping, particularly when I opened his bag to see if he'd tossed the phone there. All of his clothes were neatly pressed and organized. I shook my head and smiled. Mason loved order and my life was anything *but* orderly.

Mason's phone wasn't on the nightstand or under the bed. I stooped and peeked under the dresser, which is when I remembered what I'd found there the day before. The journal. Suddenly I couldn't wait any longer to look at it. I knew I should keep looking for Mason's phone, but surely it wouldn't hurt to take a break.

I pulled the journal out and sat on the middle of the unmade bed. Muffy jumped up with me, still quiet and unusually lethargic. I patted her head. "Did all that pasta last night make your tummy upset?"

As if on cue, a stench filled the room.

I waved my hand. "Muffy! Was that really necessary?"

The smell was so bad that I got up and moved into the nursery, sitting in the rocking chair. I opened the journal and started with the first page. Dora had been in high school when she started writing in it and her entries were sporadic. She tended to write when she was upset and stressed, which made sense. When people were happy, they were too tied up in their happiness to bother writing about it. I skimmed through bad relationships in college and stopped when she first mentioned meeting Daddy.

*I know he's twelve years older and he has a wife—a wife, for heaven's sake!—but my connection to him is unlike anything I've ever felt. I know he feels it too, although he's trying to do the honorable thing and remain faithful to his wife and baby. Still, I can see that he feels the pull. How long can he resist it?*

It was weird thinking about Daddy that way. I only remembered him as the beaten, broken man he'd become after losing Dora. I never would have guessed him to be capable of great passion and love. I flipped more pages, passing the entry I'd read the previous day.

*I can feel the baby moving now, the little flutter of feet and hands feel like angel wings. That's what this baby is, an angel sent to me. I'm sure of that. This baby was sent to save me.*

That gave me pause and filled me with guilt. If Aunt Bessie was right, my birth probably got her killed. I scanned through more pages, stopping when I saw a list titled *regrets*.

A list filled the page ranging from *ending my friendship with Angela over a fight with Steve* to *not helping grandma more after she broke her hip*. The last—*getting pregnant with Rose*—had a line marked through it.

*Many would consider having an affair with a married man and getting pregnant with his child a mistake, but I will never regret it. I've known more love and happiness in these last seven months than I've ever had in my entire life. Still, my life has been full of regrets, mistakes I hope my sweet Rose never makes. I want to make sure the path she takes is different than my own, that she's always reassured that she is deeply loved and cherished.*

As I stared down at the journal entry, a wet spot appeared on the page, slightly smearing the ink. I wiped my face, which is when I realized I'd started to cry. I set the book on a table next to the chair and lay back against the cushions, closing my eyes. *Reassured that she is deeply loved and cherished.* I had never really felt loved and cherished until meeting Joe. His love had helped me blossom into the woman I was today. Jonah insisted I had done it on my own, but I didn't believe that was entirely true. Joe had given me the gift of fun and happiness and joy. He'd loved me unconditionally. But Joe's love had been wrapped in secrets and each time a new one had unfolded, more distrust had seeped in. Part of me still loved Joe, but the bottom line was that I didn't trust him and never could again. And without trust, we had nothing.

I stood and wiped my eyes. Enough wallowing. Joe was in my past, and it was time for me to move on, whether with Mason or not.

Movement caught my eye behind the house. I parted the curtains to see a figure in a tan sheriff's uniform heading for the barn. I couldn't see his face, but he had dark hair. Deputy Miller.

I picked up the journal and stuffed it back into the drawer. I was supposed to be looking for Mason's phone and I hoped he hadn't resorted to looking for it himself. Grabbing the now cold cup of coffee, I headed down to the kitchen to grab the coffee pot before heading to the office.

Mason was still bent over his desk. "I didn't find your phone," I said.

He looked up with a worried expression. "That's so odd. I could swear I set it down right there—" he pointed to the corner of the desk "—when I came in here with Jeff. I don't remember seeing it after that. I wonder if he picked it up accidently thinking it was his own." His gaze shifted to the coffee pot in my hand and he grinned. "If you're here to give me a refill, you really are an angel sent from heaven."

The similarity to my mother's journal entry caught me off guard and I hesitated before refilling his cup.

He noticed the change in my face. "Is everything okay? Did something else happen with that deputy?"

Frowning, I shook my head. "No. Nothing like that. I read some of that journal I found, which is why it took me so long to come back down. Dora called me her angel sent to save her."

His face fell. "Rose...I'm sorry... I didn't know...."

I offered him a smile. "Of course you didn't." I waved my hand. "I'm fine. She's just beginning to feel more real to me, is all."

"Well, I'm here if you need me, okay? Don't worry about bothering me."

"Thanks."

I headed out the front door, Muffy trotting along. She ran down the steps and claimed a bush. I was going to offer fresh coffee to the deputies, but Deputy Miller wasn't on the porch. He came running around the corner of the house and skidded to a halt when he saw me.

"Ms. Gardner, I hear you're a landscaping expert and I saw a bush on the side of the house that I don't recognize. I'd like to get one for my mother. Could you come look at it and tell me what it is?"

My back stiffened. "I don't..."

Deputy Gyer sat up and gave the other man a look of disgust. "What are you thinking? She's not supposed to be outside. Now get your ass up here."

Deputy Miller slowly climbed the steps to the porch and sat in his chair. His whole body seemed to hum with agitation.

Giving me a smile, Deputy Gyer lifted his open travel mug. "If you're offering refills, I'd be obliged."

I stepped in front of Deputy Miller to top up the mug. I had already started to pour when my vision began to fade.

I was running through a field, out of breath. The sky overhead was dark and gray. Continuing to push my way through, I shouted, "I don't see them!"

"*Well, find them, dammit,*" a familiar male voice snarled.

Just as suddenly, I was back on the front porch, coffee overflowing from the mug onto the floor. "You're looking for someone."

Deputy Gyer jerked his hand back, splashing more coffee on his coat. "*What?*"

Who had he been looking for? While all fields looked similar, I was certain it was the one on my farm. And suddenly something registered—I *knew* the other voice from the vision.

I needed to tell Mason immediately, but first I needed to cover my tracks. "Isn't that what you're doing? Looking for Daniel Crocker?"

He shot me another glare before turning away to look at the driveway.

My cell phone vibrated in my pocket.

"They're trying to find him, Rose," Deputy Miller said, offering me an apologetic look. "Hopefully, this will all be over soon."

I looked away from his face and down to his chest. A necklace half-hung out of his shirt. My breath caught in my throat.

It was a St. Jude's medallion.

# Chapter Twenty

I nearly dropped the coffee pot. "Let's go inside, Muffy," I called out, worried that my voice was shaky.

"She can stay outside," Deputy Miller said. "I'll watch her."

"No." My voice broke and I told myself to get it together. "It's getting colder and I want her to come in where it's warm." I'd be the first to admit it was a lame excuse, but it was the best I could come up with on the spot. I went down two steps toward the yard and shouted, "*Muffy!*"

My little dog jerked her head up, startled. I understood why. I never shouted at her.

"Come on, girl." It was taking every ounce of control I had not to fall apart there in front of the deputies, but I needed her to come with me.

Thankfully, my short tone caught her attention and she ran up the steps.

As I turned to go back up, something on the ground caught my eye, partially hidden between the porch and the bushes. A cell phone with a cracked screen.

Mason's phone.

"Is everything all right, Ms. Gardner?" Deputy Gyer asked, sitting up straighter.

Fear bubbled in my chest and I took a deep breath to get control of myself. I climbed the steps to the porch, tripping on the last one. "Yes, of course. I just forgot I left another batch of biscuits in the oven. I don't want the house to burn down."

Wrong choice of words. A strange expression flashed over Deputy Miller's face.

I opened the front door, and I walked in after Muffy, shutting and locking the door behind us. I set the hot coffee pot on a placemat on the dining room table and ran into the office.

Mason took one look at my panicked face and jumped out of his seat. "What's wrong?"

I started crying, trying to catch my breath.

"Rose! *What happened?*"

"Deputy Miller…he…" I knew I needed to get a hold of myself, but I couldn't.

Anger flickered in Mason's eyes. "Did he act inappropriately again?"

He started for the office door, but I snagged his hand and pulled him back. "No! I had a vision."

Mason grabbed my arms, bending down so his face was level with mine. "Breathe, just breathe. It's going to be okay. What did you see?"

"He was running through a field. I think it was here on the farm. He said 'I don't see them,' and then a guy growled, 'Well, find them dammit.'" I looked up into his face. "The other man was Daniel Crocker, I'm sure of it."

Mason's face remained expressionless, but a flicker of fear passed through his eyes before determination replaced it. "Was it day or night?"

"Uh…day."

"Where was the sun?"

"I don't know, Mason." I shook my head in frustration. "I was looking at the field."

"Did you see the house?"

"No."

"So you were looking away from the house. You were probably facing north."

I stared at him, bewildered.

"Did you see any shadows?"

"I don't remember."

He pulled me over to the chair in the corner of the office and sat me down, kneeling in front of me. "Close your eyes and take a deep breath before trying to remember your vision."

I did as he instructed. The field was in front of me, the grass trampled, but this time the shadows came in focus. "Yes, I can see them."

"Which way are the shadows pointing? To your right or to your left?"

I squinted tighter. "Neither. They are kind of pointing in front of me, but not very much." I opened my eyes.

"Rose, I know that not all of your visions come true. How sure are you that this one will?"

I shook my head, fighting tears. "I don't know. I never know that part. We could change it, but I don't know how."

"How soon after you see a vision does it usually come true?"

"Sometimes soon, sometimes days later."

"So this could happen today or two days from now?"

I nodded. "But there's more. After I had my vision, I saw a necklace hanging out of Deputy Miller's jacket. It was a St. Jude's medallion."

Panic filled his eyes. "*Shit!*" Mason growled, turning to search under his desk. "Where's my goddamned cell phone? I swear to God it was *right there*." His head popped up and he turned to look at me, his eyes steely.

I wanted to break down and cry but I needed to keep it together. "I think I saw it on the ground out front."

Confusion washed over his face.

"It was between the porch and the bushes. The screen was smashed."

His face reddened with anger. "Deputy Miller was in the kitchen with you when I came back into the house. He could have taken my phone."

I sucked in deep breaths, trying not to panic.

"Where's yours?"

I dug it out of my pocket, remembering I'd missed a phone call. I looked at the screen and saw Bruce Wayne's name but there wasn't a voice mail. Shoving the phone at Mason, I took several deep breaths, close to passing out.

"Bruce Wayne?" Mason looked up from the phone. "You missed the call?"

I nodded. "The last time he called me was right before Crocker's men showed up."

He grabbed my arm and pulled me out of the chair and into the kitchen, reaching for his gun bag on the table. He pulled out a shotgun and laid it on the table.

The implications of that gun scared me even more. This was really happening. "There's something else," I said. "Before I had my vision, Deputy Miller tried to get me to go around the house with him. Alone."

Mason's face paled. "He was trying to abduct you." He stopped and punched a number into the phone, "Jeff, it's Mason. We've been compromised. It's Deputy Miller." His voice was tight and official. "No. I can't wait. He just tried to abduct Rose. I'm getting her out of here *now*." He paused. "I'm going to take the old truck and go out the back gate. I'll meet you at the Methodist church—" He looked down at the phone and tossed it onto the table. "*Goddammit!* He lost cell service."

To my irritation, I started to cry again.

Mason moved in front of me. "It's going to be okay. I won't let anything happen to you."

I nodded but I didn't believe it. If there was one thing I'd learned, it was that bad things happened to people all the time. Mason would do everything in his power to protect me, but he couldn't guarantee my safety. No one could.

I took a deep breath and held it. Strangely enough, it made me feel better. "What are we going to do?"

"You heard my plan. We'll take the truck and meet Jeff at the Methodist church parking lot in Clearwater. Moore County. Jeff's the only person in the sheriff's department I know we can trust."

"Only he didn't hear that part."

"He'll call back." Mason loaded a shotgun and laid it on the table. "I'll tell the deputies that I'm going to check the fence again, but we'll take off instead. It should buy us enough time to leave the county."

"Where will we go if he doesn't call back?"

"I don't know." He stood and put a hand behind his head. "I'll need to think about it." His voice hardened. "We should call the state police."

I stood and grabbed his hand. "I know someone in the state police we can trust."

He searched my eyes then nodded. "It won't look strange if you're the one to call him. He was your boyfriend and he's with the state police. You're scared. Spin it that way in case they're listening to your calls. Make it believable."

"You think someone is listening to our calls?"

"I have no idea, but I'm paranoid enough at this point to go there. Maybe that's why my call to Jeff was dropped."

I took a deep breath. "Are you sure you want me to call *Joe*?"

"Rose, I'm not the jealous type," he said, his voice gruff. "Even if I was, what kind of ass would I be if I didn't want you to ask for his help? The reason I didn't think about it before was because I honestly thought we were safe here." Pain covered his face. "Obviously I was wrong."

"Okay." I reached over the table for the phone and pulled up my speed dial numbers. Joe's name was still on the list, but after several rings the call went to voice mail. "Joe, this is Rose. I need to talk to you as soon as possible." I glanced up at Mason and he nodded. But I couldn't say the next part while facing him, so I spun around. "Joe, I'm in trouble and I need your help. It's about Daniel Crocker. I'm really scared." My voice broke. What would this call do to him? Joe had been devastated when I left him at the nursery. Would he think I wanted him back? "Just call me. *Please.*" I hung up and put the phone down on the table, pushing it away as though it were tainted. I tried not to think of the similarity to the call Savannah had made to Joe before she was attacked.

"You did the right thing." Mason grabbed my waist and turned me to face him, wrapping his arms around my back and pulling me into a hug.

"That call could kill him, Mason. He begged me to give him another chance. What if he thinks I want him back and then finds out I don't? What will he think of me then?"

He buried his hand in my hair, holding me close. "No matter what happened between you two, he obviously still loves you and wants you to be safe. He'll be glad you called."

"He might not want to call me back."

"If he gets the message, he will."

I looked up at him, questioning. "What do you mean *if* he gets the message?"

"His fiancée might be screening his calls. I saw the way she was watching the back room while you were in there with Joe. She's terrified that you'll take him back."

"Hilary would screen his calls?" But even as I said the words, I knew he was right. She'd already done it this past summer when she was working with Joe in Little Rock.

I grabbed fistfuls of Mason's shirt. "I really am scared." My fingers quivered, loosening my hold on his shirt.

"I know. I am too, but for an additional reason. Only five people know we're here. What if Crocker gets to Jeff? I'd like for someone on the outside to know we're in trouble. Otherwise it would be too easy for them to make us disappear and come up with a believable explanation."

I shivered.

"God, Rose. I'm sorry. I shouldn't have been so blunt."

"No, don't hide things from me. I have a right to know." The room was spinning and my vision was fading, but my irritation superseded my fear. *I will not pass out.* I sat down on the edge of the table so I wouldn't fall over and tried to take a deep breath.

"Give me the phone. I'll call the state police myself and hope I don't get cut off."

As I started to hand it to him my phone buzzed and I looked down to see a text message from Bruce Wayne.

*Get out now. They're on their way.*

Mason read the message over my shoulder. "*Dammit.*" He reached for the phone, but the screen went blank as the phone died.

I cringed. "It only had ten percent power this morning."

Mason's body tensed as he tossed the phone on the table, his voice was gruff. "We have to go. Now."

I stood, my body reacting in slow motion.

He glanced at my arms. "Get your coat." He grabbed the shotgun off the table. "But don't let the deputies see what you're doing."

I nodded and hurried into the living room to grab my jacket before returning into the kitchen.

Mason zipped up his bag and slung it over his shoulder. "Did they see you?"

"No." I glanced down at my dog, who had been unusually quiet since coming inside. "What about Muffy?" I asked, worried to hear his answer.

"We'll take her with us, of course."

Relief flowed through me.

He headed for the back door. "We need to leave now. But if we run out to the barn and the deputies see us, they'll know we know something. We don't want to make them suspicious, so we'll walk… But walk quickly."

"Okay."

I followed him outside, and he reached for me, his fingers curling around the side of my hand. When we were halfway to the barn, he turned to look back the house. I couldn't make myself do the same, terrified I'd see Deputy Miller pointing a gun at us. Instead, I glanced down at Muffy, who seemed to understand the gravity of the situation. She was sticking close to my side like she had been all morning.

When we reached the barn, Mason released my hand and gave one of the old wooden doors a hard shove. I gripped the other door and pushed too, leaning my shoulder into it when it wouldn't budge.

Once we had the doors open, Mason placed his hand on the middle of my back and pushed me toward the passenger door of the truck. He tossed the bag into the back, but then he caught sight of something that made him curse.

"What?"

He gestured to the wall. "Stay here."

I wanted to ask him what was wrong, but when I glanced down, I saw for myself. The tires were flat. Mason circled the truck before coming to a stop in front of me, anger in his eyes. "Someone's slashed all the tires."

"The deputy," I whispered. "I saw him come out to the barn."

Mason put his hands behind his head and looked around, his eyes wide with panic. "Your coat's not heavy enough. When I checked the weather forecast this morning, it said snow was moving in within a few hours."

"You don't have a heavy coat either."

He stood in the doorway, glancing between the house and the woods. "*Goddammit*. How did I let this happen?"

"What do you want to do?"

His gaze landed on mine. "Run into the woods."

I nodded. "Okay."

"Help me shut the doors. We can buy some time if they don't know we're back here."

We closed the doors from the inside, and then Mason started to rummage through the cabinets.

"Let me help, Mason. What are you looking for?"

"Anything that will help us keep warm." After he had found two saddle blankets, he grabbed his bag out of the truck and set it on the tailgate so he could pull out a rifle.

"Here." I shrank back when he tried to hand it to me. "Take it, Rose. I hope to God you don't have to use it, but I want to know you have it."

I gripped the cold metal, pointing the tip toward the ground.

"Do you know how to work the safety?"

"No."

He showed me and made me flick it on and off twice. "Are you good now?"

"Yeah." *No.*

He stuffed the blankets into the bag and slung it over his shoulder.

The sound of revving engines filled the air.

Mason rushed over to the double doors and looked through the crack. "They're here. We've got to go."

I joined Mason at the door, pressing my face against the wood slats. I watched three pickup trucks screech to a halt in front of the house. Men's voices boomed in the distance, the words muffled in the wind, but there were no gunshots. Did that mean both deputies were in league with Crocker?

Mason headed for the opposite end of the barn. "We can slip out back and head into the woods."

"Then what?"

"The forest is dense from this area of the county all the way up through the border of Moore County to the north. We can try to make it there to locate the sheriff or the state police."

"Okay."

He looked down at me. "It's going to be rough. The hills are larger here, which is why the forest is dense. It doesn't make for good farmland, so it never got developed."

"I can hike through the woods, Mason."

"That's not what I'm worried about. Crocker's guys are good ole boys. He's bound to have some experienced hunters in the group. And trackers."

The full meaning of what he was saying sunk in.

He stood behind the partially open back door, staring out into the woods. "Try as I might, I can't come up with any other ideas." His gaze shifted to my face. "What do you think?"

"Me?" I asked in shock.

"You're in this too, and from past experience, I know you think well under pressure."

I gave my head a slight shake as I tried to come up with a suggestion. "We could run for the fence at the end of the property and find a farmhouse to call the state police."

"True, but what about your vision?"

Crappy doodles. "You're right. They were looking for us in the fields." I looked up at him wide-eyed. "I don't know, Mason. I guess the only choice is for us to search for people to help us or head into the woods."

"Either way we run a risk of getting caught. The question is which gives us the best chance?"

"I don't know," I whispered.

"Then let's assume your vision is true. That means we could potentially buy some time if we head for the forest."

"Okay." I was grateful that he was including me in our decision. The need to concentrate was helping me rein in my fear. "Do you know which direction to go?"

"Ideally we'd head north to Moore County, but the fields lead north. So we can head east a bit in the woods and then turn north." He looked down at my little dog, who was sitting at my feet. "What about Muffy? Can she keep up? Will she alert them to where we are?"

I squatted and turned her to face me. "Muffy, we're going on a walk and I need you to listen to me."

Her tongue hung out of her mouth, but her eyes were focused on mine.

"No barking. And no running off. You have to stay with me." I leaned into her face. "This is very important, Muffy."

She stood up on her back legs and licked my chin.

It was the best I could do.

"Do you think she actually understands?"

"I don't know, but she's given me reason to trust her in the past. She'd gotten me out of some tight situations."

"Good enough for me."

Banging and shouting came from the direction of the house. They knew we were gone. The sooner we left the better.

"Then let's go."

Mason looked down at the gun draped over my shoulder. He pulled it off and turned it around, grimacing. "If it hangs this way, you can lift it and point. The other way you'll fumble with it."

I couldn't even imagine shooting someone, so I didn't see the point. "Maybe I shouldn't have this. What if I shoot *you* by mistake?"

He lifted the barrel and examined the side. "The safety is on. Don't touch it and we'll be fine."

Pushing the door open, he took a step out of the barn and glanced in both directions. "Okay, it's clear."

He held the door for Muffy and me. The wind felt colder than before we'd entered the barn and the sky was a darker gray. Mason carefully closed the door and followed my gaze.

"The storm's moving in quickly. That doesn't bode well for us, although the wind will make it more difficult for them to track us by sound."

We ran to the edge of the forest, clomping over the dried leaves that covered the forest floor. The brush was thick at the edge, so we would have to force our way through it.

Mason turned back to look at me. "This is going to seem counterintuitive, but I want to head south for a while before we veer into the woods. If we charge in now, they'll be able to figure out where we went in from the broken brush."

"Okay."

"The huge risk is that they'll see us from the house, but we're both wearing dark colors, so we won't jump out at them unless they know where to look."

He turned to the right and skirted the tree line while Muffy and I followed close behind. After glancing at the house, Mason picked up the pace.

Shouting broke out behind us and Mason stopped and pulled me into the shadows of the trees and down to a crouch. Muffy followed, lying on the ground next to me. I reached down and rubbed her head.

Three men burst out of the back door of the house. One of them pointed to the barn and then the field, and the others took off in the indicated directions. But my attention was squarely on the man who'd given them their orders and was standing in the middle of the yard, his hands on his hips.

"It's Daniel Crocker."

# Chapter Twenty-One

Mason's grip on my arm tightened. "Are you sure?"

"Yeah." I tried to calm my rising panic. Of course he was here. He'd been in my vision, after all.

We heard more shouting and Crocker moved to the edge of the field, Deputy Gyer going with him.

"Come on." Mason tugged on my arm. "They're following my tracks from when I checked out the field yesterday. It won't buy us much time, though. I didn't get very far."

About ten men spilled from the front of the house and headed toward the field as Mason, Muffy and I began edging down the tree line away from Crocker. We had gone about fifty feet when Mason slowed and turned toward the trees.

"There's a natural break in the brush. If we're careful, we can slip in here and conceal our tracks." He moved first, picking his way carefully and trying to step on bare spots of ground. When he made it through the narrow gap, he motioned for me to follow.

I looked back down at the house and fields. There was more shouting and I heard my name on the wind, the sound sending a shiver down my back. I was terrified, but I couldn't think about that now. We had to get away. Mason waited, his hand extended. Taking a deep breath, I picked my way across the six-foot expanse, easing myself through the narrow opening. But we were in more thick brush, and the only way for us to continue was to break the branches of the bushes around us.

"There's no helping it, Rose," Mason said, pushing deeper. "We'll just have to hope they won't realize we snuck in here." After about fifty feet, the brush gave way to partial growth. "Let's go farther east before changing direction."

"How far are we from Columbia County?" I asked. "If we keep going east we'll end up there, right?"

"It's a good thirty miles."

My shoulders sank. "And how far is Moore County?"

"Ten miles, give or take."

"So Moore it is."

"We might stumble upon a farmhouse on the way. Then we can call Jeff and the state police. If we don't, we'll keep going until we're out of the county."

"How will we know?"

He gave me a crooked smile. "That's a good question. Not too far east of here, the county line juts north. We might think we're in Moore County while we're still in Fenton. And the farther north we go, the denser the forest will become."

"How do you know so much about the county terrain?"

"It's my jurisdiction. I know the layout of the land, the towns, and the demographics of specific regions."

"And this area?"

"Mostly farmers on the outskirts of the forest, but there are some meth labs here and there in the more rural parts."

"I take it that's bad."

"The meth cooks might not like it if we trespass on their land. Especially if they figure out who I am."

"What are the chances we'll run into them?"

"If we were purposely setting out to find them, probably not likely, but since we're trying to avoid them, who knows? We haven't had the greatest luck lately. From the reports I've heard, a couple of them are holed up northeast of here, which of course is where we're heading. The problem is that they sometimes booby trap the borders, so the first sign that we're trespassing might be if we get caught."

"Let's try really hard to avoid them."

"I agree."

We continued east for another ten minutes before Mason stopped and held up a hand.

I halted, forcing my lungs to draw in a breath. Muffy bumped into my leg and pressed her body into me, looking up into my face.

"I think I hear something," he whispered.

I joined him at his side, my ears straining. After a few seconds, I heard shouting.

"They're in the woods," he said, looking behind us.

I forced myself to calm down. "What should we do?"

He spun around, taking in the landscape. "We've been traveling northeast, but we haven't been careful. If any of them have tracking experience, they'll be able to find us once they pick up our path."

"So now we know what they're gonna do. What are *we* gonna do?"

He shook his head with a slight grin. "That's my girl."

I returned his smile, amazed by my own gumption.

"Do you hear water?"

I strained to listen and beneath the men's voices, I could hear the tell-tale gurgle of a creek. "Yeah."

"It's coming from ahead. Let's turn slightly south and then intersect the creek to make it look like we're going the opposite direction. But we'll turn north, walking in the creek so we don't leave tracks."

"Mason, it's not even forty degrees outside. You want to walk in water?"

"Rose, I'm open to other ideas if you have them."

I closed my eyes and exhaled. I didn't. And I knew that I could not, under any circumstances, allow Daniel Crocker to catch me. "None. Let's go."

But I was worried about Muffy. She wouldn't willingly walk in water and she'd give us away if she walked alongside the creek.

We pushed through a new growth of brush that surrounded the two-foot-wide creek. Mason deliberately tromped down the vegetation on the bank and then stepped into the water, his body stiffening with cold. After he took a moment to recover, he turned to me. "Wait here." He went several feet down the creek, then got out and stomped on a gathering of bushes before getting back in and turning to trudge toward me. His jeans were wet up to his ankles. "I have no idea if that will work, but it was worth a try."

He reached a hand toward me and I grabbed it, trying to prepare myself for the shock of stepping into the water, but nothing could make me ready for the icy jolt that shot up my legs.

"Are you okay?" he asked.

I nodded and turned to Muffy. "Come on, girl."

She approached the creek, sniffed the water, then backed up several paces.

"Will she come in?" Mason asked.

"I don't know. I don't think so." My voice broke.

He squatted and reached out to her. "Come here, Muffy."

She slowly inched toward him, her body barely off the ground.

"That's it," he said softly, as though he were talking to a small child. "Come here, girl."

Muffy sniffed his hand and moved closer. Mason scooped her up, opened his coat, and tucked her inside, then zipped his jacket until just her head poked out. Muffy reached up to lick Mason's chin. He rubbed her snout. "That's a good girl."

My chest burned at the sight and I found it difficult to speak past the lump in my throat. "Thank you."

Mason grabbed my hand. "Well, we couldn't leave her behind."

We started to move through the twelve-inch-deep water. Mason took the lead and I followed behind, carefully picking my way along the slippery footing as the water began to get deeper. My legs turned numb as we continued to move through the water, and a couple of times Mason grabbed my arm to right me when I started to slip. Still, the voices were getting louder.

"Mason."

"I know, I'm looking for somewhere to hide on the other side of the creek, but there's not as many pine trees here and the others have lost too many leaves to provide cover."

The land began to climb, making our path through the water more precarious. Mason climbed a short incline and then turned to grab my hand once he found a level spot. He pulled me up next to him with little effort and started to climb the next section once I was secure. I didn't say anything, but it worried me how cold his hand was. Him reaching out to me in the cold water felt a little too similar to the key scene in Titanic to suit me. At least I didn't have to worry about sharing space on a piece of wood. There were plenty of downed tree trunks here.

The voices were closer and I could make out a few words.

"...picked up a trail..."

"...heading south..."

Muffy let out a low growl and Mason turned back to face me, fear in his eyes.

I leaned over and stroked her head, whispering, "Shh…" but she continued to make agitated noises.

I unbuttoned my jacket as quickly as my frozen fingers would allow. Realizing what I was doing, Mason had already unzipped his jacket and was stuffing her inside my coat. Once she was secure, he started to fasten the buttons.

Rubbing her head, I cooed in her ear, "Muffy, you have to be quiet." She was going to give us away.

But her low rumble continued and Mason shot me a worried look before turning to continue his climb.

Muffy jolted against me, scrambling until she was over halfway out of my jacket. Realizing something was wrong, Mason climbed back down as I wrestled to keep my little dog from escaping. She jumped out of my arms, onto the creek bank on the opposite side of Crocker's men.

Without thinking, I started to call out to her, but Mason clamped a hand over my mouth, pulling me back against his chest. His other hand wrapped around my waist.

Tears stung my eyes as I watched Muffy bolt south, following the creek.

"Rose, I'm sorry," he whispered in my ear. "But we have to go."

I nodded and he released my mouth and spun me around.

"I promise you that we'll find her when this is over."

I nodded again, not trusting myself to speak. My vision gave me some comfort. I knew she'd be found, even though I wished her rescuer could be someone besides Deputy Miller. Still, she trusted him and he seemed to care about her. I had to believe that while he might turn me over to Crocker, he'd be good to my little dog. In the meantime, I needed to focus on surviving this mess so I could see her again.

Returning his attention to the climb, Mason found another foothold and reached for me, grabbing my wrist to pull me up. "I think we'll be safe if we make it to the top of this."

I glanced at the ten-foot rise ahead of us, feeling a lot less confident than he sounded. "We're going too slow." I dropped his hand and started to climb up, grabbing hold of larger rocks under the water to pull myself up. The sleeves of my coat quickly became drenched.

"Rose, you're going to freeze to death if you do it that way."

"I'd rather freeze than let Daniel Crocker catch me." My way moved us up faster and I climbed over the rise, falling into a deeper pool that soaked me from the thighs down. Thankfully, I managed to keep the gun out of the water.

Mason fell in behind me. "Dammit," he grunted. "I wasn't prepared for that." He climbed onto the bank and dragged me out. The only dry parts of my body were my back and my head. I was shivering violently and Mason wrapped his arm around my shoulders, his own body shaking from cold.

He slipped his bag off his shoulders and pulled out one of the blankets, which were blessedly dry, wrapping it around my back. "I'm going over to the edge of the rise to check out where they are."

I nodded. I would have gone with him, but I was too cold to move.

He left the bag and adjusted the rifle over his arm before walking farther upstream. Keeping low, he sloshed through the shallower section of the creek and then squatted as he neared the edge of the hill. We were only about twenty feet higher than the grove below, but it was enough to give him an advantage.

My teeth rattled, but not loudly enough to drone out the voices from below.

"Rose!" Daniel called out. "Where are you, my sweet Rose?"

I wrapped my arms around myself, tugging the blanket tighter. Mason stayed perfectly still, but I noticed that he'd lifted the tip of his rifle.

"Rose, I know you're out here. Why would you run off with that assistant DA instead of waiting for me, baby? You knew I was coming."

His voice was getting louder and terror bubbled up inside me. I reached for the rifle, laying it across my lap. I wasn't sure I could actually use it, but knowing it was there made me feel a tiny bit more in control.

"I'm gonna find you, Rose, don't doubt that for a minute. But the longer it takes, the angrier I'll get, so make it easy on yourself and come out now."

Did Crocker know we were up here? His voice told me he was practically upon us. I glanced over at Mason, who was crouching, completely still, the tension in his shoulders the only sign that Crocker was getting to him.

"How much do you like that pretty lawyer, Rose? Maybe he won't be so pretty when I'm through with him."

I set the gun down and climbed to my knees, letting the blanket fall to the ground. If I gave myself up, would it save Mason? I doubted that Crocker would let him go, but how could I take that chance?

Mason glanced over his shoulder at me. "No!" he mouthed, his eyes flashing with anger.

I crawled toward the spot where Mason had crossed the creek.

"Rose! I *will* find you. And when I do, I will make you pay, baby. I'll make you pay for everything you've done." His voice rose along with his anger.

Mason spun at the waist and held his hand up. "Don't move!" he mouthed.

But I couldn't just let Crocker hurt him.

Noticing my resolve, Mason crawled toward me, stopping at the edge of the creek. "Rose," he whispered, his eyes wild and desperate. "I'm begging you to sit here and say nothing."

Tears stung my eyes. "He knows where we are, Mason," I choked out. "He's going to hurt you."

He shook his head, his jaw clenched. "No, he's bluffing. He wasn't even looking up here. Just wait."

Mason and I stared at each other, separated by three feet of water.

*"Rose!"* Daniel shouted in frustration.

Mason hurried back over to his vantage point, observing the scene below.

Tears made my already cold cheeks sting.

He turned back to me and crawled to the edge of the water. His eyes pleaded with me. "Rose, he's leaving," he whispered. "I promise. Then we'll find a house somewhere and call the state police, okay?"

My jaw quivered even more as I fought to keep from crying.

"Rose, *goddammit!*" Crocker shouted.

I closed my eyes and cringed.

"I know she's here! I can feel it." Crocker's voice carried through the grove below us. "Spread out and look for her! She's got to—"

"Daniel," another man's voice interrupted. "They found their tracks south of here, heading down the creek toward town."

I heard a loud smack and a grunt, followed by smashing leaves.

"Anyone else want to cross me?" Crocker growled.

No one answered.

Barking echoed through the trees and my eyes widened. Mason's mouth parted, probably worried about how I'd react.

Muffy.

"That's her dog. Miller—head south and see if she's with Rose." He paused. "You two head north. And you...go up that hill."

Someone was about to find us.

# Chapter Twenty-Two

Mason's eyes widened and he crossed the water, keeping low and trying not to slosh. When he reached me, he grabbed my arm and pulled me with him toward his bag. "Promise me you won't try and give yourself up to him. No matter what happens."

"Mason—"

"Rose." His face hardened. "If you don't promise me that you'll do everything in your power to hide, I'll stand up right now and tell Crocker I'm here. At least then you'll have the chance to run."

I reached for him, my nails digging into the back of his hand. "Mason, no!"

He grabbed my face with both hands. "I can't worry that you're going to do something stupid like turning yourself over in an attempt to save me. We need to be united if we have any hope of surviving. Agreed?"

I nodded, choking on my tears. "I'm just scared for you, Mason."

"And I'm scared for you, which is why I'll do everything in my power to keep him from getting you, and obviously you're willing to do the same for me. But we have to work together."

I heard brush breaking on the hill below us.

"Okay."

He gave me a quick kiss and then spun around to grab the gun and blanket I'd left behind, stuffing both into his bag. "Let's go." He slung the bag over his shoulder. Moving past me, he picked his way through the leaves, trying to keep to the bare spots. I followed his lead, having a hard time getting my numb feet to cooperate.

We moved quietly, heading for a cliff that rose ten to twelve feet.

"There's nothing up here, Crocker!" a voice shouted from behind us. I resisted the urge to turn and look for him.

Crocker's voice drifted up, faint. "Keep looking!"

The cliff edge angled back, creating a space hidden from the creek. Mason searched for a scalable section of the slope then reached for me, determination making his face hard. "Climb."

I scaled the rocks, fumbling to find a foothold since I couldn't feel my feet. The cliff was only about ten feet high in this section, but if we could get to the top and lie flat, Crocker's man probably wouldn't see us. However, I struggled to climb even three feet, shivering so hard that I couldn't get a grip on the rocks above me.

Mason moved past me and climbed to a ledge four feet up, squatting before reaching down and pulling me up. He scaled the remaining six feet of cliff and slid over the top edge. He looked down at the creek and panic filled his eyes as he held his hand out for me. "Hurry!" he grunted.

I grabbed his hands and he jerked me up and over the edge, the rocks scraping my stomach. We scooted back, lying flat on our stomachs. My heart raced as I fought to catch my breath, my whole body still shaking. Mason rubbed my back in soothing strokes while he looked down below.

I listened for signs of the man who was tracking us and heard nothing, but the way Mason's head was moving, I knew he was watching the tracker. We lay there for at least ten minutes. Each of my limbs felt like it weighed fifty pounds. Even my eyelids started to feel heavy and I succumbed to an overwhelming sleepiness.

"Rose," Mason whispered in my ear.

I blinked, wondering why I was lying on the ground.

"Rose, wake up."

He rolled me to my side and I looked up into his face. Tiny snowflakes floated around his head.

"He's gone. We need to move."

I blinked again. Where were we? Then the danger we were facing sunk in and I sat upright with a start but found myself clumsy and stiff.

He grabbed my upper arm. "He's gone and they've headed south. Our plan worked. Partially thanks to Muffy."

Crocker had sent Deputy Miller after her. Which meant that my vision about them had come true. I sent a silent prayer of thanks. "So we need to keep going?"

"Yeah." He sounded worried. "How are you feeling?"

"Sleepy and cold."

"You're showing signs of hypothermia, but it'll help if we get you moving. And I'll give you back the blanket as soon as we're off this cliff."

We scooted to the edge. Getting down was going to be more difficult than climbing up had been, especially with my new lack of coordination.

Mason turned and lowered his legs before dropping to his feet. I mimicked him and he grabbed my waist, helping me steady my feet. He scrambled down the loose rocks, holding my hand to help guide me down.

"Do we have to go down the other hill we climbed?"

"No, not yet. We can walk along this ridge for a while."

My feet felt like I was lugging bags of potatoes.

Mason opened his bag and pulled out the two blankets. He draped one around my shoulders, looking into my eyes as he did it. "We'll try to find a house, like we talked about. We need to get out of the cold." He slung the bag over his shoulder. After interlacing his fingers with mine, he began to walk. While his hands were cold, they felt warmer than mine and helped me regain some feeling in my fingers.

The hill was flat and mostly covered in pine trees, which helped keep us hidden from down below. After we'd traveled for thirty minutes or so, the land began to slope sideways. I started to slide, but Mason held me tightly to his side.

"I think it's time to go down."

He was right, but the incline was steep. As clumsy as I was, I didn't see how I could get down gracefully.

Mason started the descent first, still holding my hand, but I pulled away. He turned to me in surprise.

"I'll make us both fall. I have another way." I offered him a smile in case he was worried I'd lost my mind. "Violet and I used to roam my aunt and uncle's land, and they had some hills like these. We'd climb up, and then I'd be too scared to climb back down. Violet wasn't, but she never called me a baby. She would just take my hand and say it was a slide and that we could slide down together."

"So you plan to slide down on your butt?"

"Yeah. It beats falling flat on my face."

He shook his head with a grin. "I have a better idea. How about you grab one tree and then reach for another?"

I smirked. "It's worth a try."

I reached for a tree several feet beneath me and wrapped my arms around it, picking out which tree to lunge for next.

"So Violet wasn't always jealous of you?" Mason asked, standing by a tree next to mine.

I nearly slid past the next tree. "No, she used to be my best friend. I guess she always was until I met Neely Kate."

Mason ran several feet past me and then looked back up at me.

"Show-off."

"Were you *her* best friend?"

I lunged for another tree. "I'm not sure. I used to think so, but you know what they say about hindsight."

"Despite everything, I know she loves you, Rose."

"I know..." While I knew it was true, I still struggled with her behavior.

"Jealousy makes people do funny things."

We'd made it down about ten feet with another twenty feet to go.

"She hurt me, Mason. All this time I thought she was helping me, but she was really trying to hold me back."

"Maybe she thought she *was* helping you."

"She's always insisted that she acts the way she does to protect me. Joe told me that she was hurting me by not letting me face the world on my own two feet."

Mason held onto the tree next to me, looking into my face. "And which do you think it was?"

I slid down to the next tree. "Maybe a combination. I really don't think she ever set out to hurt me, at least up until she let everyone believe I'd stolen her money. But before that, I think she thought she was helping."

"It's all in the intent, Rose. When I file charges against someone, especially in murder cases, I have to look at the intent."

"I'm not sure I can ever totally forgive her. We gave up everything for her and she's still sneaking around and purposefully hurting me." I reached for the next tree, realizing we only had ten feet left.

Mason followed behind me. "What do you mean *we gave up everything for her?*"

My mouth dropped open. Why had I let that slip? I couldn't lie to him, but I didn't want to hurt him. I hurried down the hill, not stopping between trees.

He reached the bottom before I did. "Rose, who is *we?*"

Mason deserved the truth, even though I worried about his reaction. "Joe and me."

He blinked, all expression fading from his face. "What did you give up?"

"Mason, there's something you don't know."

"Obviously." There was no anger behind the word, but I could see a storm brewing behind his eyes. Not that I could blame him.

"You know that Joe's father forced him to run for the senate, but I didn't tell you how."

"I always presumed his father had used his past against him."

Now that we were standing still, the wind cut through my wet clothes, making me shudder.

Mason tugged my blanket more closely around me. "You can tell me while we walk."

I shook my head and grabbed his hands. "No, I need to look at you when I say this."

Worry pinched his mouth. "It sounds serious."

I took a breath. "Joe's father blackmailed him, but he did it by using me. And Violet and Mike."

"What does that mean?"

"He fabricated evidence that Mike had bribed county officials to get contracts and permits for his business."

His jaw clenched. "What else?"

"He had photos of Violet coming out of a motel with Brody MacIntosh."

"The mayor?"

I nodded.

"What did he have on you?"

I inhaled and released a long breath. "He planted evidence that made it look like I hired Daniel Crocker to murder Momma. He told Joe that he would make sure I was arrested."

Mason pulled his hands from mine. "So Joe had to break up with you and run for the senate to prevent his dad from releasing the information to the public?"

"No, he had to run, but his parents relented and said he could still marry me as long as I met their conditions." Now didn't seem like the time to discuss this, but it was too late to turn back. "I would have needed to dress and act a certain way. To disown Bruce Wayne and Jonah and probably Neely Kate. And all the while, I'd know that if I didn't do everything they said, they'd release the information. They'd release it anyway if Joe didn't agree to run."

"And you couldn't do it, right? But you told me that Joe broke up with you."

I shut my eyes for a long moment before opening them again. "He asked me to agree and then ended it when he realized I couldn't do it."

Mason watched me. "If the information was fabricated, it never would have held up in court." His voice rose. "Hell, I'm the assistant DA, Rose. I'd have to file the charges, and you know I wouldn't do it." His eyes widened. "Which means he must have found something true." He paused and his voice softened. "Violet is having an affair with Brody."

I didn't answer.

"Okay." He rubbed the back of his neck and looked away. "So neither one of you wanted to break up? You were blackmailed into it?" I heard the pain in his voice.

"Mason."

He turned back to look at me, anger in his eyes. "I deserve an answer, Rose."

"Yes, you do." I reached for his hands and held onto him. "You're right. Neither one of us wanted to break up. But after I started talking to Jonah, I realized something… Joe wasn't strong enough to stand up to his parents and fight for me. I don't doubt that his father would have carried through on his threats, but Joe was the one who got himself into the situation in the first place. And then there's the fact that he always goes back to Hilary. Even after everything she's done. That's why I agreed to talk to him in the nursery. I knew he was engaged to Hilary, and when I saw them together, I knew they were sleeping together. I told Joe that I could forgive a lot of things, but I couldn't forgive him for that. Not after what had happened to Savannah, and not after my vision."

"What vision?"

"When I was in the hospital last month, I had a vision of Joe. I saw him winning an election, but he was married to Hilary and she was pregnant."

He didn't say anything.

"When we were at the nursery, he told me that he wanted me back. I said no, Mason."

He still didn't say anything and fear raced through my blood.

"Mason, I want to be with you. You have to believe that."

"Why didn't you tell me about all of this?"

"I told you. I was scared of how you'd react."

His anger rose. "What on earth did you think I'd do? Get mad at you? *Shout*?"

"No, but Joe's family has already done enough damage to yours. I didn't want you to get involved." My voice broke. "I didn't want your career to be hurt any more than it already has with Savannah."

His face softened. "Rose."

"I know what Joe's father is capable of doing, Mason. And I knew that you wouldn't let him get away with any of it. Joe's father got you transferred to Fenton County. He got me out of jail when you and Joe couldn't. I can't even imagine what he'd do to you if you tried to fight him."

"Rose, that's my job."

"I couldn't risk it, Mason. You mean too much to me."

He reached around me and pulled me to his chest. "Do you realize that this is what Joe's visit to your nursery was all about? His father was dangling you in front of Joe to remind him of why he needs to behave." Mason paused and inhaled deeply. "Rose, as long as J.R. Simmons sits on this information, you're forever in limbo, just waiting for Joe to step out of line. You can't live like that. *I* can't live with that."

"I know, but I don't know what to do." I looked up into his face. "I'm scared for you if you try to intervene."

"And I'm scared for you if I don't." He pressed a kiss to my cold lips. "Let's get moving. Once this whole Crocker mess is taken care of, we'll find out exactly what J.R. Simmons has and figure out how to refute it." I started to protest, but he put a finger on my lips. "We'll do it so quietly that he won't know what hit him until it blows up in his face."

It was no use to argue and I relished the thought of being free of the threat.

"But no more secrets. Tell me if you're in trouble. Your safety will always supersede my anger. Okay?"

"Okay."

We trudged along for what seemed like an eternity. My legs chafed from the wet jeans clinging to my thighs and my toes were still numb and throbbing, but I felt warmer moving and my sleepiness had faded. "How far do you think we've gone?" I finally asked, desperate for the end to be in sight.

Mason paused, picking his way around a pile of rocks. "It's hard to say since walking in the woods isn't like walking down the street. It takes longer to get around the obstacles—"

"How far, Mason?"

"Maybe two miles. Heading east first took some time and distance."

My heart sank. "And you think it's ten miles to the border? And then how far until we find a house?"

He slowed and took my hand in his. "I don't know. If I remember the terrain correctly, the forest is dense along the border."

I was tired and freezing, but stopping wasn't an option and complaining wouldn't do any good. "Okay."

"I'm hoping we'll find something before too long," Mason said, scanning the trees in front of us. "If we can't find a home with a phone, maybe we can find an outbuilding where we can warm up."

"I'd rather just keep going." I didn't want to sit around and wait for Crocker to find us.

"You can't feel your feet and neither can I. It would be smarter to stop."

"Well, we'll have to find someplace first and we'll never do it standing here. Let's go."

The snow had started and stopped in fits. But it was heavier now and the sky was beginning to darken. Mason picked up the pace. "With the sky this overcast, we'll be stumbling around in the dark on uneven terrain before we know it. With this terrain, that could be dangerous."

We had been staying on high ground to lose Crocker in case he picked up our tracks, but we began to descend, hoping to find some sign of civilization. We finally reached a valley with overgrown fields. The snow had begun to accumulate and about an inch covered the ground. There were several clustered buildings in the distance. Hope soared in my heart. A farm. But it soon became apparent that the place was deserted.

As we approached the dilapidated-looking house, Mason lifted his rifle but kept the tip pointing downward. "Rose, walk behind me."

His change in stance turned my blood from cold to icy, and I did as he requested. "Do you expect any trouble?"

"No, but we're in the hollows of Southern Arkansas and this place might be remote for a reason. It's better to be safe."

One thing was certain, the house had seen better days. The wood porch was rotten and several windows were broken.

When we were within twenty feet of the house, Mason stopped. "Hello!" His voice echoed in the valley. "Anyone here? We need help."

"Do you really think there could be people inside?" I asked in a low voice. The barn behind the house looked to be in worse shape.

"Who knows? It's remote and deserted. Squatters could live here without running the risk of getting caught."

"But the house looks like it's about to fall in on itself. Wouldn't they fix it up?"

"I guess that depends on how long they planned on staying."

The wind swirled the snow on the ground and I shivered.

He called out again. "Hello! Is anyone home? We're lost in the woods and we need to call someone for help."

No one answered.

Mason climbed the four steps to the porch, stepping over one loose board and around a hole. He knocked on the screen door, which was hanging from one rusty hinge. When no one answered he opened it and turned the doorknob on the front door. It gave without him needing to apply extra force and he stepped halfway through the doorway, calling out to possible residents.

I stood at the bottom of the steps as he disappeared inside. Moments later, I heard a high-pitched cry. "*Mason*!" I shouted.

He appeared in the doorway. "It's okay. I disturbed a cat. I think the only squatters are a few stray animals."

I made my way onto the porch and through the front door, letting my eyes adjust to the dark room. The house was empty except for a kitchen chair with broken spindles and a couple of cross-stitched pictures on the walls—*There ain't no lovin' like country lovin'* and *Possum—America's dark meat*. After I read them, I understood why they had been left behind. We wandered to the back of the house. The kitchen was ransacked—half the cabinets were missing and the doors of the remaining ones were hanging open. Most of the light fixtures were gone.

"What happened here?"

"Probably a foreclosure. The owners realize they're losing everything so they take anything they think they can sell."

I couldn't imagine being that desperate.

"Let's check the rest of the house."

We moved to the second floor and I was surprised that the staircase was in such good shape. We found three empty bedrooms and a bathroom that was missing the toilet, sink, and light fixture.

Mason stood in the hallway, taking in the upstairs one more time. "This seems like a good place for us to stay the night. We can rest and warm up and set out first thing in the morning. Unfortunately, we don't have any food, but I do have a bottle of water in my bag we can share."

I nodded. "I guess we could use that broken chair to build a fire in the fireplace. And there might be more wood outside."

"We can't build a fire, Rose. Let's not give Crocker's men any reason to investigate this place."

"But they think we went south."

"They'll figure out we didn't soon enough, and then they'll fan out and look in other directions. Sure, it seems like finding us would be like finding a needle in a haystack, but we left footprints in the snow. We could be leading them straight here."

My breath caught. "Then we might as well build a fire and get warm, right? If they might find us anyway?" Now that I'd thought of building a fire, I couldn't give up the chance to get warm. "It's not like we're the only people who would build a fire on a cold, snowy night. There are other houses around. We just haven't found them."

"True…" He was wavering.

"Will they keep searching for us in the dark?"

He shook his head. "I'm not really sure. It would be difficult, and under normal circumstances, I'd say no. But we both know Daniel Crocker is anything but normal. Still, even if they look, they'll be more likely to miss our tracks in the dark."

"So let's build a fire right after the sun sets and let it die out before we go to sleep. I don't want to spend the night shivering and starving. We might not be able to take care of the starving part, but at least we can get *warm*."

He stared into my eyes.

"I'm frozen, Mason. I'll have a better chance of moving faster tomorrow if we warm up."

"You have a point." He kissed me softly.

I smiled against his lips. "So I get a fire?"

His gaze turned serious. "Do you think I could ever deny you anything?"

My smile faded. "Yes, if you thought it would protect me."

He wrapped his arms around my back and pulled me close, kissing me so intensely that I had to cling to him to stay upright.

He smiled down at me. "Let's build you that fire."

# Chapter Twenty-Three

The unheated house was cold, but it was still a shock to go outside into the bitter wind. Mason suggested I stay inside, but I didn't want to be separated from him.

We found kindling at the edge of the tree line as well as some bigger branches, but we had to search high and low for something to start the fire. Finally we found a kerosene lantern and a book of matches in the barn, along with three wool blankets. They stank to high-heaven, but they were warm. I was sure our noses would adjust.

The kerosene lantern helped as we fumbled with the fireplace. Mason had busted the one kitchen chair into pieces, but it was slow to burn, the damp branches even more so. We sacrificed one of the stinking blankets to use as tinder and finally we had a roaring fire.

I spread the two other wool blankets on the floor and slipped off my soggy shoes and set them in front of the fire. My stiff jeans followed. I doubted they'd be dry by morning, but at least they'd be less damp.

Mason sat on the hearth and turned to watch me undress.

I shrugged. "We'll warm up faster if we take off our damp clothes."

He nodded, his eyes burning.

When I dropped my jeans to the floor, he picked them up and laid them on the hearth by my shoes. I'd already shed my jacket, so I lifted my shirt over my head, kneeling on the blanket in only my bra and panties.

Mason quickly removed his clothes too and reached for the blankets we'd taken from my farm. He pulled me into his arms, and we lay on the blankets, our limbs intertwined. I slipped my toes between his calves. "Your feet are freezing," he teased.

I lifted my eyebrows in mock reprimand. "Someone made me walk in a creek."

His smile faded. "I'm sorry about that."

"It worked, right? That's what counts." I tucked my hands between his arms and his chest and he jerked backward out of reflex before settling in.

"I was sure Crocker's guy was going to find us on that bluff. It's a good thing he was sloppy or we'd be dead."

I licked my chapped lower lip and Mason's eyes followed the movement. "We can't let him catch us."

"I have no intention of letting him." His arms tightened around me. "I didn't just get you to lose you. God wouldn't be so cruel."

But God had been cruel to me for most of my life. What would stop Him in this?

I lifted my mouth to Mason's, kissing him gently until a low sound hummed in his chest. He rolled me to my back, his mouth becoming more insistent. I wrapped my arms around his neck, pulling the blanket to cover his exposed back.

He tipped his face up and stared into my eyes, the fire casting a warm glow on his face. "I feel like I'm failing you. I can't help but wonder whether we should have headed for the road."

"Mason, we both agreed to this plan. And I have no doubt that if we'd gone to the road we'd be dead or worse."

"I'm supposed to protect you."

"Who says? Why can't we protect each other?"

His kissed me with urgency, as though Crocker might show up at any minute and take me away from him. After we made love, we lay in each other's arms, still warming up with the heat of the fire. I soon drifted off to sleep.

When I awoke later, Mason wasn't next to me and the fire was a pile of glowing embers. I bolted upright, clutching the blanket to my chest.

Mason stood next to the window, his rifle slung over his shoulder. Moonlight filtered through the glass, lending a soft glow to his face. He turned to face me when he caught my movement.

"What are you doing?"

"I couldn't sleep, so I'm keeping watch."

I leaned forward to look up at the sky through the window. "The moon is out."

"The storm is breaking and the moonlight is fading in and out." He looked worried. "We didn't get much more snow, so our footprints from the woods to the house are like a neon sign."

"Do you have any idea what time it is?"

"No, but if I had to guess, I'd say around three."

"You said they probably wouldn't look for us in the woods at night. Let's get another hour or two of sleep and then take off at sunrise."

He hesitated, but I reached my hand toward him. He gave the window one last glance and then moved toward me, crawling under the blanket fully clothed. The moment he touched my skin, I squealed. "Take off your clothes! They're cold!"

"You're just trying to get me naked, Rose Gardner." He laughed and pulled off his shirt. "You are a wicked woman."

"And you like me that way." I kissed him and reached for his zipper.

"I had no idea how wicked you could be," he groaned, shimmying out of his jeans and kicking them off.

I pushed him on his back, straddled his hips, and gave him a saucy grin. "Let me show you."

When I woke a couple of hours later Mason was already up, back at the window. The sun had just begun to rise as I dressed. We on the front porch and I realized Mason had been right about our tracks. While the snow hadn't accumulated much, it was wet and heavy and our footprints were like a giant arrow pointing toward us. Mason scooped snow into our empty water bottle and put it in his bag.

"We have two choices," he said. "We can keep trudging through the valley and hope we stumble upon a house, or head back into the trees where there's less snow and it's easier to hide."

"If you don't think they're right behind us, let's go through the valley. We shouldn't be much slower than they are, so we'll hopefully find help before they catch up to us. If they even realize we went this way."

"Valley it is."

We set off north, following a gravel road that led from the house. We had traveled for twenty minutes without spotting another house or even road when a gunshot rang through the air.

We both froze, our eyes wide.

"What was that?" I asked, breathless.

"It could have been hunters."

"Is it hunting season?"

"No. Deer season isn't for another week. But this is rural Arkansas. Some citizens like to make their own rules on private property."

"If it was Crocker, why would they shoot?"

Mason looked back toward the woods behind us. "Maybe to alert the others if they found our footprints. I suspect their cell phones don't work out here."

"What do we do?"

"If it's hunters, heading for the trees in dark clothes could get us shot. But if it's Crocker, the last thing we want is for him to find us out in the open..." He paused. "It all boils down to instinct."

"And what is your gut telling you?"

"That it's Daniel Crocker."

"Mine too," I whispered, my chest about to explode.

"Let's go that way." He pointed to the tree-covered hills to the east.

I took off with Mason behind me. Once we reached the slope, we moved parallel along the side of the hill. The terrain was steep and I lost my footing several times, righting myself before I tumbled down the slope.

Voices floated through the valley. I stopped, my ears straining to pick out words.

Mason was several feet in front of me, but he turned back, watching over my shoulder. The voices grew louder and became less muffled.

"...went this way..."

"I see their footprints."

Mason's eyes widened. "Shit." He grabbed my arm and started uphill. "Let's go higher," he panted. "Now that they've found our tracks, they know we've been heading north. There's a chance we can throw them off if we keep heading east and find another valley to hike through."

"*Is* there another valley?"

"I don't know, but the area is all hills and trees, so it stands to reason that we'll find a valley if we go far enough. At least we'll be making it harder for them to find us. What do *you* want to do?"

My heart raced with fear. He was right. Anything that would help us elude Crocker was the best solution. "Go east."

He grabbed my hand and helped pull me up the hill. This one was steeper than the one we'd climbed and descended the day before. When we reached the peak, we had the option to continue along the ridge or go down the other side.

Mason gave me a long look before he started down.

The other side of the hill was the steepest yet. One glance convinced me to give up any hope of trying to go down gracefully. I tried to grab trees on the way down to slow my descent, but after I crashed into two, I sat on my butt and slid down, just like I used to do with Violet. But when I reached the bottom, I questioned the wisdom of my plan. The entire back side of my jeans was wet and muddy. But at least I didn't have any broken bones and I'd descended the fastest way possible.

My joy was short-lived when I realized we needed to mount another steep hill. We spent the next half hour climbing and descending hills until we finally came into a flat area.

"I think this is a good place for us to start changing direction."

"Okay." I leaned into a tree. I was winded and my hands and feet were freezing again.

"I haven't heard voices for at least fifteen minutes," Mason said. "I think we can rest for a few minutes." He moved next to me. "Do you want to sit?"

I shook my head. "Just let me catch my breath."

He opened his bag and handed me the half-full bottle of now-melted snow. After taking a big swig, I gave it back to him. He drained the rest, then bent down and scooped more snow into the container.

"Do you think we lost Crocker?" I asked as he scanned our surroundings.

"I don't know, but we *have* slowed them down."

"Not that Crocker would let that stop him."

Mason didn't respond, pulling me to his chest instead. His body heat seeped into mine and we stood together for a long moment. "We need to get going," he finally said in a soft voice.

I made myself step away from him. "You're right, but at least I'm warmer now."

He laughed. "I'll add transferring body heat to my résumé as one of my special skills."

We started north through the narrow valley, dodging the thick growth of trees. Snow dusted the ground, but there wasn't nearly as much as there'd been in the other valley.

"At least there's hardly any snow here," I said, grateful that we weren't leaving behind an easy trail anymore.

"The foliage is too thick overhead. That's one of the reasons it's good to be this deep in the woods."

After we traveled for another hour or so, the narrow valley began to spread out and the trees started to thin. We stayed in the denser trees for cover.

We trudged on another half an hour before Mason stopped and looked around. "Let me get our bearings and make sure we're headed in the right direction."

I squatted and leaned over my legs, trying to stifle my disappointment over the thought that we might be going the wrong way. But we were following the valley and I doubted it pointed to true north. It was inevitable that we would be slightly off course.

After a few moments, he squatted next to me and brushed a few stray hairs out of my eyes.

"How bad is it?" I asked.

"We're actually we're heading slightly northeast. Not bad at all." He paused. "Do you want to take a break?"

"Just a few more minutes."

We didn't talk, but it was a comfortable silence. We drank the bottle of melted snow, then I stood and reached down to give Mason a boost. When he grabbed my hand, my head started to tingle and my peripheral vision faded to black.

It was dark all around me, and I could hear heavy panting, which I quickly realized was my own. My hands were bound behind my back and a searing pain was shooting through my right ankle and up my leg.

I heard Daniel Crocker's voice. "I've been waiting a long time for this, Rose."

A woman's scream shot through my head.

The vision faded and I staggered as I said, "He's gonna catch us."

Mason grabbed my elbow to help me remain upright. "Did you just have a vision?"

I nodded, still in shock.

"What did you see?"

I shook my head, unable to find the words.

His grip tightened as panic filled his eyes. "*Rose!*"

I swallowed, my body shaking. "You were in the dark, and your hands were tied behind your back." I fought to take a breath, squatting again to fight the feeling of lightheadedness.

Mason sank down next to me. "What else?"

"I heard Daniel Crocker's voice. He was talking to *me*, and then I heard a scream."

"What did he say?"

I closed my eyes, trying to get the sound of the scream out of my head. "He'd been waiting for a long time for this." I swallowed. "And he called me by name."

Mason stood and jogged several feet into the valley, spinning around as he took in the terrain. "Do you know where we were?"

"No." My tears won and slid down my cheeks. "It was dark."

"Was I sitting or standing?"

"Sitting. Your back was against a wall."

"Was the floor wood? Carpet? Dirt?"

I shook my head, crying harder. "I don't know."

He knelt in front of me and took my hands. "Yes, you do. Just think about it."

I focused on what I'd felt in my vision. "It was hard. I think it was wood. And the room had strange smell. Like fish and animals."

He nodded. "That's good. Anything else?"

"It was a small space. There was light at the bottom of a door. I think you were shut in a closet." I shook my head and stood. "That doesn't tell us anything." I glanced at the bag slung over his shoulder. "I want to start carrying a gun again."

A war of emotions waged on his face.

"A handgun, not a rifle."

Mason watched me for several seconds before sliding the bag down his arm and digging out one of the handguns. He reminded me how to load it and click the safety on and off. He held onto my hand as I grabbed the weapon from him. "Promise me that if you point it at Crocker or his men, you'll do it with the intent to use it. Otherwise it might get you killed."

I tugged without answering.

"Rose."

I looked up into his eyes. "I used it last time, Mason."

He studied my face. "You shot him in the leg. This time you have to shoot to stop him. You have to shoot to kill."

I still had to wonder if I could purposely shoot someone. But if backed into a corner, I hoped I'd do what needed to be done. "Okay."

He released his hold and I double checked the safety before tucking the gun into the waistband at the small of my back.

Mason watched me with wary eyes before snagging my hand. "Let's keep going."

My fingers tightened over his. The feel of the cold gun against my skin made me feel better, which I found shocking. I had been a different person when I shot Daniel Crocker. Though it had happened less than six months ago, I felt years older than the girl who had naïvely convinced a hardened criminal to drag her upstairs. Would I have done the same thing today? I knew I would, but I'd be so much more aware of the dangers now. My fears had been so shallow before I began to truly experience life and all its great joys and disappointments.

My world had been so much smaller.

There had been so much less to lose.

# Chapter Twenty-Four

We were both exhausted and weak from hunger, but my vision had spooked us enough to pick up a faster pace. The land flattened for a while before it began to climb again, which made our trek easier. By late morning, we took a break next to a creek and drank more water.

"I think we've traveled at least four or five miles," Mason said, leaning his back against a tree.

I looked up. "So we're getting closer to Moore County."

"Yeah. I think we could be there in another few hours. Sooner if we could find more flat patches. Or a house."

I breathed out a sigh of relief. "I've lived here all my life, and I never realized you could get so lost in the woods of northern Fenton County."

"Like I mentioned, that's why the meth lab operators hide out here."

I shivered. We had a big enough enemy without throwing another one into the mix. "Let's get going."

The sun shone brightly overhead, which was a double-edged sword. While I was warmer than I'd been the day before, the thin layer of snow was beginning to melt, making our footing slippery in places and leaving muddy footprints behind us.

The terrain quickly became hilly again. The denser sections were easier to traverse since they had seen lighter snowfall, but the ground was wet no matter where we went and we kept losing our footing. We crossed the top of another hill, facing another steep climb down. I leaned over my knees. "Let me take a moment to catch my breath."

"Sure." Mason put his hands on his hips and walked along the ridge. "I think it will be easier to climb down over there." He was pointing to our right when the ground underneath him collapsed, taking him with it.

"*Mason!*" I ran over to the edge, terrified as I watched him tumble down the thirty-foot embankment and land at a heap at the bottom.

"Mason!" Trying to control my sobs of panic, I scrambled down the hill, falling onto my butt and sliding the rest of the way. "Mason!"

He lay unmoving on his side, and my heart leapt into my throat as I reached for him with shaky hands, leaning over his shoulder to look at his face. "Mason, talk to me." Blood from a cut on his forehead covered his face, and his right cheek had already begun to swell.

His eyes blinked open and his face contorted in pain.

"Can you get up?"

"Give me a second." He closed his eyes for several moments and I suddenly worried he might have a concussion. His eyes opened again. "I might need your help. I think I bruised some ribs."

My breath stuck in my chest, my worry deepening. "Okay."

I reached my arm around his shoulders and gently helped him into a sitting position. He released a cry of pain, breathing rapidly and scrunching his eyes shut. "Give me a minute." His clothes and exposed skin were covered in mud and leaves.

I pulled a leaf off his hand. "You look pretty banged up. Let me check you over."

He cracked a grin. "In a different context, I'd like the sound of that."

I smiled despite my tears. "You've got a nasty cut on your forehead." Blood was trailing from his cheek to his neck. "We have to stop the bleeding." I looked around for something to press on his wound, but we were surrounded by mud and dried leaves. The blankets were still in Mason's bag, but they had to be germ-infested. I stripped off my jacket and pulled my T-shirt over my head. The hairs on my arms stood on end when the cold air hit my bare skin.

"Rose, what are you doing?"

I folded up the shirt and pressed it to his forehead. "Can you hold this in place?"

He reached up and winced.

I picked up my jacket and shoved my arms in the sleeves, buttoning it up. "Where else do you hurt?"

He paused before looking into my face. "I think I might have broken my right leg."

"Let me see." His two legs were stretched out in front of him and I gently tugged on the hem of his jeans.

Mason groaned.

"I'm sorry," I said through my tears. He didn't answer, so I kept pulling, lifting the jeans high enough to see that his lower calf was already swollen and purple with bruising. I struggled to keep my tears in check. How would we get out of here?

Mason grabbed my hand. "Rose, listen to me. You need to keep going without me."

I stared at him in disbelief. "No."

"We're so close," he said. "If you just keep going in this direction, I think you'll end up on Moore County Road HH. You can flag down someone who can help us both."

"No." I shook my head, getting angry. "I'm not leaving you, Mason."

He paused. "I don't think I can walk."

"Then I'll help you."

His grip on my hand tightened and he winced at the movement. "Rose, you have to go. If you stay with me, there's a good chance your vision will come true. I won't be able to walk fast enough to keep us away from Crocker and his men. But if you go, you can get help."

I started to cry harder, panic swamping my head. "I can't, Mason. What if I get lost? What if I forget where you are? What if Crocker finds you first?" There was no way I could walk away and leave him here. I sat down next to him and crossed my legs.

"What are you doing?"

"Waiting for you to try to get up."

"I told you that I can't walk."

"You haven't even tried, Mason. We agreed we were in this together. I'm not going anywhere."

"Rose."

I just stared at him in silence. We stayed that way for several moments before he groaned. "Where's my rifle and the bag?" he asked, looking back at the hill.

I leaned away from the tree and scanned the area. The bag must have fallen off during his tumble and continued on its own path. It lay at the bottom of the hill about twenty feet away. The gun was halfway up the hill. "There."

"Bring them over here."

I climbed partway up the hill to retrieve the gun and then made my way over to the bag. When I reached down to pick it up, it required more effort than I'd expected. My body tilted sideways from the weight and when I reached Mason, I dropped it next to him. "How on earth have you been carrying that thing this whole time?"

"It's not that heavy."

"Braggart."

He laughed but then cringed from pain.

When I saw him fumbling with the bag's zipper, I brushed his fingers out of the way. "What do you want?"

"Pull out the ammo and let's see what I have the most of."

"Why?"

His face was taut from pain. "To figure out which guns to bring."

I smiled as tears filled my eyes. "Thank you."

"You can't carry this thing and I sure can't. We'll bring the handguns and a shotgun with some ammo and some water. We'll leave the rest behind."

"But...Crocker and his men could find it."

He continued to watch me. "That's why you need to go on without me."

"So then they'd find you *and* the bag."

"Rose, either way, I'm not going to move very far or fast."

"Then we've wasted too much time. Figure out which guns we're taking and let's go."

He exhaled and gave a slight shake to his head.

After I stacked the ammo boxes in piles next to him, he decided I'd carry the rifle and a much lighter version of the bag. He took out the blankets and put in several boxes of ammunition, leaving the rest on the ground.

"We might need to lighten it more," Mason said, grabbing the stouter shotgun. He cocked it open and removed all the bullets, handing them to me. "Put those in the bag too."

When I was ready, he reached a hand out to me, resting the butt of his gun on the ground. "Let's try this."

I squatted on his right side and slung his arm around my shoulder. Balancing his weight on his left leg, Mason used the barrel of the gun to help hoist himself up. He cried out in pain and nearly fell back down, but I bent my knees to absorb his weight and lift him upright.

He stood on his left leg, panting and cursing under his breath.

"Are you okay?"

"Give me a minute," he said through gritted teeth.

I stood next to him, at least half of his weight pressing into my shoulders. I wasn't sure how we were going to walk out of here, let alone how I would support him, the rifle, *and* the bag, but we'd find a way. We didn't have a choice.

We traveled for at least an hour without covering much distance. Mason kept getting weaker, his face paler. I was beginning to wonder if our only option was for me to leave him to get help when I spotted a building through the trees.

"Mason, look." I pointed.

He exhaled in relief. "Leave me here, but take the rifle with you to the door."

"I'm not gonna look very friendly toting a rifle to their front door."

He shook his head, already lowering himself to the ground. I struggled to keep him from landing too quickly. "Yeah, I guess you're right. But I'm worried about how they'll react to a complete stranger showing up on their doorstep in the middle of nowhere. Some of these people live in the middle of nowhere for a reason."

I handed him the gun. "I'm not getting into a shootout, at least not if I can avoid it. I'll look less suspicious if I'm not carrying a weapon." I turned to leave and he grabbed my hand, flinching with pain from the sudden movement.

"Be careful, Rose."

I leaned down and pressed a kiss to his lips. "I will."

The one-story ranch house was old and worn, but it didn't look abandoned like the last house, which gave me hope. I knocked on the storm door and stepped back onto the gravel path. While I waited, I glanced down at my clothes, suddenly worried about how I would look to anyone in the house. I was a sight. Most of my clothes were covered in mud and my jacket sleeve was bloody from the cut on Mason's forehead.

After ten seconds, I knocked again, louder this time. When no one answered, I banged on the door and shouted, "Is anyone home?"

Several seconds later, Mason called out, "See if the door's unlocked."

My jaw dropped. "The other place was obviously abandoned, but someone lives here. I can't just walk into someone's house!"

"Rose, this is an emergency. I'm the Fenton County Assistant DA and I'm sure as hell not pressing charges. Do whatever it takes to get inside."

Taking a deep breath, I opened the storm door and tried the door knob. "Locked."

"Go around back and see if there's a door open somewhere else. If not, we'll have to break a window."

I would hate for us to resort to literally breaking in, but a quick examination revealed that the back door was locked, so it didn't seem like there were a lot of options.

I walked over to Mason and found him slumped against a tree trunk, his eyes clenched shut. Squatting next to him, I placed the back of my hand against his forehead where he wasn't cut. His eyelids blinked open and he gave me a startled look.

"It's okay," I said, moving my hand down to his cheek. "The doors are locked, but the back door has lots of window panes. I'm going break one of the panes and reach in to open the door."

"Be careful," he groaned. "Bust out all the glass and then pull your hand into your sleeve before you put it through the hole."

"You sound like an experienced felon," I teased.

A hint of an ornery smile cracked his lips. "Guilty by association."

"I'll be right back."

I didn't find a rock that was big enough, but I found a broken tree branch that did the trick. The sound of the shattering glass echoed loudly and I expected someone to jump out of the woods and attack us. But no one did, and I managed to get in without cutting my hand.

The door opened onto a dated kitchen and I nearly cried from relief when I saw a phone on the wall. As I lifted the receiver, I was struck with the fear that the phone wouldn't work, but the dial tone filled my ear. I suddenly wondered whom to call. I couldn't call 911 because the call would most likely go to the sheriff's department, and I didn't know the number of the state police. But I *did* know the number of a state policeman.

I punched in Joe's phone number, thanking my lucky stars that I'd memorized it and hadn't become reliant on speed dial. His phone rang three times and I was sure it was about to go to voice mail when a man answered, sounding groggy. "Who is this?"

"Joe?" I asked, worried I'd called the wrong number.

"*Rose?*"

He had actually answered. I started crying out of relief. "Joe, I need help. Crocker found us and Mason got hurt..." My last words were nearly incomprehensible.

"Rose, slow down."

I was grateful that he sounded more like my Joe. I tried to catch my breath. "Okay."

"Take it slow. What happened?"

"Daniel Crocker broke into my house while I was sleeping and left a threatening note. So the sheriff's department had Mason and me go out to my birth mother's farm to hide until they caught him. They even gave us a guard. Only the sheriff's department has a leak and at least one of the deputies told Crocker where we were. Then he showed up."

"Oh God, Rose." I heard the shock in his voice. "Are you okay?"

I started to cry again. "No. We've been running from Crocker for the past day and a half in the hills of northern Fenton County. He's closing in on us, but Mason fell down a hill and broke his leg."

"Did you call 9-1-1?"

"No, I don't know who's working for Crocker in the sheriff's office. Mason thinks the sheriff himself might be involved. At this point he only trusts the chief deputy."

"Where are you? How are you calling me?"

"We found a house, but no one was home. Mason told me to break in. He thinks we're a couple of miles from the Moore County border and that we'd intercept Highway HH if we kept moving."

"What's the terrain like where you are?"

"It's all pine trees and hills."

"It's a house? Look around for an address. Maybe there's something inside that will give us a clue about where you are."

I scanned the kitchen counter and found several pieces of mail. My fumbling fingers sorted through the stack. "There's an address! 524 Ever Pine Road, Sweet Knob, Arkansas."

"Good! Stay where you are, Rose. I'm coming."

"Should I call the state police?"

"No, I'll take care of it."

I breathed a sigh of relief, then something hit me. "You seemed surprised to hear that Crocker was after me. I called you yesterday and left a message. You didn't get it?"

He paused. "You did *what?*"

"I called you and left a voice message begging you to call me back, but the phone died and we left it at the farmhouse, so I wasn't sure if you got the call."

"I didn't get it, Rose." He sounded horrified. "I would have had the state police looking for you yesterday if I did."

I wanted to tell him it was okay, but it wasn't. Someone was to blame. "It was Hilary, wasn't it?" I asked, my anger rising. "She intercepted the call and deleted the voice mail."

"Rose you don't know—"

"*You're still defending her?*" I shouted. "Even now? Even in this?" It was just one more betrayal. "My life is in danger, Joe, and she deleted my voice mail out of petty jealousy."

"No. She wouldn't do that. She has too much to lose." But while his tone was hard, I heard a waver of uncertainty. "I told her that if she ever interferes with another one of my calls, we'll be done for good. She wouldn't risk it."

"*Do you even hear yourself right now?* How many times have you told her that, yet look where you are right now?"

He didn't answer, which was answer enough.

I steeled my back. "Give me the number for the state police."

"*What?*"

"I want the state police to come save me. How can I rely on you? Hilary might ask you stay home to pick out a china pattern."

"Don't be ridiculous, Rose!"

All the fight fled from me, leaving only disappointment. "I'm not the one being ridiculous. Now give me the number."

To his credit, he rattled it off and I scratched the digits down on the envelope.

"Thank you for your help. I need to hang up and call the state police."

"Rose—" But I hung up before he could say anything else.

I held onto the telephone receiver, which was resting in the cradle, and leaned my forehead on it. Why was I so disappointed in him? I already knew Joe and Hilary were back together—our meeting at the nursery had been proof enough of that. Joe would *always* go back to Hilary. He was like a carrier pigeon and she was his home base. I couldn't be with someone like that, someone who was captive to his past.

I needed Mason.

With a huge sigh, I straightened and picked up the receiver to call the state police. I punched in the number, but the phone call didn't go through. I hung up and put the receiver to my ear, but this time there was no dial tone. I hung up and tried again. Still nothing.

Panic raced up my spine and I dropped the phone, running out the still-open back door toward the spot where I'd left Mason. On the other side of the house, Deputy Gyer stepped away from the building, holding a large pocketknife in his hand. A severed utility line dangled behind him. He turned to me with a wicked smile.

"Rose, long time no see," he laughed. "You're a hard woman to find."

# Chapter Twenty-Five

Deputy Gyer was in on it too.

Recovering from the shock, I turned and ran for the trees behind the house, but he quickly caught up and snaked an arm around my waist, hauling me up to his chest.

"I think you've done enough running, little Rose." He reached between us and pulled the handgun out of the waistband of my pants. "Crocker warned me you liked to hide guns on you. Looks like he was right."

He dragged me toward the house and I kicked and squirmed, trying to break free. After I landed a solid kick to his shin, he grunted and grabbed a fistful of my hair, jerking his hand back.

I released a cry of pain and he growled in my ear. "You've caused me nothing but trouble since I showed up at your farm yesterday morning. Crocker wasn't happy that we let you get away. While he told us to keep you alive, he didn't say anything about what shape he wants you in. Don't think I won't beat the shit out of you to get you to cooperate."

He practically carried me into the house and I craned my neck, desperate to see whether Mason was still in the woods. There wasn't any sign of him. Deputy Gyer dragged me into a bedroom and my fear escalated, especially when I saw that another man was already in the room. He looked like a teenager and he was sporting a busted lip.

Gyer shot him a look of disgust, shaking his head. "What the hell happened to you?"

He turned bright red. "He put up a fight."

"*How?* He's got a busted leg and looked too weak to kick a kitten." Deputy Gyer set me down and I tried to elbow him in the groin. He twisted my arms around my back with enough force to make me cry out. "Good thing I took care of this hellcat myself because Crocker would have both our asses if she got away."

The teen glared at me.

Gyer shoved me toward an open walk-in closet. I struggled not to fall on top of Mason, who was sprawled face-first on the floor, his hands tied behind his back.

"Mason!"

"You just sit tight while we wait for Crocker to show up," Detective Gyer said with a sneer. Then he slammed the door shut and we were plunged into darkness.

"Mason." I blindly reached for him, coming into contact with his arm.

"I'm sorry, Rose." He sounded devastated.

"Don't apologize. You didn't do anything wrong." I rubbed his back.

"Did you get a chance to call anyone?"

I closed my eyes and tried to keep from bursting into tears. "Yes. But I didn't know the number for the state police, so I called Joe."

"Did you leave another message?"

"No, he answered and I even found this house's address on a stack of mail in the kitchen."

"So he's sending help?"

I stayed silent.

"Rose, what happened?"

"He told me he was coming and he'd call the state police."

"Then why do you sound so worried?"

"Because he didn't get my call yesterday and when I told him that Hilary must have deleted the voice mail, he got defensive of her. I got angry..."

"And?"

"And I told him not to bother coming, that I'd call the state police myself. I made him give me the number."

"But you didn't get a chance to call."

I heaved a long breath. "No."

"It's okay. Joe will probably call them anyway. Just to make sure they got the message."

I wasn't so convinced, but I didn't want to think about what was going to happen if he didn't. "We need to move you, Mason. You're lying flat on your face. Do you want to lie down or sit up?"

"Can you help me sit up?"

"Yeah." I grabbed his arms and we maneuvered him into a sitting position, his back propped against the wall. I tried to undo the binding on his hands, but it was a zip tie.

"I can't get it undone."

"Do you still have your gun?" he asked.

"No. Deputy Gyer, the guy who showed up to help Deputy Miller, took it. Crocker had warned him that I might have a hidden gun."

"Deputy Gyer? He's one of them too?"

"It looks like it."

"We never stood a chance." He sounded disgusted. "Okay. Let's figure out something we can use to defend ourselves. Check the hangers."

I stood and felt around, my eyes slowly adjusting to the darkness. We had to be in a spare bedroom; there were linens stacked on the shelves and just a few articles of clothing hanging from the rod. "There are about ten plastic hangers."

"No wire?"

"No."

"Will the pole that's holding them come out of its brackets?"

I lifted the rod, banging the end into the wooden shelf above it. "Yeah."

"Be careful," he whispered. "We don't want them to realize we're up to something."

"What am I going to do with this?"

"Fight like hell."

He was right. I couldn't sit calmly and wait for Crocker to show up and get his revenge. But I was scared to death. I laid the pole on the floor and after a bit more rustling around, found two shorter poles in brackets, one stacked over the other. "Now what?"

"Keep searching the closet and see if you can find something to cut this zip tie."

I searched the entire closet, finding only more linens and clothing and two objects that felt like stuffed animals only with real fur and they stunk to high heaven. "There's nothing." My voice broke. I sat next to Mason, discouraged. "Mason, I'm scared."

"I know. I am too."

I laid my head on his shoulder, trying to keep from crying. "You know what I regret most?" I asked.

"What?"

"I regret not visiting the farm sooner. I love it there. I've been doing a lot of thinking, and if we get out of here alive, I think I'm going to move to the farm."

Mason rested his cheek on my head, his breathing slightly labored. "Not *if*, Rose. We *will* get out of this."

I wasn't so certain. "I also regret not telling Violet off sooner. That was a long time coming."

"She deserved it, that's for sure."

"And I regret not telling you about Joe's father and the evidence he falsified."

"When we get out of this, it'll be on the top of my list of things to deal with." His tone was stern.

I still didn't want him to get tangled up in the whole mess, but this hardly seemed like the time to say so.

"I have regrets too," he said softly. "I regret being so harsh with you when we first met."

"Mason…"

"And I regret that Joe met you first. I lived in Henryetta before you two started dating. In theory, I could have met you before you and Joe became involved."

"I'm not the same person I was then, Mason. I'm not sure you would have noticed me."

"Joe did."

"Because he thought I was a suspect. He only paid attention because it was part of his job. He insists that's not true, but he'd lived next to me for a month before we so much as exchanged a word. The first time we spoke was when I knocked on his door after I found Momma's body."

We were silent for a moment.

"I can't regret Joe," I whispered. "He's part of who I am today."

He kissed my forehead. "And I would never ask you to regret him. I didn't mean it that way. I just wish that we could have had more time together."

"What would you have done if Joe and I didn't break up?"

"I would have moved on eventually, I suppose. The fact that I could see cracks in your relationship gave me hope, although I never wanted you to be hurt, Rose."

"I know."

"And I regret not being a better brother to Savannah. Maybe if I'd been there for her more she wouldn't have made so many bad choices."

"Mason, I'm sure you were a great brother. Look what you did after she was murdered. You found the guy and beat him up."

"And you know I regret that too…"

"Enough regrets," I sighed. "We can't change the past. We can only look toward the future." I turned my head and gave him a soft kiss.

"If something happens to you…" His voice broke. "My biggest regret of all will be that I never got the chance for a future with you."

I grabbed his face with both hands and kissed him, showing him how much I regretted that too.

Suddenly, the closet door flew open and sunlight flooded the small room. I jerked backward, edging behind Mason as I tried to make out who was in the doorway.

"Hello, my sweet Rose."

I nearly passed out from fright.

It was Daniel Crocker.

# Chapter Twenty-Six

Getting her warmed up for me, Mr. Assistant DA?" Crocker asked with a laugh. His smile fell as his gaze landed on me. "Aren't you going to say hello, Rose? Be careful or I'll think you aren't happy to see me."

He looked different from when I'd last seen him up close. His dark brown hair was shorter and he had several days' growth on his face that had more gray in it than I remembered. He had more lines on his forehead and around his mouth too, but the change in his eyes struck me the most. They had been hard before with a bit of madness, but now they looked flat-out crazy.

I struggled to catch my breath, my body shaking with fright.

"Crocker, listen to me," Mason said, using his professional voice. "You haven't even been to trial yet. I can work out some kind of deal for you."

He cocked his head with an amused grin. "What kind of deal?"

Mason paused. "We can drop the racketeering charges and one count of attempted murder."

Crocker started laughing. "You're kidding me. That's all she's worth to you?"

Mason flinched.

I wrapped my fingers around his arm and rose to my knees. "He's not dropping anything. You deserved every one of those charges."

A demented grin lit up his face. "I plan to earn a few more before I go back."

"I'll drop the murder charges," Mason blurted out. "You'd be left with the drug charges, nothing more."

My grip on his arm tightened. "Mason, you can't do that!"

"And I'll make sure you don't face any charges for escaping."

Crocker turned his head to study Mason. "Hmm…"

Could Mason get away with doing that? The entire state was watching this case. He'd ruin his career. For me.

"It's very tempting," Crocker said, his index finger stroking his chin as he looked at me. "But I'd still be in prison for a very long time. Without the comfort of a woman. And we both know how much I love women."

I shuddered.

"There's nothing keeping you here," Mason said, insistent. "You can escape and find all the women you want. Rose and I will even misdirect the state police. I give you my word."

"But there's something you're not taking into consideration," Crocker said, all amusement falling away from his face. "There's only one woman I'm interested in right now." He held out his hand to me, beckoning.

I shrank back and Mason scooted away from the wall, trying to shield me. "The state police are on their way, Crocker. If you leave now, you might still have a chance to escape. Otherwise, you're sure to be captured."

Crocker shook his head. "You've been in here for nearly half an hour. The way the state police have canvassed this county, they would have been here by now if they were coming. You're bluffing."

My heart sank. He was right. They should have been here by now. That meant Joe really hadn't called them. Now we'd be killed and it was all because of my temper.

"Come on, Rose," Crocker growled. "I'm tired of waiting."

I reached down, my fingers brushing the shorter wooden pole. I had no delusions of escaping three men, but I wasn't about to make things easy for them.

Crocker stepped into the closet and Mason tried to block his path, distracting his attention. I swept up the pole as I stood, shoving it into Crocker's stomach with all my strength.

He stumbled, letting out a whoosh of air and a growl.

I raised the pole to strike him across the back, but he grabbed it and jerked it from my hands, shoving me across the bed. I rolled off the edge and landed hard on the floor, releasing a grunt.

Crocker walked back to the closet and kicked Mason in the chest.

I rushed forward. "*No! Stop!*" I grabbed Crocker's arm as he kicked Mason again. "Stop! I'll do what you want. Just leave him alone. *Please.*"

Mason's eyes grew wild with fear. "Rose! No!"

I was still clinging to Crocker's arm when he turned to look at me. "You're telling me you'll cooperate? With *everything?*"

Squaring my shoulders, I stared into Crocker's wild eyes. "Yes."

"Rose!" Mason shouted. I didn't look at him. I couldn't.

Crocker dragged me out of the closet and shut the door, bracing a chair under the doorknob. He turned to me with a grin.

"I want you to let him go," I said. "You have to promise not to hurt him."

Surprise flickered in his eyes as he jutted his head back in disgust. "I don't *have* to do anything."

I started to unbutton my jacket and forced myself to calm down. I'd figure a way out of this. I'd managed to last time. "How good do you want it?"

His eyes followed my hand to where my jacket hung open at my waist, exposing my bra and bare abdomen. "Fine. We won't touch him when we're done here."

"Rose! No!" Mason shouted through the closet door.

"You won't hurt him at all."

Mason banged on the closet door, shouting my name.

Crocker looked back at the door and then grinned at me. "None of us will hurt him at all."

I took several steps backward and reached for the door. "Let's go to somewhere more private."

Crocker crossed the room and slammed the door shut, turning me so my back was propped against it. He pressed his chest against mine. "I like this room just fine."

My eyes widened in understanding and fear.

His hand snaked into my hair and wrapped around a handful of strands. "I've been waiting a long time for this, Rose."

He jerked hard and I couldn't stop my scream.

This was my vision.

It was coming true.

"Rose!" Mason shouted, banging on the door.

Crocker grinned and covered my mouth with his. I'd forgotten what a sloppy kisser he was, even without any alcohol. In my horror, I forgot about my agreement to cooperate. "You don't seem very enthusiastic, Rose. Have you forgotten our deal already?" He jerked my hair again.

"No," I wheezed out, unable to hide my terror.

Crocker fed on my fear, his eyes lighting with excitement. After releasing my hair, he lowered his hands to my waist, skimming both hands slowly up my sides while watching my face. "I've been thinking about this for months, Rose. Many different ways."

I kept my gaze on his, forcing myself to calm down. "My expectations aren't quite as high," I heard myself saying.

He dropped his hands and slapped my face before I realized what was happening. I released a cry of pain, trying to ignore Mason's continued shouting.

Crocker dug his fingers into my upper arms. "I don't consider that cooperative, Rose."

"You want me to lie and tell you how good you are?"

He hit me again and I couldn't stop my groan. I knew I shouldn't antagonize Crocker, but I'd rather be beaten than the alternative.

As if reading my mind, he pulled the jacket down my arms and tossed it to the floor. "We're wasting valuable time, sweet Rose." His mouth lowered to mine, and I tried to show more enthusiasm this time.

I had to figure a way out. I opened my eyes and took an inventory of the room. A bed, a dresser, sheer curtains hanging on the window. A bedside table with a ceramic lamp and an old-fashioned alarm clock. The discarded wooden rod on the floor. None of the pieces were coalescing into a plan.

Crocker stripped off his shirt and stood in front of me bare-chested, a huge bruise forming on his stomach. His eyes followed my gaze and his eyebrows rose. "You shouldn't have done that, Rose." He reached down and picked up the pole.

I turned and ran for the door. I managed to get it open, but Crocker caught me in the hall and slammed me into the wall. Panic raced through my body and I tried to swallow the sob in my throat.

"Where are you going, Rose? You said you'd cooperate."

I looked down at the wooden rod still in his hand. "You're going to hurt me."

He spun me around, his grin maniacal. "You said you'd cooperate in *everything*."

Mason's life depended upon it, but for the life of me, I wasn't sure I could willingly allow him to beat me with that pole. "But how can I be *totally* cooperative if you hurt me first?" My voice betrayed me by shaking, but I had his attention. "I've learned a few things since you last saw me. I'm more experienced now."

He tossed the pole onto the wooden floor, clanging on the wood floor in the hallway. "I better be impressed." He reached for the button on my jeans and unzipped them. "Take them off."

Swallowing my fear, I hooked my thumbs on my waistband.

"Actually," Joe's authoritative voice startled me. "I think she should leave them on."

I swiveled to see Joe at the end of the hallway, pointing his handgun at Crocker.

I released a cry of relief. Joe had come anyway.

"Rose, why don't you walk toward me real slow." Joe inched forward, his eyes and gun still on Crocker.

I moved toward him, keeping my attention on Crocker. When I reached Joe, he slid an arm around my waist and pulled me to his chest. "Did he hit you?" he said, his voice harsh.

Crocker laughed. "What are you going to do about it, McAllister? You hid behind her last time. You gonna hide behind her again?"

Joe started to lunge for Crocker, but I grabbed fistfuls of his jacket and held tight. "No! He's not worth it."

Crocker leaned over, laughing hard. "You're not man enough to shoot me."

Joe backed up, dragging me with him. "Let's discuss my lack of manhood out here where there's more room."

Crocker followed, grinning at Joe like he was a Christmas present. "I thought you two had broken up, but the way you're holding her tells me otherwise."

Joe didn't answer. Instead, he pried my hands from his jacket and pushed me behind him. "Our personal life is none of your business."

"I've spent the last five months making Rose very much my business."

Joe tensed and I put a hand on his shoulder. "Please don't."

"Listen to her, Joe. I'll just kick your ass, and then Rose and I will pick up where we left off."

Joe started to unzip his jacket. "I want you to put this on and go outside," he said to me.

"What about the two other guys?"

"I've taken care of them."

I shook my head. "I need to help Mason."

Crocker sneered. "She was making out with the DA when I found her in the closet. His hands were *all* over her."

Joe tensed again. "Go get him."

Watching me with a leer, Crocker's eyebrows lifted in appreciation. "As you can see, he had her half undressed and ready for me. I can't say I blame him."

Joe's face reddened.

"He's lying, Joe! He's trying to piss you off."

"Go get him," he growled again. He waved his gun at Crocker. "Move away from the hall."

Lifting his hands in surrender, he backed away from the hall and into the center of the living room.

I ran into the bedroom and pulled the chair out from underneath the doorknob, throwing the closet door open. "Mason."

He lay on the floor in front of the door, blinking to adjust to the light. "Rose? I heard shouting. How—"

"Joe's here."

"What about the rest of the state police?"

"Not yet."

I helped him sit up. "Did he hurt you very badly?"

He grimaced and took a deep breath, then looked into my eyes. "I should be asking you that question."

"I'm fine."

His mouth pressed together tightly enough to blanch the skin around his lips.

"I need to find something to cut that tie so you can balance enough to stand."

He nodded.

When I ran into the hall, Crocker was still taunting Joe. "—fantasizing about her for months. One version she's—"

I disappeared into a bathroom and found a small pair of scissors in the drawer before hurrying back into the bedroom to cut through the plastic cord. After I snapped it, Mason rubbed his wrists for a second and then reached for me. We held each other for a long moment, and then I helped him up.

"I'm sorry," I whispered when he gasped.

"Just give me a moment to recover."

I wasn't sure how long we had left before Joe ripped Crocker apart with his bare hands.

We hobbled to the door and Mason stopped just inside the doorway.

"Put on your jacket."

After I did, he wrapped his arm around my shoulder again and we eased through the door.

Crocker turned his attention to us. "Here come the lovebirds now. You should have been here, Officer Joe. Mr. DA was about to drop every charge against me to protect Rose's virtue. Even the murder charges if I promised not to touch her."

Mason ignored the insult. "Joe, how soon until the state police arrive?"

"I don't know. I called Chief Deputy Dimler to bring him into the loop. He told me they'd contacted him to coordinate the capture."

I lowered Mason onto a kitchen chair. "Where is everyone, then?" I wheezed out. "They should be here by now."

"Good question." Joe scowled.

"Rose, you covered up," Crocker mock frowned. "I want to see your pretty—"

"*Shut. Up.*" Joe shouted.

The front door opened and Chief Deputy Dimler came through the door, wearing civilian clothes and pausing to take in the scene. "Good job, Detective Simmons." He turned his attention to Mason and me. "Mason, good to see you're alive and well." But something seemed off. He was too nonchalant.

Mason picked up on it too—I could tell from the stiffness of his shoulders.

The chief deputy stopped next to Joe and pulled his gun out of its holster. "Why don't you wait outside for the rest of the state police officers and I'll take over here?"

Jeff unzipped his jacket, revealing a necklace that was hanging halfway out of his T-shirt.

A St. Jude's medallion.

# Chapter Twenty-Seven

My mouth dropped open.

Joe's eyebrows lifted. "Rose, what's wrong?"

"It was you all along," Mason said, his words laced with a mixture of disappointment and anger. "You were the leak."

I pointed at his necklace, which Jeff was already stuffing inside his shirt. "He's wearing a St. Jude's medallion. All of Crocker's men wear them."

Joe shook his head. "No. They didn't when I was part of their group."

"They do now. I've seen it myself and Jonah confirmed it."

"Mason, seriously. Are you suggesting I'm one of Crocker's men?" Jeff laughed good-naturedly. He lifted his hand to his chest. "We're friends. We've been working this case together for months. We play basketball together. Hell, you came over to my house and watched the Little Rock-LSU game." He shook his head. "Being lost in the woods has made you a bit paranoid, which is understandable. I'll let it slide. No hard feelings."

Mason didn't look convinced. "Where'd you get it?"

"I'm a good Catholic boy. I go to mass every Sunday. My grandmother gave it to me for protection when I joined the sheriff's department."

Joe turned his attention to the chief deputy, his eyes narrowing. "That's odd, considering St. Jude is the patron saint of lost objects."

Jeff flashed him a smile then he and Crocker rushed Joe at once. The gun went off and Mason flew off the chair, tackling me to the floor as I screamed. The three men continued to tussle and there was another shot.

"Mason. I need to find a gun," I shouted.

"No." He grunted in pain as he pressed me to the floor. "You'll get shot."

"We're in big trouble if they overpower Joe." I shoved him off. I was sorry to hurt him, but I needed one of those guns.

"Look outside," Mason called after me. "The guy who found me didn't take the bag."

I ran out the back door toward the grouping of trees where I'd left Mason. The bag was several feet behind the tree where he had waited for me. My hand was shaking so hard it took me two attempts to open it, but I found a handgun inside with a full clip. I grabbed more clips and stuffed them into my pockets before heading back to the house.

I crept through the back door and hid behind the kitchen table as I assessed how the situation had changed. Mason had raised himself into a sitting position on the floor and was halfway between the living room and the kitchen. My heart leapt into my throat when I saw Joe lying on the floor, his face beaten. Jeff stood to the side looking unhappy as Crocker delivered another kick to Joe's ribs.

"We've got a DA and a state police detective here, not to mention the fact that Joe Simmons is running for state senate and is the son of a very powerful political player, Crocker." Jeff ran a hand through his hair and released a low whistle. "We're in deep shit."

"You were in deep shit long before now. We'll kill these two and dispose of them in the hills where they'll never be found, then I'll take Rose with me."

I rushed forward, the gun trained on Crocker. "I'm not going anywhere with you. Now get away from him."

Mason swung around to look at me.

Crocker turned in surprise and smiled. "Rose, you came back to the party." Then he kicked Joe again.

Joe released a grunt and spat blood onto the floor.

I held the gun higher, aiming at Crocker's chest, my finger on the trigger. Mason had told me I'd better be prepared to use it if I pointed it at Crocker or one of his men. I only hoped I was.

"You can't shoot me," Crocker said, amused. "It's not self-defense."

"Mason?" I asked.

"Do it," he said in a menacing voice.

Crocker looked surprised for a second, but he kicked Joe again in defiance. "You won't shoot me, Rose."

My hand shook.

Joe moaned on the floor, curling up in a defensive position, his eyes closed.

Crocker followed my gaze to Joe then looked back at me with a smirk. "If you shoot me, Chief Deputy Dimler will shoot *you*. And I don't think that's what you want."

I didn't answer.

"You're too scared, Rose," Crocker purred. "But that's okay. It's not easy killing a man. Watching his life bleed out."

My stomach clamped and I hesitated as he started to creep toward me. Now he was just six feet away.

"Shoot him!" Mason shouted.

"I know what you want, Rose." He smiled. "You want to protect both the D.A. and McAllister." He held his hands out at his sides. "So let's make a deal where no one gets hurt." He took another step toward me. "If you put your gun down, Dimler promises to let your boyfriends go."

"And me?"

He gave me his cocky grin. "You leave. With me."

"I don't think so."

Crocker lunged for the gun.

I took a deep breath and squeezed the trigger. The blast filled the room and Crocker fell backward, tripping over Joe's legs and landing on the floor. I swung the gun toward Dimler, whose gun was trained on me.

He moved his hands to his sides, the gun pointed against the wall, and took a step toward me. "Rose." He smiled. "You can get away with shooting an escaped criminal, but not the chief deputy sheriff. Now put down the gun."

"Mason?" My voice rose with fright.

"*Don't listen to him.*"

Jeff's face pleaded with me. "Rose, I know how this looks, but you don't know the whole story."

"It looks like you've partnered with Daniel Crocker and you told him where we were hiding. Why? And why didn't you just tell him immediately? Why wait?"

"We were...negotiating. And as for why, do you know how much a sheriff makes? Not very damn much, I'll tell you that. How the hell am I supposed to pay for all of my kid's medical bills?"

"Answer this," Mason said, his voice hard. "Why have me work on finding the leak if you were planning to turn me over to Crocker with Rose?"

Jeff turned to look at Mason. "I didn't *want* you involved in this. I told you to let me take her into our protection." He pointed his gun at me again. "And I told *you* to convince him to stay out of the whole situation. We both know who's going to win this standoff. So if Mason gets hurt in all of this, that's on *your* head."

I gasped.

Keeping his gun trained on me, Jeff glanced back at Mason. "Crocker didn't even know you and Rose were involved. Hell, *I* didn't know you were involved until after Crocker visited her house. I never intended for you to be dragged into this."

He took two more steps toward me.

Mason shook his head. "But the investigation...If you were the leak, why have me keep working on it?"

"I was surprised when you approached me this summer, but I figured I could use it to my advantage. I hoped to pin everything on the sheriff. I'm your friend, Mason. We can work this out."

Mason's mouth dropped open. "If you believe that, you never really knew me at all."

"Stop being so idealistic for once," Jeff scoffed. "This is how the real world works. We can both take over—you as DA and me as sheriff. We can rule Fenton County."

Mason shook his head in disbelief. "There's no way in hell I'll agree to that."

Jeff took another step toward me and tossed his gun to the floor.

"Stop right there." I jabbed the gun in his direction. "I'll shoot you."

"Will you? Now I'm unarmed, Rose. You could get in *big* trouble, and these two—" he pointed to Mason and Joe with a sly grin "—aren't exactly unbiased witnesses. How would you like to do some prison time?"

I swallowed the lump of fear that had lodged in my throat.

"See, Rose? You don't want to shoot me." He was four feet in front of me now, reaching out his hand. "Just give me the gun."

"Don't listen to him, Rose," Mason grunted. "No one will ever press charges."

Changing tactics, Dimler dropped to his knees and put Mason in a chokehold, positioning his body behind Mason's. "Put down the gun or I'll strangle him."

My hands shook.

"Just put it down and we'll have a reasonable discussion."

Mason's face was turning red.

"You'd kill your own friend?" I asked in disbelief.

"He's the one who turned his back on me." Jeff cocked his head to look at me. "I'm guessing you're not a good enough shot to make sure you miss Mason."

"No," Joe said, his words slurred. "But I am."

A gunshot rang out and Dimler slumped to the ground with a groan, blood seeping from his right shoulder.

Mason hunched forward, gasping for air.

My gaze turned to Joe, who was propped up on his left elbow, the gun in his right hand still pointed at the deputy.

I ran to Mason first, setting my gun on the floor beside him. "Are you okay?"

"I'm fine." His voice was hoarse. "Check on Joe and call the state police with his cell phone." He picked up my gun and pointed it at the still-moving chief deputy.

I rushed over to Joe and sat next to him, fear washing over me at the sight of his bloody and swollen face. "Joe." I choked down tears. "Are you okay?"

He forced open a swollen eye and pushed himself into a sitting position, grunting in the process. "Never been better, darlin'." His familiar term of endearment made me cry harder.

"Hey." He covered my hand with his, exposing his bloody and swollen knuckles. "Don't cry. I've been worse."

"What do you want me to do?"

"Help me get up, and I'll go outside and call the state police. I'll get better reception out there." Joe glanced at Mason, who had scooted back toward the kitchen.

Mason nodded at him. "I'll keep an eye on these two, although I don't think Crocker is going anywhere."

Crocker lay sprawled on the floor, his shirt soaked with blood. His eyes were open, his face expressionless.

"I killed him," I said, my body swaying with the realization.

"Get her out of here." Mason barked.

Joe climbed unsteadily to his feet and reached a hand toward me. "Come on, darlin'. Let's get you some fresh air."

I took his hand, being careful of his knuckles, and he pulled me out the door and into the front yard. He led me to a wrought iron and wood slat bench under a tree. "Head between your knees," he said after I sat. "Just like the night we first met."

I lowered my head and took in deep gulps of air.

He sat down next to me, rubbing my back in slow, soft circles. "You didn't have a choice, Rose. You saved my life. Thank you."

I sat up, tears streaming down my face. "I couldn't let him kill you."

He winked—or tried to with his swollen eye. "I appreciate that."

I took a deep breath.

"Can you get my cell phone out of my pants pocket?" he said. "I'd get it myself but…" He held up his bloody hand.

I nodded.

He stood and moved in front of me. I reached into his right pocket and pulled his phone out. The familiarity of knowing which pocket he kept his cell phone in made me uncomfortable, as well as the intimate contact. I held it out to him without comment.

Joe sat down and called Brian, his good friend in the state police department, filling him in on what had happened.

When he hung up, he handed me the phone and I held it in my lap.

We sat in silence for several moments.

"You came," I whispered. "Even when I was ugly and told you not to."

"Of course I did, Rose," he said, his voice husky. "How could I not? I don't care where you are or who you're with. I'll always come if you ever need me."

"Thank you." I started crying again.

His stared into my eyes and lifted a hand to my cheek. "I love you, Rose. And I always will."

While I knew he meant it, I couldn't trust him to stay. Hilary had sunk her claws in too deeply years before we ever met. I closed my eyes. I couldn't do this now. Especially after everything I'd shared with Mason. "Joe. Don't."

Sirens blared in the distance.

"I have to." His hand slipped into my hair, pulling my face closer to his until only a foot separated us. "I'm going to figure out a way to prove my father's evidence is falsified, and I'm going to quit the senate race. You mean more to me than anything in my entire life ever has."

"Joe." I shook my head sadly. "We're done."

"No!" He became more insistent. "We're *not*. We only broke up because of my father. If I fix this, then he won't be an issue. Everything will be fixed."

"No, it *won't*. Everything won't be fixed. There will always be Hilary."

"I'll break up with her!"

"How many times have you broken up with her? Every single time you go back. We've been broken up for just over a month and you ran back to her after two weeks or less."

"That's not fair, Rose. You're with Mason now!"

"The key difference is that Hilary is toxic and Mason is anything but." I swallowed. "Mason encourages me to grow and face my past. He believes I can face the hard things. He respects me and my opinions and treats me as an equal."

"Are you saying I don't?"

"Joe—" I turned to face him "—you see me as the innocent naïvely woman you met months ago. Mason sees me for the person I am now."

He started to protest.

"No." I curled my hand around his neck, the act itself feeling intimate and familiar. "You can't help it. You were always upset by how Violet wanted to protect me from the world, but *you* tried to protect me from it too. You always put limits on what you thought I could do. Mason doesn't do that. He encourages me to try things myself."

"Do you really expect me to be okay with you dating him?" he asked in disbelief.

I didn't point out that he'd moved on first. Instead, I swallowed the new lump in my throat and lowered my voice. "Part of me will always love you, Joe. But we're done. I've moved on. I just hope that you'll stop running back to Hilary someday. You deserve better." I stood. "I hope you have a happy life, Joe. I hope you find what you're looking for."

I started to walk away, but he snagged my wrist and pulled me to him, wrapping his arms around my waist and pressing his cheek to my abdomen. "You're what I'm looking for, what I've always been looking for."

My fingers threaded through his hair out of instinct. I pulled them out and cupped his head, trying to keep from sobbing. "Then I hope you find something else."

Police and sheriff cars pulled up in front of the house, and officers started to pour out of their cars. Several ambulances followed behind, their sirens on and lights flashing.

Joe stood and turned to look at me, tears in his eyes. "I'll figure out a way to fix this." Then he left to tell the officers what had happened.

I went back inside the house. Mason's eyes filled with worry when he saw me. "Rose, go back outside."

Several state policemen pushed past me and one of them grabbed my arm. "Miss, you need to wait outside. This is a crime scene."

Yeah, this was *my* crime scene.

But Mason nodded and motioned for me to leave.

I went outside and sat back down on the bench, watching the commotion in a daze. A state police officer sat down and began to take my statement. Part way through, the paramedics rolled the chief deputy's gurney out and lifted it into the first ambulance. Several minutes later, another paramedic came out with Mason's. I jumped up and ran over to him, grabbing his hand as they wheeled him to the ambulance.

"Mason, I'm coming with you."

The paramedic at the head of his gurney shook her head. "I'm sorry. Only the patient is allowed in the back."

Mason's grip tightened on mine and he glanced up at the woman and said, "Maggie, either she comes with me in the back or I'm getting off this gurney."

"Mr. Deveraux," Maggie protested, shooting me a glare. "You need medical attention."

"Then let Rose ride with me."

Her eyes narrowed as she looked at me. "It goes against protocol."

Mason reached for the buckle of the strap securing him to the bed. "Then stop and let me off."

The paramedics stopped and Maggie tried to push Mason back down. "You can't even walk on that leg."

"If you think I'm getting in this ambulance without her, you've got another think coming. It will be days before I let her out of my sight."

Maggie moved to the side of the gurney, glaring at me. "If you cared anything about him at all, you wouldn't interfere with his medical care."

The other paramedic motioned Maggie to the side and they got into a heated conversation.

I glanced over my shoulder at them and then back to Mason. "Another member of the Mrs. Mason Deveraux hopefuls?"

He grimaced.

"Why do I think that dating you is going to make me the enemy of half the Fenton County female population?"

Mason winked. "Since when did you back down from a challenge?"

"You're not really going to refuse to ride in the ambulance if I can't come with you, are you?"

He grinned. "You're damn right I am. I almost always get my way."

Laughing, I shook my head, then leaned down to kiss him, letting my lips linger on his. "Well, then you've met your match, mister."

The paramedics wandered back and Maggie didn't look at all happy. "We'll bend the rules this time for you, Mr. Deveraux."

Mason shot me an *I told you so* grin before they rolled his cart into the ambulance. I climbed in after him, shaking my head. For the whole ride, Maggie fussed over him, pretending I wasn't there and that we weren't holding hands, flirting up a storm.

After we arrived at the hospital, the staff got Mason settled into an exam room in the ER, and I took the seat next to his bed, shaking my head. "I remember this happening a little over a month ago. Only I was the one in the bed."

The corners of his mouth tilted up. "We shouldn't make a habit of this."

"Deal."

I laid my head against his arm.

"Joe still loves you," Mason whispered in my ear.

"I know," I whispered back.

He was quiet for a moment. "You know that I want you to be happy, Rose."

My head popped up. "What does that mean?"

"It means I don't want you to feel obligated to be with me. I know you didn't want to break up with him."

I leaned down to kiss him. He reached behind my head, holding me in place as he kissed me back more thoroughly.

"You can't get rid of me that easily. I'm exactly where I want to be, Mason." I looked around and rolled my eyes. "Well, maybe not in this room, but with you."

His serious eyes searched mine. "Are you sure?"

"I've never been more sure of anything in my life."

He kissed me for several minutes more, until a nurse cleared her throat. "Okay, love birds. There are enough rumors flying around about you without adding fuel to the fire."

I lifted my head, blushing.

"And what rumors would those be?" Mason asked good-naturedly.

"That you're madly in love."

"That was fast," I joked and turned to look at Mason. But the expression on his face told me it was true. Mason was in love with me. He probably had been for months.

Mason's arm tightened around my waist.

"Well, you two will have to live without each other for a few minutes while I take Mr. Deveraux to x-ray." She headed for the door. "And I take it he'll be going home with you, Ms. Gardner?"

Mason looked uncomfortable, but I smiled softly at him. "Yes."

The nurse left and Mason grabbed my hand. "Rose, that's not necessary. I'm sure my mom will come and help."

"Good. Do you think she'd mind helping us move into the farmhouse?"

"What?"

"I meant what I said earlier. I've decided to move into the farmhouse. And since you don't have anywhere to live, I want you to stay with me."

His mouth opened and he hesitated.

"It doesn't have to be permanent, Mason. You can come and stay while you're recovering, or until you get a new place to live. But I want you to come with me. It feels right with you there. Like home."

"Rose... I don't know what to say."

"Then just say yes."

He smiled, happiness radiating from his face. "Yes."

Then I kissed him to seal the deal.

# Chapter Twenty-Eight

Two weeks later, I parked my truck behind Bruce Wayne's beat-up Pinto in front of Mary Louise's house. I climbed out and cinched the belt on my coat as I picked my way across the yard in heeled boots.

Bruce Wayne was in the backyard, bent over his shovel as he started to dig Mary Louise's new garden pond. The oval shape was spray-painted in the grass and he tossed a scoop of dirt onto the canvas tarp next to it.

"How's it goin'?" I asked.

Bruce Wayne looked up. "I thought you were going by the hospital, Miss Rose."

"I am, but I wanted to stop and check on you first."

He stopped digging and leaned on his shovel, giving me a sheepish grin. "I already promised I wouldn't run off again. You don't need to keep checking on me twice a day."

"Yeah, well, you promised me that once before and you up and did it again."

His gaze shifted to the dirt pile as he shuffled his feet. "I already told you that I did it for you."

"I know. And thank you." I spanned the distance between us and pulled him into a hug. He remained stiff for a second then his back softened a bit.

"It was nothin'," he murmured as he pushed me away.

"Going undercover on your own to spy on Daniel Crocker to protect me? I wouldn't call that *nothin'*. You put yourself in danger, Bruce Wayne."

He looked into my eyes. It was one of the rare instances of direct eye contact I'd experienced with him. "Friends look out for each other." He looked away and swallowed. "You taught me that."

I planted a kiss on his cheek. "Yes, we do, Bruce Wayne," I forced past the lump in my throat. "Yes, we do."

He turned back to digging. "It was the only way I knew to protect you."

When Crocker's men planned his jail break, they made Bruce Wayne come back to Weston's Garage to give them information about me. He'd given them some accurate information he deemed harmless while misleading and flat-out lying to them about anything important. But when Crocker had gotten angry about not finding me, Bruce Wayne had borne the brunt of his frustration. The bruises he'd sported the first week after his return were proof enough of that.

"I'm glad you're back," I said, wiping a tear from my cheek. "I missed you."

"I missed you too," he said, refusing to look up at me.

"I'll see you tomorrow."

"Have a good night. And tell Neely Kate hi."

"I will."

When I arrived at the hospital with a wrapped present, Neely Kate was in the waiting room on the maternity floor. She squealed with excitement when she saw me. "It's about time! You're late!"

"Only by five minutes. I stopped to check on Bruce Wayne."

She grinned. "Well, if you were on time, I could have been holding her five minutes ago."

"That baby isn't going anywhere," I teased.

"They grow up fast, Rose." She looped her arm through mine. "Come on already!"

The door was already cracked open when we got to Heidi Joy's room, and we could see both mother and baby in the bed. She must have heard us approach because she looked up with a smile. "Well, hello, you two. Come on in. I just got her to sleep."

I pushed the door open and Neely Kate immediately rushed over to the bed. Heidi Joy was wearing a silky pink nightgown and the baby was wrapped in a soft pink receiving blanket. My friend's face glowed with happiness.

"She's so cute," Neely Kate gushed. "Was your labor hard?"

Heidi Joy looked down at the little round face. "She might be my sixth child, but it was my hardest labor yet and movin' in the middle of it didn't help matters. Andy's sure I went into labor just to get out of havin' to help. Shows what *he* knows," she scoffed. "What woman would *willingly* subject herself to twenty-five hours of labor just to get out of moving? Now Andy's gonna put things away where I don't want 'em while his mother spoils those boys rotten." She glanced down at the baby's face. "In any case, I didn't think this baby was ever gonna come. But she came in her own sweet time."

"What's her name?" Neely Kate asked.

"Clementine. Clementine Joy."

"Can I hold her?"

"Of course." Heidi Joy handed the baby to Neely Kate, who sat in the chair next to the bed.

"She's so sweet," Neely Kate said, sticking her pinky finger into Clementine's little fist.

I sat on the edge of the bed and studied Heidi Joy's face. "How are you doing? Really?"

"I'm tired. But I'm happy." She leaned closer and grinned. "Especially since I got my tubes tied. No more babies."

"I'm happy for you. On both accounts." I handed her the present. "Here, open it. Only it's for you and Andy, not Clementine."

She carefully unwrapped the small box and grinned when she opened it and pulled out the coupon book. "Free babysitting? I love it!"

"You call me anytime you need me."

A sly grin spread across her face. "Will Mason come with you?"

"I don't know." I smiled back. "Maybe. He's getting around better than we expected with his crutches. But he went back to work the day after his surgery. He didn't give himself time to recuperate, so he gets really worn out."

Neely Kate's head popped up and she lifted a neatly trimmed eyebrow. "Are you sure you don't play a part in wearing him out?"

I looked down and blushed.

Heidi Joy grabbed my hand. "You were lucky you weren't both killed."

I sighed, trying to put the nightmare behind me. "I know. I don't know how I would have made it if I didn't have Mason with me."

"And you saved his life too," Neely Kate added.

"We saved each other." In more ways than one, when I thought about it.

"So, Joe...?" Heidi Joy asked.

My mouth tipped up into a sad smile. "We're done. My decision."

Neely Kate stood and handed me the bundle. "Do you want to hold her?"

"Yeah." I took Clementine, snuggling her in the crook of my arm. "She's so precious, Heidi Joy."

"Maybe you and Mason will get married and have babies," Heidi Joy said.

"Maybe..."

"Well, she won't be having them first," Neely Kate said in a knowing voice.

I lifted my gaze to her beaming face.

"I'm pregnant! I just found out this morning."

We squealed and the baby stirred, but I bounced her until she settled down.

"So I guess it wasn't those hot wings making you sick after all," I said.

She groaned. "They sure didn't help."

"When are you due?"

"June."

Heidi Joy waved her hand. "Girl, you're gonna be so hot, but it won't be as bad as if you were due in August. Trust me. I know."

The baby wiggled and made faces again and I bounced her and cooed, leaning over to breathe in her sweet baby smell.

"You're a natural, Rose," Neely Kate said.

"I get plenty of practice with my niece and my nephew." I kissed the baby's head and then handed her back to Heidi Joy. "Maybe someday," I said.

I listened to my two friends talk about pregnancies and labor for ten minutes before I stood. "I need to get home and pack before Mason gets off work. He's been overdoing it.

Plus, the sooner I get everything packed, the sooner I can get out to the farm."

Heidi Joy grabbed my wrist. "You look really happy, Rose."

"You know what? I really am. Who would have thought?" I smiled and leaned down to kiss the baby's head one last time. "I'll see you guys later."

With a last glance at my friends, I left the room and was surprised to see Violet walking toward me.

"Rose."

I stopped in front of her, feeling awkward. We'd hardly spoken since our argument. I knew we needed to address it, but Violet changed the subject whenever I tried.

She had on a pretty green dress and was carrying a present wrapped in white paper and a pink tulle bow. "You look pretty, Vi." It was true—she could be a model from a magazine.

Violet smoothed her skirt. "Thanks, so do you. How's the packing going?"

"Good. Almost done. We'll be out by the time you move in next week."

"Can Mason help much with his leg in that brace?"

"He's helping as much as he can, but the big shakeup in the sheriff's department has created a lot of extra work for him." Not to mention his sadness over his friend's betrayal.

Violet pressed her lips together in disapproval. "He's always working, Rose. He's a workaholic."

I bristled. "He has an important job."

She tilted her head, narrowing her eyes in a pointed gaze. "I just think he should be home more. Your relationship is so new and he's obviously crazy about you. But then again, Joe was crazy about you too and look how that turned out."

Anger burned in my chest. "What are you insinuating, Violet?"

Her eyes widened. "Nothing."

I put my hand on my hip. "I know you'll never approve of anyone I'm with, Vi. I don't know why you're so mean to me, but Jonah's helped me realize that it's not up to me to figure that out." I leaned toward her and lowered my voice. "But just know that you cannot steal my joy. I do not give you that power. I want your support and approval, but I don't *need* it."

She lifted her chin and her eyes were filled with sadness when she met my gaze. "You're right. I'm sorry."

My mouth dropped open.

"I've done some soul-searching myself lately." Her gaze dropped to the floor. "I haven't told you this yet because I wasn't sure it would come to anything, but Mike and I are seeing a marriage counselor."

The shocks just kept coming. "That's…great."

"Yeah." She glanced up. "My attorney insisted I go to help my divorce case, so we started about a month ago as part of mediation, but then when the sheriff sent the kids and me to Aunt Bessie and Uncle Earl's farm, they had Mike go with us. And while we were out there…we started working some things out."

"What about Brody?"

"He broke up with me a couple of weeks ago." Her face reddened. "He's planning to go back to his wife."

"Oh." I knew she loved Brody and I thought he loved her. "So if you and Mike are trying to work things out, are you still moving into Momma's house?"

She shrugged. "Yeah, Mike and I aren't rushing things. We're gonna date. Can you imagine that?" She flashed me a smile like old times, and then it fell. "Anyway, we're just seeing each other and I can't pay the mortgage on the house by myself, so this is good. This will work."

But I knew how much she liked her house in her cookie-cutter neighborhood. I knew how hard it was for her to give it up.

"I'm really sorry about your house, Violet."

Tears filled her eyes and she nodded, looking at her gift.

"I don't like fighting with you."

Her face lifted to mine. "Me, neither. I'm trying to be a better sister, Rose, believe it or not. Don't give up on me."

I shook my head, tears filling my eyes. "I could never give up on you. You were there for me before anyone else. I would have never survived growing up without you." And for all our recent troubles, I could never forget the love and support she'd given me when I had felt so unloved and alone. Mason had said it was all about intent, and when we were scared little girls, huddled in the dark, her intent had been pure, unconditional love. She could have sided with Momma and she never did. "I love you, Violet."

Her chin quivered. "I love you too." Then she brushed past me. "Tell Mason that I said hello."

I drove home, marveling over our conversation. The possibility of Violet and Mike getting back together made me happy. They had been a couple so long it was hard to think of them with other people. I suddenly wondered if people had felt the same way about Joe and me.

When I pulled onto my street, I was surprised to see Mason's car parked in front of my house. We'd had lunch together and he told me he would have to work late. Happiness bubbling in my chest, I burst through the side door. He stood next to the kitchen table, putting a newspaper-wrapped item in a cardboard box. His crutches were leaned against the table and his leg was propped on a chair.

"Mason! What are you doing home?"

He reached for me, pulling me against his chest, his mouth finding mine. He kissed me for a good minute before he lifted his head. "This is why I'm home. I've missed your lips."

"My lips visited you for lunch."

He laughed. "That was *hours* ago." Then he kissed me again to show me how much he missed me.

Muffy came running around the corner, jumping up on my legs. I squatted to pet her. "I missed you too, girl." She had stuck close to me ever since Deputy Miller had returned her.

While Bruce Wayne had performed his undercover mission without supervision, Deputy Miller had been undercover in a more official capacity. Crocker's men had approached him about joining the group a couple of months earlier ago. He had immediately notified the state police and, at their request, joined the group as an informant. But since he was low level, with little information, he hadn't known about Chief Deputy Dimler's connection. That morning at the farm when he'd acted so strangely, Deputy Miller had been trying to warn us that Crocker was coming. He was worried the house was bugged, which was why he hadn't been more direct.

I stood after giving Muffy one last rub behind the ears. "You don't have to pack up my things, Mason. And you shouldn't be on your feet."

"I've had my foot propped up all day, which you saw when we had lunch in my office earlier. And as far as helping you pack, the sooner it's done, the sooner you can get out there. I know how excited you are about the move."

I placed a gentle kiss on his mouth. "Thank you." I put my hands on my hips and looked around the room. "I'm almost done, and then we can make another run out to the farm."

"Have you decided what to do with the furniture?"

"Not yet. Since there's already furniture out at the farm, I don't need everything, but I like my living room furniture, so I want to take it. I may see if Bruce Wayne and David want some of it. Theirs is pretty worn. In any case, I need to move it somewhere. Violet has her own stuff."

"Then I guess you have a week or so to figure it out. She's still moving in next week, right?"

"Yeah."

Mason hobbled into the kitchen and looked out the window over the sink. "Heidi Joy and Andy got moved out okay yesterday?"

"Andy had to finish up after she had the baby. Miss Mildred says the new renter is moving in tomorrow."

"Any word on who it is?"

"None."

Mason laughed. "How is that possible? That woman knows everything."

"I know, and I can tell that the not knowing is eating her alive."

I lifted the box and headed for the side door. "I'm going to start loading the truck."

"Rose, I wish you would have let me hire someone to move you. I hate that you're doing all this work and I can't help carry things."

I leaned over to kiss him. "No. It's my stuff, so you're not paying for it. And I need every spare penny I have to fix up the farmhouse. Now push the door open for me."

He opened it and shook his head. "You're bossy."

My eyebrows rose and I lowered my voice. "And you know you like me that way."

A wicked grin lit up his face. "Yeah, especially late last night."

I bumped his hip, gasping in mock surprise. "Mr. Deveraux. You have a reputation to maintain."

"Then it's a good thing Mildred wasn't looking through the window with her binoculars."

"I wouldn't put it past her." Laughing, I took the box out to the truck and slid it into the truck bed. I was heading back into the house when a familiar car pulled into the driveway next to mine. My breath caught in my throat.

Joe got out of his car and circled toward me, grinning ear to ear. "Hi, Rose. How are you recovering?"

I absently touched the faded bruises on my face. I was wearing makeup and they weren't visible, but I knew they were there. "I'm fine. How about you? You were injured worse than I was."

He kicked a patch of gravel. "You can't keep me down."

The way he said it made me wonder if there was some hidden meaning behind his words. "I was sorry to hear you lost the election."

Determination filled his eyes. "I wasn't. I told you I was going to quit the race, but I was so far behind in the polls, I figured I'd just let it run its course. My father hates losing, so it was a bonus."

"What are you doing here? You could have called me on the phone to catch up."

He rested his butt against the hood of his car. "I heard Heidi Joy moved out. Have any idea who's moving in?"

"Unbelievably, not even Miss Mildred knows."

Grinning, he jingled his keys. "Hi, neighbor."

My mouth dropped open. "*You?* You're the one who rented this house?"

"I couldn't believe my good luck when I heard it was available. I figured it was serendipity. I guess we'll be next-door neighbors again."

I shook my head. "But...how? I don't understand."

"After the chief deputy sheriff got arrested and the sheriff lost several other men in the Crocker mess, he offered me a job. You're looking at the new Chief Deputy Sheriff of Fenton County."

My heart sank, although I didn't know why. Joe and I were broken up, so what did I care? Maybe because the fact that he was going to take a sheriff's position before he broke up with me was bittersweet. "That's great, Joe. Congratulations."

"After I lost the election, I told my dad I was taking this job. He didn't like it, but he gave me his approval." His voice lowered. "So you're safe."

"For now."

Worry flashed in his eyes for a moment. "Hopefully forever."

We both knew that his father was saving the leverage for when he needed Joe to toe the line next time.

"So Hilary's not moving in with you?" I couldn't see her willingly moving into the tiny house. After discovering Joe's financial situation, I found it hard to believe *he* would live there.

"No." His voice was hard. "She's gone."

I didn't say anything.

"I know you don't believe me, but it's true." He stood and moved closer to me, his hands lifting slightly as though to reach for me before falling to his sides. "I'm here to prove to you that I can be the man you need me to be."

I closed my eyes and shook my head. "Joe."

"I know you say we're over, but I refuse to accept that. You taught me to fight for what I want and not to let it go. What I want is you."

I looked up into his face. "What about what *I* want, Joe?"

Before he could answer, the side door of my house opened and Mason hobbled toward us on his crutches. "Well, hello, Joe. What a surprise to see you here." He stopped next to me, wrapping an arm around my waist.

"I'm moving into my old house," Joe said with a grin, his gaze landing on Mason's hand at my waist then rising. "Rose and I are neighbors again." The challenge in his voice was clear.

"Well then, your timing is perfect," Mason said, his friendly tone not matching the look in his eyes. "Seeing as how Rose is moving out to her mother's farm."

Joe's smile fell. "Is that true?"

I nodded. "Violet's moving in here next week."

"But I'm sure Violet will appreciate having you for a neighbor." Mason leaned down and kissed my temple, his lips lingering for several seconds. "I'll go finish packing your bathroom."

As Mason walked away, Joe's eyes narrowed in determination. "We'll be working together quite a bit now, Mason. Seeing as how I'm the new chief deputy sheriff."

Holding onto the door, Mason paused for a second and then turned at the waist, flashing Joe a firm smile. "I'm looking forward to it."

And just like that, my life got even more complicated.